T'nT
TELZEY & TRIGGER

The Complete Federation of the Hub
Volume 2

JAMES H. SCHMITZ

EDITED BY ERIC FLINT

co-edited by Guy Gordon

"Company Planet" first published May 1971 in *Analog*; "Resident Witch" first published in May 1970 in *Analog*; "Compulsion" first published June 1970 in *Analog* (note: the Prologue to "Compulsion" was originally published as a separate short story under the title "The Pork Chop Tree" in February 1965 in *Analog*; "Glory Day" first published June 1971 in *Analog*; "Child of the Gods" first published March 1972 in *Analog*; "Ti's Toys" first published under the title "The Telzey Toy" May 1971 in *Analog*; "The Symbiotes" first published September 1972 in *Analog*; all copyright to the estate of James H. Schmitz

Afterword, © 2000 by Eric Flint; "That Certain Something," © 2000 by Guy Gordon.

A Baen Book

Baen Publishing Enterprises
P.O. Box 1403
Riverdale, NY 10471

ISBN: 0-671-57879-0

Cover art by Bob Eggleton

First printing, July 2000

Distributed by Simon & Schuster
1230 Avenue of the Americas
New York, NY 10020

Production by Windhaven Press, Auburn, NH
Printed in the United States of America

CONTENTS

Company Planet 1

Resident Witch 49

Compulsion 93

Glory Day 163

Child of the Gods 207

Ti's Toys 263

The Symbiotes 329

Afterword, by Eric Flint 391

That Certain Something,
    by Guy Gordon 395

COMPANY PLANET

1

Fermilaur was famous both as the leading body remodeling center of the Hub and as a luxurious resort world which offered relaxation and scenery along with entertainment to fit every taste, from the loftiest to the most depraved. It was only three hours from Orado, and most of Telzey's friends had been there. But she'd never happened to get around to it until one day she received a distress call from Fermilaur.

It came from the mother of Gikkes Orm. Telzey learned that Gikkes, endowed by nature with a pair of perfectly sound and handsome legs, had decided those limbs needed to be lengthened and reshaped by Fermilaur's eminent cosmetic surgeons if she was ever to find true happiness. Her parents, who, in Telzey's opinion, had even less good sense than Gikkes, had let her go ahead with it, and her mother had accompanied her to Fermilaur. With the legs remodeled according to specification, Gikkes had discovered that everything else about her now appeared out of proportion. Unable to make up her mind what to do, she became greatly upset. Her mother, equally upset, equally helpless, put in an interstellar call to Telzey.

Having known Gikkes for around two years, Telzey wasn't surprised. Gikkes didn't quite rate as a full friend, but she wasn't a bad sort even if she did get

3

herself periodically into problem situations from which somebody else had to extricate her. Telzey decided she wouldn't mind doing it again. While about it, she should have time for a look at a few of Fermilaur's unique restructuring institutions and other attractions.

Somewhat past the middle of the night for that locality, she checked in at a tourist tower not far from the cosmetic center where the Orms were housed. She'd heard that Fermilaur used resort personnel to advertise its remodeling skills, the general note being that having oneself done over was light-hearted fashion fun and that there was nothing to worry about because almost any cosmetic modification could be reversed if the client wished it. The staff of the tower's reception lobby confirmed the report. They were works of art, testimonials to the daring inventiveness of Fermilaur's beauty surgeons. Telzey's room reservation was checked by a slender goddess with green-velvet skin, slanted golden eyes without detectable pupils, and a shaped scalp crest of soft golden feathers which shifted dancingly with each head motion. She smiled at Telzey, said, "May I suggest the services of a guide, Miss Amberdon?"

Telzey nodded. "Yes, I'll want one." There were no cities, no townships here. The permanent population was small, mostly involved with the tourist trade and cosmetic institutions, and its maintenance systems were underground, out of sight. Much of the surface had been transformed into an endlessly flowing series of parks in which residential towers and resort and remodeling centers stood in scenic isolation. Traffic was by air, and inexperienced visitors who didn't prefer to drift about more or less at random were advised to employ guides.

The goddess beckoned to somebody behind Telzey's back.

"Uspurul is an accredited COS Services guide and

thoroughly familiar with our quadrant," she informed Telzey. "I'm sure you'll find her very satisfactory."

Uspurul was a quite small person, some four inches shorter than Telzey, slender in proportion. Like the receptionist, she looked like something COS Services might have conjured up out of exotic mythologies. Her pointed ears were as expressively mobile as a terrier's; a silver horse's tail swished about with languid grace behind her. The triangular face with its huge dark eyes and small delicate nose was unquestionably beautiful but wasn't human. It wasn't intended to be. She might have been a charming toy, brought to life.

Which was all very well, as far as Telzey was concerned. More important seemed a shadowy swirl of feeling she'd sensed as Uspurul came up to the reception desk—a feeling which didn't match in the least the engaging friendliness of the toy woman's smile. It wasn't exactly malice. More something like calculating cold interest, rather predatory. Telzey took note of nuances in the brief conversation that followed, decided the two were, in fact, more anxious to make sure she'd employ Uspurul as guide than one should expect.

Somewhere else, that could have been a danger signal. A sixteen-year-old with a wealthy family made a tempting target for the criminally inclined. The resort world, however, had the reputation of being almost free of professional crime. And, in any case, it shouldn't be difficult to find out what this was about—she'd discovered during the talk that Uspurul's mind appeared to be wide open to telepathic probing.

"Why not have breakfast with me in my room tomorrow?" she said to the guide. "We can set up a schedule then." And she could ferret out at her leisure the nature of the interest the remodeled myths seemed to take in her.

They settled on the time, and Telzey was escorted

to her room. She put in a call to Mrs. Orm from
there, learned that Gikkes would be in treatment at
the main center of Hute Beauticians during the early
part of the morning and was anxious to see Telzey
and get her opinion of the situation immediately
afterward. Mrs. Orm, having succeeded in transfer-
ring the responsibility for decisions to somebody else,
appeared much less distraught.

Telzey opened one of her suitcases, got out a
traveler's lock and attached it to the door of the room,
which in effect welded the door to the adjoining wall.
The only thing anyone trying to get in without her
cooperation could accomplish was to wake up half the
tower level. She continued unpacking reflectively.

Fermilaur didn't have a planetary government in
the usual sense. It was the leasehold of COS, the
association of cosmetologists which ran the planet. Its
citizen-owners, set up in a tax-free luxury resort and
getting paid for it, had reason to be happy with the
arrangement, and could have few inducements to
dabble in crime. The Hub's underworld reputedly had
its own dealings with COS—bodies, of course, could
be restructured for assorted illegal purposes. But the
underworld didn't try to introduce its usual practices
here. COS never denied reports that criminal pros
found attempting to set up shop on the leasehold
vanished into its experimental centers. Apparently, not
many cared to test the validity of the reports.

Hence, no crime, or almost no crime. And crime
of the ordinary sort hardly could be involved in the
situation. The receptionist and the elfin guide never
had seen her before. But they did seem to have
recognized her by name, to have been waiting, in fact,
for her to show up.

Telzey sat down on the edge of the bed.

The two were COS employees. If anyone had an
interest in her here, it should be COS.

The tower reservation had been made in her name

five hours ago on Orado. Five hours was plenty of
time for a good information service to provide inquir-
ers with the general background of the average
Federation citizen. Quite probably, COS had its own
service, and obtained such information on every first-
time visitor to Fermilaur. It could be useful in a
variety of ways.

The question was what might look interesting
enough in her background to draw COS's attention
to her. It wasn't that the Amberdon family had money.
Almost everybody who came here would meet that
qualification. There were, Telzey decided, chewing
meditatively on her lower lip, only two possible points
of interest she could think of at the moment. And
both looked a little improbable.

Her mother was a member of the Overgovernment.
Conceivably, that could be of significance to COS.
At present, it was difficult to see why it should be.

The other possibility seemed even more remote.
Information services had yet to dig up the fact that
Telzey Amberdon was a telepath, a mind reader, a
psi, competent and practicing. She knew that, because
if they ever did dig it up, she'd be the first to hear.
She had herself supplied regularly with any datum
added to her available dossiers. Of the people who
were aware she was a psi, only a very few could be
regarded as not being completely dependable. Unfortunately, there were those few. It was possible, though
barely so, that the item somehow had got into COS's
files.

She could have a problem then. The kind of people
who ran COS had to be practical and hardheaded.
Hardheaded, practical people, luckily, were inclined
to consider stories about psis to be at least ninety-
nine percent superstitious nonsense. However, the
ones who didn't share that belief sometimes reacted
undesirably. They might reflect that a real psi, competent, practicing, could be eminently useful to them.

Or they might decide such a psi was too dangerous to have around.

She'd walk rather warily tomorrow until she made out what was going on here! One thing, though, seemed reasonably certain—COS, whatever ideas it might have, wasn't going to try to break through the door to get at her tonight. She could use a few hours of rest.

She climbed into bed, turned over, and settled down. A minute or two later, she was asleep.

2

After breakfast, Telzey set off with Uspurul on a leisurely aircar tour of the area. She'd explained she'd be visiting an acquaintance undergoing treatment at Hute Beauticians later on, and then have lunch with another friend who'd come out from Orado with her. In the afternoon, she might get down finally to serious sightseeing.

With Uspurul handling the car and gossiping merrily away, Telzey could give her attention to opening connections to the guide's mind. As she'd judged, it was an easy mind to enter, unprotected and insensitive to telepathic probing. One fact was promptly established then, since it was pervasively present in Uspurul's thoughts. COS did, in fact, take a special interest in Telzey, but it wasn't limited to her. She had plenty of company.

The reason for the interest wasn't apparent. Uspurul hadn't wanted to know about it, hardly thought of it. The little female was a complex personality. She was twenty-two, had become a bondswoman four years earlier, selling her first contract to COS Services for the standard five-year short-term period. People who

adopted bondservant status did it for a wide range of
reasons. Uspurul's was that a profitable career could
be built on bond contracts by one who went about it
intelligently.

She'd chosen her masters after careful deliberation.
On a world which sold luxury, those who served also
lived in relative luxury, and as a COS guide she was
in contact with influential and wealthy people who
might be used for her further advancement. Her next
contract owner wouldn't be COS. She was circum-
spect in her behavior.

More was done on Fermilaur than cultivating an
exclusive tourist trade and cosmetic clientele, and it
wasn't advisable to appear inquisitive about the other
things. COS didn't mind rumors about various barely
legal or quite illegal activities in which it supposedly
engaged; they titillated public interest and were good
for business. But underlings who became too knowl-
edgeable about such obscure matters could find it
difficult to quit.

Uspurul intended to remain free to quit when her
contract period ended. For the past year, she'd been
on the fringes of something obscure enough. It had
brought her a string of satisfactory bonuses, and there
was nothing obviously illegal about what she did or
COS Services did. As long as she avoided any indication of curiosity it seemed safe.

She still acted as guide. But she was assigned now
only to female tourists who appeared to have no
interest in making use of the remodeling facilities.
Uspurul's assignment was to get them to change their
minds without being obvious about it. She was skillful
at that, usually succeeded. On a number of occasions
when she hadn't succeeded, she'd been instructed to
make sure the person in question would be at a
certain place at a certain time. She'd almost always
been able to arrange it.

Now she was using the morning's comfortable

schedule to keep up a flow of the light general chatter through which she could most readily plant the right notions in a hesitant visitor's mind.

"I was thinking I might have a little remodeling myself while I was here," Telzey remarked, by and by. She took out a small mirror, looked into it critically, arching her brows. "Nothing very important really! But I could have my brows moved higher, maybe get the eyes enlarged." She clicked the mirror to an angle view, pushed back her hair on the left side. "And the ears, you see, could be set a little lower—and the least bit farther back." She studied the ear a moment. "What do you think of their shape?"

"Oh, I wouldn't have them change the *shape!*" said Uspurul, thinking cheerfully that here came an easy bonus! "But they might be a tiny bit lower. You're right about that."

Telzey nodded, put the mirror away. "Well, no rush about it. I'll be looking around a few days first."

"Someone like you doesn't really need remodeling, of course," Uspurul said. "But it is fun having yourself turned into exactly what you'd like to be! And, of course, it's always reversible."

"Hmmm," said Telzey. "They did a beautiful job on you. Did you pick it out for yourself?"

Uspurul twitched an ear, grinned impishly.

"I've wanted to do *that* since I was a child!" she confessed. "But, no—this was COS Services' idea. I advertise for the centers, you see. A twenty-two thousand credit job, if I had to pay for it. It'd be a little extreme for the Hub generally, of course. But it's reversible, and when I leave they'll give me any other modification I want within a four thousand credit range. That's part of my contract."

She burbled on. Telzey didn't have the slightest intention of getting remodeled, but she wanted Uspurul and COS Services to think she did until she was ready to ship out. It would keep the situation more relaxed.

It remained a curious situation. The people to whom Uspurul reported were satisfied if a visitor signed up for any kind of remodeling at all, even the most insignificant of modifications. That hardly looked like a simple matter of drumming up new business for the centers, while the special attention given some of those who remained disinterested was downright on the sinister side. The places to which Uspurul steered such tourists were always resort spots where there were a good many other people around, coming and going places—in other words, where somebody could easily brush close by the tourist without attracting attention.

What happened there? Something perhaps in the nature of a hypno spray? Uspurul never saw what happened and didn't try to. When she parted company with the tourist that day, there'd been no noticeable effects. But next day she'd be given a different assignment.

Of course, those people weren't disappearing. It wasn't *that* kind of situation. They weren't, by and large, the kind of people who could be made to vanish quietly. Presumably they'd been persuaded by some not too legal method to make a remodeling appointment, and afterward went on home like Uspurul's other clients. They might all go home conditioned to keep returning to Fermilaur for more extensive and expensive treatments; at the moment, that seemed the most probable explanation. But whatever the COS Services' operation was, Telzey reflected, she'd simply make sure she didn't get included in it. With Uspurul's mind open to her, that shouldn't be too difficult. Back on Orado then, she'd bring the matter to the attention of Federation authorities. Meanwhile she might run across a few other open minds around here who could tell her more than Uspurul knew.

The man she was meeting for lunch—a relative on her mother's side—was an investigative reporter for one of the newscast systems. Keth had his sharp nose into many matters, and exposing rackets was one of his specialties. He might be able to say what this was about, but the difficulty would be to explain how she'd come by her information without mentioning telepathy. Keth didn't know she was a psi. Nor could she do her kind of mental research on him—she'd discovered on another occasion that he was equipped with a good solid commercial mind shield. Keth doubted that anyone could really see what was in another person's mind, but he took precautions anyway.

The remodeling counselors at the Hute Beauticians center had told Gikkes Orm quite candidly that if she was to be equipped with the leg type she wanted, overall body modifications were indicated to maintain an aesthetic balance. Gikkes hadn't believed it. But now the cosmetic surgeons had given her a pair of long, exquisitely molded legs, and it seemed the counselors were right.

The rest of her didn't fit.

"Just look at those shoulders!" she cried, indicating one of two life-sized models which stood against the far wall of the room. They showed suggested sets of physical modifications which might be performed on Gikkes. "I love the legs! But—"

"Well, you might be a little, uh, statuesque," Telzey acknowledged. She studied the other model. Sinuous was the word for that one. A dancer's body. "But, Gikkes, you'd look great either way, really! Especially as the slinky character!"

"It wouldn't be *me!*" Gikkes wailed. "And how much work do you think I'd have to put in to *stay* slinky then? You know I'm not the athletic type."

"No, I guess you're not," Telzey said. "When did

you first get the idea that you wanted your legs changed?"

It appeared Gikkes had been playing around with the notion for several years, but it was only quite recently that it had begun to seem vital to her. It was her own idea, however—not an obsession planted on a previous trip to Fermilaur. Telzey had been wondering about that. The solution shouldn't be too difficult. Off and on for some while, Telzey had made use of suitable occasions to nudge Gikkes in the general direction of rationality. It had to be done with care because Gikkes wasn't too stable. But she had basic intelligence and, with some unnoticed guidance, was really able to handle most of her problems herself and benefit from doing it. Telzey picked up the familiar overall mind patterns now, eased a probe into the unhappy thought muddle of the moment, and presently began her nudging. Gikkes went on talking.

Twenty minutes later, she said ruefully, "So I guess the whole remodeling idea was a silly mistake! The thing to do, of course, is to have them put me back exactly as I was."

"From all you've told me," Telzey agreed, "that does make sense."

Mrs. Orm was surprised but relieved when informed of her daughter's decision. The Hute staff wasn't surprised. Remodeling shock and reversal requests weren't infrequent. In this case, reversal was no problem. Gikkes' experiment in surgical cosmetology probably had reduced her life expectancy by an insignificant fraction, and the Orm family was out a good deal of money, which it could afford. Otherwise, things would be as before.

A level of the Hute center restaurant was on Keth Deboll's private club circuit, which in itself guaranteed gourmet food. It was a quietly formal place where the employees weren't trying to look like anything but people. Keth's bony inquisitive face, familiar to newsviewers over a large section of the Hub, presumably didn't go unrecognized here, but nobody turned to stare. He deliberated over the menu, sandy brows lifting in abrupt interest now and then, and ordered for both of them, rubbing his palms together.

"You'll like it," he promised.

She always did like what Keth selected, but this time she barely tasted what she put in her mouth, as she chewed and swallowed. He'd mentioned that top COS executives patronized the place, and that he rather expected to be meeting someone before lunch was over.

She'd been wondering how she could get close enough to some top COS executive to start tapping his mind. . . .

She was sliding out discreet probes before Keth had placed his order. After the food came, only a fraction of awareness remained in her physical surroundings. Keth would eat in leisurely silent absorption until the edge was off his appetite, and she might have her contact made by that time.

Several minds in the vicinity presently seemed as open to contact as Uspurul's. None of them happened to be a COS executive. Something else was in the vicinity—seven or eight mind shields. Unusual concentration of the gadgets! Her probes slipped over them, moved on, searching—

"You might get the opportunity," Keth's voice was saying. "Here comes a gentleman who could arrange it for you."

Awareness flowed swiftly back to the outer world as she reoriented herself between one moment and the next. Keth had reached the point where he didn't mind talking again, had asked—what? Ah, yes, had asked what plans she had for the day. She'd responded automatically, that she was hoping to get a look at some of Fermilaur's less publicized projects. . . . Who could arrange it?

She looked around. A handsome, tall, strong-faced man was coming toward their table. On his right shoulder perched a small creature with blue and white fur, adorned with strings of tiny sparkling jewels. The man's dark eyes rested on Telzey as he approached. He nodded to her, smiled pleasantly, looked at Keth.

"Am I intruding?" It was a deep, soft-toned voice.

"Not at all," Keth told him. "We're almost finished—and I'd intended trying to get in touch with you during the afternoon. Telzey, this is Chan Osselin. He handles publicity for COS and incidentally owns Hute Beauticians. . . . Telzey Amberdon, an old friend. We came out from Orado together. If you have the time, join us."

Osselin drew a chair around and sat down. His scalp hair was short, deep black, like soft animal fur. Telzey wondered whether it was a product of remodeling, felt rather certain then that it wasn't. The small animal on his shoulder stared at Telzey out of large pale eyes, yawned and scratched a rounded ear with a tiny clawed finger. The stringed jewels decorating it flashed flickering rainbows of fire.

"I heard of your arrival a few hours ago," Osselin said. "Here on Adacee business?"

Keth shrugged. "Always on Adacee business."

"Um. Something specific?"

"Not so far. Something new, unpublicized, sensational."

Osselin looked reflective. "Sensational in what way?"

"Questionable legality wouldn't have to be part of it," Keth said. "But it would help. Something with shock effect. None of your pretty things."

"So COS is to be exposed again?" Osselin seemed unruffled.

"With some new angle," said Keth. "On some new issue."

"Well," Osselin said, "I'm sure it can be arranged. . . ."

Telzey, absently nibbling the last crumbs of her dessert, drew back her attention from what was being said. She'd known Chan Osselin's name as soon as she saw him. She'd seen him before as an image in Uspurul's mind. One of COS's top men. Uspurul wouldn't willingly have brought herself to the attention of someone like Osselin. People of that kind were to be avoided. They had too much power, were too accustomed to using it without hesitation or scruple.

There was no trace of the dead, psi-deadening, effect of a mind shield about Osselin—

Telzey reached out toward the deep sound of his voice, paying no attention to the words, groping cautiously for some wash of thought which might be associated with the voice.

She had no warning of any kind. A psi hammer slammed down on her, blacking out her vision, leaving her shaken and stunned.

3

She drew in a slow, cautious breath. Her psi screens had locked belatedly into a hard shield; another assault of that kind could have no great effect on her now. But none came. She realized she'd lowered her head in protective reflex. Her hair hid her face, and the voices of the men indicated they weren't aware that anything in particular had happened. Vision began to return. The section of the tabletop before her grew clear, seemed to sway about in short semi-circles. A last wave of giddiness and nausea flowed over her and was gone. She'd be all right now. But that had been close—

She kept her face turned away as she reached for her bag. The makeup cassette showed she'd paled, but it wasn't too noticeable. Listening to a thin, angry whistling nearby, she touched herself up, put the cassette away, and finally raised her head.

The furry thing on Osselin's shoulder stared at her. Abruptly it produced its whistling sounds again, bobbing up and down. Osselin stroked it with a finger. It closed its eyes and subsided. He smiled at Telzey.

"It gets agitated now and then about strangers," he remarked.

She smiled back. "So it seems. What do you call it?"

"It's a yoli. A pet animal from Askanam. Rare even there, from what I've been told. This one came to me as a gift."

"Supposed to be a sort of living good luck charm, aren't they?" said Keth.

"Something like that. Faithful guardians who protect their master from evil influences." Osselin's dark eyes crinkled genially at Telzey. "I can't vouch for their effectiveness—but I do seem to remain undisturbed by evil influences! Would you care to accompany us to a few of the specialized labs a little later, Miss Amberdon? You should find them interesting."

Keth was to be shown a few projects COS didn't talk about otherwise, which might give him the kind of story he wanted. They preferred that to having him dig around on Fermilaur on his own. She told Osselin she'd be delighted to go along.

The yoli appeared to be falling asleep, but she sensed its continuing awareness of her. A psi guard—against psis. Its intelligence seemed on the animal level. She couldn't make out much more about it, and didn't care to risk trying at present. It probably would react as violently to an attempted probe of its own mind as to one directed against its master.

And now she might be in personal danger. The number of shields she'd touched here suggested some sophistication in psi matters. Ordinarily it wouldn't disturb her too much. Mechanical anti-psi devices could hamper a telepath but weren't likely to lead to the detection of one who'd gained some experience, and other telepaths rarely were a problem. The yoli's psi senses, however, had been a new sort of trap; and she'd sprung it. She had to assume that Osselin knew of his pet's special quality and what its behavior just now signified. A man like that wasn't likely to be indifferent to the discovery that someone had tried to reach his mind. And the yoli had made it clear who it had been.

If she dropped the matter now, it wasn't likely that Osselin would drop it. And she wouldn't know what he intended to do then until it was too late. . . .

Some time later, as the tour of the special labs began, there was an attention split. Telzey seemed aware of herself, or of part of herself, detached, a short distance away. That part gazed at the exhibits, smiled and spoke when it should, asked questions about projects, said the right things—a mental device she'd worked out and practiced to mask the sleepy blankness, the temporary unawareness of what was said and done, which could accompany excessive absorption on the psi side. On the psi side, meanwhile, she'd been carrying on a project of her own which had to do with Osselin's yoli.

The yoli was having a curious experience. Shortly after Telzey and Keth rejoined Osselin, it had begun to pick up momentary impressions of another yoli somewhere about. Greatly intrigued because it had been a long time since it last encountered or sensed one of its kind, it started searching mentally for the stranger, broadcasting its species' contact signals.

Presently the signals were being returned, though faintly and intermittently. The yoli's excitement grew. It probed farther and farther for the signals' source, forgetting now the telepath it had punished for trying to touch its master. And along those heedlessly extended tendrils of thought, Telzey reached delicately toward the yoli mind, touched it and melted into it, still unperceived.

It had taken time because she couldn't risk making the creature suspicious again. The rest wasn't too difficult. The yoli's intelligence was about that of a monkey. It had natural defenses against being controlled by another's psi holds, and Telzey didn't try to tamper with those. Its sensory centers were open to her, which was all she needed. Using its own impressions of how another yoli, a most desirable other yoli, would appear to it, she built up an illusion that it was in satisfying communication with such a one and left the image planted firmly in its mind along with a few other befuddling concepts. By that time, the yoli was no longer aware that she existed, much less of what she was up to.

Then finally she was able to turn her attention again to Osselin. Caution remained required, and she suspected she might be running short of time. But she could make a start.

The aircar floated three thousand feet above foggy valley lands—Fermilaur wilderness, tamed just enough to be safe for the tourist trade. Tongue tip between lips, Telzey blinked at the clouds, pondering a thoroughly ugly situation. There was a sparse dotting of other cars against the sky. One of them was trailing her; she didn't know which. It didn't matter.

She glanced impatiently over at the comm grille. Keth Deboll was in conference somewhere with

Osselin. She'd left a message for him at his residential tower to call her car's number as soon as he showed up. She'd left word at her own tower to have calls from him transferred to the car. In one way or the other, she'd be in contact with him presently. Meanwhile she had to wait, and waiting wasn't easy in the circumstances.

Chan Osselin couldn't sense a telepathic probe. Except for that, she might have been defeated and probably soon dead. She'd found him otherwise a difficult mental type to handle. His flow of conscious thoughts formed a natural barrier; it had been like trying to swim against a current which was a little too strong. She kept getting pushed back while Osselin went on thinking whatever he was thinking, unaware of her efforts. She could follow his reflections but hadn't been able to get past them to the inner mind in the time she had available. . . . And then she'd been courteously but definitely dismissed. The guided tour was over, and the men had private business to discuss. Shortly after she left them, she'd lost her contact with Osselin.

She'd absorbed a good deal of scattered information by then, could begin fitting it together. As she did, the picture, looking bad enough to start with, got progressively worse—

Normally, even people who accepted that there might be an occasional mind reader around had the impression that telepathy couldn't pick up enough specific and dependable information to be a significant threat to their privacy. That might have been the attitude of the top men in COS up to a year ago. Unfortunately, very unfortunately for her, they'd had a genuine psi scare then. They spotted the psi and killed him, but when they realized how much he'd learned, that they almost hadn't found him out in time, they were shaken. Mind shields and other protective devices were promptly introduced. Osselin hated shields; like many others he found them as uncomfortable as a tight shoe. When an Askab lady provided him with a guard yoli, he'd felt it was safe to do without a shield.

He still felt safe personally. That wasn't the problem. COS had something going, a really important operation. Telzey had caught worried flashes about it, no more and not enough. The Big Deal was how Osselin thought of it. They couldn't afford the chance of having the Big Deal uncovered. Keth Deboll was a notoriously persistent and successful snoop; a telepathic partner would make him twice as dangerous. The fact that the two had appeared on Fermilaur together might have no connection with the Big Deal, but who could tell? COS was checking on both at present. If they couldn't be cleared, they'd have to be killed. Risky, but it could be arranged. It would be less risky, less suspicious, than carrying out a double mind-wipe and dumping them on some other world, which might have been an alternative in different circumstances.

And that was it! Telzey wet her lips, felt a chill quivering again through her nerves, a sense of death edging into the situation. She didn't see how they could be cleared. Neither did Osselin, but something might turn up which would make it unnecessary to dispose of them. The Amberdon girl's demise or disappearance shouldn't cause too much trouble, but Deboll was another matter. Too many people would start wondering whether he hadn't been on the trail of something hot on Fermilaur, what it could be. This would have to be very carefully handled! Meanwhile COS was taking no chances. Neither of the two would be allowed to leave the planet or get near an interstellar transmitter. If they made the attempt, they'd get picked up at once. Otherwise, they could remain at large, under surveillance, until the final decision was made. That should turn up any confederate they might have here.

The final decision was still some hours away. How many, Telzey didn't know. Osselin hadn't known it yet. But not very many, in any case. . . .

Osselin himself might be the only way out of this. Their information on psis was limited; they thought of her only as a telepath, like the other one, and didn't suspect she could have further abilities which might endanger them. She had that advantage at present. Given enough time, she should be able to get Osselin under control. She'd considered trying to restore mental contact with him at long range, wherever he happened to be. But she wasn't at all certain she could do it, and the yoli made it too risky. Its hallucinations should be self-sustaining for some hours to come if nothing happened to disturb it seriously. She had to avoid disturbing it in resuming contact with Osselin, which meant working with complete precision. A fumble at long range could jolt the creature out of its dreams and into another defensive reaction.

She didn't know what effect that would have on Osselin, but at the very least it might give him the idea to equip himself with a mind shield as a further safeguard until they'd dealt with the telepath. She'd be stopped then.

She had to be *there*, with Osselin, to be sure of what she was doing. If she got in touch with him and told him she'd like to talk to him privately, he'd probably want to hear what she had to say. But he'd be suspicious, on guard. It would be easier for Keth to find a plausible reason for another meeting, easier if Keth was around to keep some of Osselin's attention away from her. . . . The comm grille burred. She gave a gasp of relief as her hand flicked out to switch it on.

4

Keth took a little convincing then. He'd set their aircar down on a grassy hillside, and they'd moved off until it was a hundred yards below them. He'd turned on this and that antisnoop device. From eight feet away, their voices were an indistinguishable muddle of sound, their features blurred out.

"We can talk," he'd said.

Telzey talked. He listened, intent blue eyes blinking, face expressionless. Twice he seemed about to interject something, then let her go on. Finally he said, "Telzey, you're obviously not joking, and I don't believe you've suddenly become deranged. Did you ever try to read my mind?"

She nodded.

"Yes, once. Half a year ago. I thought you were up to something and wanted to find out what it was."

"Oh? What did you find?"

"That you use a mind shield, of course. I didn't waste any more time."

Keth grunted. "All right! You're a telepath. If the situation is what it looks like, we have a problem. The check on me won't tell COS anything. Adacee isn't leakproof, but all they'll learn there is what I told Osselin. I came to Fermilaur to get a good story. Nothing specific. Any story as long as it's good enough. Can they find anything in your background to confirm that you're a mind reader?"

Telzey shrugged, shook her head. "I've been careful. What there was has been pretty well covered up. It's very unlikely they'll find anything. The trouble is Osselin's already pretty well convinced of it—he goes by the yoli's psi sense. And, of course, they can't prove that I'm *not* one."

"No. Not without linking you into a lie detector system. If they go that far, they'll already have decided to go all the way with us. At any rate, they haven't made up their minds yet. I parted from Osselin on apparently friendly terms. If the verdict's favorable, nothing at all will have happened."

"Unless we try to reach a spaceport," Telzey said. "Or to get in touch with somebody somewhere else."

"Yes, they wouldn't allow that. And, of course, they can seal off the planet as far as we're concerned. In effect, they own it." Keth considered. "There's a man I might contact here, but that would only pull him into the trouble. How about other, uh, functional telepaths?"

Telzey shook her head.

"Starting cold, it probably would be hours before I located one. We don't have that much time. They mightn't want to help anyway. It could cost them *their* cover."

Keth rubbed his chin. "If it gets to the point of running, a space yacht might get us off."

"COS Services handles the yacht rentals," Telzey reminded him.

"Not what I was thinking of," Keth said. "Plenty of people come here in private yachts. Last year, I got out of a somewhat similar situation that way. It shouldn't be impossible to borrow one, but it probably wouldn't be easy." He reflected. "That Big Deal of COS—the story they *think* we might be snooping around here for? You got no clue from Osselin what that might be?"

She shook her head. "There's an awful lot of money involved, and there's something illegal about it. They'll protect it, whatever it takes. They think you might have picked up some clues to it somewhere and brought me to Fermilaur to help dig up more. But that's all I can say. Everything else connected with it was too blurred to make out."

"Finance, politics, business—the big money areas," Keth said, watching her. "Nothing about some secret

Hub-wide system to gather hot inside information at top levels there."

Telzey stared at him. "Oh, my!" she said after a long moment.

Keth said, "You went white, Telzey. What is it?"

"That guide I had this morning! Uspurul." Telzey put her hand to her mouth. "I was reading *her* mind. There was something odd going on. I didn't think there was any connection, but I wanted to check with Uspurul again to be sure. I tried to get in touch with her an hour ago. COS Services said she was on another assignment, couldn't be reached."

"You don't think she's on another assignment?"

"Uh-uh! No. She didn't know it, but she's connected with their Big Deal! Hot inside information— When they started checking this afternoon on what I've been doing here since I landed, they'd have picked her up to see what a telepath could have got from her."

Keth said, "The kind of lie detector that pushes unconscious material to view. . . . So just what did you learn from her?"

Telzey recounted the essentials. Keth nodded slowly. He'd paled somewhat himself.

"That will have tipped the fat into the fire!" he said.

A secret Hub-wide information gathering system on the distaff side. . . . Wives, mistresses, daughters of the Federation's greats streamed in to Formilaur. Were tagged on arrival, maneuvered into making a remodeling appointment if that hadn't been their intention.

"Anesthesia, unconsciousness, in-depth interrogation," Keth said. "Anything they know of significance is filed immediately. The ones who can be typed as foolproof COS agents and have sufficiently valuable connections go home under a set of heavy compulsions, go to work. When their work's done, they come back, get debriefed. Leaving no trace of what's happened, in case of subsequent checks. Yes, a big setup! COS's capital investment program should be spectacularly successful!"

Now and then suspicion might turn on an unwitting agent. When it happened, the agent appeared to go into amnesiac withdrawal and committed suicide at the first opportunity. It wasn't something the people involved would want to talk about. But there'd been such a case among Keth's acquaintances, and he'd learned of another very similar one, discovered both women had gone through remodeling centers on Fermilaur in recent months. It seemed worth following up. He'd come to Fermilaur to do it.

"I dislike turning my back on a story before it's in the bag," he said. "But I can pick this up at the other end now. We'd better get set to run while we can, Telzey! The decision they'll reach is to do us in. From their viewpoint, there won't be much choice."

"A yacht?" she said.

"Yes. Noticed a few boat parks while I was moving around this morning, and—"

"Keth, how much chance would we have of getting away?"

He hesitated, grimaced.

"It depends. Even odds perhaps, if we act now. Less if we wait."

She shook her head. "We can do better! Chan Osselin's really top man in COS, isn't he?"

Keth looked at her. "Yes. Barrand's president of the association. I've heard Osselin could have the job any time he wants. What he says pretty well goes anyway. Why?"

"You've got to think of some reason to see him again immediately, with me. I need more time to work on him, to really get into his mind."

"What will that do for us?"

"If I get through to him, Osselin will get us off

Fermilaur," Telzey said. "He's in a better position to do it than anyone else."

Keth considered her.

"It seems you're something more than a telepath," he remarked.

"They don't know it."

"All right. How much time would you need?"

She shook her head.

"An hour—thirty minutes—twenty minutes—two hours . . . I don't know. It's always different, and Osselin isn't easy. But we'll have much better than even odds there!"

"Well, there's no need to arrange for a meeting," Keth said. He looked at his watch. "We've got a dinner appointment at Osselin's house two and a half hours from now, our local time. He emphasized that I was to bring my charming young friend along. Two people want to meet us. One's Barrand, the COS president I mentioned. The other's Nelt, vice-president and executive officer. They and Osselin are the trio that runs COS. Presumably the decision on what to do about us will be made at that time."

"Yes, probably," Telzey said. "But let's get there early, Keth."

"By about half an hour? I'm sure Osselin won't object. I've thought of further details about the projects he showed me that I'd like to discuss with him." He added as they turned back to the aircar, "But we're not scratching the space yacht idea just yet!"

"We're not?"

"No. COS *might* decide to lower the boom before we have a chance to sit down to dinner this evening. And you see, there're three special yacht types. Racing boats . . ."

The three yacht types had one thing in common: an identical means of emergency entry. It was designed for use in space but could be operated when the vessel was parked if one knew how. Keth did, though it wasn't

general knowledge. "It's quick," he said. "We can do
it from the car. Since we haven't spotted the people
who are trailing us, they're doing it at a discreet distance. The chances are we'll be inside and going up
before they realize what we're thinking about. So let's
put in the next hour looking around for yachts like that!
If the situation looks favorable, we'll snatch one."

Telzey agreed. Keth was an expert yachtsman.

It appeared, however, that no yachts in that cat-
egory happened to be in the general area that day.
After an hour, Telzey transferred her belongings to
the residential tower where Keth was registered. It
seemed better not to become separated now. They
settled down to wait together until it would be time
to go to Osselin's residence.

5

Osselin's yoli was still in timeless communion with the
yoli of its dreams but beginning to show indications
of uneasiness. The imagery had become static and
patchy here and there. Telzey freshened it up. The
yoli murmured blissfully, and was lost again.

Since their last meeting, Osselin had added a piece
of pertinent equipment to his attire—a psi recorder,
disguised as a watch and fastened by a strap to his
brawny wrist. Its complex energies registered as a very
faint burring along Telzey's nerves. She'd come across
that particular type of instrument before. It was
expensive, highly touted in deluxe gambling establish-
ments and the like. It did, in fact, indicate any of
the cruder manipulations of psi energy, which had
earned it a reputation for reliability. One of its draw-
backs was that it announced itself to sufficiently
sensitive psis, a point of which the customers weren't

aware. And here it was no real threat to Telzey. The psi flows she used in investigative work were well below such a device's registration levels.

Barrand and Nelt had showed up presently, bringing two stunning young women with them. The girls, to Telzey's satisfaction, were gaily talkative creatures. Barrand was short, powerfully built. Nelt was short and wiry. Both had mind shields. Both wore psi recorders of the same type as Osselin's, though theirs weren't in sight. And like Osselin they were waiting for the tactile vibrations from the recorders which would tell them that psi was being used.

So they weren't really sure about her.

She'd split her attention again. Keth knew about that now, knew what to do to alert her if she didn't seem to be behaving in a perfectly normal manner. With suspicious observers on hand, that had seemed an advisable precaution. Keth and the ladies carried most of the conversation—the ladies perhaps putting up unwitting verbal screens for their escorts, as Keth was maintaining one to give Telzey as much freedom for her other activities as possible. Now and then she was aware that the COS chiefs studied her obliquely, somewhat as one might watch a trapped but not entirely predictable animal. The psi recorders remained inactive. She made progress along expanding lines with Osselin, sampled a series of dishes with evident appreciation, joined occasionally in the talk— realized dinner was over.

"Of course, I want to see Sorem!" she heard herself say. "But what in the world is a guilt-smeller?"

Nelt's lovely companion made fluttering motions with tapered white hands. "I'll keep my eyes closed until he's gone again!" she said apprehensively. "I looked at him *once* with his helmet off! I had nightmares for a month."

The others laughed. Osselin reached around for the yoli, perched at the moment on the back of his chair.

He placed it on his lap. "I'll keep my pet's eyes closed, too, while he's in the room," he said, smiling at Telzey. "It isn't easily frightened, but for some reason it's in deathly fear of Sorem. Guilt-smeller . . . well, Sorem supposedly has the ability to pick anyone with a strong feeling of guilty apprehension out of a group." He shrugged.

"He's unnatural," Nelt's lady told Telzey earnestly. "I don't care what they say—Sorem never was human! He couldn't have been."

"I might let him know your opinion of him," Barrand rumbled.

The girl paled in genuine fright. "Don't! I don't want him to notice me at all."

Barrand grinned. "You're in no danger—unless, of course, you have something to hide."

"Everybody has *something* to hide!" she protested. "I—" She broke off.

Faces turned to Telzey's right. Sorem, summoned unnoticed by Barrand, had come into the room. She looked around.

Sorem wore black uniform trousers and boots; a gun was fastened to his belt. The upper torso was that of a powerful man, narrow at the waist, wide in the shoulders, with massively muscled arms and chest. It was naked, hairless, a lusterless solid black, looking like sculptured rock. The head was completely enclosed by a large snouted helmet without visible eye slits.

This figure came walking toward the table, helmet already turning slowly in Telzey's direction. In Osselin's mind, she had looked at the head inside the helmet. Black and hairless like the body, the head of an animal, of a huge dog, yellow-eyed and savage. Barrand's bodyguard—a man who'd liked the idea of becoming a shape of fear enough to undergo considerable risks in having himself transformed into one. The great animal jaws were quite functional. Sorem was a triumph of the restructuring artists' skills.

The recorders had indicated no stir of psi throughout dinner. But they thought that perhaps she simply was being cautious now. Sorem was to frighten her, throw her off guard, jolt her into some revealing psi response. So she would show fear—which mightn't be too difficult. Sorem's mind was equipped with a shield like his employer's, but a brutish mirth and cruelty washed through it as he made it plain his attention was on her. Telzey glanced quickly, nervously, around the table, looked back at him. Keth's face was intent; he didn't know what would happen, whether it wasn't their executioner who had been called into the room. Sorem came up, steps slowing, a stalking beast. Telzey stopped breathing, went motionless, staring up at him. Abruptly, the helmet was swept away; the dog head appeared, snarling jaws half open. The eyes glared into Telzey's.

The yoli squealed desperately, struggling under Osselin's hand.

There were violent surges of psi energy then. The yoli wasn't fully aware of what was happening, but a nightmare shape had loomed up in its dreams, and it wanted to get away. Telzey couldn't afford to let it wake up now, and didn't. The three psi recorders remained active for perhaps forty-five seconds. Then she'd wiped the fright impressions from the yoli's mind, made it forget why it had been frightened. . . .

"It must have recognized your creature by his scent," Osselin was saying. "I had its eyes covered."

He stroked the yoli's furry head. It still whimpered faintly but was becoming reabsorbed by its fantasies. Sorem had turned away, was striding out of the room. Telzey watched him go, aware of Barrand's and Nelt's speculating eyes on her.

"If I'd been able to breathe," she gasped suddenly, "I'd have made more noise than that little animal!"

The beautiful COS dolls tried to smile at her.

❖   ❖   ❖

"Their recorders couldn't distinguish whether those psi jolts came from the yoli or from me," Telzey said. "And with the racket the yoli was making, it really was more likely it was doing it."

"So the final decision still is being postponed?" Keth said.

"Only on how to go about it, of course. The other two want to know whether I'm a psi or not, what we've learned, whether we were after the Big Deal in the first place. Osselin thinks that's no longer so important. He wants to get rid of us in a way that's safe, and take his chances on everything else. He's giving Barrand and Nelt a few more hours to come up with a good enough reason against his plan—but that's the way it's to be."

Keth shook his head. "He thinks that?"

"Yes, he thinks that."

"And at the same time he's to make sure that it's *not* the way it's to be? Isn't he aware of the contradiction?"

"He's controlled," Telzey said. "He's aware of what I let him be aware. It just doesn't occur to him that there is a contradiction. I don't know how else to explain that."

"Perhaps I get the idea," Keth said.

They were in Osselin's house. Barrand and Nelt and their retinue had left shortly after the incident with Sorem and the yoli, having plans for the evening. Osselin had asked Keth and Telzey to stay on for a while.

The difference of opinion among the COS chiefs was based on the fact that Osselin was less willing to risk a subsequent investigation than his colleagues. The forcing lie detector probes Barrand and Nelt wanted would involve traceable drugs or telltale physical damage if the subjects turned out to be as intractable as he suspected these subjects might be. A gentle anesthesia quiz wasn't likely to accomplish much here. It would be necessary to get rid of the bodies afterward. And the abrupt disappearance of Keth Deboll and a companion on Fermilaur was bound to lead to rather stringent investigations even as a staged accident. Osselin intended to have them killed in a manner which could leave no doubt about the accidental manner of their death. A tragic disaster.

"What kind of disaster?" Keth asked.

"He's got engineers working on that, and it's probably already set up," Telzey said. "We'll be seen walking in good health into the ground level of our tower. Depending on the time we get there, there'll be fifty to a hundred other people around. There's an eruption of gas-equipment failure. A moment later, we're all dead together. Automatic safeguards confine the gas to that level until it can be handled, so nobody else gets hurt."

Keth grunted. "Considerate of him."

Objectively considered, it was a sound plan. The tourist tower was full of important people; various top-level cliques congregated there. There'd be then a substantial sprinkling of important victims on the ground level. Even if sabotage was suspected, nothing would suggest that Keth and Telzey had been its specific targets.

On a subterranean level of Osselin's house was a vault area, and he was in it now. They hadn't accompanied him because anyone else's body pattern would bring the vault defenses into violent action. Telzey remained in mental contact; she hadn't quite finished her work on Osselin, though there wasn't much left to do. He was sewed up as tightly as she'd ever sewed anyone up. But he remained a tough-minded individual, and she wanted to take no chances whatever tonight. Things seemed under control and moving smoothly. But she wouldn't breathe easily again until Fermilaur vanished in space behind them.

In one respect, things had gone better than they'd had any reason to expect. "Will you settle for a complete file on the Big Deal?" she'd asked Keth. "The whole inside information gathering program? The file goes back almost three years, which was when it started. Names, dates, the information they got, what they did with it. . . ."

Osselin kept duplicate copies of the file in the vault. She'd told him to bring up one copy for Keth and forget he'd had that copy then. After that, it would be a question of getting off Fermilaur—not too easy even with Osselin's cooperation. He couldn't simply escort them to a spaceport and see that they were let through. They were under COS surveillance, would be trailed again when they left the house. COS police waited at the ports. If anything began to look at all suspicious, Barrand and Nelt would hear about it at once, and act at once.

Osselin obviously was the one best qualified to find a way out of the problem, and Telzey had instructed him to work on it. He came back up from the vault presently, laid two small objects on a table, said matter-of-factly, "I have some calls to make on the other matter," and left the room again.

Keth shook his head. "He seems so normal!"

"Of course, he seems normal," Telzey said. "He feels normal. We don't want anybody to start wondering about him."

"And this is the COS file?" Keth had moved over to the table.

"That's it."

The objects were a pair of half-inch microcubes. Keth smiled lovingly at them, took out a card case, opened it, ran his thumbnail along a section of its inner surface. The material parted. "Shrink section," he remarked. He dropped the cubes inside, sealed the slit with the ball of his thumb. The case was flat again and he returned it to an inner pocket.

Telzey brushed her hair back from her face. The room wasn't excessively warm, but she was sweating. Unresolved tensions. . . . She swore mentally at herself. It was no time to get nervous. "How small are they now?" she asked.

"Dust motes. I get searched occasionally. You drop the whole thing into an enlarger before you open it again, or you're likely to lose whatever you've shrunk." He glanced at his watch. "How far has he got on that other matter?"

"I haven't been giving much attention to it. I'm making sure I have him completely tied up—I'll probably have to break contact with him again before we're off Fermilaur."

"You still can't control him at a distance?"

"Oh, I might. But I wouldn't want to depend on that. He seems to have the details pretty well worked out. He'll tell us when he gets back."

"The pattern will be," said Osselin, "that you've decided to go out on the resorts. What you do immediately after you leave the house doesn't matter. Live it up, mildly, here and there, but work around toward Hallain Palace, and drop in there an hour and a half from now. If you don't know the place, you'll find its coordinates on your car controls."

"I can locate Hallain Palace," Keth said. "I left money enough there five years ago."

"Tonight you're not gambling," Osselin told him. "Go to the Tourist Shop, thirteenth level, where two lamps have been purchased against Miss Amberdon's GC account."

"Lamps?" repeated Keth.

"They're simply articles of the required size. You'll go to the store's shipping level with them to make sure they're properly packaged, for transportation to Orado. They're very valuable. You'll find someone waiting for you with two shipping boxes. You'll be helped into the boxes, which will then be closed, flown directly to Port Ligrit, passed through a freight gate under my seal, and put on board an Orado packet shortly before takeoff. In space, somebody will let you out of the boxes and give you your tickets." Osselin looked at Telzey. "Miss Orm and her mother are on their way to another port, accompanied by two Hute specialists who will complete Miss Orm's modeling reversion at her home. They'll arrive at the Orado City Terminal shortly after you do. You can contact them there."

"How far can you trust him?" Keth asked, as Osselin's house moved out of sight behind their car.

"Completely now," Telzey said. "Don't worry about that part! The way we're still likely to run into trouble is to do something at the last moment that looks suspicious to our snoops."

"We'll avoid doing it then," said Keth.

Telzey withdrew from contact with Osselin. He considered the arrangements to be foolproof, providing they didn't deviate from the timetable, so they probably were foolproof. Tracer surveillance didn't extend into enclosed complexes like Hallain Palace, where entrances could be watched to pick them up again as they emerged. By the time anyone began to look through the Palace's sections for them, they'd have landed on Orado. There'd be nothing to indicate then what had happened. Osselin himself would have forgotten.

They stopped briefly at a few tourist spots, circling in toward Hallain Palace, then went on to the Palace and reached it at the scheduled time. They strolled through one of the casinos, turned toward the Tourist Shop section. At the corner of a passage, three men in the uniform of the Fermilaur police stepped out in front of them.

There was a hissing sound. Telzey blacked out.

6

Barrand said, "Oh, you'll talk, of course. You'll tell us everything we want to know. We can continue the interrogation for hours. You may lose your minds if you resist too stubbornly, and you may be physically destroyed, but we'll have the truth from both of you before it gets that far."

It wasn't the escape plan that had gone wrong. Barrand and Nelt didn't know Osselin was under Telzey's control, or that she and Keth would have been off Fermilaur in less than an hour if they hadn't been picked up. They'd simply decided to override Osselin and handle the situation in their own way, without letting him know until it was too late to do anything about it. Presumably they counted on getting the support of the COS associates when they showed that the move had produced vital information.

Their approach wasn't a good one. Telzey had been fastened to a frame used in restructuring surgery, while Keth was fastened to a chair across the room. Frame and chair were attachments of a squat lie-detecting device which stood against one wall. A disinterested-looking COS surgeon and an angular female assistant sat at an instrument table beside Telzey. The surgeon had a round swelling in the center of his forehead, like a lump left by a blow. Apparently neither he nor the assistant cared to have the miracles of cosmetology applied to themselves.

They were the only two people in the room who weren't much concerned about what was going on. Telzey couldn't move her head very far and had caught only one glimpse of Nelt after she and Keth were brought awake. But Barrand remained within her range of vision, and his heavy features were sheened occasionally with a film of sweat. It was understandable. Barrand had to get results to justify his maneuver against Osselin. He might have regarded this as an opportunity to break down Osselin's prestige and following in the association. And so far Barrand could be certain of only one thing. He was, in fact, dealing with a psi.

He looked as if he almost wished he hadn't made the discovery.

From Telzey's point of view, it couldn't be avoided. Regaining contact with Osselin might be the only possible way to get them out of the situation, and she didn't know whether she could do it in time. The subtle approach was out now. While Keth, doing his part again, argued angrily and futilely with Barrand and Nelt, she'd been driving out a full-sweep search probe, sensitized to Osselin's mind patterns. Barrand's expression when he stared at her told her his psi recorder was registering the probe. So, of course, was Nelt's, whose impatiently muttering voice Telzey could hear in the section of the room behind her. He was keeping it low, but it was fairly obvious that he was hurrying along preliminary briefing instructions to the lie detector as much as he could without confusing the device or giving it insufficient information to work with. They were anxious to have it get started on her.

She hadn't picked up a trace of Osselin yet. But almost as soon as she began reaching out for him, she'd run into a storm of distress signals from another familiar mind.

It had turned into a bad day for Uspurul. Shortly after noon, she was called in to COS Services' regional office. Something happened there. She didn't know what. A period of more than an hour appeared to have lapsed unnoticed, and nobody was offering any explanations. She'd heard of amnesia treatments, but why should they have given her one? It frightened her.

She pretended that everything seemed normal, and when she was told to go to her quarters and rest for a few hours because she might be given a night assignment, she was able to convince herself that the matter was over—she'd been brushed briefly by some secret COS business, put to some use of which she was to know nothing, and restored to her normal duties.

An hour ago then, she'd been told to check out an aircar for a night flight to the Ialgeris Islands, registering Miss Amberdon and a Mr. Deboll as her passengers. That looked all right. Amberdon was still her assignment. The Ialgeris tour, though a lengthy one, requiring an expert guide because it involved sporadic weather risks, was nothing unusual. She took the car to one of the Barrand centers where she was to pick up the passengers. There she was conducted to a sublevel room and left alone behind a closed door. Misgivings awoke sharply again. There was no detectable way of opening the door from within the room.

Why should they lock her in? What was happening? Uspurul became suddenly, horribly, convinced that she'd been drawn deep into one of those dark COS activities she'd hardly even let herself think about. A fit of shaking came over her and it was some minutes then before she could control her muscles. Shortly afterward, the door opened. Uspurul stood up quickly, putting on a servile smile. The smile was wiped away by the shock of realizing that the man in the door was Nelt—one of the biggest of the COS big shots, one of the people she least wanted to see at present. Nelt beckoned her out into the passage.

Uspurul stepped out, legs beginning to shake again, glanced up the passage and felt she'd dropped into a nightmare. Barrand, the COS president, stood thirty feet away at an open door, speaking to a man in surgeon's uniform. Beside them was a float table, and

on it lay two covered figures. Uspurul didn't doubt
for an instant that they were those of her prospec-
tive passengers. Neither they nor she were to reach
the Ialgeris Islands. Tomorrow the aircar would be
reported lost in a sea storm, as a number were each
year in spite of all precautions—

The surgeon moved the float table through the
door, and Barrand followed it. Nelt turned away and
walked along the passage toward the room, leaving
Uspurul standing where she was. For a moment,
hopes flickered wildly in her. She might be able to
get out of the center unnoticed, find a place to hide—
stay alive!

A great black-gloved hand came down on her
shoulder. Uspurul made a choked screeching noise.
Nelt didn't look around. He went on into the room
and the door closed.

Sorem, whose black-uniformed tall figure Uspurul
had seen once at a distance, Barrand's bodyguard,
whose head was always covered in public by a large,
disturbingly shaped helmet, unlocked the door to an
adjoining room, went in with Uspurul and shoved her
down on a bench. She'd heard stories about Sorem.
Half fainting, staring fascinatedly at him, she hoped
he wouldn't take off the helmet.

But he did, and the yellow-eyed black dog head
grinned down at her.

The lie detector was asking its patterned series of
trap questions on the matters it had been instructed
to investigate, and Telzey was answering them. It was
nerve-stretching work. They'd stripped her before
fastening her to the frame, and she'd been warned
that if she refused to answer or the detector stated
she wasn't telling the truth, the surgeon was ready
to restructure one of her arms as a start.

She'd split her awareness again, differently, deeply.
The detector's only contact was with a shadow

mentality, ignorant of the split, memoryless, incapable
of independent thought. A mechanism. When a question was asked, she fed the mechanism the answer
she wanted it to give, along with the assurance that
it was the truth. It usually was not the truth, but the
mechanism believed it was. Psi sealed Telzey's mind
away otherwise both from the detector's sensors and
from crucial body contacts. There were no betraying
physical reactions.

It took much more concentration than she liked—
she'd still found no mental traces of Osselin, and a
purposeful search probe absorbed concentration
enough itself. But she needed time and was more
likely to gain time if she kept their attention on her,
away from Keth. He wasn't being questioned directly,
but Telzey suspected the detector was picking up
readings from him through the chair to which he was
fastened and comparing them with the readings it got
from her. There was a slight glassiness in Keth's look
which indicated he'd gone into a self-induced trance
as soon as the questions began, couldn't hear either
questions or answers, hence wasn't affected by them.
He'd said he could hold out against a lie detector by
such means for a while. But a sophisticated detector had ways of dealing with hypnotic effects, and the
COS machine obviously was an advanced model. She
should keep it working away at her as long as possible.

The questions ended abruptly. Telzey drew a long,
slow breath.

She might have caught a touch of Chan Osselin's
mind just then! She wasn't sure. The stress of maintaining her defense against the detector had begun
to blur her sensitivity.

The lie detector's voice said, "Deboll does not
respond to verbal stimuli at present. The cause can
be analyzed if desired. Amberdon's response to each
question registered individually as truthful. The overall

question-response pattern, however, shows a slight but definite distortion."

"In other words," Barrand said from behind Telzey, "she's been lying."

"That is the probability. The truth registration on individual questions is not a machine error. It remains unexplained."

Barrand and Nelt moved into Telzey's range of vision, looked down at her. Nelt shook his head.

"I don't like that," he said uneasily.

"Nor I," said Barrand. "And we can't be sure of what else she's doing. Let's speed up the procedure! Have the detector get Deboll out of whatever state he's in and start questioning him immediately. Put on full pressure at the slightest hesitation. Take the girl off the machine for the time being." Barrand looked at the surgeon. "Get to work. To begin with, I want the left arm deboned to the wrist and extended."

The surgeon's look of disinterest vanished. He drew back the sliding top of the instrument table. "A functional tentacle?"

Barrand grunted. "She's to stay alive and able to talk. Aside from that, keep her functional if you can, but it's not of primary importance. Let her watch what's happening." He added to Telzey, "We'll stop this as soon as you demonstrate to our satisfaction that you're willing to cooperate."

All the energy she could handle was reaching for Osselin's mind now. But the trace, if it had been one, had vanished. The sculpting frame moved, bringing her down and around. The surgeon's face appeared above her. An arm of the frame rose behind him and she saw herself in the tilted mirror at its tip.

"Don't let her lose consciousness," Barrand was saying to the surgeon's assistant. "But keep the pain level high—close to tolerance."

The skin on the odd lump in the center of the surgeon's forehead quivered and drew back to either side. The lump was a large dark bulging eye. It glanced over at Telzey's face independently of the other two eyes, then appeared to align itself with them. Part of Telzey's mind reflected quite calmly that a surgeon might, of course, have use for an independent eye—say one which acted as a magnifying lens.

But this was getting too close. Barrand and the detector weren't giving her the time she'd hoped to have.

"*Chan Osselin!*" She blasted the direct summons out, waited for any flicker of reaction that could guide her back to him.

Nothing.

Uspurul had been in an entertainingly hysterical commotion for a few minutes, but then she'd simply collapsed. Sorem wasn't sure whether she was conscious or not. When he prodded her with a finger, she made a moaning noise, but that could have been an automatic response. Sullenly, he decided to leave her alone. If she happened to die of fright here, it wouldn't really matter, but Barrand would be annoyed.

Sorem stood up from the bench on which he'd been sitting, hitched his gun belt around, looked down at the child-sized figure sprawled limply on the floor, eyes half shut. He nudged it with his boot. Uspurul whimpered. She still breathed at any rate. The black dog head yawned boredly. Sorem turned away toward the door, wondering how long it would be before they got what they wanted in the detector room.

Uspurul opened her eyes, looked for him, rolled up quietly on her feet.

Sorem had good reflexes, but not abnormally good ones; he was, after all, still quite human. And, at the moment, he was less than alert. He heard a faint, not immediately definable sound, felt almost simultaneously a violent jerk at his gun belt. He whirled, quickly enough now, saw for an instant a small face glare up at him, then saw and heard no more. The big gun Uspurul held gripped in both hands coughed again, but the first shot had torn the front of Sorem's skull away.

Telzey couldn't see the door opening into the lie detector room, but she was aware of it. For an instant, nobody else in the room was aware of it; and after that, it hardly mattered. Sorem had fancied a hair-triggered gun, and Uspurul was holding the trigger down as she ran toward Barrand and Nelt, swinging the gun muzzle about in short arcs in front of her. Most of the charges smashed into floor and wall, but quite enough reached the two COS chiefs. Nelt, already down, moments from death, managed to drag out his own gun and fire it blindly once. The side of Uspurul's scalp was laid open, but she didn't know it. Nelt died then. Barrand already was dead. Uspurul stopped shooting.

"Deboll," the lie detector's voice announced in the room's sudden silence, "is now ready for questioning."

Telzey said softly to the surgeon, "We don't exactly need you two, you know, but you won't get hurt if you do as I tell you. She'll do whatever I want."

"She will?" the surgeon breathed. He watched Uspurul staring at him and his assistant from twelve feet away, gun pointed. They'd both frozen when the shooting started. "What are we to do?"

"Get me off this thing, of course!"

He hesitated. "I'd have to move my hands . . ."

"Go ahead," Telzey said impatiently. "She won't shoot if that's all you're doing."

The frame released her moments later. She sat up, slid off it to the floor. Across the room, Keth cleared his throat. "You," Telzey said to the bony assistant, "get *him* unfastened! And *don't* try to get out of the room!"

"I won't," the assistant said hoarsely.

❖   ❖   ❖

"My impression," Keth remarked some hours later, "was that we were to try to stall them until you could restore your mental contact with Osselin and bring him to the rescue."

Telzey nodded. "That's what I wanted. It would have been safest. But, like I told you, that kind of thing isn't always possible. Barrand wouldn't let me have the time. So I had to use Uspurul, which I *didn't* like to do. Something could have gone wrong very easily!"

"Well, nothing did," said Keth. "She was your last resort, eh?"

"No," Telzey said. "There were a few other things I could have done, but not immediately. I wasn't sure any of them would work, and I didn't want to wait until they were carving around on me, or doped you to start talking. Uspurul I could use at once."

"Exactly how did you use her?" Keth asked.

Telzey looked at him. He said, "Relax! It's off the record. Everything's off the record. After all, nobody's ever likely to hear from me that it wasn't the famed Deboll ingenuity that broke the biggest racket on Fermilaur!"

"All right, I'll tell you," Telzey said. "I knew Uspurul was around almost as soon as we woke up. She's very easy psi material, so I made good contact with her again, just in case, took over her mind controls and shut subjective awareness down to near zero. Sorem thought she'd fainted, which would come to the same thing. Then when I had to use her, I triggered rage, homicidal fury, which shot her full of adrenaline. She needed it—she isn't normally very strong or very fast. That gun was really almost too heavy for her to hold up."

"So you simply told her to take the gun away from Barrand's monster, shoot him and come into the next room to shoot Barrand and Nelt?" Keth said.

Telzey shook her head.

"Uspurul couldn't have done it," she said. "She'd

never touched a gun in her life. Even in a frenzy like that, she couldn't use violence effectively. She wouldn't know how. She didn't know what was going on until it was over. She wasn't really there."

Keth studied her a moment. "You?"

"Me, of course," Telzey said. "I needed a body that was ready to explode into action. Uspurul supplied that. I had to handle the action."

"You know, it's odd," Keth said after a moment. "I never would have considered you a violent person."

"I'm not," Telzey said. "I've learned to use violence." She reflected. "In a way, being a psi is like being an investigative reporter. Even when you're not trying very hard, you tend to find out things people don't want you to know. Quite a few people would like to do something about Keth Deboll, wouldn't they? He might talk about the wrong thing any time. By now I've come across quite a few people who wanted to do something about me. I don't intend to let it happen."

"I wasn't blaming you," Keth said. "I'm all in favor of violence that keeps me alive."

They were on a liner, less than an hour from Orado. Once they were free, Telzey hadn't continued her efforts to contact Osselin mentally. They located a ComWeb instead, had him paged, and when he came on screen, she told him what to do. The story was that Sorem had gone berserk and killed Barrand and Nelt before being killed himself. Keth had made his own arrangements later from the liner. Adacee and various authorities would be ready to slam down on the secret COS project within a week.

Telzey's restrictions on Osselin should hold easily until then. The surgeon and his assistant had been given standard amnesia treatments to cover the evening. They could deduce from it that they'd been involved in a detector interrogation dealing with secret matters, but nothing else. It wasn't a new experience, and they weren't likely to be curious. Uspurul was aboard the liner.

"You know, I don't really have much use for a bondswoman," Keth remarked, thinking about that point.

"You won't be stuck with her contract for more than a year," Telzey said. "Keth, look. Don't you owe me something?"

He scratched his jaw. "Do I? You got us out of a mess, but I doubt I'd have been in the mess if it hadn't been for you."

"You wouldn't have had your COS story either."

Keth looked nettled.

"Don't be so sure! My own methods are reasonably effective."

"You'd have had the full story?"

"No, hardly that."

"Well, then!" Telzey said. "Uspurul's part of the story, so she can be your responsibility for a while. Fair enough? I'd take care of her myself if I didn't have my hands full."

"Why take care of her at all?"

"Because not everyone in COS is going to believe Osselin's version of what happened. They don't dare do anything about him, but there was enough to show Uspurul was involved somehow in what went on tonight. She's a rotten little creature in some ways, but I'd sooner not think of her being worked over by COS interrogation methods. They can break down amnesia treatments sometimes, so Osselin wanted to have her killed immediately to be on the safe side." Telzey added, "Uspurul's got a really good brain, and you'd be surprised at the things she's learned working for COS Services! Adacee should find her an asset. Give her half a chance, and she might make a great newscaster!"

"Adacee and I thank you," said Keth.

RESIDENT WITCH

1

Telzey checked in at the Morrahall Hotel in Orado City that evening, had an early dinner, and thereupon locked herself into her room. The impression she'd left at Pehanron College was that she would be spending the night with her family. Her parents, on the other hand, naturally assumed she was at the college. She'd programmed the ComWeb to have calls coming in at the college, at home, or to her car, transferred to the hotel room—if the caller, having been informed that she was busy and much preferred not to be disturbed before morning, felt there was justification enough for intruding on her privacy.

The semifinals of the annual robochess district championship series had begun, and she was still well up among the players. There should be two or three crucial games tonight, very little sleep. She wanted *all* the seclusion she could get.

She got into a casual outfit, settled down at the set, dialed herself into the series. Five minutes later, she was fed an opening move, an easy-looking one. She countered breezily. Six moves on, she was perspiring and trying to squirm out of an infernally ingenious trap. Out of it, though not unscathed, just ahead of deadline, she half closed a rather nasty little trap of her own.

Time passed in blissful absorption.

Then the ComWeb rang.

Telzey started, frowned, glanced at the instrument. It rang again. She pushed the Time Out button on the set, looked at her watch, switched on the Com-Web. "Yes?" she said.

"A caller requests override, Miss Amberdon," the ComWeb told her.

"Who is it?"

"The name is Wellan Dasinger."

"All right." Telzey clicked in nonvisual send, and Dasinger's lean tanned face appeared in the screen. "I'm here," she said. "Hello, Dasinger."

"Hello, Telzey. Are we private?"

"As private as we can be," she assured him. Dasinger was the head of Kyth Interstellar, a detective agency to which she'd given some assistance during the past year, and which in turn was on occasion very useful to her.

"I need information," he said. "Quite urgently— in your special study area. I'd like to come out to Pehanron and talk to you. Immediately, if possible." This was no reference to her law studies. Dasinger knew she was a psi; but neither he nor she referred to psi matters directly on a ComWeb. He added, "I realize it can't be the most convenient hour for you."

Dasinger wasn't given to overstatement. If he said a matter was quite urgent, it was as urgent as matters could get. Telzey depressed the Concede button on the robochess set, thereby taking herself out of the year's series. The set clicked off. "The hour's convenient, Dasinger," she said. "So is the location."

"Eh?"

"I'm not at the college. I took a room at the Morrahall for the night. You're at the agency?"

"I am." The Kyth offices were four city block complexes away. "Can I send someone over for you?"

"I'll be down at the desk in five minutes," Telzey told him.

She slipped into sportswear, fitted on a beret, slung her bag from her shoulder, and left the room.

There were three of them presently in Dasinger's private conference room. The third one was a Kyth operator Telzey hadn't met before, a big blond man named Corvin Wergard.

"What we want," Dasinger was saying, "is a telepath, a mind-reader—the real thing. Someone absolutely dependable. Someone who will do a fast, precise job for a high fee, and won't be too fussy about the exact legality of what he's involved in or a reasonable amount of physical risk. Can you put us in contact with somebody like that? Some acquaintance?"

Telzey said hesitantly, "I don't know. It wouldn't be an acquaintance; but I *may* be able to find somebody like that for you."

"We've tried the listed professionals," Wergard told her. "Along with some unlisted ones who were recommended to us. Mind-readers; people with telepathic devices. None of them would be any good here."

Telzey nodded. No one like that was likely to be much good anywhere. The good ones stayed out of sight. She said, "It might depend on exactly what you want the telepath to do, why you want him to do it. I know it won't be anything unethical, but he'll want to be told more than that."

Dasinger said, "It may concern a murder already carried out, or a murder that's still to come. If it's the last, we want to prevent it. Unfortunately, there's very little time. Would you like to see the file on the case? It's a short one."

Telzey would. It was brought to her.

The file was headed: *Selk Marine Equipment.* Which was a company registered on Cobril, the water world eighteen hours from Orado. The brothers Noal and Larien Selk owned the company, Larien having been involved in it for only the past six years. For the past four years, however, he alone had been active in the management. Noal, who'd founded the company, had been traveling about the Hub during that time, maintaining a casual connection with the business.

A week ago, Noal had contacted the Kyth Agency's branch on Cobril. He'd returned unexpectedly, found indications that Larien was siphoning off company funds, and apparently investing them in underworld enterprises on Orado. He wanted the agency to start tracing the money on Orado, stated he would arrive there in a few days with the evidence he'd accumulated.

He hadn't arrived. Two days ago, Hishee Selk, Larien's wife, appeared at the agency's Cobril branch. She said Larien had implied to her that Noal had tried to make trouble for him and would pay for it. From his hints, she believed Larien had arranged to have Noal kidnapped and intended to murder him. She wanted the agency to find Noal in time to save his life.

The Selk file ended there. Visual and voice recordings of the three principals were included. Telzey studied the images, listened to the voices. There wasn't much obvious physical resemblance between the brothers. Larien was young, athletically built, strikingly handsome, had an engaging smile. Noal, evidently the older by a good many years, seemed a washed-out personality—slight, stooped, colorless. Hishee was a slender blonde with slanted black eyes and a cowed look. Her voice matched the look; it was low and uncertain. Telzey went through that recording again, ignoring Hishee's words, absorbing the voice tones.

She closed the file then. "Where's the rest of it?"

"The rest of it," said Dasinger, "is officially none

of the Kyth Agency's business at the moment. Hence it isn't in the agency files."

"Oh?"

"You know a place called Joca Village, near Great Alzar?"

She nodded. "I've been there."

"Larien Selk acquired an estate in the Village three months ago," Dasinger said. "It's at the northeast end, an isolated cliffside section overlooking the sea. We know Larien is there at present. And we've found out that Noal Selk was in fact kidnapped by professionals and turned over to Larien's people. The probability is that he's now in Larien's place in Joca Village. If they try to move him out of there, he'll be in our hands. But that's the only good prospect of getting him back alive we have so far. Larien has been given no reason to believe anyone is looking for his brother, or that anyone but Hishee has begun to suspect Noal is missing. That's our immediate advantage. We can't afford to give it up."

Telzey nodded, beginning to understand. Joca Village was an ultraexclusive residential area, heavily guarded. If you weren't a resident or hadn't been issued a pass by a resident, you didn't get in. Passes were carefully checked at the single entrance, had to be confirmed. Overhead screens barred an aerial approach. She said, "And you can't go to the authorities until you have him back."

"No," Dasinger said. "If we did, we'd never get him back. We might be able to pin murder on Larien Selk later, though that's by no means certain. In any case, it isn't what we're after." He hesitated, said questioningly after a moment, "Telzey?"

Telzey blinked languidly.

"Telzey—" Dasinger broke off, watching her. Wergard glanced at him. Dasinger made a quick negating motion with his hand. Wergard shifted his attention back to Telzey.

"I heard you," Telzey said some seconds later. "You have Hishee Selk here in the agency, don't you?"

Wergard looked startled. Dasinger said, "Yes, we do."

"It was her voice mainly," Telzey said. "I picked her up on that." She looked at Wergard. "Wergard can't really believe this kind of thing is real."

"I'm trying to suspend my doubts," Wergard said. "Bringing in a mind-reader wasn't my idea. But we could use one only too well here."

Dasinger said, "All right to go on now, Telzey?"

"Oh, yes," she said. "I was gone for only a moment. Now I'm making contact, and Hishee looks wide open. She's very easy!" She straightened up in her chair. "Just what do you want your mind-reader to do?"

Dasinger said to Wergard, "What Telzey means is that, having seen what Hishee Selk looks like, and having heard her voice, she gained an impression of Hishee's personality. She then sensed a similar impression around here, found a connection to the personality associated with it, and is now feeling her way into Hishee's mind. Approximately correct, Telzey?"

"Very close." For a nonpsi, Dasinger did, in fact, have a good understanding of psi processes.

"Now as to your question," he went on. "When Larien Selk bought the place in Joca Village, he had it equipped with security devices, installed by Banance Protective Systems, a very good outfit. During the past week, Banance added a few touches—mainly a Brisell pack and its handler. At the same time, the Colmer Detective Agency in Great Alzar was employed to provide round-the-clock guards, five to a shift, stationed directly at the house, behind the pack. However, we've obtained copies of the Banance security diagrams which show the setup on the grounds. And, of course, there are various ways of handling guards."

"You mean you can get into Joca Village and into the house?"

"Very likely. One of the residents is an agency client and has supplied us with Village passes. Getting in the Selk estate and into the house without alerting security presents problems, but shouldn't be too difficult. Everything is set up to do it now, two or three hours after nightfall at Joca Village. It's after we're inside the house that the matter becomes really ticklish."

Wergard said, "It's a one-shot operation. If we start it, it has to come off. We can't back away, and try again. Either Noal will be safe before his brother realizes somebody is trying to rescue him, or he'll have disappeared for good."

Telzey considered. It was easy enough to dispose of a human being instantly and tracelessly. "And you don't *know* Noal's in the house?" she said.

"No," Dasinger said. "There's a strong probability he's there. If we can't do better, we'll have to act on that probability tonight, because every hour of delay puts his life—if he's still alive—in greater danger. If he isn't there, Larien is the one person in the house who's sure to know where he is. But picking up Larien isn't likely to do Noal any good. He's bound to have taken precautions against that, and again Noal, wherever he is, will simply vanish, along with any evidence pointing to him. So we come back to the mind-reader—somebody who can tell us from Larien's mind exactly where Noal is and what we can do about it, before Larien knows we're in the house."

"Yes; I see," Telzey said. "But there're a number of things I *don't* understand here. Why does Larien—" She broke off, looked reflective a moment, nodded. "I can get that faster from Hishee now! It's all she's thinking about."

2

Larien Selk, legally and biologically Noal's junior by
twenty-five years, was, in the actual chronology of
events, the older brother. He'd been conceived first
by three years. The parents were engaged in building up a business and didn't want to be burdened with
progeny taxes. The Larien-to-be went to an embry-
onic suspense vault. When Noal was conceived, the
family could more readily afford a child, and the
mother decided she preferred giving natural birth to
one.

So Noal was born. His parents had no real wish
for a second child. They kept postponing a decision
about the nameless embryo they'd stored away, and
in the end seemed almost to have forgotten it. It
wasn't until they'd died that Noal, going through old
records, found a reference to his abandoned sibling.
Somewhat shocked by his parents' indifference, he
had Larien brought to term. When his brother grew
old enough to understand the situation, Noal
explained how he'd come to take his place.

Larien never forgave him. Noal, a shrewd enough
man in other respects, remained unaware of the fact.
He saw to it that Larien had the best of everything—
very nearly whatever Larien wanted. When he came
of age, Noal made him a partner in the company he'd
founded and developed. Which put Larien in a position to begin moving against his brother.

Hishee was his first move. Hishee was to have
married Noal. She was very young, but she was fond
of him and a formal agreement wasn't far away. Then
Larien turned his attention on Hishee, and the formal agreement was never reached. Hishee fell violently in love.

Noal accepted it. He loved them both; they were
near the same age. But he found it necessary to

detach himself from them. He waited until they married, then turned the effective management of the company over to Larien, and began traveling.

Larien set out casually to break Hishee. He did an unhurried thorough job of it, gradually, over the months, eroding her self-esteem and courage in a considered variety of ways. He brought her to heel, continued to reduce her. By the time Noal Selk came back to Cobril, Hishee was too afraid of Larien, too shaken in herself, to give her brother-in-law any indication of what had happened.

But Noal saw it. Larien had wanted him to see it, which was a mistake. Larien wasn't quite as well covered in his manipulation of the company's assets as he'd believed.

Noal, alerted to Larien's qualities, became also aware of that. He made a quiet investigation. It led him presently to the Kyth detective agency.

Then he disappeared.

Dasinger said dryly, "We'd put you on the Kyth payroll any time, Telzey! It took us some hours to extract half that information from Hishee. The rest of it checks. If Larien thinks it's safe, he'll see Noal broken completely before he dies. No doubt he's made ingenious arrangements for that. He's an ingenious young man. But the time we have for action remains narrowly limited."

"He doesn't know Hishee's gone?" Telzey asked.

"Not yet. We have that well covered. We had to take her out of the situation; she'd be in immediate danger now. But it's an additional reason for avoiding delay. If Larien begins to suspect she had courage enough left to try to save Noal, he'll destroy the evidence. He should be able to get away with it legally, and he knows it."

Telzey was silent a moment. There were some obscure old laws against witchcraft, left deliberately unchanged, very rarely applied. Aside from that, the Federation was officially unaware of the existence of psis; a psi's testimony was meaningless. Legally then, it was probable enough that Larien Selk could get away with the murder of his brother. She doubted he'd survive Noal long; the private agencies had their own cold rules. But, as Dasinger had said, that wasn't what they were after.

She said, "Why do you want to plant the telepath in the house? If he's good enough, he should be able to tap Larien's mind from somewhere outside Joca Village, though it probably would take a little longer."

Wergard said, "One of the Banance security devices is what's known technically as a psi-block. It covers the outer walls of the house. Larien shares some of the public superstitions about the prevalence of efficient mind-reading instruments. Presumably the block would also stop a human telepath."

She nodded. "Yes, they do."

"When he's outside one of his psi-blocked structures, he wears a mind shield," Wergard said. "A detachable type. If we'd known about this a little earlier, we might have had an opportunity to pick him up and relieve him of it. But it's too late now."

"Definitely too late," Dasinger agreed. "If you think you can find us a telepath who's more than a hit-and-miss operator, we'd take a chance on waiting another day, if necessary, to bring him in on it. But it would be taking a chance. If you can't get one, we'll select a different approach and move tonight."

Telzey said, "A telepath wouldn't be much good to you if Larien happens to be probe-immune. About one in eight people are."

"Seven to one are good odds in the circumstances," Dasinger said. "Very good odds. We'll risk that."

"They're better than seven to one," Telzey told him. "Probe-immunes usually don't know that's what they are, but they usually don't worry about having their minds read either. They feel safe." She rubbed her nose, frowning. "A Psychology Service psi could do the job for you, and I can try getting one. But I don't think they'll help. They won't lift a finger in ordinary crime cases."

Dasinger shook his head. "I can't risk becoming involved with them here anyway. Technically it's an illegal operation. The Kyth Agency won't be conducting it unless we come up with evidence that justified the illegality. I resigned yesterday, and Wergard and some others got fired. We'll be acting as private citizens. But that's also only a technicality, and the Service is unpredictable. I don't know what view they'd take of it. We might have them blocking us instead of helping. Can you find someone else?"

She nodded. "I can get you a telepath. Just one. The other psis I know won't touch it. They don't need the fee, and they don't want to reveal themselves— particularly not in something that's illegal."

"Who's the one?" Wergard asked.

"I am, of course."

They looked at her a moment. Wergard said, "That isn't what we had in mind. We want a pro who'll take his chances for the money he's getting. We needed information from you, but no more than that."

Telzey said, "It looks like it's turned into more than that."

Wergard said to Dasinger, "We can't get her involved."

"Corvin Wergard," Telzey said.

He looked back at her. "Yes?"

"I'm not reading your thoughts," she said. "I don't have to. You've been told who I am, and that I'm sixteen years old. So I'm a child. A child who comes of a very good family and has been very carefully raised. Somebody really too nice to get shot tonight, if something goes wrong, by a Colmer guard or Joca Security people, or ripped up by Brisells. Right?"

Wergard studied her a long moment. "I may have had such notions," he said then. "Perhaps I've been wrong about you."

"You've definitely been wrong about me," Telzey told him. "You didn't know enough. I've been a psi, a practicing psi, for almost a year. I can go through a human life in an hour and know more about it than the man or woman who's living it. I've gone through quite a few lives, not only human ones. I do other things that I don't talk about. I don't know what it all exactly makes me now, but I'm not a child. Of course, I *am* sixteen years old and haven't been that very long. But it might even be that sometimes people like you and Wellan Dasinger look a little like children to me. Do you understand?"

"I'm not sure," Wergard said. He shook his head. "I believe I'm beginning to."

"That's good. We should have an understanding of each other if we're to work together. The agency would save the fee, too," Telzey said. "I don't need it. Of course, there may come a time when I'll ask you to stick your neck out for something I'd like to have done."

Wergard asked Dasinger, "Has that been the arrangement?"

Dasinger nodded. "We exchange assistance in various matters." He added, "I still don't want you in this, Telzey. There will be risks. Not unreasonable ones; but our people are trained to look out for themselves in ways you're not. You're too valuable a person to be jeopardized on an operation of this kind."

"Then I can't help you help Noal Selk," she said. "I'd like to. But the only way I can do it is by going along with you tonight. It would take more time than you have to hunt around for somebody else."

Dasinger shook his head. "We'll use a different approach then. With a little luck, we can still save Noal. He isn't your problem."

"How do you know?" Telzey said. "He mightn't be if he were someone I'd only heard about. If I helped everybody I could help because I happen to be a psi, I'd have no time for anything else the rest of my life. There isn't a minute in the day I couldn't find someone somewhere who needs the kind of help I can give. I'd keep busy, wouldn't I? And, of course, everything I did still wouldn't make any real difference. There'd always be more people needing help."

"There would be, of course," Dasinger agreed.

She smiled. "It gave me a bad conscience for a while, but I decided I wasn't going to get caught in that. I'll do something, now and then. Now, here I've been in Hishcc Sclk's mind. I'm still in her mind. I know her, and Noal and Larien as she knows them—perhaps better than most people know the members of their family. So I can't say their problem isn't my problem. It wouldn't be true. I simply know them too well."

Dasinger nodded. "Yes, I see now."

"And I," said Wergard, "made a large mistake."

Dasinger looked at his watch. "Well, let's not waste time. The plan goes into operation in thirty minutes. Telzey, you're going high style—Joca Village level. Wergard, take her along, have her outfitted. Scratch Woni. We won't need her."

3

The only entry to the secluded Selk estate in Joca Village was a narrow road winding between sheer cliff walls. Two hundred yards along the road was a gate; and the gate was guarded by Selk employees.

Up this road came a great gleaming limousine, preceded by a cry of golden horns. It stopped near the gate, and Larien Selk's three guards moved forward, weapons in their hands, to instruct the intruders to turn back. But they came prepared to give the instruction in as courteous a manner as possible. It was unwise to offer unnecessary offense to people who went about in that kind of limousine.

Its doors had opened meanwhile; and, gaily and noisily, out came Wergard in a Space Admiral's resplendent and heavily decorated uniform; Dasinger with jeweled face mask, a Great Alzar dandy; Telzey, finally, slender and black-gowned, wearing intricate silver headgear. From the headgear blazed the breath-stopping beauty of two great star hyacinths, proclaiming her at once to be the pampered darling of one who looked on ordinary millionaires as such millionaires might look on the lowest of bondsmen.

Weapons most tactfully lowered, the guards attempted to explain to these people—still noisily good-natured, but dangerous in their vast arrogance and wealth and doubly unpredictable now because they were obviously high on something—that a mistake had been made, that, yes, of course, their passes must be honored, but this simply didn't happen to be a route to the estate of the Askab Odarch. In the midst of these respectful explanations, an odd paralysis and confusion came to the guards. They offered no objection when men stepped out from behind the limousine, gently took their weapons and led them toward the small building beside the gate, where Wergard already was studying the gate controls. The study was a brief one; the gate's energy barrier, reaching up to blend into the defense shield of Joca Village above, winked out of existence a minute later and the great steel frames slid silently back into the rock walls on either side. The instruments which normally announced the opening of the gate to scanners in the Selk house remained inactive.

The limousine drifted through and settled to the

ground beside the road. The gate closed again, and the vehicle was out of sight. Joca Village security patrols would check this gate, as they did the gates of all Village residents, several times during the night, and leaving the limousine outside would have caused questions. Whether suspicions were aroused otherwise depended mainly on whether someone began to wonder why Larien Selk's three gate guards were men who hadn't been seen here before. Measures had been taken to meet that contingency, but they were measures Dasinger preferred not to bring into play at present. The goal was to get Telzey into the house quickly, find out where Noal Selk was, pick him up if he was here and get back out with him, with no more time lost than could be helped. Whether or not his brother came along would be determined by what they discovered. With luck in either case, they'd be out of Joca Village again, mission accomplished, before the next patrol reached the Selk estate.

Only Dasinger, Wergard, and Telzey had gone through with the limousine. They emerged from it quickly again, now in fitted dark coveralls, caps and gloves, difficult to make out in the nighttime half-dark of the cliff road, and with more sophisticated qualities which were of value to burglars seeking entry into a well-defended residence. They moved silently along the road in the thick-soled sound-absorbing boots which went with the coveralls, Wergard carrying a sack. The road led around a turn of the cliffs; and a hundred yards beyond the turn, Dasinger said, "You might give them the first blast from here."

They stopped. The rock wall on the left was lower at this point, continued to slope downward along the stretch of road ahead. Wergard opened the sack and took out a tube a foot long and about three inches in diameter. He lifted the tube, sighting along it to a point above the cliffs on the left, pressed a trigger button. Something flicked silently out of the mouth of the tube and vanished in the dark air. They went on fifty yards, stopped again, and Wergard repeated the performance. The next time they stopped, the cliff on the left had dwindled to a rocky embankment not much more than twelve feet high. Larien Selk's big house stood in its gardens beyond the embankment, not visible from here.

They stood listening.

"It's got them," Wergard said then, low-voiced. "If it hadn't, they'd be aware of us by now, and we'd hear them moving around."

"Might as well give them a third dose, to be sure," Dasinger remarked.

"Why not?" Wergard agreed. He took a third tube from the sack, adjusted its settings, squinting through the dusk, then discharged its contents up across the embankment. The copies of the diagrams, briefly borrowed from the files of Banance Protective Systems, had showed that beyond the fence above the embankment was the area patrolled by a dozen Brisell dogs, dependable man-killers with acute senses. The three canisters Wergard had fired into the area were designed to put them out of action. They contained a charge stunning canine olfactory centers, approximately equivalent, Telzey had gathered, to the effect which might have been achieved by combining the most violent odors obtainable in their heaviest possible concentration, and releasing the mix in a flash of time. The canine mind thus treated went into prolonged dazed shock.

"Getting anything so far?" Dasinger asked her.

She nodded. "There is a psi-blocked area around. It seems to be where the house is. If Noal and Larien are here, they're in that area."

She'd kept bringing up impressions of both Selk brothers on the way from Orado City—things she knew about them from Hishee Selk's recalls and reflections, and from the visual and auditory recordings her own

senses had registered. After they'd passed through the
gate, she'd been searching mentally for anything which
might relate to those impressions, blocking off her
awareness of Wergard and Dasinger. There'd been
occasional faint washes of human mind activities here-
abouts, but they carried unfamiliar patterns. She'd
fastened on the most definite of those and was developing the contact when Dasinger addressed her.

She mentioned this now, added, "It's one of the
Colmer guards outside the house. Nobody's expecting trouble there. I can't tell yet what he's thinking,
but nothing's worrying him."

Dasinger smiled. "Good! Keep your inner ears
tuned to the boy! That could be useful. Let's move
on—starting from here, as ghosts."

He reached under his collar as he spoke, abruptly
became a bulkier smoky figure, features distorted
though still vaguely distinguishable. There was a visual
dispersion effect connected with the coverall suits,
increasing with distance. Wergard and Telzey joined
him in apparent insubstantiality. They went around
the embankment, came to the fence.

It was more than a fence. Closely spaced along the
rails topping it, twenty feet above, were concealed
pickup devices which registered within the house. The
diagrams had listed and described them. Now reasonable caution and the equipment in the suits of the
three trespassers should give the devices nothing to
register.

They moved slowly along the fence, twelve feet
apart, not speaking here though they carried distorters
which smothered voice tones within the distance of
a few feet, until Wergard, in the lead, reached a
closed gate where the road they'd been following
turned through the fence. His wavering contours
stopped there; and Telzey and Dasinger also stopped
where they were. Wergard was the burglary expert;
his job was now to get them through the gate. It was

locked, of course. The relays which opened the lock
were in the house, and the lock itself was a death
trap for anyone attempting to tamper with it. However, nobody had seemed concerned about those
details, and Telzey decided not to worry either.
Wergard was doing something, but she couldn't determine what. His foggy shape blurred out a quarter of
the gate. Which wasn't bothering Wergard; the effect
wasn't a subjective one. Telzey could see a faint haze
about herself, which moved as she did. But it didn't
interfere with her vision or blur her view of herself.
She looked over at the house, still more than half
hidden here by intervening trees.

It was a large windowless structure. A pale glow
bathed the lower section of the front wall. That came
from a lit area they'd have to cross. Closer to them,
on this side of the trees, the ground was shadowy,
heavily dotted with sizable shrubs, through which she
could make out the outlines of a high hedge. This was
where the Brisell pack prowled. She thought she could
distinguish something moving slowly on the ground
between two shrubs. It might be one of the dogs.
Otherwise there was no sign of them.

A voice suddenly said something.

Telzey didn't move. She hadn't heard those words
through her ears but through the ears of her contact.
He was replying now, the sound of his own voice less
distinct, a heavy rumble. She blinked, pushing probes
out quickly into newly accessible mind areas, orient-
ing herself. The contact was opening up nicely. . . .

A hand tapped her shoulder. She looked up at
Dasinger beside her. He indicated the gate, where
Wergard had stepped back and stood waiting for
them. The gate was open.

The thing she'd thought she'd seen moving occasionally on the ground between two shrub clusters
was one of the Brisells. He was lying on his side as
they came up, and, except for jerking his hind legs

slightly, he wasn't moving just then. Two other dogs, not far from him, had been out of sight behind the shrubs. One turned in slow circles, with short, staggering steps. The other sat with drooping head, tongue lolling far down, shaking himself every few seconds. They were powerful animals with thick necks, huge heads and jaws, torsos protected by flexible corselets. None of them paid the slightest attention to the human ghost shapes.

Dasinger beckoned Telzey and Wergard to him, said softly, "They'll be no good for an hour or two. But we don't know that our business here will be over in an hour or two. We'll get their handler in the shelter now. Then it should be worth a few minutes finding the rest of the pack and putting them out till tomorrow with stun charges."

Wergard nodded; and Dasinger said to Telzey, "Stay here near those three so we don't lose you."

"All right."

She watched them hold their guns briefly to the heads of the dogs. Then the blurred shapes moved soundlessly off, becoming more apparitional with each step. In moments, she couldn't see them at all. The dogs lay unmoving now; and nothing else stirred nearby. She went back to her contact. Human thought whispers which came from other minds were reaching her from time to time, but she didn't try to develop those touches. The man she'd started working on was in charge of the Colmer Agency group and stationed near the entry of the house, directly beyond the lit area. She should get the best results here by concentrating attention on him.

His superficial thoughts could be picked up readily by now. It was the thinking of a bored, not very intelligent man, but a dangerous and well-trained one. A human Brisell. He and his group were in the second hour of an eight-hour stint of guard duty. He was looking forward to being relieved. Telzey gave the vague flow of thoughts prods here and there, turning them into new directions. She got a self-identification: his name was Sommard. He and the other Colmer guards knew nothing of what went on inside the home, and weren't interested. On arrival, they'd been admonished to constant alertness by a Mr. Costian. Sommard figured Mr. Costian for a nervous nut; the place obviously was well protected without them. But that wasn't his business, and he was doing his duty, however perfunctorily. His attention never wandered far. Two other guards stood to his right and left some fifty yards away, at the corners of the house. The remaining two were at the rear of the building where there was a service entry. . . . That checked with what the Kyth Agency had established about the defense arrangements.

There was a sudden wash of mental brightness. It steadied, and Telzey was looking out of Sommard's eyes into the wide illuminated court below the house where the estate road terminated. Keeping watch on that open area, up to the fence on the far side and the locked road gate in the fence, was his immediate responsibility. If anyone not previously authorized by Mr. Costian to be there appeared in the court, there'd be no challenge. He'd give his companions and the people in the house a silent alert, and shoot the intruder. Of course, no one would appear there! He yawned.

Telzey let the view of the court go, made some preparations, reduced contact, and glanced at her watch. It had been four and a half minutes since the Kyth men left her. She began looking about for them, presently saw a haziness some twenty feet away, condensing slightly and separating into two shapes as it drew closer. A genuine pair of ghosts couldn't have moved more quietly. "The section's taken care of," Dasinger was saying then. "Anything to report?"

Telzey told them what she'd learned. Dasinger

nodded. "Costian's been Larien Selk's underworld contact on Orado. It's probable that the pros delivered Noal to him." He scratched his chin. "Now what's the best way to take the agency guards out gently? We have no dispute with Colmer."

Wergard said, "Going through the gate's still possible, but it'll call for fast moving once we're through or we'd risk disturbance. The long way around past the cliffs seems safer to me."

Telzey shook her head.

"That won't be necessary," she said.

Sommard presently shut his eyes for no particular reason except that he felt like it. The road gate across the court opened slightly, stayed open a few seconds, closed quietly again. Sommard then roused himself, looked briskly about. He glanced at his two colleagues, stationed at the corners of the house on either side of him. They stood unmoving, as bored as he was. All was well. He scratched his chest, yawned again.

Thirty feet from him, invisible as far as he was concerned, Telzey settled herself on the low balustrade above the court, looked at him, reached back into his mind. She waited. Something like a minute passed. The guard at the corner to Sommard's left took two stumbling steps to the side and fell backward.

Sommard's awareness blanked out in the same instant. His knees buckled; he slid down along the wall against which he had been leaning, went over on his side and lay still.

Telzey looked around at the guard at the other house corner. He was down and out, too, and Wergard and Dasinger were now on their way along the sides of the house to take care of the two guards at the rear. She stood up and went over to Sommard. What she'd done to him was a little more complicated than using a stun gun, a good deal gentler than a stun gun's jolt. The overall effect, however, was the same. He'd go on sleeping quietly till morning.

She stayed beside him to make it easier for Dasinger to find her when he came to take her to the back of the house. There was an entry there which led to the servants' quarters below ground level. They would use that way to get into the house. There should be only three men in the servants' quarters tonight—Larien Selk's second gate guard team. They might be asleep at present. The estate's normal staff had been transferred to other properties during the past week. In the upper house were Costian, Larien Selk, probably Noal Selk, and two technicians who kept alternate watch on the instruments of the protective system. That was all.

Getting into the house wasn't likely to be much of a problem now. But the night's work might have only begun.

4

"I'm getting traces of Larien," Telzey said.

"And Noal?" Dasinger asked.

"I'm not sure. There was something for a moment—but—" Her voice trailed off unsteadily.

"Take your time." Dasinger, leaning against a table ten feet away, watching her in the dim glow of a ceiling light, had spoken quietly. They'd turned off the visual distorters; the ghost haze brought few advantages indoors. Wergard had found the three off-duty gate guards asleep, left them sleeping more soundly. He'd gone off again about some other matter. Telzey and Dasinger were to stay on the underground level until she'd made her contacts, established what the situation here was.

She leaned back in her chair, closed her eyes, sighed. There was silence then. Dasinger didn't stir. Telzey's face was pale, intent. After a while, her breathing grew ragged. Her lips twisted slowly. It might have been a laborious mouthing of words heard in her mind. Her fingers plucked fitfully at the material of the coveralls. Then she grew quiet. Wergard returned soundlessly, remained standing outside the door.

Telzey opened her eyes, looked at Dasinger and away from him, straightened up in the chair, and passed her tongue over her lips.

"It's no use," she said in a flat, drained voice.

"You couldn't contact Noal?"

She shook her head. "Perhaps I could. I don't know. You'll have to get the psi block shut off, and I'll try. He's not in the house." She began crying suddenly, stopped as suddenly. A valve had opened; had been twisted shut. "But we can't help him," she said. "He's dying."

"Where is he?"

"In the sea."

"In the sea? Go ahead."

She shrugged. "That's it! In the sea, more or less east of Joca Village. It might be a hundred miles from here, or two thousand. I don't know; nobody knows. Larien didn't want anybody to know, not even himself."

Wergard had come into the room. She looked over at him, back at Dasinger. "It's a bubble for deep water work. Something the Selks made on Cobril. Marine equipment. Larien had it brought in from Cobril. This one has no operating controls. It was just dropped off, somewhere."

An automated carrier had been dispatched, set on random course. For eight hours it moved about the sea east of the mainland; then it disintegrated and sank. At some randomly selected moment during those eight hours, relays had closed, and the bubble containing Noal Selk began drifting down through the sea.

She told them that.

Dasinger said, "You said he's dying . . ."

She nodded. "He's being eaten. Some organism— it tries to keep the animals it feeds on alive as long as it can. It's very careful . . . I don't know what it is."

"I know what it is," Dasinger said. "When was it injected?"

"Two days ago."

Dasinger looked at Wergard. Wergard shrugged, said, "You might find something still clinically alive in the bubble five days from now. If you want to save Noal Selk, you'd better do it in hours."

"It's worth trying!" Dasinger turned to Telzey. "Telzey, what arrangements has Larien made in case the thing got away from him?"

"It isn't getting away from him," she said. "The bubble's got nondetectable coating. And if somebody tried to open it, it would blow up. There's a switch in the house that will blow it up any time. Larien's sitting two feet from the switch right now. But he can't touch it."

"Why not?" Wergard asked.

Telzey glanced at him. "He can't move. He can't even think. Not till I let him again."

Dasinger said, "The destruct switch isn't good enough. Isn't there something else in the house, something material, we can use immediately as evidence of criminal purpose?"

Telzey's eyes widened. "Evidence?" For a moment, she seemed about to laugh. "Goodness, yes, Dasinger! There's all the evidence in the world. He's got Noal on screen, two-way contact. He was talking to Noal when I started to pick him up. That's why—"

"Anyone besides Costian and the two techs around?" Dasinger asked Wergard.

"No."

"Put them away somewhere," Dasinger said. "Telzey and I will be with Larien Selk."

They weren't going to find the bubble. And if some accident had revealed its location, they wouldn't have got Noal Selk out of it alive.

They hadn't given up. Dasinger was speaking to the Kyth Agency by pocket transmitter within a minute after he'd entered Larien's suite with Telzey, and the agency promptly unsheathed its claws. Operators, who'd come drifting into Joca Village during the evening, showing valid passes, converged at the entry to the Selk estate, set up some lethal equipment, and informed Village Security the section was sealed. Village Security took a long, thoughtful look at what confronted it in the gate road, and decided to wait for developments.

Dasinger remained busy with the transmitter, while Wergard recorded what Larien's two-way screen showed. Telzey, only half following the talk, spoke only when Dasinger asked questions. She reported patiently then what he wanted to know, information she drew without much difficulty from Larien's paralyzed mind—the type of nondetectable material coating the deep water device; who had applied it; the name of the Cobril firm which installed the detonating system. They were attacking the problem from every possible angle, getting the help of researchers from around the planet. On Cobril, there was related activity by now. Authorities who would be involved in a sea search here had been alerted, were prepared to act if called on. The Kyth Agency had plenty of pull and was using it.

The fact remained that Larien Selk had considered the possibilities. It had taken careful investigation, but no special knowledge. He'd wanted a nondetectable coating material and a tamper-proof self-destruct system for his deep water device. Both were available;

and that was that. Larien had accomplished his final purpose. The brother who'd cheated him out of his birthright, for whom he'd been left in a vault, ignored, forgotten, incomplete, had been detached from humanity and enclosed in another vault where he was now being reduced piecemeal, and from which he would never emerge. As the minutes passed, it became increasingly clear that what Dasinger needed to change the situation was an on-the-spot scientific miracle. Nothing suggested there were miracles forthcoming. Lacking that, they could watch Noal Selk die, or, if they chose, speed his death.

Telzey bit at her lip, gaze fastened on Larien, who lay on a couch a dozen feet from her. They'd secured his hands behind his back, which wasn't necessary; she'd left her controls on him, and he was caught in unawareness which would end when she let it end. That strong, vital organism was helpless now, along with the mind that had wasted itself in calculating hatred for so many years.

There was something here she hadn't wanted to see . . .

A psi mentality needed strong shutoffs. It had them, developed them quickly, or collapsed into incoherence. The flow of energies which reached nonpsis in insignificant tricklings must be channeled, directed, employed—or sealed away. Shutoffs were necessary. But they could be misapplied. Too easily, too thoroughly, by a mind that had learned to make purposeful use of them.

There was something she'd blocked out of awareness not long ago. For a while, she'd succeeded in forgetting she'd done it. She knew now that she had done it, but it was difficult to hold her attention on the fact. Her mind drew back from such thoughts, kept sliding away, trying to distract itself, trying to blur the act in renewed forgetfulness.

She didn't want to find out what it was she'd shut

away. By that, she knew it was no small matter. There was fear involved.

Of what was she afraid?

She glanced uneasily over at the screen showing the brightly lit metallic interior of the bubble. Wergard stood before it, working occasionally at his recordings. She hadn't looked at the screen for more than a few seconds since coming into the room. It could be turned to a dozen views, showing the same object from different angles and distances. The object was a human body which wasn't quite paralyzed because it sometimes stirred jerkily, and its head moved. The eyes were sometimes open, sometimes shut. It looked unevenly shrunken, partly defleshed by what seemed a random process, skin lying loosely on bone here and there, inches from the swell of muscle. However, the process wasn't a random one; the alien organism within the body patched up systematically behind itself as it made its selective harvest. Outside tubes were attached to the host. The body wouldn't die of dehydration or starvation; it was being nourished. It would die when not enough of it was left to bind life to itself, or earlier if the feeding organism misjudged what it was doing. Dasinger had said its instincts were less reliable with humans because they weren't among its natural food animals.

Or Noal Selk would die when it was decided he couldn't be saved, and somebody's hand reached for the destruct switch.

In any case, he would die. What the screen showed were the beginnings of his death, whatever turn it took in the end. There was no reason for her to watch that. Noal, lost in the dark sea, in his small bright-lit tomb unknown miles from here, was beyond her help, beyond all help now.

Her eyes shifted back to Larien. It happened, she decided, at some point after she'd moved into his mind, discovered what he had done, and, shocked,

was casting about for further information, for ways
to undo this atrocity. Almost now, but not quite, she
could remember the line of reflections she'd followed,
increasingly disturbed reflections they seemed to be.
Then—then she'd been past that point. Something
flashed up, some horrid awareness; instantly she'd
buried it, sealed it away, sealed away that entire area
of recall.

She shook her head slightly. It remained buried!
She remembered doing it now, and she wouldn't
forget that again. But she didn't remember what she
had buried, or why. Perhaps if she began searching
in Larien Selk's mind . . .

At the screen, Wergard exclaimed something.
Telzey looked up quickly. Dasinger had turned away
from the table where he'd been sitting, was starting
toward the screen. Sounds began to come from the
screen. She felt the blood drain from her face.

Something was howling in her mind—wordless
expression of a terrible need. It went on for seconds,
weakened abruptly and was gone. Other things
remained.

She stood up, walked unsteadily to the screen. The
two men glanced around as she came up. An enlarged
view of Noal Selk's head filled the screen. There were
indications that the feeder had been selectively at
work here, too; but there wasn't much change in the
features. The eyes were wide open, staring up past
the pickup. The mouth was lax and trembling; only
wet, shaky breathing sounds came from it now.

Wergard said, "For some moments, he seemed fully
conscious. He seemed to see us. He—well, the speaking apparatus isn't essential to life, of course. Most
of that may be gone. But I think he was trying to
speak to us."

Telzey, standing between them, looking at the
screen, said, "He saw you. He was trying to ask you

to kill him. Larien let him know it could be done any time."

Dasinger said carefully, "You *know* he was trying to ask us to kill him?"

"Yes, I know," Telzey said. "Be quiet, Dasinger. I have to think now."

She blinked slowly at the screen. Her diaphragm made a sudden, violent contraction as a pain surge reached her. Pain shutoff went on; the feeling dimmed. Full contact here.

Her mouth twisted. She hadn't wanted it! Not after what she'd learned. That was what she hadn't allowed to come into consciousness. She'd told herself it wasn't possible to reach Noal where he was, even after they'd shut off the psi block in the walls of the house. She'd convinced herself it was impossible. But she'd made the contact, and it had developed, perhaps as much through Noal's frenzied need as through anything she'd done; and now she'd been blazingly close to his mind and body torment—

She brushed her hand slowly over her forehead. She felt clammy with sweat.

"Telzey, is something wrong with you?" Dasinger asked.

She looked up at their watchful faces.

"No, not really. Dasinger, you know you can't save him, don't you?"

His expression didn't change. "I suppose I do," he acknowledged. "I suppose we all do. But we'll have to go on trying for a while, before we simply put him to death."

She nodded, eyes absent. "There's something I can try," she told them. "I didn't think of it before."

"Something *you* can try?" Wergard said, astonished. His head indicated the screen. "To save him *there*?"

"Yes. Perhaps."

Dasinger cleared his throat. "I don't see . . . what do you have in mind?"

She shook her head. "I can't explain that. It's psi. I'll try to explain as I go along, but I probably won't be able to explain much. It may work, that's all. I've done something like it before."

"But you can't—" Wergard broke off, was silent.

Dasinger said, "You know what you're doing?"

"Yes, I know." Telzey looked up at them again. "You mustn't let anyone in here. There mustn't be any disturbance or interference, or everything might go wrong. And it will take time. I don't know how much time."

Neither of them said anything for some seconds. Then Dasinger nodded slowly.

"Whatever it is," he said, "you'll have all the time you need. Nobody will come in here. Nobody will be allowed on the estate before you've finished and give the word."

Telzey nodded. "Then this is what we'll have to do."

5

She had done something like this, or something nearly like this, before . . .

Here and there was a psi mind with whom one could exchange the ultimate compliment of using no mental safeguards, none whatever. It was with one of those rare, relaxing companions that she'd done almost what she'd be doing now. The notion had come up in the course of a psi practice session. One was in Orado City, one at the tip of the Southern Mainland at the time. They'd got together at the thought level, and were trying out various things, improving techniques and methods.

"I'll lend you what *I* see if you'll lend me what *you* see," one of them had said.

That was easy enough. Each looked suddenly at what the other had looked at a moment ago. It wasn't the same as tapping the sensory impressions of a controlled mind. Small sections of individual awareness, of personality, appeared to have shifted from body to body.

It went on from there. Soon each was using the other's muscles, breathing with the other's lungs, speaking with the other's voice. They'd got caught up in it, and more subtle transfers continued in a swift double flow, unchecked: likes and dislikes, acquired knowledge, emotional patterns. Memories disintegrated here, built up there; vanished, were newly complete—and now quite different memories. Only the awareness of self remained—that probably couldn't be exchanged, or could it?

Then: "Shall we?"

They'd hesitated, looking at each other, with a quarter of the globe between them, each seeing the other clearly, in their exchanged bodies, exchanged personalities. One threadlike link was left for each to sever, and each would become the other, with no connection then to what she had been.

"Of course, we can change right back—"

Yes, but could they? Could they? Something would be different, would have shifted; they would be in some other and unknown pattern—and suddenly, quickly, they were sliding past each other again, memories, senses, controls, personality particles, swirling by in a giddy two-way stream, reassembling, restoring themselves, each to what was truly hers. They were laughing, but a little breathlessly, really a little frightened now by what they'd almost done.

They'd never tried it again. They'd talked about it. They were almost certain it could be done, oh, quite safely! They'd be two telepaths still, two psis. It should be a perfectly simple matter to reverse the process at any time.

It should be. But even to those who were psis, and in psi, much more remained unknown about psi than was known. Anyone who gained any awareness at all understood there were limits beyond which one couldn't go, or didn't try to go. Limits beyond which things went oddly wrong.

The question was whether they would have passed such a limit in detaching themselves from their personality, acquiring that of another. It remained unanswered.

What she had in mind now was less drastic in one respect, seemed more so in another. She would find out whether she could do it. She didn't know what the final result would be if she couldn't.

She dissolved her contact with Noal. It would be a distraction, and she could restore it later.

Larien Selk was fastened securely to his couch. Dasinger and Wergard then fastened Telzey as securely to the armchair in which she sat. She'd told them there might be a good deal of commotion here presently, produced both by herself and by Larien. It would be a meaningless commotion, something to be ignored. They wouldn't know what they were doing. They had to be tied down so they wouldn't get hurt.

The two men asked no questions. She reached into a section of her brain, touched it with paralysis, slid to Larien Selk's mind. In his brain, too, a selected small section went numb. Then the controls she'd placed on him were flicked away.

He woke up. He had to be awake and aware for much of this, or her work would be immeasurably, perhaps impossibly, increased. But his wakefulness did result in considerable commotion, though much less than there would have been if Larien had been able to use his voice—or, by and by, Telzey's. She'd silenced both for the time being. He couldn't do more than go through the motions of screaming. Nor could he move around much, though he tried very hard.

For Larien, it was a terrifying situation. One moment, he'd been sitting before the screen, considering whether to nudge the console button which would cause a stimulant to be injected into Noal and bring him back to consciousness again for an hour or two. He enjoyed talking to Noal.

Then, with no discernible lapse in time, he sensed he was lying on his back, arms and legs stretched out, tied down. Simultaneously, however, he looked up from some point in midair at two tense-faced men who stood between him and the screen that peered into Noal's bubble.

Larien concluded he'd gone insane. In the next few minutes, he nearly did. Telzey was working rapidly. It wasn't nearly as easy work as it had been with a cooperating psi; but Larien lacked the understanding and ability to interfere with her, as a psi who wasn't cooperating would have done. There was, of course, no question of a complete personality exchange here. But point by point, sense by sense, function by function, she was detaching Larien from all conscious contacts with his body. His bewildered attempts to retain each contact brought him into a corresponding one with hers—and that particular exchange had been made.

The process was swift. It was Larien's body that struggled violently at first, tried to scream, strained against its fastenings. Telzey's remained almost quiescent. Then both twisted about. Then his, by degrees, relaxed. The other body continued to twist and tug, eyes staring, mouth working desperately.

Telzey surveyed what had been done, decided enough had been done at this level. Her personality, her consciousness, were grafted to the body of Larien Selk. His consciousness was grafted to her body. The unconscious flows had followed the conscious ones.

She sealed the access routes to memory storage in the Telzey brain. The mind retained memory without the body's help for a while. For how long a while was something she hadn't yet established.

Time for the next step. She withdrew her contact with Larien's mind, dissolved it. Then she cut her last mind links to her body. It vanished from her awareness. She lay in Larien Selk's body, breathing with its lungs. She cleared its throat, lifted the paralysis she'd placed on the use of its voice.

"Dasinger!" the voice said hoarsely. "Wergard!"

Footsteps came hurrying over.

"Yes, *he's* over *there*. I'm here . . . for now. I wanted you to understand so you wouldn't worry too much."

They didn't say anything, but their faces didn't look reassured. Telzey added, "I've got his—its voice cut off. Over there, I mean."

What else should she tell them? She couldn't think of anything; and she had a driving impatience now to get on with this horrid business, to get it done, if she could get it done. To be able to tell herself it was over.

"It'll be a while before I can talk to you again," Larien Selk's voice told Wergard and Dasinger.

Then they vanished from her sight. Larien's eyes—no longer in use—closed. Telzey had gone back to work. Clearing the traces of Larien's memories and reaction patterns from his brain took time because she was very thorough and careful about it. She wanted none of that left; neither did she want to damage the brain. The marks of occupancy faded gradually, cleaned out, erased, delicately annihilated; and presently she'd finished. She sent out a search thought then to recontact the mind of Noal Selk in the brightly lit hell of his bubble, picked up the pattern almost at once, and moved over into his mind.

He was unconscious, but something else here was conscious in a dim and limited way. Telzey turned her attention briefly to the organism which had been implanted in Noal. A psi creature, as she'd thought. The ability to differentiate so precisely between what was and was not immediately fatal to a creature not ordinarily its prey had implied the use of psi. The organism wasn't cruel; it had no concept of cruelty. It was making a thrifty use of the food supply available to it, following its life purpose.

She eased into the body awareness from which Noal had withdrawn, dimming the pain sensations which flared up in her. It was immediately obvious that very extensive damage had been done. But a kind of functional balance lingered in what was left. The body lived as a body.

And the mind still lived as a mind, sustaining itself by turning away from the terrible realities about it as often as Noal could escape from pain into unconsciousness. She considered that mind, shifting about it and through it, knowing she was confronting the difficulty she'd expected. Noal wouldn't cling to this body; in intention, he already was detached from it. But that was the problem. He was trying, in effect, to become disembodied and remain that way.

He had a strong motivation. She should be able to modify it, nullify it eventually; but it seemed dangerous to tamper with Noal any more than she could help. There wasn't enough left of him, physically or mentally, for that. He had to want to attach himself fully and consciously to a body again, or this wasn't going to work. She could arouse him, bring him awake . . .

He would resist it, she thought.

But she might give him something he wouldn't resist.

Noal dreamed.

It was a relaxed dream, universes away from pain, fear, savage treachery. He remembered nothing of

Larien. He was on Cobril, walking along with a firm, quick stride in warm sunlight. He was agreeably aware of the strength and health of his body.

Something tugged at him.

Vision blurred startlingly. Sound faded. The knowledge came that the thing that tugged at him was trying to drag him wholly away from his senses, out of himself, into unfeeling nothingness.

Terrified, he fought to retain sight and sound, to cling to his body.

Telzey kept plucking him away, taking his place progressively in the still functional wreckage left by the organism, barring him more and more from it. But simultaneously she made corresponding physical anchorages available for him elsewhere; and Noal, still dreaming, not knowing the difference, clung to each point gained with frantic determination. She had all the cooperation she could use. The transfer seemed accomplished in moments.

She told him soothingly then to go on sleeping, go on dreaming pleasantly. Presently, agitations subsiding, he was doing it.

And Telzey opened Noal Selk's gummily inflamed and bloodshot eyes with difficulty, looked out into the metallic glittering of the bubble, closed the eyes again. She was very much here—too much so. Her pain shutoffs were operating as far as she could allow them to operate without hampering other activities, but it wasn't enough. A sudden fresh set of twinges gave her a thought then; and she put the busy psi organism to sleep. At least, that part of it shouldn't get any worse.

But she'd have to stay here a while. In this body's brain was the physical storehouse of Noal's memories, the basis of his personality. It was a vast mass of material; getting it all transferred in exact detail to the brain she'd cleared out to receive it was out of the question. It probably could be done, but it would take hours. She didn't have hours to spare.

The essentials, however, that which made Noal what he was, should be transplanted in exact detail. She started doing it. It wasn't difficult work. She'd doctored memories before this, and it was essentially the same process.

It was simply a question of how much she could get done before she had to stop. The physical discomforts that kept filtering into her awareness weren't too serious a distraction. But there was something else that frightened her—an occasional sense of vagueness about herself, a feeling as if she might be growing flimsy, shadowy. It always passed quickly, but it seemed a warning that too much time was passing, perhaps already had passed, since she'd cut herself off from her own brain and body and the physical basis of memory and personality.

She paused finally. It should do. It would have to do. Her mind could absorb the remaining pertinent contents of this body's brain in a few minutes, retain it until she had an opportunity to feed back to Noal whatever else he might need. It would be second-hand memory, neither exact nor complete. But he wouldn't be aware of the difference, and no one who had known him would be able to tell there was a difference. She couldn't risk further delay. There was a sense of something that had been in balance beginning to shift dangerously, though she didn't yet know what it was.

She began the absorption process. Completed it. Went drifting slowly off, then through nothing, through nowhere. . . . Peered out presently again through puzzled sore eyes into the gleaming of the bubble.

Hot terror jolted through her—

"Dasinger!"

Dasinger turned from the couch on which the Larien body lay, came quickly across the room. "Yes?"

Wergard indicated the other figure in the armchair.

"This one seems to be coming awake again!"

Dasinger looked at the figure. It was slumped back as far as the padded fastenings which held its arms clamped against the sides of the chair permitted. The head lolled to the left, eyes slitted, blood-smeared mouth half open. "What makes you think so?" he asked.

The figure's shoulders jerked briefly almost as he spoke.

"That," Wergard said. "It's begun to stir."

They watched, but the figure remained quiet now. Wergard looked at the screen. "Some slight change there, too!" he remarked. "Its eyes were open for a while. A minute ago, they closed."

"Coinciding with the first indication of activity here?" Dasinger asked.

"Very nearly. What about the one on the couch?"

Dasinger shrugged. "Snoring! Seems to smile now and then. Nobody could be more obviously asleep."

Wergard said, after a moment, "So it must be between these two now?"

"If she's been doing what we think, it should be. . . . There!"

The figure in the chair sucked in a hissing breath, head slamming up against the backrest. The neck arched, strained, tendons protruding like tight-drawn wires. Dasinger moved quickly. One hand clamped about the jaw; the other gripped the top of the skull. "Get something back in her mouth!"

Wergard already was there with a folded wet piece of cloth, wedged it in between bared teeth, jerked his fingers back with a grunt of pain. Dasinger moved his thumb up, holding the cloth in place. The figure was in spasmodic violent motion now, dragging against the fastenings. Wergard placed his palms above its knees, pressed down hard, felt himself still being shifted about. He heard shuddering gasps, glanced up once and saw blue eyes glaring unfocused in the contorted face.

"Beginning to subside!" Dasinger said then.

Wergard didn't reply. The legs he was holding down had relaxed, gone limp, a moment before. Howling sounds came from the screen, turned into a strangled choking, went silent. He straightened, saw Dasinger take the cloth from Telzey's mouth. She looked at them in turn, moved her puffed lips, grimaced uncomfortably.

"You put your teeth through your lower lip a while ago," Dasinger explained. He added, "That wasn't you, I suppose. You *are* back with us finally, aren't you?"

She was still breathing raggedly. She whispered, "Not quite . . . almost. Moments!"

Animal sounds blared from the screen again. Their heads turned toward it. Wergard went over, cut off the noise, looked at the twisting face that had belonged to Noal Selk. He came back then and helped Dasinger free Telzey from the chair. She sat up and touched her mouth tentatively, reminding Wergard of his bitten finger. He looked at it.

Telzey followed his glance. "Did I do that, too?"

"Somebody did," Wergard said shortly. He reached for one of the cloths they'd used to keep her mouth propped open, wrapped it around the double gash. "How do you feel, Telzey?"

She shifted her shoulders, moved her legs. "Sore," she said. "Very sore. But I don't seem to have pulled anything."

"You're back all the way?"

She drew a long breath. "Yes."

Wergard nodded. "Then let's get this straight. Over there on the couch, asleep—that's now Noal Selk?"

"Yes," Telzey said. "I'll have to do a little more work on him because he doesn't have all his memory yet. But it's Noal—in everything that counts, anyway."

"He doesn't have all his memory yet," Wergard repeated. "But it's Noal!" He stared at her. "All right. And you're you again." He jerked his thumb at the screen. "So the one who's down in the bubble now is Larien Selk?"

She nodded.

"Well—" Wergard shrugged. "I was watching it," he said. He looked at Dasinger. "It happened, that's all!"

He went to the screen console, unlocked the destruct switch, and turned it over. The screen went blank.

The three of them remained silent for some seconds then, considering the same thought. Wergard finally voiced it. "This is going to take a remarkable amount of explaining!"

"I guess it will," Telzey said. "But we won't have to do it."

"Eh?" said Dasinger.

"I know some experts," she told him. She climbed stiffly out of the chair. "I'd better get to work on Noal now, so we'll have that out of the way."

The Operator on Duty at the Psychology Service Center in Orado City lifted his eyebrows when he saw Telzey walking toward his desk in the Entry Hall. They'd met before. He pretended not to notice her then until she stopped before the desk.

He looked up. "Oh, it's you," he said indifferently.

Yes, it's me," said Telzey. They regarded each other with marked lack of approval.

"Specifically," asked the Operator, "why are you here? I'll take it for granted it has to do with your general penchant for getting into trouble."

"I wouldn't call it that," Telzey said. "I may have broken a few Federation laws last night, but that's beside the point. I'm here to see Klayung. Where do I find him?"

The Operator on Duty leaned back in his chair and laced his fingers.

"Klayung's rather busy," he remarked. "In any case, before we bother him you might explain the matter of breaking a few Federation laws. We're not in that much of a hurry, are we?"

Telzey considered him reflectively.

"I've had a sort of rough night," she said then. "So, yes—we're in exactly that much of a hurry. Unless your shields are a good deal more solid now than they were last time."

His eyelids flickered. "You wouldn't be foolish enough to—"

"I'll count to two," Telzey said. "One."

Klayung presently laid Telzey's report sheets down again, sat scratching his chin. His old eyes were thoughtful. "Where is he at present?" he asked.

"Outside the Center, in a Kyth ambulance," Telzey told him. "We brought Hishee along, too. Asleep, of course."

Klayung nodded. "Yes, she should have almost equally careful treatment. This is a difficult case."

"You can handle it?" Telzey asked.

"Oh, yes, we can handle it. We'll handle everything. We'll have to now. This could have been a really terrible breach of secrecy, Telzey! We can't have miracles, you know!"

"Yes, I know," Telzey said. "Of course, the Kyth people are all right."

"Yes, they're all right. But otherwise—"

"Well, I know it's going to be a lot of trouble for you," she said. "And I'm sorry I caused it. But there really wasn't anything else I could do."

"No, it seems there really wasn't," Klayung agreed. "Nevertheless—well, that's something I wouldn't recommend you try very frequently!"

Telzey was silent a moment.

"I'm not sure I'd try it again for any reason," she admitted. "At the end there, I nearly didn't get back."

Klayung nodded. "There was a distinct possibility you wouldn't get back."

"Were you thinking of having Noal go on as Noal?" Telzey inquired.

"That should be the simplest approach," Klayung said. "We'll see what the Makeup Department says. I doubt it would involve excessive structural modifications. . . . You don't agree?"

Telzey said, "Oh, it would be simplest, all right. But—well, you see, Noal was just nothing physically. He's got a great body now. It would be a shame to turn him back to being a nothing again."

Klayung looked at her a moment.

"Those two have had a very bad time," Telzey continued. "Due to Larien. It seems sort of fair, doesn't it?"

"If he's to become Larien Selk officially," Klayung remarked, "there'll be a great many more complications to straighten out."

"Yes, I realize that."

"Besides," Klayung went on, "neither Noal nor Hishee might want him to look in the least like Larien."

"Well, they wouldn't now, of course," Telzey agreed. "But after your therapists have cleared up all the bad things Larien's done to them, it might be a different matter."

Klayung's sigh was almost imperceptible. "All right. Supposing we get the emotional and mental difficulties resolved first, and then let the principals decide for themselves in what guise Noal is to resume his existence. Would that be satisfactory?"

Telzey smiled. "Thanks, Klayung!" she said. "Yes, very satisfactory!"

COMPULSION

Prologue: The Pork Chop Tree

In research laboratory 3230 of the Planetary Quarantine Station two thousand miles out from the world of Maccadon, Professor Mantelish of the University League stood admiringly before a quarantine object. It had been unloaded from his specimen boat some hours ago and aroused from the state of suspended animation in which he had transported it back to the Hub from its distant native world.

It was a plant-form and a beautiful one, somewhere between a tree and a massive vine in appearance, its thick, gray-sheened trunk curving and twisting up to a point about twenty-five feet above the conditioning container in which it was rooted. Great heart-shaped leaves of a deep warm green sprang from it here and there; and near the top was a single huge white flower cup. A fresh and pleasant fragrance filled the laboratory.

Mantelish, an immense old man, scratched his scalp reflectively through his thick white hair, his gaze shifting from this point to that about the plant. Then his attention centered on a branch immediately above him where something had begun to move. A heavy, tightly coiled tendril swung slowly out from the branch, unwinding with a snaky motion until it lay flat in the air. Simultaneously, three new leaves, of a lighter green and smaller than the mature ones about them, unfolded along the tendril's length and spread away from it.

"So it started right in growing again as soon as you woke it up!" a voice said behind Mantelish.

He looked around. A slim red-headed girl in shorts had entered the laboratory and was coming over to him.

"Yes, it did, Trigger," he said. "As I've suspected, it will speed up or slow down its growth and reproduction processes in accordance with the area it finds available to it."

"Until it's covered a planet." Trigger studied the new tendril a moment. "Pretty ambitious for a tree, isn't it?"

Mantelish shrugged. "It's a prolific and highly adaptable life form. Do you happen to know where Commissioner Tate is at present?"

"Dissecting one of the specimens from the other boat," said Trigger. "I stopped by there just now, and he told me not to come in . . . what he was doing was pretty gooey and I wouldn't want to see it. He said he'd be along in a few minutes. There was something he wanted to find out about the thing. Have you fed baby those slow-down hormones you were talking about?"

"Yes. They're having the expected effect. The new branch you saw it put out is the only indication of growth it's given during the past twelve minutes."

"So that will work, eh?"

"Under laboratory conditions we certainly can control its growth," Mantelish said. "But let's not be too hasty. Much more definite safeguards will be required before there can be any question of releasing the tree to the public. There's the matter of curbing its various forms of propagation, particularly the periodic release of self-propelled airborne seeds. Under present circumstances, our beautiful tree could become a very definite nuisance on any Hub world to which it was introduced."

"Well, those are problems which simply will have to be solved!" Trigger said. "Because everyone who has a garden is going to want to have one of them. You hear that, pet?" She stepped out on the conditioning container, ran her palms lightly along the tree's trunk. "You're not only about the most *edible* thing around," she told it, "and you're not only beautiful— you also have a wonderful personality. You're going to become a great big fad everywhere in the Federation!"

Mantelish laughed. "Trigger, you're crooning to it."

"Well, I feel like crooning to it," she said. "I feel very affectionate toward it. Did I tell you that on the trip back, when it was in stasis and I couldn't go near it, I'd dream about the trees every night?"

"No."

"I did. There I'd be climbing around in that wonderful forest again, or stretching out for a nap on one of the leaves—and they curl up around you so nicely when you lie down on them! You know, I think I'll climb up baby right now . . ."

"Why not?" said Mantelish. "If it weren't for my weight, I might try it myself."

"If you ate just what you got from the tree," Trigger told him, "you'd trim down fast." She caught a branch above her, swung herself over to a level section of the main trunk, and walked along it till it curved upward. Then she clapped her hands to the trunk and went up quickly all fours style like a cat to the highest point where the tree turned level again. She stood up there, reached for the white flower cup overhead and drew it toward her.

"When did the bud open?" she asked.

"Almost immediately after I brought it out of stasis," Mantelish said, looking up. "Is it in seed?"

Trigger peered into the cup.

"Full of seeds! But they're still soft and unfeathered. We're not going to let you puff those away on the wind, baby. You have to become civilized now. Ah!" She reached back of the flower, plucked something from its stem.

"What have you found?" asked Mantelish.

"Some of the black cherry things," said Trigger. "I do believe baby remembered how much I like them and grew them especially for me." She sat down on the trunk, legs dangling, popped one of the black cherry things into her mouth. "Did you get the reports on the samples you sent back?"

"Yes, they were waiting for me here," Mantelish said.

"Well?"

He shrugged. "They confirm officially what we already know. Almost every part of the trees has a high nutritional value for the human organism."

"Yes, of course. But what do they say about the flavors?"

"The reports don't mention flavors, Trigger. They weren't checking on that."

"Well, they should have been checking on it," said Trigger. "The flavors certainly are important. So is the variety—something new being put out every few days, so that you could get your meals from one tree all your life and never grow tired of the diet! Along with hammock leaves, and warm cubbyholes in the trunks to snuggle up in when it rains too hard. . . . You know what the very special thing is, though? It's the feeling that you're so welcome to everything—that the trees like you and want you to be around!"

Mantelish cleared his throat. "I had that impression occasionally. It's quite curious. Others also reported it."

"Of course, they reported it. It's a very definite thing. I had the feeling strongly all the time we were there." Trigger patted the trunk beside her. "And I'm getting it—very strongly—from baby right now. It's *glad* I'm sitting up here with it again!"

Mantelish shook his head slowly.

"It would be difficult to prove," he said, with some uneasiness in his tone, "that your imagination isn't simply running away with you there. . . ."

"Well, I don't think it's my imagination," Trigger told him. "And you know, it shouldn't really be too surprising. Because there the trees are—and everyone agrees they're a highly evolved life-form. But they're the only highly evolved life-form on their world. All the other creatures we saw around looked as dull as anything alive can get."

Mantelish frowned. "I didn't find them at all dull," he remarked. "It was a fauna of well-adapted parasites. A successful parasite, of course, may appear oversimplified to the untrained eye. But with the trees' forests almost covering that world, there would be little reason for other organisms to develop qualities that might have made them more intriguing to you. After all, the trees supply them with everything they require."

"Yes, and the trees evidently don't mind feeding the rest of the planet, or they wouldn't be so edible," Trigger agreed. "Just the same, those parasites must become pretty boring company. I think the trees would like to have more interesting guests around for a change—that's why they try to let us know we're welcome."

"Well, those are fancies, Trigger," Mantelish said deprecatingly.

"You think so? I don't. And I think we should accept their invitation. I think the Federation should declare that whole world a vacation land! They could put big fast ships on the run and bring in people by the tens of thousands for a month or so . . . families with children, anyone who wants a change, especially people who feel run-down or tensed up. It would be

wonderful for everybody! Everything would be free—
and the trees would love it—"

Trigger broke off, looked over at the entrance,
smiled. "Hi, Commissioner!" she said. "We were dis-
cussing—anyway, I was—what could be done with the
tree world."

"That's a rather good question," said Commissioner
Tate.

Trigger got to her feet, and half walked, half slid,
back down along the tree's thick serpent trunk to the
ground as Commissioner Tate came across the laboratory toward them. He'd been in charge of the
Federation expedition which discovered and investi-
gated the planet of the trees, and had returned to
the Hub with Mantelish and Trigger in another specimen boat crammed with assorted organisms for biological study.

"Got several bits of news for you two," he said.

"About what?" Mantelish asked.

The Commissioner glanced up at the tree. "In a
way, about our little friend here. A transmitter call
from Expedition Headquarters reached my boat while
we were coming in on Maccadon around six hours
ago. One thing they reported was that three members of the paleontological team we left digging
around down there have walked off the job."

"Walked off the job?" Trigger repeated.

"Yes," said the Commissioner. "This was a few days
ago. They left a note which said in effect not to
bother them. They'd found the world of their dreams,
and they weren't coming back."

Trigger said after a moment, "Well, one can hardly
blame them for that."

"No. I wouldn't blame them. However, I've notified
Patrol Command. They've got a few ships cruising
about the area they can get to the planet in under a
week, with instructions to round up our three strays
and bring them back to the Hub. They won't have gone

far, of course." He smiled briefly. "All they want is to prowl around among the trees and be happy. They'll be found somewhere within a mile of the camp."

"I suppose so," Trigger said hesitantly. She paused, frowning. "But do we really have any right, legal or otherwise, to interfere with them if that's their decision? It's not an off-limits world. Why shouldn't they just be considered the first settlers there? After all, the trees would give human beings everything they need to live as well as they could live anywhere else."

"So they would," said the Commissioner. "Well, there's the second part of the report I had. The paleontological team hadn't been looking for anything of the sort, of course, but they've come across a couple of ruins and begun to uncover them."

"Ruins?" said Mantelish, surprised.

"Yes," the Commissioner said. "Those three wouldn't be the first human settlers on that world, Trigger. The ruins are about eight hundred years old, and there's enough to show quite definitely that they were once occupied by human beings."

Trigger looked startled. "Human beings—where would they have come from?"

"Presumably it was one of the groups that were pushing out from the Old Territory during the period the Hub was being settled. Interstellar drives and transmitters weren't too efficient at the time. I got in contact with the Charting Bureau and had them run a check on an area around the trees' world representing a current week's cruising range. An early colonial group which wanted to settle a number of worlds without losing contact among themselves shouldn't have scattered farther than that. The Bureau ran the check and called me back. They had the information I wanted. Charting records show that two other terratype planets within the area I inquired about are also covered with a blanket of apparently homogenous forest vegetation."

Trigger asked, "You mean those early colonists transplanted the trees to those two other worlds?"

"Evidently they did."

Mantelish nodded. "A reasonable supposition. If no restrictions were placed on it, the tree should cover the land areas of a terratype world to which it was introduced rather rapidly."

"Well, I can understand that," said Trigger. "But why the ruins?" There was uneasiness in her voice. "Even eight hundred years ago, they must have had methods enough to keep the trees out of places they didn't want them to be."

"No doubt they had the methods," the Commissioner agreed.

Trigger looked at him, her face troubled. "You're thinking of the three men who walked off the job back there?"

"What else? They'd never be settlers in the ordinary sense, Trigger. They simply turned their backs on civilization. The colonists did the same thing. They deserted their settlements, went to live among the trees."

"But not all of them!" Trigger protested. "Some people might want to spend their lives like that, and if that's what they like, why not? But a whole group of colonists doesn't simply leave everything they've built up and go away."

"Not under normal circumstances," the Commissioner agreed. "But the circumstances were far from normal. You've talked about a feeling you have that the trees want us around. The evidence we've been getting indicates you're right . . . they do want us around, and they do something about it. It hadn't occurred to me before to look for the symptoms, but I'd say now that in the short period we were there, all of us who were in regular contact with the trees became somewhat addicted to them."

"Addicted?" Trigger looked up at the tree, back

at the Commissioner, expression startled, then reflective.

"Yes," she said slowly. "I've become addicted to them, anyway! Not too seriously. It's mainly liking to be near them, feeling that they like you to be there . . . that they're beautiful friendly things that want to take care of you. . . ."

He nodded. "I know. And in the case of our wandering paleontologists, those feelings simply become strong enough to override their ordinary good sense. The colonists, who were constantly surrounded by the trees, had no chance of escaping the effect indefinitely. We have to assume they all succumbed to it."

Trigger said after a moment, "But what happened to them afterwards? You'd think with the trees to look after them, their descendants should still have been there when we arrived."

"I wondered about that, too," said the Commissioner. "And there was another matter. If the tree is covering three terratype worlds in that section of space, the odds are two to one that the world on which we found it is one of those to which it was carried by the human colonists."

Mantelish shook his head emphatically.

"No!" he said. "It's quite obvious that the tree did originate on that world. You overlook the fact that the fauna there is so completely adapted to it that—" He paused, eyes narrowing abruptly. He scowled absently at the Commissioner for a moment. "Unless—" he began.

The Commissioner nodded. "*Unless!* That was my thought. In so short a time—a mere eight hundred years—the wide assortment of creatures we found there couldn't possibly have changed from an independent existence to one in which they had become parasites on the trees, physically modified to the extent that they could no longer have survived away from their hosts . . . unless the life-form which likes to have other life-forms around has methods which go beyond simple addiction to keep guests permanently with it.

"I took three of the specimens in my boat apart on a hunch. The third of them was the thing which looks a good deal like a limp, gangly hundred-pound frog. It's practically blind, and it has about the same amount of brains as a frog. Of course, it doesn't need much intelligence to crawl from leaf to leaf and along the tree's branches. But most of its internal arrangements are still essentially human."

There was silence for some seconds. Then Trigger said faintly, "But that's horrible!"

The Commissioner shrugged. "From our point of view, it may appear rather horrible. From that of the creature, if it had a point of view, it probably would seem to be leading a very comfortable and satisfactory life. The trees are generous and dependable hosts."

Trigger's gaze shifted to the tree, followed the flow of the curving trunk up to the great white flower cup nodding benignly above them. "It's not their fault," she said suddenly. "They don't understand what they're doing. Will they all have to be killed?"

The Commissioner looked at her. "I find myself hoping some other solution will be found, Trigger. Possibly one will be. For the present, those worlds will be quarantined; but they can't be kept quarantined indefinitely. The danger is too great—the trees literally could destroy any civilization into which they were introduced. So we don't know what the outcome of this will be. But the situation will be studied carefully before any definite decision is made."

"And whoever studies the trees," remarked Mantelish, "will become addicted to them."

"No doubt. But now that we're aware of the factor, we should be safe from undue effects."

The three of them stood silently watching the tree. And the tree stood there and loved them.

The Commissioner drew a long, sighing breath. "Reasonably safe, that is," he concluded.

1

There'd been a dinner party at the Amberdon town house in Orado City that night. Telzey was home for the weekend but hadn't attended the party. Graduation exams weren't far away, and she'd decided she preferred to get in additional study time. It was mainly a political dinner anyway; she'd been at enough of those.

Most of the guests had left by now. Four of them still sat in the room below her balcony alcove with Gilas and Jessamine, her parents. They'd all strolled in together a while ago for drinks and conversation, not knowing someone was on the balcony. The talk was about Overgovernment business, some of it, from the scraps Telzey absently picked up, fairly top-secret stuff. She wasn't interested until a man named Orsler started sounding off on something about which he was evidently very much annoyed. It had to do with the activities of a young woman named Argee.

Telzey started listening then because she disliked Orsler. He was an undersecretary in Conservation, head of a subdepartment dealing with uncolonized and unclaimed worlds and the life-forms native to them. Telzey had scouted around in his mind on another occasion and discovered that those remote, unsuspecting life-forms had a dubious champion in Orsler. He was using his position to help along major exploitation schemes, from which he would benefit substantially in roundabout ways. She'd decided that if nobody had done anything about it by the time the schemes ripened, she would. She gave the Overgovernment a little quiet assistance of that kind now and then. But the time in question was still several months away.

Meanwhile, anything that vexed Orsler should make enjoyable hearing. So she listened.

The group below evidently was familiar with the subject. There was a treelike creature, recently discovered somewhere, which was dangerous to human beings. Orsler's department had it tentatively classified as "noxious vermin," which meant it could be dealt with in any manner short of complete extermination. Miss Argee, whose first name was Trigger, had learned about this; and though she lacked, as Orsler pointed out bitterly, official status of any kind, she'd succeeded in having the classification changed to "quarantined, pending investigation," which meant Orsler's department could do nothing about the pseudotrees until whatever investigations were involved had been concluded.

"The girl is simply impossible!" Orsler stated. "She doesn't seem to have the slightest understanding of the enormous expense involved in keeping a planet under dependable quarantine—let alone three of them!"

"She's aware of the expense factor," said another guest, whose voice Telzey recognized as that of a Federation Admiral who'd attended Amberdon dinners before. "In fact, she spent some time going over it with me. I found she had a good grasp of logistics. It seems she's served on a Precol world and has been on several long-range expeditions where that knowledge was put to use."

"So she's annoyed you, too!" said Orsler. "If any citizen who happens—"

"I wasn't annoyed," the Federation Admiral interrupted quietly. "I rather enjoyed her visit."

There was a pause. Then Orsler said, "It's amazing

that such an insignificant matter could have been carried as far as the Hace Committee! But at least that will put a prompt end to Argee's fantastic notions. She's a Siren addict, of course, and should be institutionalized in her own interest."

Federation Councilwoman Jessamine Amberdon, who served on the Hace Ethics Committee, said pleasantly, "I'd prefer to think you're not being vindictive, Orsler."

"I?" Orsler laughed. "Of course not!"

"Then," said Jessamine, "you'll be pleased to know that the Committee is handling this as it handles all matters properly brought before it. It will await the outcome of the current investigations before it forms a conclusion. And you needn't be concerned about Miss Argee's health. We have it on good authority that while she was at one time seriously addicted to the Sirens, she's now free of such problems. Her present interest in them, in other words, is not motivated by addiction."

Orsler evidently didn't choose to reply, and the talk turned to other subjects—regrettably, from Telzey's point of view. Orsler had found no support, and had been well squelched by Jessamine, which she liked. But now she was intrigued. Treelike Sirens which addicted people and rated a hearing in the Ethics Committee were something new.

She could ask Jessamine about it later, but she'd have to admit to eavesdropping then, which her mother would consider not quite the right thing to have done. Besides, one of the minds down there could tell her. And having been in Orsler's mind before, reentry would be a simple matter

Unless there happened to be a Guardian Angel around. Frequently enough, they hovered about people in upper government levels, for one reason or another. She'd picked up no trace of their presence tonight, but they were rather good at remaining unnoticed.

Well, she'd find out. She dropped an entry probe casually toward Orsler.

And right enough:

"Telzey Amberdon, you stop that!"

It was a brisk, prim thought-form, carrying distinct overtones of the personality producing it. She knew this particular Guardian Angel, or Psychology Service psi operator, who probably was in a parked aircar within a block or two of the Amberdon house—a hard-working, no-nonsense little man with whom she'd skirmished before. He was no match for her; but he could get assistance in a hurry. She didn't complete the probe.

"Why?" she asked innocently. "You're not interested in Orsler, are you?"

"He's precisely the one in whom I'm interested!"

"You surprise me," said Telzey. "Orsler's a perfect creep."

"I won't argue with that description of him. But it's beside the point."

"A little mental overhauling wouldn't hurt him," Telzey pointed out. "He's no asset to the Federation as he is."

"Undersecretary Orsler," the Angel told her sternly, "is not to be tampered with! He has a function to perform of which he isn't aware. What happens after he's performed it is another matter—but certainly no business of yours."

So they knew of Orsler's planetary exploitation plans and would handle it in their way. Good enough!

"All right," Telzey said amiably. "I have no intention of tampering with him, actually. I only wanted to find out what he knows about those Sirens they were talking about."

A pause. "Information about the pseudotrees is classified," said the Angel. "But I suppose that technicality means little to you."

"Very little," Telzey agreed.

"Then I suggest that your mother knows more about the subject than anyone else in the room."

Telzey shrugged mentally. "I don't snoop in Jessamine's mind. You know that."

A longer pause. "You're really interested only in the Sirens?" asked the Angel.

"And Trigger Argee."

"Very well. I can get you a report on the former."

"How soon?"

"It will be in your telewriter by the time you reach your room. As for Miss Argee, we might have a file on her, but you can hardly expect us to violate her privacy to satisfy your curiosity."

"I wouldn't ask you to violate anyone's privacy," Telzey said. "All I'd like is her background, what kind of person she is—the general sort of thing I could get from a good detective agency tomorrow."

"I'll have a scan extract made of her file," the Angel told her. "You'll receive it in a few minutes."

The blue reception button on the ComWeb was glowing when Telzey came into her room. She closed the door, pulled up the report on the Sirens, and sat down. The report began flowing up over the reading screen at her normal scanning rate.

An exploration group had discovered the Sirens on a terratype world previously covered only sketchily by mapping teams. They were the planet's principal life-form, blanketing the landmasses in giant forests. The explorers soon discovered that a kind of euphoria, a pleasurable feeling of being drawn to them, was experienced by anyone coming within a few hundred yards of the pseudotrees. So they began referring to this life-form as the Sirens.

It appeared that the Sirens induced other creatures to become dependent on them, and that even a highly evolved species then degenerated very rapidly to the point of becoming a true parasite, unable to survive away from its hosts. A space scan disclosed that two other worlds in that stellar area were also covered with Siren forests. On those worlds, too, there seemed to be no creatures left which hadn't become Siren parasites, and the indication was that their original human discoverers had introduced them to two associated colonies. In effect, all three human groups then had been wiped out. Their modified descendants could no longer be regarded as human in any significant sense.

The discovery of the Sirens wasn't publicized. General curiosity might be dangerous; there was a chance that Sirens could be transplanted to a civilization which wouldn't recognize their strange qualities until it was virtually destroyed. Various Overgovernment departments began making preparations for the sterilization of the three worlds. It seemed the only reasonable solution to the problem.

But there was somebody who wouldn't accept that.

The report didn't give the name of the former expedition member who argued that it wasn't the Sirens but their dangerous potential which should be eliminated, that they had intelligence, though it was intelligence so different from humanity's that it had been impossible for them to recognize the harm they did other creatures.

That couldn't be proved, of course. Not on the basis of what was generally known.

But neither could it be disproved—and the Overgovernment had been systematically alerted to the fact all along the line. A stop order went out on the preparation of sterilization measures . . .

Telzey's lips quirked approvingly. Unless it could be shown that there was no alternative, or that a present emergency existed, the extermination or near-extermination of a species, let alone that of a species possessing sentient intelligence, was inexcusable under Federation law. The former expedition member had made a very good move. Investigations were now being conducted at various levels, though progress was hampered by the fact that investigators, unless given special protection, also became liable to Siren addiction.

"At present," the report concluded, "no sufficiently definite results appear to have been obtained."

The ComWeb had emitted a single bright *ping*-note a minute or two earlier, and the blue button was glowing again. Telzey erased the material on the Sirens and brought up the report on the determined former expedition member.

This extract was considerably shorter. Trigger Argee was twenty-six, had a high I.Q., had been trained in communications, administration, basic science, survival techniques, and unarmed combat at the Colonial School on Maccadon, had served in Precol on the world of Manon, and been employed in an administrative capacity on three U-League space expeditions. She was twice a pistol medalist, responsible, honest, had a good credit rating, and maintained a fashionable on-and-off marriage with an Intelligence Colonel. She'd been recently issued a temporary Class Four Clearance because of volunteer activities in connection with a classified Overgovernment project. Previous activities, not detailed in the extract, qualified her for a Class One Clearance if the need for it should arise.

The last was intriguing. Of the high-ranking people in the room below the balcony alcove, probably only Jessamine Amberdon held the Overgovernment's Class One Clearance. It might explain why Undersecretary Orsler and others had been unable to check the Siren crusade. Telzey erased this report also and made a mental note to check occasionally on the progress being made in the project.

When she got back down to the alcove, they were still talking in the room below, but it appeared that Orsler and his Guardian Angel had made their departure, the Angel presumably having provided

Orsler with an unconscious motivation to leave. He believed in taking no chances with his charges.

Telzey grinned briefly, quietly gathered up her study materials and carried them back to her room.

2

The Regional Headquarters of the Psychology Service on Farnhart was housed in a tall structure of translucent green, towering in wilderness isolation above a northern ocean arm. Pilch stood in a gray Service uniform at a window of the office on the eightieth level which she'd taken over from the Regional Director that morning, gazing at the storm front moving in from the east. She was a slender woman, rather tall, with sable hair and ivory features, whose gray eyes had looked appraisingly on many worlds and their affairs.

"Trigger Argee," announced the communicator on the Director's desk behind her, "is on her way up here."

Pilch said, "Show her through to the office when she arrives." She went to the desk, placed a report file on it, turned to the side of the room where a large box stood on a table. Pilch touched one of the controls on the box. Its front wall became transparent. The lit interior contained what appeared to be a miniature tree planted in a layer of pebbly brown material. It stood about fifteen inches high, had a curving trunk and three short branches with a velvety appearance to them, and a dozen or so relatively large leaves among which nestled two white flower cups. It was an exquisitely designed thing, and someone not knowing better might have believed it to be a talented artist's creation. But it was alive; it was a

Siren. Three months before, it had been a seedling. Left to itself, it would have stood three times Pilch's height by now. But its growth had been restrained, limiting it still to a seedling's proportions.

The office door dilated, and a mahogany-maned young woman in a green and gold business suit came in. She smiled at Pilch.

"Glad to see you!" she said. "I didn't know you were on Farnhart until I got your message."

Pilch said, "I arrived yesterday to handle some Service business. I'll leave again tonight. Meanwhile, here's your specimen, and copies of our investigators' reports."

"I'm sorry no one found anything positive," Trigger said. "I was beginning to feel we were on the right track finally."

"We won't assume it's the wrong track," said Pilch. "The results aren't encouraging, but what they amount to is that the xenotelepaths we had available weren't able to solve the problem. Various nonhuman xenos were called in to help and did no better. Neither, I'll admit, did I, when I was checking out the reports on the way here."

Trigger moistened her lips. "What *is* the problem?"

"Part of it," Pilch said, "is the fact that the investigations produced no indication of sentient intelligence. The Sirens' activities appear to be directed by complex instinctual drives. And aside from that, your specimen is a powerhouse of psi. The euphoria it broadcasts is a minor manifestation, and we can assume that its ability to mutate other organisms is psi-based. But it remains an assumption. We haven't learned enough about it. Most of the xenos were unable to make out the psi patterns. They're very pronounced ones and highly charged, but oddly difficult to locate. Those who did recognize them and attempted to probe them experienced severe reactions. A few got into more serious trouble and had to be helped."

"What kind of trouble?" Trigger asked uneasily.

"Assorted mental disturbances. They've been straightened out again."

"Our little friend here did all that?"

"Why not? It may be as formidable as any adult Siren in that respect. The euphoric effect it produces certainly is as definite as that of the older specimens."

"Yes, that's true." Trigger looked at the box. "You're keeping a permanent psi block around it?"

"Yes. It can be turned off when contact is wanted."

Trigger was silent a moment, watching the Siren. She shook her head then. "I still don't believe they don't have intelligence!"

Pilch shrugged. "I won't say you're wrong. But if you're right, it doesn't necessarily improve the situation. The psi qualities that were tapped appear to be those of a mechanism—a powerful mechanism normally inaccessible to alien psi contact. When contact is made, there is instant and violent reaction. If this is a reasoned response, the Siren seems to be an entity which regards any psi mind not of its own species as an enemy. There's no hesitation, no attempt to evaluate the contact."

"It may be a defensive reaction."

"True," Pilch said. "But it must be considered in conjunction with what else we know. The three Siren worlds appear sufficient evidence that the goal of the species is to take over all available space for itself. It has high mobility as a species, and evidently can cover any territory that becomes available to it with startling speed. As it spreads, all other life-forms present are converted to harmless parasites. This again, whether it's an instinctive process or a deliberate one, suggests the Siren is a being which tolerates only its own kind. Its apparent hospitality is a trap. It isn't a predator; it makes no detectable use of other forms of life. But it interrupts their evolutionary development and, in effect, eliminates them from the environment."

Trigger nodded slowly. "It's not a good picture."

"It's a damning picture," said Pilch. "Translated to human terms, this is, by every evaluation, a totally selfish, paranoid, treacherous, indiscriminately destructive species, a deadly danger to any other species it encounters. What real argument for its preservation can be made?"

Trigger gave her a brief smile.

"I'll argue that the picture is wrong!" she said. "Or, anyway, it's incomplete. If the Sirens, or their instincts, simply wanted to eliminate other creatures, there'd be no need for that very complicated process of turning them into parasites. One good chromosomal error for each new species they came across, and there'd be no next generation of that species around to annoy them!"

"Yes," Pilch said. "That's one reason, perhaps the only substantial reason so far, for not being too hasty about the Sirens." She paused. "Have you been getting any encouraging reports on the physical side of the investigation?"

Trigger shook her head. "Not recently. The fact is, the labs are licked—though some of them won't admit it yet."

"What we've learned about the specimen," said Pilch, "indicates they'll be forced to admit it eventually. If it weren't basically a psi problem, all the talent you've rounded up and put to work should have defanged the Sirens before this. The problem presumably will have to be solved on the psi level, if it's to be solved at all."

"It does seem so," Trigger agreed. She hesitated. "I'm trying to keep the labs plugging away a while longer mainly to gain time. If it's official that they've given up, the push to sterilize the Siren worlds will start again."

"It may be necessary to resort to that eventually," said Pilch. "They can't be left at large as they are. Even if the closest watch is maintained on those three worlds, something might go wrong."

"Yes, I know. It still would be a mistake, though," Trigger said. "Exterminating them might seem necessary because we hadn't been able to think of a good solution. But it would be a mistake, and wrong."

"You're convinced of it?"

"I am."

"Why?"

Trigger shook her head. "I don't know. Since I became unaddicted, I haven't even liked the Sirens much. It's not that I dislike them—I simply feel they're completely alien to me."

"How do you react now to the euphoria effect?" Pilch asked.

Trigger shrugged.

"It's an agreeable feeling. But I know it's an effect, and that makes it an agreeable feeling I'd sooner not have. It doesn't exactly bother me, but I certainly don't miss it when it's not there."

Pilch nodded. "There've been a few other occasions," she remarked, "when you've acted in a way that might have appeared dead wrong to any other rational human being. It turned out you were right."

"I know. You think I'm right about this?"

"I'm not saying that. But I feel your conviction is another reason for not coming to overly hurried conclusions about the Sirens." Pilch indicated the container. "What plans do you have for the specimen now?"

"I'm beginning to run a little short of plans," Trigger admitted. "But I'll try the Old Galactics next. They're a kind of psi creature themselves, and they're good at working with living things. So I'll take the specimen to them."

Pilch considered. "Not a bad idea. They're still on Maccadon?"

"Very probably. They were there six months ago, the last time I visited Mantelish's garden. They weren't planning to move."

"When are you leaving?"

"Next ship out. Some time this afternoon."

Pilch nodded. "I'll be passing by Maccadon four days from now. I'll drop in then and contact you. And don't look so glum. We're not at the end of our rope. If it seems the Old Galactics can't handle the Sirens, I'll still have a few suggestions to make."

"Very glad to hear it!"

"And while we're on Maccadon," Pilch continued, "I'll have you equipped with a mind shield."

"A mind shield?" Trigger looked dubious. "I know they're all using them in the labs, but . . . well, I had to wear one for a while last year. I didn't like it much."

"This will be a special design," Pilch told her. "It won't inconvenience you. If you're going to start escorting the specimen around again, you should have a good solid shield, just in case. We know that now."

3

In the rolling green highlands south of the city of Ceyce on Maccadon, Trigger's friend Professor Mantelish maintained a private botanical garden. It was his favorite retreat when he wanted to relax, though he didn't manage to get there often. Trigger herself would drop in now and then and stay for a week or two, sleeping in the room reserved for her use in the big white house which stood near the center of the garden.

The garden was where the Old Galactics lived. Only Trigger and Pilch knew they were there. Mantelish might have suspected it, though he'd never said so. Very few other people even knew of their existence. They'd had a great culture once, but it had been destroyed in a vast war which was fought and over with in the Milky Way before men learned how to dig mammoth pits. Not many Old Galactics survived that period, and they'd been widely scattered and out of contact, so that they had only recently begun to gather again. The garden appeared to be their reassembly area, and a whole little colony of them was there by now, arriving by mostly mysterious methods from various regions of the galaxy. That any at all of the fierce race which had attacked their culture still existed was improbable. The Old Galactics had formidable powers; and when they finally decided something needed to be eliminated, they were very thorough and patient about it.

Communication between them and humans was at best a laborious process. Trigger had done them a service some time before, and had learned how to conduct a conversation with Old Galactics on that occasion. They seemed to live on a different time scale. When you wanted to talk to them, you didn't try to hurry it.

So when she arrived at the garden with the Siren, she went first to her room in the house, steered the container on its gravity float to a table, settled it down on the tabletop and switched off the float. Then she unpacked, taking her time and putting everything away, arranging books she'd brought along on the shelves beside others she'd left here on her last visit. Afterward, Mantelish's housekeeper brought a lunch to the room, and Trigger ate that slowly and thoughtfully. Finally she selected a book and sat down with it.

All this time, she'd been letting the Old Galactic with whom she was best acquainted know she was here, and that she had a problem. She didn't push it, but simply brought the idea up now and then and let it, so to speak, drift around for a moment. Shortly after she'd settled down with the book, she got an acknowledgment.

The form it took was the image of one of the big trees in the garden, which came floating up in her mind. It wasn't the tree the Old Galactic had been occupying when she was here last, but they changed quarters now and then. She sent him a greeting, slipped the book into her jacket pocket, and left the room, towing the Siren container behind her.

By then, it was well into the spring afternoon. Three Tainequa gardeners were working near the great tree as she approached, small brown-skinned men, members of a little clan Mantelish had coaxed into leaving its terraced valley on Tainequa and settling on Maccadon to look after his collection. Trigger smiled and said hello to them; and they smiled back and then stood watching thoughtfully as she went on toward the tree, selected a place where she could sit comfortably among its roots, grounded the container, and took the book from her pocket.

When she looked up, the three Tainequas were walking quietly off along the path she'd come, carrying their tools, and in a moment they'd disappeared behind some shrubbery. Trigger wasn't surprised. The Tainequa valley people were marvelously skilled and versatile gardeners—entirely too good at their craft, in fact, not to understand very well that Mantelish's botanical specimens flourished to an extent even their talented efforts didn't begin to explain. And while they knew nothing about Old Galactics, they did believe in spirits, good and evil.

If they'd thought the local spirits were evil, the outrageous salary Mantelish was obliged to pay the clan couldn't have kept it on Maccadon another hour. Benevolent spirits, however, are also best treated with respect by mortal man. The Tainequas worked diligently elsewhere in the garden, but they kept their distance from the great trees which obviously needed no care from them anyway. And when Trigger sat familiarly down beside one, any Tainequa in sight went elsewhere. She wasn't quite sure what they thought her relationship with the spirits was, but she knew they were in some awe of her.

Under the circumstances, that was convenient. She didn't want anyone around to distract her. Actually, the Old Galactics did almost all the real work of carrying on the conversation, but she made it easier by remaining simultaneously relaxed and attentive and not letting her thoughts stray. So while she was looking down at the book on her knees, she wasn't reading. Her eyes, unfocused, blinked occasionally at nothing. She'd been invited to come; she'd come, and was waiting.

She waited, without impatience. Until presently: *Describe the problem.*

She didn't sense it as words but as meaning, and sensed at the same time that there was more than one of them nearby, her old acquaintance among them. They liked the great trees of the garden as dwellings, their substance dispersed through the substance of the tree, flowing slowly through it like sap. They had their own natural solid shape when they chose to have it. And sometimes they took on other shapes for various purposes. Now a number of them had gathered near the base of the tree, still out of sight within it, to hear what she wanted.

She began thinking about the Sirens. The small one here in its container, and its giant relatives, mysterious and beautiful organisms, spread about three worlds in towering forests. She thought of how humans had encountered the Sirens and discovered how dangerous they were to other life, so dangerous that their complete extermination was beginning to look like the only logical way of dealing with them, and of her feeling that this would be totally wrong even if it seemed in the end to be inevitable. She didn't try to organize her thinking too much; what would get through to the Old Galactics were general impressions. They'd form their own concepts from that.

What do you want done?

She thought of the possibility that the Sirens had intelligence, and of reaching that intelligence and coming to an understanding with them so they would stop being uselessly destructive. Or, if they were creatures capable only of acting out of instinct, then ways might be found to modify them until they were no longer dangerous. The Old Galactics were great scientists in their own manner, which wasn't too similar to the human manner. Perhaps, Trigger's thoughts suggested, they would be able to succeed with the Sirens where humans so far had failed. She thought about the difficulties Pilch's xenotelepaths had encountered in trying to contact her specimen on the mental level, and of the fact that most humans had to be protected by psi blocks or mind shields against Siren euphoria.

There was stillness for a while then. She knew she'd presented the matter sufficiently, so she simply waited again. About an hour and a half had passed since she first sat down under the tree, which meant that from the Old Galactics' point of view they'd been having a very brisk conversational exchange.

By and by, something was told her.

Trigger nodded. "All right," she said aloud. She switched on the container's gravity float, moved it so that it stood next to the base of the big tree, and there grounded it again. Then she shut off the psi block, turned the front side transparent, opened the top, and sat down on a root nearby from where she could watch the Siren.

✧   ✧   ✧

The euphoric effect became noticeable in a few seconds, strengthened gradually, then remained at the same level. It was always pleasurable, though everybody seemed to experience it in an individual manner. For Trigger it usually had been a light, agreeable feeling, which seemed a perfectly natural way to feel when she had it—a sense of well-being and contentment, an awareness that it came from being around Sirens, and a corresponding feeling of liking for them. In the course of time, that had been quite enough to produce emotional addiction in her; and other people had been much more directly and strongly affected. "That's it," she said now, for the Old Galactics' benefit.

There was no response from them; and time passed again, perhaps fifteen or twenty minutes. Then something began to emerge from the bark of the big tree above the container.

Trigger watched it. In its solid form, an Old Galactic looked something like a discolored sausage; and this was what now appeared to be moving out from the interior of the tree. It was a very slow process. It took a minute or two before Trigger could make out that this wasn't her acquaintance, who was sizable for his kind, but a much smaller Old Galactic, probably not weighing more than half a pound. It got clear of the tree at last, moved down a few inches until it was level with the top of the container, curved over to it, and started gliding down inside. Eventually then the sausage shape reached the base of the Siren, touched it, began melting into it.

Something else was said to Trigger. She hesitated questioningly a moment, then placed her wrist against the side of the root on which she was sitting and left it there. A minute or two afterward, a coolness touched the inside of her wrist. She couldn't see what caused it, but she knew. She also knew from experience that it harmed a human body no more than it harmed a tree to have an Old Galactic's substance dispersed through it; they were unnoticeable, and if there was anything wrong with the body when they entered, they would take care of it before they left, precisely as they tended to the botanical specimens in Mantelish's garden.

In this case, they weren't concerned about Trigger's health, which was excellent. But they evidently felt, as had Pilch, that if she was going to be involved with a Siren, she should have the protection of a mind shield; and an Old Galactic specialist was now to begin providing her with their equivalent of one. He should be finished with the job in a few days. Trigger asked some questions about it, was given explanations, and presently agreed to let the specialist go ahead.

The rest of the afternoon passed uneventfully, as far as she was concerned. They'd told her after a while to restore the psi block and close the container. She was glad to do it. It was unlikely that a Tainequa would approach this section of the garden again today and get within range of the euphoria effect, but one never knew just what might happen if an area was exposed to the effect for any extended period of time. After that, the Old Galactics ignored her. She read in her book a while, stretched out in the grass near the tree for a nap, read some more. Eventually it was getting near evening, and there still had been no indication that the Old Galactics intended to interrupt whatever they were doing. Trigger went to the garden house, came back with her supper, a sleeping bag, and a few more books. She ate, read until dark, then opened the bag, got into it, and fell asleep.

She dreamed presently that she was back in a great Siren forest on a faraway world, swimming in the euphoria experience, but now frightened by it because she was aware she was becoming addicted. She made a violent effort to escape, and the effort brought her awake.

She knew where she was immediately then. A cloudbank covered the sky, with the starblaze gleaming through here and there; the garden lay quiet and shadowy around her. But the sense of Siren euphoria hadn't faded with the dream.

Trigger turned over, slipped partly out of the sleeping bag, and sat up. She couldn't make out the Siren container too well in the shade of the great tree, but she could see that it had been opened; and the psi block obviously was switched off. She had a moment of alarm. Then Old Galactic thought brushed slowly past her.

They weren't addressing her, and she couldn't make out any meaning. But she saw now that several dark sausage shapes of varying sizes were on the container. A vague thought pulse touched her mind again. It was ridiculous to think of Old Galactics becoming excited about anything; but Trigger had the impression that the little group on the container was as close to excitement as it could get. One of them evidently touched the psi block control then because the euphoria effect went out.

She sat there a while longer watching them and wondering what they were doing; but nothing much happened and she had no more thought impressions. Presently they began to move back to the big tree and into it. The last one shifted the control that closed the container before turning to follow his companions. Trigger got down into the bag again and went back to sleep. When she woke up next, it was cool dawn in the garden, everything looking pale and hazy. And the Old Galactics were speaking to her.

She gathered that the matter looked quite favorable, but that they couldn't give her definite information yet. One of them was still inside the Siren, analyzing it. She was to take the container back to her room now, and return with it in the evening. Then they would be able to tell her more.

4

"Well?" Pilch inquired, when they met two days later in Ceyce.

"They can do it," Trigger said. "They couldn't explain how—at least not in a way I understood."

"You hardly look overjoyed," Pilch observed. "What's the hitch?"

Trigger shrugged. "The time element. They live so long they never really seem to understand how important time is to us. Getting the Sirens tamed down would take them a while."

"How much of a while?"

"That was a little blurry. Anything having to do with time tends to be with them. But I'm afraid they meant something like a couple of centuries."

Pilch shook her head. "We can't wait that long!"

"I know," Trigger said. "What I told them was that I was in a little bit of a hurry with the Sirens, so I'd better shop around for faster results."

"How did they react?"

"They seemed to think it was a good idea. So—I'm on the move again." Trigger smiled soberly. "What are the other approaches you had in mind?"

"At the moment, I have two suggestions," said Pilch. "There are a few Service xenos in whom I'd have some confidence in the matter. They're among our best operators. However, they're on an assignment outside the Hub. Even if they were to interrupt what they're doing—which they shouldn't—it would take them well over a month to get here."

"I'll be glad to take the specimen to them," said Trigger.

Pilch nodded. "We may wind up having you do just that. On the other hand, you may need to go no farther than Orado. There's a psi there who's a very capable xenotelepath. She isn't in the Service and doesn't let it be generally known that she's a psi. But if she feels like it, it's quite possible she'll be able to determine whether the Sirens have intelligence, and whether it's a type and degree of intelligence that will permit communication with them. If that should turn out to be the case, of course, we'd be over the first great hurdle."

"We certainly would be!" Trigger agreed. "How do I get in touch with her?"

Pilch produced a card. "Here's her name and current address. Send her an outline of the situation, inquire whether she'd like to investigate the specimen for you, and so forth. If she'll do it, she's your best present bet."

"I'll get at it immediately." Trigger studied the card, put it in her purse. "Telzey Amberdon. How much can I tell her?"

"Anything you like. Telzey's come by more information about the Federation's business than most members of the Council should have. But she doesn't spill secrets. I'll give you a Class Four Clearance to send her, to keep it legitimate."

"What kind of fee will she want?" asked Trigger. "I might have to make arrangements."

"I doubt she'll want a fee. Her family has plenty of money. She'll work for you if the proposition catches her interest. Otherwise, she won't."

"I should be able to make it sound interesting enough," Trigger remarked. "Supposing she gets herself into trouble over this like some of your xenos?"

Pilch said, "Nobody's suffered permanent damage so far. If she winds up needing therapeutic help, she'll get it. I wouldn't worry too much. Telzey's a little monster in some respects. But I'll be around the area a while, and you can contact me through any Service center." She looked at her timepiece. "We'll go to the Ceyce lab now, and get you equipped with your mind shield."

"Well, as to *that*," said Trigger, "I already have one. Not quite, but very nearly."

"Eh?"

Trigger explained about her resident Old Galactic, and that he'd been doing something to her nervous system for the past two days. They went to the Service lab anyway; Pilch wanted to know just what was being done to Trigger's nervous system. Tests established then that she, indeed, had a shield. It permitted contact with her conscious thoughts but sealed off the rest of her mind with a block which stopped the heaviest probe Pilch tried against it. However, it was a block which became nonexistent when Trigger didn't want it there.

"Any time I decide to get rid of it permanently, it will start fading away," Trigger said.

Pilch nodded. "I noticed there'd been provision made for that." She reflected. "Well, you won't need the shield I'd intended for you. They're giving you something that seems more effective. So I'll be running along."

She left. Around evening of that day, Trigger's Old Galactic let her know he'd finished his work. She went back to his home tree and held her wrist against it until he'd transferred again, thanked them all around for their trouble, and returned to her room. The report to Telzey Amberdon was already prepared. It didn't mention the Old Galactics but was candid about almost everything else, specifically the subject of risks. Trigger flew in to Ceyce and had the report dispatched to Orado at an interstellar transmitter station.

Telzey Amberdon should receive it some six hours later.

That night, after the lights were out in the garden house and Trigger was asleep in her room, a visitor came to Mantelish's garden. Three Tainequas on their way to their quarters saw, but didn't notice, the cloaked shape moving toward them under the starblaze, went on talking in their soft voices, unaware of the shadow drifting across their minds, unaware of the visitor passing them a few feet away.

Pilch moved deeper into the garden and into the dimness under the great trees. Now and then she stopped and stood quietly, head turning this way and that, like a sensing animal, and went on in a new direction. At last, she halted before the tree where Trigger had conferred with the Old Galactics, and stayed there.

Awareness stirred in the tree, slowly focused on her. There was a long pause. An inquiry came.

Pilch identified herself. After a time, the identification was acknowledged. *Your purpose?*

She brought up assorted unhurried impressions of Trigger's Siren specimen, of the Siren worlds, of the effects produced by Sirens, of their inaccessibility to psi contact. . . .

Yes. The Hana species.

What did they know of it?

Pilch gathered presently that they'd never encountered a Hana before this. They'd had reports. Not recent ones. They'd believed the species was extinct.

Was it as dangerous as it appeared to be?

Yes. Very dangerous.

The slow exchange continued. In Pilch's mind, impressions formed. Time, space, and direction remained wavering, unstable concepts. But, by any human reckoning, it must have been very long ago, very far away in the galaxy's vastness, that a race of conquerors brought Hanas to many civilized worlds.

Presently those worlds were destroyed. The Hanas had swifter weapons than their ability to produce euphoria and mindless dependency in other species. Pilch watched as psi death lanced out from them, and all other minds in a wide radius winked out of existence. She saw great psi machines brought up to control the Hanas, and then those machines shredded into uselessness as their own energies stormed wildly through them. On a planet, while a semblance of its surface remained, the Hana species seemed indestructible, spreading and proliferating like a shifting green flood, sweeping up into furious life here as it was annihilated there.

They died at last when distant space weapons seared all worlds, many hundreds of worlds by then, on which they were to be found until no life of any kind remained possible. Then the great race the Hana had fought hunted long and far, to make sure none remained alive in the universe.

But it appeared that one remote planet, at least, had been overlooked in that search.

Near daybreak, a small aircar lifted from a forested hillside a little to the north of Mantelish's garden and sped away toward Ceyce. Trigger awoke an hour later, had breakfast, watched a few Tainequas moving about the garden from the veranda of her room, settled down to read. Around noon, the ComWeb in Mantelish's office on the ground floor began ringing. Trigger hurried down, took a message from the receiver.

It appeared Telzey Amberdon's time next week would be mainly occupied with college graduation exams. However, she did want to see Miss Argee's Siren and discuss her plan with her, and would be pleased to meet her on Orado. If it happened to be convenient to Miss Argee, she had the coming weekend free—that being Days Seventy-one and Seventy-two of the standard year.

It was now Day Seventy. Trigger called the Psychology Service Center in Ceyce and left a message for Pilch. She packed quickly, loaded the Siren container into her aircar, and headed for Ceyce Port. Within the hour, she was on her way to Orado.

5

Trigger met Telzey Amberdon next morning in a room she'd taken in the Haplandia Hotel at the Orado City Space Terminal. She was startled for a moment by the fact that Telzey seemed to be at most seventeen years old. On reflection, she decided then that a capable young psi, one who knew more Federation secrets than most Council members, might mature rather rapidly.

"Ready to be euphorized?" she asked, by and by.

Telzey nodded. "Let's check it out."

Trigger switched off the psi block on the Siren container, and Siren euphoria began building up gradually in the room. Telzey leaned forward in her chair, watching the Siren. Her expression grew absent as if she were listening to distant voices. Trigger, having seen a similar expression on Pilch now and then, remained silent. After a minute or two, Telzey straightened, looked over at her.

"You can shield it again," she said.

Trigger restored the psi block. "What was it like?"

"Very odd! There was a wisp of psi sense for a moment—just as you switched off the block."

Trigger looked interested and thoughtful. "No one else reported that."

"It was there. But it was gone at once, and I didn't get it again. The rest was nothing. Almost like a negation of psi! I felt as if I were reaching into a vacuum."

Trigger nodded. "That's more or less how the

Service xenos described the sensation. I brought along a file of their reports. Like to see them?"

Telzey said she would. Trigger produced the file; and Telzey sat down at a table with it and began scanning through the reports. Trigger watched her. A likable sort of young person . . . Strong-willed probably. Intelligent certainly. Capable of succeeding where Pilch's xenos had failed? Trigger wondered. Still, Pilch wouldn't have referred to her as a little monster without reason.

The little monster presently closed the file and glanced over at Trigger.

"That certainly *is* a different kind of psi creature!" she remarked. "Different from anything I've come across, anyway. I don't know if I can do anything with it. I'm not your last hope, am I?"

Trigger smiled briefly. "Not the last. But the next ones more than a month's travel time away."

"Do you want me to try? Now that you've seen me?"

Trigger hesitated. "It's not exactly a matter of wanting anyone to try."

"You're worried, aren't you?" Telzey asked.

"Yes, I'm worried," Trigger acknowledged. "I seem to be getting a little more worried all the time."

"What about?"

Trigger bit her lip gently. "I can't say specifically. It may be my imagination. But I don't think so. It's a feeling that we'd better get this business with the Sirens straightened out."

"Or something might happen?"

"That's about it. And that the situation might be getting more critical the longer it remains unsettled."

Telzey studied her quizzically. "Then why aren't you anxious to have me try the probe?"

Trigger said, "There hasn't been too much trouble so far. In the labs, where they've been trying to modify the Sirens biologically, there's been no trouble at all. Except, of course, that some people got addiction symptoms before they started using psi blocks and mind shields. But you see, all they've accomplished in the labs is to put some checks on the Sirens." She indicated the container. "Like stopping this one's growth, keeping the proliferation cycles from getting started, and so on. Meanwhile, there've been indications that the chromosomal changes involved have gradually begun to reverse—which, I've been told by quite a number of people, is impossible."

Telzey said, "The midget here might start to grow again?"

"Yes, it might. What it means is that the labs haven't really got anywhere. Now, the Psychology Service xenos didn't get too far either, but they did learn a few definite things about the Siren. They got into trouble immediately."

Telzey nodded.

"And you," Trigger said, "are supposed to be better than the Service xenos. You should be able to go further. If you do, it's quite possible you'll get into more serious trouble than they did."

Telzey said after a moment, "You think the Siren doesn't intend to change from what it is? Or let us find out what it really is?"

"It almost looks that way, doesn't it?"

"On the psi side it might look that way," Telzey agreed. She smiled. "You know, you're not trying very hard to push me into this!"

"No," Trigger said. "I'm not trying to push you into it. I don't feel I should. I feel I should tell you what I think before you decide."

Telzey looked reflective. "You told other people?"

Trigger shook her head. "If I started talking about it generally, it might turn us back to the extermination program. I think that's the last thing that should happen." She added, "Pilch probably knows. She's looked around in my mind now and then, for one reason and another. But she hasn't said anything."

"Pilch is the one who recommended me to you?" Telzey asked.

"Yes. Have you met?"

Telzey shook her head. "I've never heard of her. What's she like?"

Trigger considered.

"Pilch is Pilch," she said. "She has her ways. She's a very good psi. She seems to be one of the Service's top executives. She's a busy lady, and I don't think she'd bother herself for a minute with the Sirens if she thought they weren't important. She told me there was a definite possibility you'd be able to get into communication with our specimen—that's assuming, of course, there's something there that can communicate." Trigger thought again, shrugged. "I've known Pilch nearly two years, but that's almost all I can tell you about her."

Telzey was silent for over a minute now, dark-blue eyes fixed reflectively on Trigger.

"If I told you," she said suddenly, "that I didn't want to get involved in this, what would you do?"

"Get packed for a month's travel plus," Trigger said promptly. "I don't think it will be at all safe to push ahead on the psi side here, but I think it will be safer generally than not pushing ahead."

Telzey nodded.

"Well, I am getting involved," she said. "So that's settled. We'll see if Pilch is right, and it's something I can handle—and whether you're right, and it's something that has to be handled. I can't quite imagine the Sirens as a menace to the Federation, but we'll try to find out more about them. If I don't accomplish anything, you can still pack up for that month's trip. How much time can you spend on Orado now?"

Trigger said, "As much time as it takes, or you're willing to put in on it."

Telzey asked, "Where will you stay? We can't very well work in the Haplandia."

"We certainly can't," Trigger agreed. "We'd have half the hotel in euphoria if we left the Siren unshielded for ten minutes. I haven't made arrangements yet. The labs where they work on Sirens are all a good distance away from population centers, even though the structures are psi-blocked. So I'll be looking for a place that's well out in the country, but still convenient for you."

"I know a place like that."

"Yes?"

"My family has a summer house up in the hills," Telzey said. "Nobody will be using it the next couple of months. There's Ezd Malion, the caretaker; but he and his wife have their own house a quarter of a mile away."

Trigger nodded. "They'll be safe there. Unless there are special developments. The Siren euphoria couldn't do more than give them sunny dispositions at that distance."

"That's what I thought from the reports," said Telzey. "And we can keep the Malions away from the house while we're working. There's nobody else around for miles. It's convenient for me—I can get there from college in twenty minutes. . . . If there isn't something you want to do, why don't we move you and the Siren in this afternoon?"

6

The Hana dwarf dreamed in its own way occasionally. Its life of the moment had been a short one and might not be extended significantly; but its ancestral memory went back for a number of generations before it began to fade, and beyond that was a kind of memory to which it came only when it withdrew its attention wholly from the life of the moment and its requirements. It had taken to doing it frequently since realizing it was on a Veen world and no longer in contact with its kind.

That form of memory went back a long way to the world on which the Hanas originated, and even to the early period of that world when they gained supremacy after dangerous and protracted struggles with savage species as formidable as they. They came at last to the long time in which the world remained in harmony and they kept it so, living the placid and thoughtful plant existence they preferred, but not unaware of what went on outside. Disruptions occurred occasionally when some form of scurrying mobile life, nervously active, eternally eating or being eaten, began to become a nuisance, to crowd out others, or attempt to molest the Hanas. Then the Hanas would beckon that overly excitable species to them and start it on the path which led it eventually to the quietly satisfactory existence of the plant.

It was a good time, and the Hana dwarf now lived there often for a while before returning, strengthened, to the life of the moment and the knowledge of being among the Veen. There was little else to do. The Veen held it enclosed in a cage of energy, difficult to penetrate and opened only when they came with their prying minds and mind machines to seek out and enslave the captured Hana mind, precisely as they had done in other days. They'd learned much in the interval, if not greater wisdom and less arrogance. The Hana dwarf was aware of the manipulations which stopped its growth and prevented it from developing and distributing its seed. But such things were of no significance. They could be undone. The question was whether the Veen could reach its mind.

It hadn't believed they could. It was more

formidably armed than any Hana had been in the times of the Veen War; if its defenses failed, the touch of its thought would kill other minds in moments. But it was less sure now. The Veen's first probes barely reached its defenses, broke there; and a brief period of quiet followed. But they were persistent. Indications came that another attempt was being carefully prepared, with mind qualities involved which had not been noticeable before.

It would warn them, though Veen had not yet been known to respond sensibly to a warning. They were the race which knew no equals, which could tolerate only slaves. If they persisted and succeeded, the Hana would emerge to kill, and presently to die. A single pulse would be enough to notify the Three Worlds, long since alerted, and waiting now with a massed power never before encountered by Veen, that the Veen War had been resumed.

The Hana shaped its warnings and set them aside, to be released as seemed required. Then, with its several deaths prepared, it, too, waited, and sometimes dreamed.

Toward evening, four days after Trigger and the Siren specimen moved into the Amberdon summer-house, Telzey was on her way there by aircar. It had been a demanding day at college, but she was doing very well in the exams. When she left Pehanron, she'd felt comfortably relaxed.

Some five minutes ago then, her mood shifted abruptly. An uneasy alertness awoke in her. It wasn't the first time she'd felt that way during the past few days.

The Siren? From behind a psi block and over all these miles? Not likely, but perhaps not impossible either. She hadn't made much headway in the investigation over the weekend and the last two evenings, and hadn't tried to. That was a strange being! Under the mechanical euphoric effect seemed to lie only the empty negation which had met her first probe. The Service's translating machines had reported nothing at all, but most of the Service xenotelepaths also had sensed the void, the emptiness, the vacuum. Some of them eventually found something in the vacuum. They weren't sure of what they'd found; but they'd stirred up a violence and power difficult to associate with the midget Siren. Mind shields had been hard tested. Some shields weren't tight enough or resistant enough; and as a result, the Service had a few lunatic xenos around for a while.

Even without Trigger's forebodings, it wouldn't have looked like a matter to rush into. When the exams were over, Telzey could settle down to serious work on the Siren. All she'd intended during the week was to become acquainted with it.

In doing even that much, had she allowed it to become acquainted with her? She wasn't sure. Something or other, at any rate, seemed to have developed an awareness of her. Otherwise, she'd had no problems. The addictive effect didn't bother her; that could be dampened or screened out, and whatever lingered after a period of contact was wiped from her mind in seconds.

The something-or-other did bother her.

Telzey turned the aircar into the mouth of a wide valley. It was between winter and spring in the hills, windy and wet. Snow still lay in the gullies and along the mountain slopes, but the green things were coming awake everywhere. The Amberdon house stood forty miles to the north above the banks of a little lake. . . .

There was this restlessness, a frequent inclination to check the car's view screens, though there was almost no air traffic here. Simply a feeling of something around! Something unseen.

When it happened before, she'd suspected there might be a psi prowling in her mental neighborhood, somebody who was taking an interest in her. Since such uninvited interest wasn't always healthy, she'd long since established automatic sensors which picked up the beginnings of a scanning probe and simultaneously concealed and alerted her. The sensors hadn't gone into action.

So it shouldn't be a human psi hanging around. Unless it was a psi with a good deal defter touch than she'd encountered previously. Under the circumstances, that, too, wasn't impossible.

If it wasn't a human psi, it almost had to be a Siren manifestation.

The feeling faded before she reached the house and brought her Cloudsplitter down to the carport. Another aircar stood there, the one Trigger had rented for her stay on Orado.

During the past two evenings, they'd established a routine. When Telzey arrived from college, she and Trigger had dinner, then settled down in the room Gilas Amberdon used as a study when he was in the house. Its main attraction was a fine fireplace. They'd talk about this and that; meanwhile the Siren's unshielded container stood on a table in a corner of the room, and Telzey's thoughts drifted about the alien strangeness, not probing in any way but picking up whatever was to be learned easily. She soon stopped getting anything new in that manner; what was to be learned easily about the Siren remained limited. Some time before midnight, they'd restore the psi block, and Telzey went off to Pehanron.

But before she left, they turned on the lights in the grounds outside for a while. The very first night, the day Trigger and the Siren moved in, they'd had a rather startling experience. They were in the study when they began to hear sounds outside. It might have been tree branches beating against the wall in the wind, except that no tree grew so close to the house there. It might even have been an unseasonable, irregular spattering of hail. The study had no window, but the adjoining room had two, so they went in, opened a window and looked out.

At once, something came up over the sill with a great wet flap of wings and tail and drove into the room between them, bowling Telzey over. Trigger yelped and slammed the window shut as another pair of wings boomed in from the windy dusk with more shadowy shapes behind it. When she looked around, Telzey was getting to her feet and the intruder had disappeared into the house. They could hear it flapping about somewhere.

"Are you hurt, Telzey?"

"No."

"What in the world is that thing? There's a whole mess of them outside!"

"Eveers. They're on spring migration. A flock was probably settling to the lake and got in range of the Siren."

"Good Lord, yes! The Siren! We should have realized—what'll we do with the one in the house?"

"The first thing we'd better do is get the Siren shielded," said Telzey.

Trigger cocked her head, listening. "The, uh, eveer is in the study!"

Telzey laughed. "They're not very dangerous. Come on!"

The eveer might not have been a vicious creature normally, but it had strong objections to being evicted from the study and put up a determined fight. They both collected beak nips and scratches, were knocked about by solid wing strokes and thoroughly muddied by the eveer's wet hide, before they finally got it pinned down under a blanket. Then Trigger crouched on the blanket, panting, while Telzey restored the psi block. After that, the eveer seemed mainly interested in getting away from them. They carried it to the front door between them, bundled in the blanket, and opened the door. There they recoiled.

A sizable collection of Orado's local walking and flying fauna had gathered along the wall of the house. But the creatures were already beginning to disperse, now that the Siren's magic had faded; and at the appearance of the two humans, most of them took off quickly. Trigger and Telzey shook the eveer out of the blanket, and it went flapping away heavily into the night.

It took them most of an hour to tend to their injuries and clean up behind it. After that, they ignored unusual sounds outside the house when the container's psi block was off.

Other things were less easy to ignore.

The night Telzey started back to Pehanron after the weekend was the time she first got the impression that something unseen was riding along with her. Psi company, she suspected, though her sensors reported nothing. She waited a while, relaxed her mind screens gradually, sent a sudden quick, wide search-thought about, with something less friendly held in readiness, in case it was company she didn't like. The search-thought should have caught at least a trace of whoever or whatever was there. It didn't.

She remained behind her screens then, waiting. The feeling grew no stronger; sometimes it seemed to weaken. But it was a good five minutes before it faded completely.

It came back twice in the next two days. Once in the house while she was in the study with Trigger, once on the way to the house. She didn't mention it to Trigger; but that night, when it was getting time for her to leave, she said, "I think I'll sleep here tonight and start back early in the morning."

"Be my guest," Trigger said affably. She hesitated, added, "The fact is I'll be rather glad to know you're around."

Telzey looked at her. "You get lonesome at night in this big old house?"

"Not exactly lonesome," Trigger said. "I've never minded being by myself." She smiled. "Has your house ever had the reputation of being haunted?"

"Haunted? Not for around a hundred years. You've had the impression there's a spook flitting about?"

"Just an odd feeling occasionally," Trigger said. She paused, added in a changed voice, "And by coincidence, I'm beginning to get that feeling again now!"

They stood silent then, looking at each other. The feeling grew. It swelled into a sensation of bone-chilling cold, of oppressive dread. It seemed to circle slowly about them, drawing closer. Telzey passed her tongue over her lips. Psi slashed out twice. The sensation blurred, was gone.

She turned toward the Siren container. Trigger shook her head. "The psi block's on," she said. "It was on the other times, too. I checked."

And the psi block was on. Telzey asked, "How often has it happened?"

Trigger shrugged. "Four or five times. I'll come awake at night. It'll last a minute or two and go away."

"Why didn't you tell me?"

"I didn't want to disturb you," Trigger said. "It wasn't as strong as this before. I didn't know what it was, but it didn't seem to have anything to do with the Siren." She smiled, a trifle shakily. "An Amberdon ghost I could stand."

"Let's sit down," Telzey said. "It wasn't an Amberdon ghost, but it was a ghost of sorts."

They sat down. "What do you mean?" Trigger asked.

Telzey said, "A psi structure. Something with some independent duration. A fear ghost. A psi mind made it, planted it. It was due to be sensed when we sensed it."

Trigger glanced at the container. "The Siren?"

"Yes, the little Siren." Telzey blinked absently, fingering her chin. "There was nothing human about that structure. So the Siren put it out while the block was off. It's telling us not to fool around with it . . . But now we *will* have to fool around with it!"

Trigger looked questioningly at her.

"It means you were right," Telzey said. "The Siren has intelligence. It knows there's somebody around who's trying to probe it, and it doesn't want to be probed. It's tried to use fear to drive us away. Any psi mind that can put out a structure like that is very good! Dangerously good." She shook her head. "I don't think anyone could say exactly what a whole world of creatures who can do that mightn't be able to do otherwise!"

"Three worlds," said Trigger.

"Yes, three worlds. So the Siren operation can't just stop. They don't know enough about us. They might think we're very dangerous to them, and, of course, we are dangerous. The three worlds are there, and sooner or later somebody's going to do something stupid about them. And something will get started—if it hasn't started already." She glanced at Trigger, smiled briefly. "Until now, I was thinking it might be only your imagination! But it isn't. This is a really bad matter."

Trigger said after a moment, "I wish it had been only my imagination!" She looked at the Siren container. "You still think you can handle it?"

Telzey shrugged. "I wouldn't know by myself. But I'm sure Pilch gave that careful consideration."

Trigger reflected, tongue tip between lips, nodded. "Yes, she must have. It seems you've been pushed into something, Telzey."

"We've both been pushed into something," Telzey said.

Trigger sighed. "Well, I can't blame her too much! It has to be done, and the Service couldn't do it—at least not quickly enough. But I won't blame you at all if you want to pull out."

"I might want to pull out," Telzey admitted. "It's more than I'd counted on. But I'd be going around worrying about the Sirens then, like you've been doing. We know more now to be worried about."

"So you're staying?"

"Yes."

Trigger smiled. "I can't say I'm sorry! Look. It's getting late, and you'll have to be off to college early. Let's talk about strictly non-eerie things for a little, and turn in."

So they talked about non-eerie matters, and soon went to bed, and slept undisturbed until morning, when Telzey flew off to Pehanron College.

That evening, she slipped a probe lightly into the psi-emptiness of the Siren—an area she'd kept away from since her first contact with it. She thought presently it didn't seem quite as empty as it had. There might be something there. Something perhaps like a vague, distant shadow, only occasionally and briefly discernible.

She withdrew the probe carefully.

"Let's leave the psi block on until I've finished with the exams," she told Trigger later. "I've picked up as much as I can use for a start." She wasn't so sure now of the psi block's absolute dependability when it came to the Siren. But it should act as a temporary restraint.

Trigger didn't comment. Telzey slept in the house the rest of the week, and nothing of much significance happened. What remained of the exams wasn't too significant either; she went breezing through it all with only half her attention. Then the end of the week came, and she moved into the summerhouse. In three weeks, she'd be attending graduation ceremonies at Pehanron College. Until then, her time was her own.

7

It was early on the first morning after the exams then that Telzey had her first serious session with the Siren. She'd closed the door to the study and moved an armchair to a point from where she could observe the container. Trigger wasn't present; she'd stay out in the house to avoid distracting Telzey, and to handle interruptions like ComWeb calls. Ezd Malion, the caretaker, usually checked in before noon to get shopping instructions.

Telzey settled herself in the chair, relaxed physically. Mentally there'd be no relaxing. If the Siren entity followed the reaction pattern described in the Service reports, she shouldn't be running into immediate problems. But it might not stay with the pattern.

Her probe moved cautiously into the psi-emptiness. After a time, she gained again the impression of a few days before: it wasn't as empty as it had appeared at first contact. Something shadowy, distant, seemed to be there.

She began to work with the impression. What did she feel about it? A vague thing—and large. Cold perhaps. Yes. Cold and dark . . .

It was what she felt, no more than that. But her feelings were all she had to work with at this stage. Out of them other things could develop. There was this vague, dark, cold largeness then, connected with the Siren on the study table. She tried to gain some impression of the relationship.

An impression came suddenly, a negative one. The relationship had been denied. Afterward, the darkness seemed to have become a little colder. Telzey's nerves tingled. There was no change otherwise, but she'd had a response. Her psi sensors reached toward the fringes of the darkness, seemed to touch it, still found nothing that allowed a probe. She had a symbol of what was there, not yet its reality. But the search had moved on a step.

Then there was an interruption. She knew suddenly she wasn't alone in the study. This was much more definite than any previous feeling that there might be someone or something about. She still sensed nothing specific, but the hair at the nape of her neck was trying to lift, and the skin of her back prickled with awareness of another's presence in the room.

Telzey didn't look around, knowing she'd see no one if she did. Instead, she flicked a search probe out suddenly. As suddenly the presence was gone.

She sat quiet a moment, returned her attention to the symbol. Nothing there had changed. She withdrew from it, stood up, turned the container's psi block back on, and looked at her watch. About an hour had passed since she'd entered the study.

She found Trigger in the conservatory, tending to the plants under the indoor sun. "Trigger," she said, "did you happen to be thinking about me a few minutes ago?"

"Probably," Trigger said. "I've been thinking about you right along, wondering how you were doing. Why?"

"Has there ever been anything to indicate you might be a psi?"

Trigger looked surprised.

"Well," she said, "I understand everybody's a bit of a psi. So I suppose I'm that. I've never done anything out of the ordinary, though. Except perhaps—" She hesitated.

"Except perhaps what?" Telzey asked.

Trigger told her about the Old Galactics and her contacts with them.

"Great day in the morning!" Telzey said, astounded, when Trigger concluded. "You certainly have unusual acquaintances!"

"Of course, no one's to know they're there," Trigger remarked.

"Well, I won't tell."

"I know you won't. You think it might mean I'm a kind of telepath?"

"It might," Telzey said. "It wouldn't have to. They may simply have themselves tuned in on you." She stood a moment, reflecting. "I ran into a heavy-duty psi once who didn't have the faintest idea he was one," she said. "It was a problem because all sorts of extraordinary things kept happening to him and around him. Right now, anything like that could be disturbing."

Trigger looked concerned. "Have there been disturbances?"

"I haven't noticed anything definite," Telzey said untruthfully. "But I've been wondering."

"Could you find out about me if I undid that mind shield they gave me?"

Telzey sat down. "Let's try."

Trigger wished the shield out of existence. Some little time passed. Then Telzey said, "You can put the shield back."

"Well?" Trigger asked. "Am I?"

"You are," Telzey said absently. "I thought you might be, from the way you've been worrying about the Sirens." She shook her head. "Trigger, that's the most disorganized psi mind I've ever contacted! I wonder why Pilch never mentioned it."

Trigger hesitated. "Now that *you've* mentioned it," she said, "I believe Pilch did suggest something of the kind on one occasion. I thought I'd misunderstood her. She didn't refer to it again."

"Well, if you like," said Telzey, "we can take a week off after we're through with the Siren, and see if we can't make you operational."

Trigger rubbed her nose tip. "Frankly, I doubt that I'd want to be operational."

"Why?"

"You and Pilch seem to thrive on it," Trigger said, "but I've met other psis who weren't cheery people. I suppose you can pick up a whole new parcel of problems when you have abilities like that."

"You pick up problems, all right," Telzey acknowledged.

"That's what I thought. And I," Trigger said, "seem to find all the problems I can handle without adding complications. Could that disorganized psi mind of mine do anything to disturb you when you're trying to work with the Siren?"

Telzey shook her head. Trigger, psi-latent, hadn't been unconsciously responsible for those manifestations, couldn't have been. Neither was the Siren. This time, there'd been, for a moment, a decidedly human quality about the immaterial presence.

So the Psychology Service was keeping an eye on proceedings here. She'd half expected it. And they'd assigned an operator of exceptional quality to the job—*she* couldn't have prowled about an alerted telepath and remained as well concealed.

Nor, Telzey thought, was that the only concealed high-quality psi around. While Trigger was talking about the Old Galactics, she'd recalled that flick of mind-stuff she caught the moment the Siren container came unshielded in the Haplandia Hotel.

It seemed the Old Galactics, too, had an interest in the Siren specimen, and were represented in the summerhouse. . . .

Did either of them know about the other? Did the Siren entity know about either of them, or suspect it had an occupant? It was nothing she could mention to Trigger—there was too much psi involved all around, and Trigger's surface thoughts were accessible to any telepath who wanted to follow them.

She'd have to await developments—and meanwhile push ahead toward the probe. Around that point, everything should start falling into place. It would have to.

She told Trigger what she'd accomplished so far, added, "I've probably got the contact process started. This afternoon I'll pick the symbol up again and see." She yawned, stretched slowly. "How about we go for a long walk before lunch? This is great hiking country."

They went down to the end of the grounds, past the house where Ezd Malion and his wife lived, and on to the banks of the lake. The sun was out that morning; it was chilly, blustery, refreshing. They followed narrow trails used more often by animals than by people. It was over an hour before they turned back for lunch.

Early in the afternoon then, Telzey went into the study and closed the door. She emerged four hours later. Trigger regarded her with some concern. "You look pretty worn out!"

"I am pretty worn out," Telzey acknowledged. "It was hard work. Let's go have some coffee, and I'll tell you."

She'd picked up her symbol with no trouble—a good sign. She settled her attention on it, and waited. There'd been changes, she decided presently. It was as if a kind of life were seeping into the symbol, accumulating there. Another good sign. No need to push it now; she was moving in the right direction.

That might have gone on about an hour. Physically Telzey was feeling a little uncomfortable by then, which again could be counted, technically, a good sign, though she didn't like it. There was a frequent shivering in her skin, moments when breathing seemed difficult, other manifestations of apprehension. What it meant was that she was getting close.

Then there was an instant when she wasn't close, but there. Or *it* was there. The symbol faded as what had been behind it came slowly through. This was no visualization, but reality as sensed by psi. It was the darkness, the cold, in the false emptiness. It simmered with silent power. It was eminently forbidding.

It was there—then it wasn't there. It seemed to have become nonexistent.

But she needed no symbols to return to it now. What she had contacted, she could contact again. It was in her memory; and memory was a link. She could draw herself back to it.

She did, quickly lost it once more. Now there were two links. All she needed was patience.

Any feeling of passing time, all awareness of the room about her, of the chair in which she sat, even of her body, was gone. She was mind, in the universe of mind where she moved and searched, tracing the thing she had contacted, finding it, establishing new connections between herself and it. She lost it again and again, but each time it was easier to find, less difficult to hold. It was a great fish, and she a tiny fisherman, not fastening the fish to herself, but herself to the fish. Finally, the connection was stable, unchanging. When she was sure of that, she broke it. She could resume it whenever she chose.

At that point, she became conscious of the other reality, of her physical self and her surroundings.

And—once more—of having uninvited company.

This time, she ignored the presence. It faded quietly from her awareness as she opened her eyes, sat up in the armchair. . . .

"I think we're almost there," she told Trigger. "The thing's a structure, a psi structure. It's what the Service xenos found and tried to probe. And I can believe it bounced them—it's really charged up!"

"You're going to try to probe it?" Trigger asked.

Telzey nodded. "I'll have to. There's been no mind trace of the Siren, so that structure must act as its shield. I'll have to try to work through it. How, I won't know till I find out what it's like." She was silent a moment. "If it bounces me, too, I don't know what else we can do," she said. "But we'll start worrying about that then. I do have very good shields. And if I can get one solid contact with the Siren mind, we may have the problem solved. Unless they're basically murderous, of course. But I agree with you that they don't really seem to be that."

There were other factors involved. But that was still nothing to talk to Trigger about. "So everything's set up for the probe now," Telzey concluded. "Next time I'll try it. But I want to be a lot fresher for that, so it won't be tonight. We'll see how I feel tomorrow."

They turned in early. Telzey fell into sleep at once like drifting deep, deep down through a cool dark quiet sea. . . . Some time later then, she found herself standing in the Siren's container.

It wasn't exactly the container, though there was a shadowy indication of its walls in the distance. A kind of cold desert stretched out about her, and she stood at the base of the Siren. A Siren which twisted enormously up into an icy sky, gigantic, higher than a mountain, huge limbs writhing. A noise like growing thunder was in the air; the desert sand shook under her, and her feet were rooted immovably in the sand. Then she saw that the Siren was tilting, falling toward her, would crush her. She heard herself screaming in terror.

She awoke.

She sat up in bed, breathing in quick short gasps. She looked around the dark room, reached for the light switch. As she touched it, light blazed in the hall beyond the door. "Trigger?" she called.

From the direction of Trigger's room came a shaky, "Yes?"

"Wait a moment!" Telzey climbed out of bed,

started toward the door. Trigger met her there, robe wrapped around her, face pale, hair disheveled. "What's the matter?" Telzey asked.

Trigger tried to smile. "Had a dream—a nightmare. *Whew!* Going down to the kitchen for some hot milk to settle myself." She laughed unsteadily.

"A nightmare?" Telzey stared at her. "Wait—I'll come along."

They'd had the same dream. A dream apparently identical in all respects, except that in Trigger's dream, it was Trigger who was about to be crushed by the toppling monster Siren. Sitting in the kitchen, sipping their hot milk, they discussed it, looking at each other with uncertain eyes. Something had come into their minds as they slept

"That Old Galactic shield of yours," Telzey pointed out, "is supposed to keep anything from reaching your subconscious mind processes—which includes the dream mechanisms."

Trigger gave her a startled glance.

"Unless I allow it!" she said. "And I think I did allow it."

"What?"

Trigger nodded, frowned, trying to remember. "I was half asleep," she said slowly. "Something seemed to be telling me to dissolve the shield. So I did."

"Why?"

Trigger shrugged helplessly. "It *seemed* perfectly all right! I wasn't surprised or alarmed—not until I started dreaming." She reflected, shook her head. "That's all I remember. I suppose there was another of those ghost structures floating around?"

Telzey nodded. "Probably." She couldn't recall anything that had happened before she started dreaming. "Some general impression—warning, threat," she said. "With a heavy fear charge."

"How could we have turned that into the same dream?"

Telzey said, "We didn't. Your mind was wide open. I'm a telepath." A dream could be manufactured in a flash, from whatever material seemed to match the impulse that induced it. "One of us whipped up the dream," she said. "The other shared it. We came awake almost at once then."

"That Siren," said Trigger after a moment, "really doesn't want to be probed."

"No, not at all. And it may be aware that I've got as far as its shield."

Two other psi minds around here, Telzey thought, should also be aware of that fact. The Psychology Service would hardly be trying to discourage her from the probe. But the observer the Old Galactics had left planted in the Siren might have some reason for doing it—and might have the ability to induce a warning nightmare. She wished she had some clue to the interest that ancient race was taking in the Sirens.

They finished their milk, sat talking a few minutes longer, decided there was no sense sitting up the rest of the night, and went back to bed. They left the light on in the hall outside their rooms. Somewhat to Telzey's surprise, she felt herself fall asleep again almost as soon as her head touched the pillow.

8

They awoke to a disagreeable day. The sky was gloomy; a wind blew in cold gusts about the house; and there were intermittent falls of rain. Breakfast was a silent affair, as each was withdrawn into her own thoughts. When they'd finished, Trigger went to a window and looked out. Telzey joined her. "Gruesome weather!" Trigger remarked darkly. "I feel depressed."

"So do I," said Telzey.

Trigger glanced at her. "You don't think it's the weather, do you?"

"No."

"It's in the house all around us," Trigger said, nodding. "I've felt it since I woke up. As if there were something unpleasant about that I might see or hear at any moment. More of that ghost stuff, isn't it?"

"Yes. It may wear off." But Telzey wasn't so sure it would wear off, and whether the entity behind the psi block wasn't reaching them now through the block. This was a subtler assault on their nerves, the darkening of mood, uneasiness, a prodding of anxieties—all too diffused to counter.

An hour later, it didn't seem to be wearing off. "You shouldn't try the probe while you're feeling like this, should you?" Trigger asked.

Telzey shook her head. "Not if I can help it—but I don't think I should put it off too long either."

They were vulnerable, and they'd stirred something up. Even left alone, it wouldn't necessarily settle down. It might keep undermining their defenses for hours, or shift to a more definite attack. The probe must be attempted, and soon. The Sirens existed, were an unpredictable factor; something had to be done. If she waited, she might be reduced to incapability. That could be the intention.

"Let's go outside and tramp around a while," Trigger said. "Maybe it will cheer us up. I usually like a good rainy day, really."

They donned rain capes and boots, went down to the lake. But the walk didn't cheer them up. The wind stirred the cold lake surface, soughed through the trees about them. The sky seemed to be growing darker; and the notion came to Telzey that if she looked closely enough, she'd be able to make out the giant Siren of their dream writhing among distant clouds. She stopped short, caught Trigger by the arm.

"This isn't doing any good!" she said. "It's focused on us, and we're dragging it around with us here. Let's go back, pick up swim gear, and clear out! I know a beach where it won't be rainy and cold. We can be there in an hour."

They sped south in the Cloudsplitter, came down on a beach lying golden and hot under a nearly cloudless sky. The wind that swept it was a fresh and happy one. They swam and tumbled in the surf, spirits lifting by the minute. They came out and sunned, talked and laughed, swam again, collected a troop of bronzed males, let themselves be taken to lunch, shook off the troop, fled fifty miles east along the beach, went back to the water for a final dip where breakers rose high, and emerged exhausted and laughing ten minutes later. "*Now* let's go tackle that Siren!"

They flew north again, dropping down at a town en route to buy two tickets to the currently most popular live show in Orado City. Just what would happen when the probe began seemed a rather good question. Enough had happened, at any rate, to make them feel the Malions shouldn't be anywhere in the area at the time. They stopped off at the caretaker's house, explained they'd intended taking in the show that night, but found they couldn't make it; so there were two expensive tickets on hand which shouldn't go to waste. . . . Ezd and wife were on their way to Orado City thirty minutes later.

Parked at the northern end of the grounds, Telzey and Trigger watched the caretakers leave. The Cloudsplitter lifted then, slid down into the carport of the summerhouse. They went in by a side entrance.

The house was quiet. If anything had taken note of their return, it gave no indication. They got arranged quickly in the study. Trigger would be sitting in on this session. The finicky part of the work was done; someone else's presence, the subtle whisper of half-caught surface thoughts and emotional flickerings nearby when her sensors were tuned fine, could no longer be a distraction to Telzey. And company would be welcome to both of them now. Trigger took a chair to the right of the one Telzey had been using, a dozen feet away. "Ready?" Telzey asked from beside the Siren container.

Trigger settled herself. "When you are."

Telzey switched off the psi block. Something came into the study then. Telzey glanced at Trigger. No, Trigger hadn't noticed. Telzey went slowly to her chair, sat down.

The presence was back. *That* didn't surprise her. But Trigger . . .

She looked over at Trigger. Trigger gave her a sober smile. There was alert intelligence in her expression, along with concern she wasn't trying to hide. Trigger, undeniably, was in that chair, aware and awake. But in a sense she'd vanished a moment ago. The normal tiny stirrings of mind, of individuality, had ceased. There was stillness now, undisturbed.

Telzey slid a probe toward the stillness. It didn't seem to touch anything, but it was stopped. She drew it back.

A shield of totally unfamiliar type. Trigger evidently didn't realize it was there. But it sealed her off from outside influences like indetectable heavy armor.

Things had begun to add up. . . .

Telzey checked her own safeguards briefly. Mind screens which might be the lightest of veils, meant only to obscure her from psi senses while she peered out, so to speak, between them. Or, on other occasions, tough and resilient shields which had turned the sharpest probe she'd ever encountered and held up under ponderous onslaughts of psi energy. They could shift in an instant from one extreme to the other. Sometimes, though rarely now, they disappeared completely.

She restored contact—and it was back at once before her: the cold darkness, the emptiness that wasn't empty, the sense of forbidding, repelling power. She scanned cautiously along the impression but could make out no more about it than before.

So then the initial probe! A sensing psi needle reached, touched, drove in, withdrew. As it withdrew, something wrenched briefly and violently at Telzey.

She waited. The xenotelepathic faculty was an automatic one, operating in subconscious depths beyond her reach. She didn't know why it did what it did. But when she touched an alien mind, it began transforming alien concepts to concepts sufficiently human in kind so that she understood them; and if she wanted to talk to that mind, it turned her concepts into ones the alien grasped. Usually the process was swift; within a minute or two there might be the beginnings of understanding.

No understanding came here. Her screens had gone tight as something gripped and twisted her. When she relaxed them deliberately again, nothing else happened.

A deeper probe then. She launched it, braced for the mental distortion.

It came. The shields stiffened, damping it, but she had giddy feelings of being dragged sideways, stretched, compressed. And the probe was being blocked. She drew it back. Strangeness writhed for a moment among her thoughts and was gone. Echo, at last, of alien mind—of the mind that wanted no contact!

The sense of violent distortion ended almost as soon as her probe withdrew. The dark lay before her again, sullen and repelling. A psi device, assembled by mind. A shield, a barrier. A formidable one. But she'd touched for a moment the fringes of the alien mind concealed by the barrier, and now contact with it, whether it wanted contact or not, might be very close. She'd have to do more than she'd done. She decided to trust her shields.

She paused then, at a new awareness.

She wasn't alone. The presence had followed. More than a presence now. Mind, human mind, behind heavy shielding.

"What do you want?" Telzey asked.

Thought replied. "After you make the contact, you may need support."

She would. "Can you give it?"

"I believe so. Be ready!" The impression ended.

Telzey moved in her shields toward the dark barrier, reached it. The barrier awoke like a rousing beast. Her probe stabbed out, hard and solid. The barrier shook at her savagely, and mind-strangeness flickered again through her thoughts. She caught it, tagged it, felt incomprehensibility and an icy deadliness in the instant before it was gone. Now there had been contact—a thread of psi remained drawn between herself and the alien mind, a thin taut line which led through the barrier. Following the line, she moved forward into the barrier, felt a madness of power surge up about her.

"Link with me quickly before—"

Vast pressures clamped down. Telzey and the other spun together through the thunders of chaos.

She'd joined defenses before the barrier struck. With whom, she didn't know, and there was no time just now to find out. But she'd felt new strength blend with hers in that moment, and the strength was very, very useful. For here was pounding confusion, a blurring and blackening of thought, a hideous distorting and twisting of emotion. The barrier was trying to eject her, force her back, batter her into helplessness. It was like moving upstream through raging and shifting currents.

But the double shield absorbed it. And her psi line held. For a time she wasn't sure she was moving at all through the psi barrier's frenzies. Then she knew again that she was—

9

She was lying in bed in a darkened room and didn't have to open her eyes to know it was her bedroom in the summerhouse. She could sense its familiar walls and furnishings about her. How she'd got there, she didn't know. Her mind screens were closed; not drawn into a tight shield, but closed. Automatic precautionary procedure.

Precaution against what?

She didn't know that either.

Something evidently had happened. She felt very unpleasantly weak; and it wasn't the weakness of fatigued muscles. Most of her strength seemed simply absent. There were no indications of physical damage otherwise. But her mental condition was deplorable! What had knocked out her memory?

The answer came slowly.

The Hana had knocked out her memory.

With that, it was all back. Telzey lay quiet, reflecting. That incredible species! Waiting on the three worlds they'd filled wherever they could grow, worlds transformed into deadly psi forts—waiting for the return of an enemy they'd fought, how long ago? Fifty thousand human years? A hundred thousand?

They'd been convinced the Veen would be back and attempt again to enslave or destroy them. And they'd been ready to receive the Veen. What giant powers of attack and defense they'd developed in that long waiting while their minds lay deeply hidden! When an occasional psi entity began to search them

out, it was hurled back by the reef of monstrous
energies they'd drawn about themselves. None had
ever succeeded in passing that barrier.

Until we did, Telzey thought.

They had; and the Hana mind, nakedly open,
immensely powerful, believing they were Veen who
had penetrated its defenses, began killing them.
They'd lasted a while, under that double shield. They
couldn't have lasted very long even so, because life
was being drained from them into the Hana mind in
spite of the shield; but there was time enough for
Telzey's concept transforming process to get into
operation. Then the Hana realized they weren't Veen,
weren't enemies, didn't intend to attack it; and it
stopped killing them.

Things had begun to get rather blurred for Telzey
around then. But she'd picked up some additional
details—mostly about the other who'd come through
the barrier with her.

She relaxed her screens gradually. As she'd suspected, that other one was in the room. She opened
her eyes, sat up unsteadily in bed, turned on the room
lights.

Pilch sat in a chair halfway across the room, watching her. "I thought you'd come awake," she remarked.

Telzey settled back on the bed. "How's Trigger?"

"Perfectly all right. Asleep at present. She was
behind a rather formidable shield at the time of
contact."

"The Old Galactic's," said Telzey.

"Yes."

"What was *it* doing here—in the Hana?"

"A precaution the Old Galactics decided on after
they realized what the Hana was," Pilch said. "If our
psi investigations failed and the Hana began to cut
loose, it would have died on the physical side. They
have fast methods."

Telzey was silent a moment. "As I remember it,"

she said then, "you weren't in much better shape than I was when I passed out."

"True enough," agreed Pilch. "We were both in miserable shape, more than half dead. Fortunately, I'm good at restoring myself. At that, it took me several days to get back to par."

"Several days?"

"It's been ten days since you made the contact," Pilch told her.

"Ten days!" Startled, Telzey struggled back up to a sitting position.

"Relax," said Pilch. "No one's missed you. Your family is under the impression you're vacationing around, and it won't occur to the caretakers to come near the house until we're ready to let them resume their duties. Which will be quite soon. I know you still feel wrung out, but you've been gaining ground very rapidly tonight. A few more hours will see you back to normal health. That was no ordinary weakness."

Telzey studied her thoughtfully.

"You use anyone about any way you like, don't you?" she said.

"You, too, have been known to use people, Telzey Amberdon!" Pilch remarked. "You and Trigger, in your various ways, share the quality of being most effective when thrown on your own resources. It seemed our best chance, and it was. None of our xenos could have done precisely what you did at the critical moment, and I'm not at all sure the contact could have been made in any other manner."

She glanced at the watch on her wrist, stood up and came over to the bed.

"Now you're awake and I'm no longer needed here. I'll be running along," she said. "Trigger can fill you in. If there's some specific question you'd like me to answer, go ahead."

"There's one question," Telzey said. "How old are you, Pilch?"

Pilch smiled. "Never you mind how old I am."

"You were there before they founded the Federation," Telzey said reflectively.

"If you saw that," said Pilch, "you've also seen that I helped found the Federation. And that I help maintain it. You might keep it in mind. Any time a snip of a psi genius can be useful in one of my projects, I'll use her."

Telzey shook her head slightly. "I don't think you'll use me again."

Pilch's knowing gray eyes regarded her a moment. Then Pilch's hand reached down and touched her cheek. Something like a surge of power flowed through Telzey and was absorbed. She blinked, startled.

Pilch smiled.

"We'll see, little sister! We'll see!" she said.

Then she was gone.

"Are you angry with her?" Trigger asked, an hour later, perched on the edge of Telzey's bed while they both took cautious sips from cups of very hot broth. It was early morning now, and they were alone in the house. The Hana and the Old Galactic had left with Pilch's people days ago, and Trigger had gathered they were going first to bring the news that the Veen War was over to the other Hanas currently in Hub laboratories. Afterward, they'd all be off together to the Hana planets to make arrangements which would avoid further problems.

Telzey shook her head.

"I'll forgive her this time," she said. "She took a chance on her own life helping me get through the Hana shield, and she knew it. Then she seems to have spent around a week of her time here, to make sure I'd recover."

Trigger nodded. "Yes, she did. You were looking pretty dead for a while, Telzey! They said you'd be all right, but I wasn't at all certain. Then Pilch appeared and took over, and you started to pick right up." She sighed. "Pilch has her ways!"

Telzey sipped her broth meditatively. The Hanas hadn't been the only ones who'd had trouble with the Veen. It appeared that conflict wasn't much more than a minor skirmish on the fringes of the ancient war which blazed through the empire of the Old Galactics and destroyed it, before the survivors of those slow-moving entities brought their own weapons into full play and wiped out the Veen. "The Old Galactics weren't too candid with you either, were they?" she said.

"No, they weren't," said Trigger. She regarded Telzey soberly. "It looks as though we got a bit involved in galactic politics for a while!"

Telzey nodded. "And I personally plan to keep out of galactic politics in the future!"

"Same here," Trigger agreed. "It doesn't—" She raised her head quickly as the ComWeb chimed in the hall. "Well, well! We seem to have been restored to the world! Wonder who it is. . . ."

She hurried from the room, came back shortly, smiling. "That Pilch!"

"Who was it?"

"Ezd Malion. Calling to say he was going to town early and did we want any groceries."

"No idea that it's been ten days since he talked to us last?" asked Telzey.

"None whatever! He's just picking up where he was told to leave off."

Telzey nodded.

"That's about what we'll be doing," she said. "But at least we know we're doing it."

GLORY DAY

1

The last thing she remembered feeling was a horrid, raging, topsy-turvy confusion. Her mind seemed simultaneously ripped apart and squeezed to a pulp. She hadn't been able to begin to think. Then there'd been nothing.

Now there was something again. The confusion was gone. She found herself here, and thinking—

Lying on her back on some soft surface, dressed. There was light beyond her eyelids which she wasn't going to open just yet. The attack on Casmard's space yacht hadn't killed her, or injured her physically. What about the others?

Her mind screens opened cautiously.

Trigger was close by, probably in the same room, asleep. Sleeping comfortably. There were no immediate indications of Casmard, which wasn't surprising since she'd never tried to touch his mind before. She didn't start searching for him. If neither she nor Trigger had been harmed in the attack on the yacht, he should be all right, too, at the moment.

But there'd been a fourth person on the yacht— a man named Kewen, Casmard's navigator in the Husna Regatta. Telzey did want to know immediately about him.

She put out search thoughts designed to awaken a response in the subconscious levels of Kewen's mind if they touched it. Eventually, one of them did.

Telzey followed it up, and eased herself very gently into that mind. Kewen also was placidly asleep. She studied his mental patterns carefully for a time, secured a number of controls on them. Before she was done, she was picking up occasional washes of faint thought from other sources. There were minds of psi type about, apparently unscreened, apparently non-telepathic.

That should be significant; in any case, it could produce immediate information. Finished with Kewen, Telzey waited for the next wisp of other-thought, touched it when it came, blended awareness with it, moved toward an unguarded psi mind and ghosted inquiringly around there.

She gained information—and what she learned increased her caution. She withdrew from the psi as imperceptibly as she'd approached.

Then at last, almost an hour after she'd first come awake, she opened her eyes.

There was diffused light glow on the ceiling, barely required here. Daylight coming through a large shuttered window on the right made a pattern of bright lines on the carpet. She was lying on a couch, and Trigger lay on a couch across the room from her, red-bronze hair spilling over her face. They were dressed in the clothes they'd worn on Casmard's yacht before the attack. Arranged along the floor in the center of the room was the luggage they'd had on the yacht.

Telzey gave Trigger's half-shielded mind a nudge, and Trigger woke up. She'd been close to awaking for some while. She lifted her head, looked over at Telzey, came up on an elbow and looked around. Her glance held on the row of luggage. She sat up, put a cautioning finger to her lips, got off the couch and went over to the luggage. She opened one of the suitcases.

Telzey joined her there. Trigger was unsealing a

secret compartment in the suitcase. She brought out a cosmetics purse which she set aside, then a small bag which she opened. There were a number of rings in it. Trigger selected two, gave one to Telzey, put the other on her finger, returned the bag to the compartment, and closed that and the suitcase.

She put the cosmetics purse in her jacket pocket and watched Telzey very carefully fit on the second ring.

"That on-and-off husband of mine," Trigger said then in a normal voice, "is a security gadget nut. He insists I carry what he calls the minimum line around with me when we're not together. Every so often it turns out to be a good idea. We're distorted and scrambled now, so I guess we can talk. What's happened?"

"I've found out a few things," Telzey said. "Better get your O.G. shield closed tight, and keep it tight."

"Done," said Trigger. "Psi stuff around, eh?"

Telzey nodded. "Quite a lot of it! I don't know what that means yet, but it could mean trouble. About what happened to us—somebody seems to have turned a stun beam on the yacht and knocked us out before they grappled and boarded."

"A rough beam that was!" Trigger said.

"What did it feel like to you?"

"Well . . . let's say as if my head turned into a drum half the size of the universe and somebody was pounding on it with clubs. But I'm all right now. Do you know who did it, where we are, and what's happened to the Askab and the navigator?"

"More or less, I do," Telzey said. "We're on Askanam, in the Balak of Tamandun—Casmard's balak. More specifically, we're in a section of a palace which belongs to the man who's been Regent of Tamandun in Casmard's absence. He was presumably responsible for the attack on the yacht."

"To have Casmard kidnapped?"

"Apparently. I'm pretty sure Casmard's somewhere in the palace, and I know Kewen is. We're here because we happened to be on the yacht with Casmard."

Trigger said, after a moment, "From what I've heard of Askanam politics, that doesn't look too good."

"I'm afraid it isn't good," Telzey agreed. "When we're missed, all anyone will know is that Casmard's yacht appears to have vanished in interstellar space with all aboard."

"How does the psi business fit in?"

"I don't know yet. There're a number of psis of assorted types not very far from us. Anywhere up to two dozen of them. One had an unguarded mind and I tapped it. But I discovered then that some of the others were screened telepaths. I could have been detected at any moment, so I pulled out before I got as much information as I wanted. I'm not sure why they're here. There was something about a Glory Day—a big annual holiday in Tamandun—coming up. Something else about arena games connected with Glory Day festivities." Telzey shook her head. "Those psis aren't Askanam people. At least, the one I was tapping isn't. She's a Federation citizen."

"They might be helpful then," Trigger suggested.

"They might. But I'd want to find out more about them before I let them know I'm also a Federation psi who's probably in a jam. And I'll have to be careful about that because of the telepaths."

Trigger nodded. "Sounds like you're right! You'd better stay our secret weapon for a while. Particularly—are the psis in the building, too?"

"No, I'm sure they're not in the building. They're close to us, but not that close."

"But there's a connection between them and Casmard's Regent?"

"I'm almost sure of that."

"Well—" Trigger shrugged. "Let's freshen up and

change our clothes before we have visitors. What do you wear on Askanam in the palace of a Regent who might be thinking of featuring you in the upcoming arena games?"

"Something quietly conservative, I suppose," Telzey said.

"All right. Just so it goes with my purse." The cosmetics purse didn't contain cosmetics but Trigger's favorite gun, and was equipped with an instant ejection mechanism. Conceivably, it could act as their other secret weapon here. "The door on the left looks like it should open on a refresher—"

2

In certain confidential Overgovernment files, Askanam was listed among the Hub's experimental worlds. Officially, it was a world which retained a number of unusual privileges in return for acknowledging the Federation's basic authority and accepting a few balancing restrictions. Most of its surface was taken up by the balaks of the ruling Askabs, ranging in size from something not much larger than a township to great states with teeming populations. It was a colorful world of pomp and splendor, romance, violence, superstition and individualism. The traditionally warlike activities of the Askabs were limited by Federation regulations, which kept Askanam pretty much as it was though individual balaks not infrequently changed hands. Otherwise Federation law didn't extend to the balaks. Hub citizens applying for entry were advised that they were going into areas where they would receive no Federation protection.

Telzey was aware that the arrangement served several purposes for the Overgovernment. Askanam

was populated largely by people who liked that kind
of life, since nothing prevented them from leaving.
They were attracted to it, in fact, from all over the
Hub. Since they were a kind of people whose romantic notions could cause problems otherwise, the
Overgovernment was glad to see them there. Askanam
was one of its laboratories, and its population's ways
were more closely studied than they knew.

For individuals, of course, that romantic setup
could turn into a dangerous trap.

Telzey discovered an intercom while Trigger was
freshening up, and after they were dressed again, they
used it. They were connected with someone who said
he was the Regent Toru's secretary, extended the
Regent's welcome to the Askab Casmard's yacht
guests, trusted they were well rested, and inquired
whether they would be pleased to join the Askab and
his cousin for breakfast.

They would, and were guided through a wing of
the palace to a room where a table was set for four.
The Askab Perial Casmard waited there, smiling and,
to all appearances, at ease. Three other men were
with him, and he introduced them. The Regent Toru,
tall, bony and dark. Lord Ormota, with a bristling red
beard, Servant of the Stone. Finally a young, strongly
built man with a boyishly handsome face, who was
Lord Vallain.

The Regent said, "I waited only to meet you and
to express my regrets if any inconvenience has been
caused you. I hope your visit to the Balak of Tamandun
will be very pleasant otherwise. Political considerations
made it necessary to bring you here, as the Askab will
explain." He added to Casmard, "Your taste in guests
is impeccable, dear cousin!" Then he bowed to Telzey
and Trigger and left the room, accompanied by Lord
Ormota.

They took their seats, and breakfast was served.
When the waiters had left, Casmard said, "I regret

deeply that you two are involved in this matter! We can speak freely, by the way. I'm using a distorter, and Toru, in any case, would have no interest in what we have to say. He's certain there's nothing we can do."

"Is it a very bad situation?" Trigger asked.

"Yes, quite bad!" Casmard hesitated, then shook his head. "I would be both insulting you and treating you unfairly by offering you false reassurances. The fact is then that Toru undoubtedly intends to have all four of us killed. He believes you're my women and that he can put additional pressure on me because of it."

"Pressure to do what?" asked Telzey.

"To renounce my right to the title of Askab of Tamandun, abdicate publicly in his favor. The reasoning is that my interests are no longer here. That's perfectly true, of course. It's been eight years since I last set foot on Askanam. For more than half my life, I've been a Federation citizen in all but legal fact. I've built up a personal fortune which makes me independent of the revenues of Tamandun. To act as the Balak's Askab in practice is something I'd find dull, indeed!"

Trigger said, "Then why not simply abdicate?"

"For two reasons," Casmard told her. "One is that, while I've intended to do it for some time, I also intended to wait another year and then make Vallain, who is my cousin as is Toru, my successor. He would have been of suitable age to become Askab then. He doesn't share my dislike for the role, and, as Askabs go, he would make a far better ruler for Tamandun than Toru. I still feel some slight responsibility toward the Balak."

"Which is why I've joined you on Toru's death list," Vallain informed Telzey and Trigger. He didn't appear greatly disturbed by the fact. "Very many people would prefer me to the Regent."

✧   ✧   ✧

"Well, and there you have my second reason," Casmard went on. "After my formal abdication has been obtained and announced and Toru has himself installed as Askab, he'll lose no time in terminating my existence. If any of you are still alive at that time, you'll die with me."

Trigger cleared her throat. "You mean he might kill us first?"

Perial Casmard looked distressed. "Unfortunately, that's quite possible. You three are in more immediate danger than I am. Since I've never given evidence of the blood-thirstiness which is supposed to distinguish a proper Askab, Toru feels that fear is a tool which can be used to influence me. He may decide to make object lessons of you."

"Casmard," said Vallain, "what difference does it really make? We can't get off the palace grounds. We can't get out a message. We're not even being watched. The Regent is so sure of us that he can afford to treat us as guests until we die. He'll become the Askab of Tamandun on Glory Day, and none of us will survive that day. Since it's inevitable, don't let it upset you."

"When's Glory Day?" Telzey asked.

Vallain looked at her. "Why, tomorrow! I thought you knew."

Telzey pushed her chair back, stood up.

"Trigger and I saw some beautiful gardens from a window on our way here," she said. "Since the Regent doesn't seem to mind, I think we'll walk around there and admire them a while." She smiled. "My appetite might be better a little later!"

Casmard said uneasily, "I believe you would be safer if you stayed with me."

"How much safer?" Telzey said.

Vallain laughed. "She's right, Cousin! Let them go. The gardens are beautiful, and so is the morning. Let them enjoy the time they have left." He added to

Telzey and Trigger, "I would ask your permission to accompany you, but in view of the situation, there are some matters I should take care of. However, I'll show you down to the gardens."

Casmard stood up.

"Then be so good as to wait for them here a few minutes," he told Vallain. "There's something I'd like them to have."

He led the way from the room, turned presently into another one and shut the door after Telzey and Trigger had entered.

"All things may be the tools of politics," he remarked. "On Askanam, the superstitions of the people are a tool in general use by those who seek or hold power—and they themselves often aren't free of superstition. When I was a child, my father, the Askab, made me promise to keep certain small talismans he'd had our court adept fashion for me on my person at all times. They were to protect me from tricks of wizardry. I've kept them as souvenirs throughout the years—and now I want to give one to each of you, for somewhat the same reason my father had."

He took two star-shaped splinters of jewelry no larger than his thumbnail from a pocket, gave one to Telzey and the other to Trigger.

"Well, thanks very much, Casmard!" Trigger said. "They're certainly very beautiful." She hesitated. "Do you—"

Casmard said, "You're thinking of course, that the danger we're in is affecting my mind. However, I can assure you from personal knowledge that superstitions, on occasion, may cloak something quite real. I'm not speaking of technological fakery which is much employed here. You've heard of psis, of course. Sophisticated people in the Federation tend to believe that the various stories told about them are again mainly superstition. But having made a study of the subject, I've concluded that many of those stories have a foundation in fact. My parents' court adept, for example, while he professed to deal in magic and to control supernatural entities, evidently was a psi. And I'm sure that a considerable number of psis are active on Askanam to an extent they couldn't be elsewhere. The general belief in sorcery covers their activities—is simply reinforced by them.

"I don't know whether Toru has an adept working for him at present. But it's possible. It's also possible that he feels it would be an effective move to have you two appear to be the victims of sorcery. Frankly, I have no way of knowing whether the talismans actually offer protection against psi forces—but, at least, they can do you no harm. So will you keep them on your persons as a favor to me? I feel we should take every possible precaution available at present."

He left them at the door to the breakfast room, and Vallain showed them the way down to the gardens and told them how to find him, or Casmard, later when they felt like it. A number of other buildings were visible on the palace grounds, and Telzey asked a few questions about them. Then Vallain excused himself pleasantly and went away.

"If I were Toru," Trigger remarked as they started off along a path, "I wouldn't trust our Lord Vallain without a guard."

Telzey nodded. "He's planning something. That's why he didn't want us to be around this morning. I'm not sure about Perial Casmard either. He's really a tough character."

"What are you planning?" Trigger asked.

"I want to locate that group of psis as soon as possible—they should be in one of the buildings on the grounds. If I can get close to them, I can start doing some precision scanning. It's not too likely they'd notice that. Until we know something about them, it's hard to figure out what we can do."

"The telepaths could spot you if you went to work directly on the Regent?"

"Well, they might. Especially with a number of them around. We don't know how the group would react to that." Telzey shook her head. "But Toru could be too tough a job anyway in the time we have left! He and that Servant of the Stone don't seem to have any illusions about Askanam adepts either—they've imported good solid Federation mind shields of a chemical type and are using them. We might get better results if I don't waste time trying to work through that stuff. At any rate, we have to find out how the psis fit in first."

"Do Casmard's talismans do anything?"

Telzey shrugged. "They could make someone who believes in them feel more secure, of course. But that's all they can do."

3

The palace grounds were very extensive and beautifully tended—a varied succession of terraced gardens, large and small. There wasn't a human being in sight anywhere. They followed curving paths in and out of tree groves, around artificial lakes, up and down terrace stairs of polished and tinted stone. Trigger inquired presently, "Are you working?"

Telzey shook her head. "Just waiting for some indication from the psis at the moment. So far there hasn't been a sign. What did you want to talk about?"

"Two things," said Trigger. "I had a notion about aircars—but it seems to me now that aircars aren't permitted in the balaks."

"That's right. No sort of powered flight is," Telzey said. "They use gliders in some places, and I remember

Casmard saying a few Askabs have tried importing a flying animal that's big enough to carry a man. They're not very manageable though."

Trigger nodded. "That kills the notion! I doubt gliders or flying animals would do us much good if we could find them. But then, you know—I'm wondering why no one else seems to be in the gardens at present . . ."

"I've wondered a little about that too," Telzey acknowledged. She added, "Did you hear something a moment ago?"

Trigger glanced at her. "Just the general sort of creature sounds we've been hearing right along."

"This was a spitting noise."

Telzey broke off, and both of them came to a stop. They'd been approaching a stand of shade trees and, about sixty feet away, an animal suddenly had come out from the trees on the path they were following.

It stood staring at them. It was a short-legged animal some twelve feet long, tawny on top and white below, with a snaky neck and sharp snout. The alert eyes were bright green. It was a beautiful creature and an extremely efficient-looking one.

Trigger said very softly, "It may not be dangerous, but we'd better not count on that. If we move slowly off to the left, away from it—"

The animal bared large white teeth and made the spitting noise Telzey had heard. This time it was quite audible. Then, in an instant, it was coming straight at them. It moved with amazing speed, short legs hurling it along the path like a projectile, head held high above the body. Trigger slapped the side of the cosmetics purse at her belt, and the gun it concealed seemed to leap simultaneously into her hand. She turned sideways, right arm stretched straight out.

The animal made a blaring sound as the green eyes vanished in momentary scarlet flashes of light. The long body knotted and twisted, rolled off the path.

The sound ended abruptly. The animal went limp. Trigger lowered the gun, stood watching it a few seconds.

"Five head shots," she said quietly then. "That's a tough creature, Telzey! Any idea what it is?"

"Probably something they use in arenas." Telzey's breath was unsteady. "It certainly wasn't a garden pet!"

"No. And I suppose," Trigger said, "somebody was watching to see what would happen, and is still watching. We pretend we think it was an accident, eh?"

"We might as well. It wouldn't do much good to complain. They know about your gun now."

"Yes, that's too bad. It couldn't be helped."

They walked closer to the creature. From fifteen feet away, Trigger put another bolt into the center of its body. It didn't stir. They went up to it, looked at the blood-stained great teeth.

"At a guess," Trigger said, "the Regent wanted a couple of mangled bodies to shock Casmard with. Let's see if we can find out where it came from."

They followed the path in among the trees. A metal box stood there, open at one end, large enough to have contained the animal. There was no one in sight.

"They brought it up in a car and let it out when we were close enough," Telzey said. "If it had done the job, they would have knocked it out with stun guns and taken it away again. So it was Toru."

"You were thinking it might have been the psis?"

"It might have been. But if they were controlling it, it would have been moving about under its own power. And they—"

"What's that?" The gun was in Trigger's hand again.

"Psi stuff," Telzey said after a moment. "Don't do anything—it can't hurt us!"

Long green tentacles had lifted abruptly out of the earth, enclosing them and the metal box in a writhing ring. The tentacles looked material enough, and there were slapping, slithering sounds when they touched one another.

There came another sound. It might have been a sighing of the air, a stirring in the treetops above them. At the same time, it seemed to be a voice.

"Don't move!" it seemed to be saying. "Don't move at all! Stay exactly where you are until Dovari tells you what to do . . ."

Trigger moistened her lips. "All illusions, eh?"

"Uh-huh—illusions."

Someone knew they were here and was manipulating the visual and auditory centers of their brains. Very deftly, too! Telzey held her attention on the thought projections, drifted with them, reached the projecting mind.

Unscreened, unprotected mind, concentrated on what it was doing, expecting no trouble. She reflected, sent a measured jolt through it. Its awareness abruptly went dim; the illusions were gone.

Trigger was looking at her. "What did you do?"

"Knocked out the sender for a little while."

"And now?"

"I don't know. The psis have discovered us and are taking an interest in us. I've let them know I'm a psi who doesn't want to play games, but I didn't do their illusionist any real harm when I could have done it. Let's go on the way we were going. We'll see what they try next. Better keep that shield good and tight!"

"It's tight as it can get," Trigger assured her. She had no developed psi talents; but she'd been equipped by a psi mind with a shield which was flatly impenetrable when she wanted it that way. They seemed adequately covered for the moment.

They continued along the path they'd been following. Trigger remained silent, watching the area about them, hand never far from the gun purse. Another sudden onslaught by a loosed arena killer didn't seem too likely; but the palace grounds almost might have been designed to let danger lurk about unseen.

Telzey said presently, "They're probing at us now. Carefully, so far, but I'm picking up a few things."

She, too, was being careful. There were at least half a dozen screened telepathic minds involved here—perhaps a few more. They seemed experienced and skilled. The best they weren't, Telzey thought; they shouldn't have been quite so readily detectable— though it was possible, of course, that they didn't much care whether she detected them or not. There was one psi mind around, at any rate, from which she could catch no thought flickering at all, but only the faintest suggestion of a tight shield with a watchful awareness behind it, unnoticeable if she hadn't been fully alert for just such suggestions.

That mind seemed highly capable. She concentrated on it, ignoring the others more or less at the moment, prowled lightly about the shielding. Then, for an instant, she caught an impression of the personality it concealed. Her eyes flickered in surprise. That personality was no stranger! Here—on Askanam? But she knew she hadn't been mistaken.

She directed a thought at the shield, self-identification accompanying it. "Sams! Sams Larking!"

A moment's startled pause, then:

"Telzey! You're the one old Toru was trying to do in?"

"That's what it looks like." She gave him a mental picture of the short-legged animal. Quick thought flow returned. Confirmation—a short while ago, on the Regent's orders, a cheola from the arena pens had been transported to the palace grounds. One of the telepaths had been curious to see what Toru intended with the dangerous creature, and entered the mind of the vehicle's driver. When he reported that the cheola apparently had been killed by its intended victims, the group became interested.

"At that point, we didn't know there was a psi involved," Sams concluded. "Come on over and see us! They all want to meet you."

Telzey hesitated. The probing attempts of the others had stopped meanwhile. "Where are you?"

"You've been moving in the right direction. When you come into the open again, it's the building ahead and to your left. The Old Palace. We're the only ones quartered here at present. I'll meet you at the door. Toru doesn't have any other surprises prepared for you in the gardens, by the way. We've been checking, and will cover for you."

"All right."

Thought contact broke off. Telzey told Trigger what had happened. Trigger studied her face. "You don't seem delighted," she observed. "Isn't your acquaintance going to help us?"

"Well . . . I'm not at all sure. It might depend on why he and the others are here. Sams tends to look out for his own interests first."

"I see. So we stay on our toes and keep shields tight. . . ."

"I think we'd better."

4

"I've been arranging this for a year," Sams Larking said. "Toru is stingy, but he knows he has to come up with the best in arena games on Glory Day—particularly on the Glory Day he plans to be announced as Tamandun's new Askab to the multitudes. I offered him the best the Hub could provide at a price that delighted his shriveled soul. We've brought in the greatest consignment of fighters and performers, human and animal, in Tamandun's history! Hatzel"—

he nodded at a chunky man with a round expression-less face on the other side of the big room—"will be sitting in the Regent's box with Toru, as Lord of the Games tomorrow. We've arranged the whole show. Toru keeps purring over the schedule. He feels he'll be the envy of Askanam."

Trigger said, "From what I've heard, more than half of the people you brought in for the arena should be dead before the games are over."

"Considerably less than half in this case," Sams told her. "We picked the best, as I mentioned. Local fight-ers aren't in their class!" He studied her a moment. "You disapprove? They all know the odds. They also know that the ones who survive the games will be heroes in Tamandun—wealthy heroes. Some will have a good chance of making it to the nobility. They know that more than one Askanam arena favorite wound up among the Askabs. They're playing for high stakes. I feel that's their business."

Telzey glanced around the room. Eighteen in all, half of them telepaths, the others an assortment of talents. In effective potential among non-psis it was an army. Dovari, the illusionist, had regained con-sciousness before they reached the building. She was a slender woman with a beautiful and, at present, thoroughly sullen face.

"What are you people playing for?" Telzey asked. "You can hardly be making a profit on your deal with the Regent."

Sams shook his head. "That's not what we're after. You've heard of the Stone of Wirolla?"

Telzey nodded. "Casmard's mentioned it. Some old war relic with supposedly magical qualities. They used to sacrifice people to it by cutting out their hearts."

"The Regent's revived that practice," Sams said. "It's a form of execution now, reserved for criminals of note and for special occasions. The Stone then indi-cates its satisfaction with both offering and occasion through supernatural manifestations in the Grand Arena. The manifestations have been on the feeble side—Toru's too miserly to have had equipment for anything really spectacular installed. But it's traditional. The people love it."

"And?" Telzey said.

"This Glory Day, the manifestations will be spectacular. We have the talent for it assembled in this room. I'm grateful you didn't do more than tap Dovari because she'll be responsible for much of it. But we aren't confining ourselves to illusions, by any means! It's going to be a terrible shock to Toru when he sees his miracle gadgets producing effects he knows they can't possibly produce—all in honor of the new Askab showing how highly the Stone of Wirolla approves of him! As it happens, that won't be Toru. At the end of Glory Day, I'll be Askab of Tamandun!"

He added, "And you see around you Tamandun's new top nobles—psi rulers of one of the wealthiest balaks of Askanam. You and Miss Argee are herewith invited to join their ranks! I've told the group of your ability, and they're ready to welcome you." He glanced at Dovari. "With the possible exception of our illusionist! However, she'll soon get over her irritation."

Telzey shook her head. "Sams, you're crazy!" She looked around the room. "All of you must be, to let him talk you into something like this."

Sams didn't lose his smile. "What makes you say that?"

"The Psychology Service, for one thing. You start playing around with psi stuff openly, they'll be here to investigate. You don't think they'll let you use it to control Tarnandun, do you?"

"As a matter of fact, I do," Sams told her. "I checked out our Askanam maneuver with them. Anything too obvious that could be attributed to psi is out, of course. But there's no objection to goings-on that in Tamandun will have the flavor of the supernatural and at more sophisticated levels will be passed off as superstitious gullibility. We'll have to keep to our balak, but, with those restrictions, what we do here is our business."

"If they're letting you do it," Telzey said, "they've been letting other psis do it."

He nodded. "Oh, they have. I said I've been preparing this for some time. I've been around Askanam and I know that plenty of psis have established themselves in the culture here and are operating about as freely as they like. But almost all of that's on a minor level. We'll be the first group that really gets things organized."

"You might have been the first to get shuffled out here as a group," Telzey said.

Sams's eyes narrowed slightly. "Meaning?"

"Isn't it obvious? The Federation exempts Askanam from normal restrictions because it's a simple way to keep a specific class of lunatics corralled. The experiment's worked out, so it's being continued. The Service evidently has expanded it to include irresponsible psi independents. Put them where whatever they do can't really add much to the general mess! I wouldn't feel flattered if they told me I could make Tamandun my playground but was to make sure I stayed there. What kind of playground is it? Being little gods among some of the silliest people in the Hub is going to bore you to death— or you're lunatics!"

"I have no liking," Dovari remarked, "for the girl's insults."

The man called Hatzel said, "There could be a difference of opinion about the opportunities waiting for us in Tamandun. But the point is, Sams, that you seem to be mistaken in believing Miss Amberdon would be interested in lending her talents to the group's goals."

"I still hope to be able to persuade her," Sams told him.

"Why not try it, Telzey? It may not be at all what you think. You can always pull out, of course, if you find you don't like the life."

"If I thought I might like it," Telzey said, "there'd still be the fact that Tamandun already has an Askab."

Hatzel said, "For the moment only. That's Toru's affair, not ours. As Lord of the Games, I'll be attending the Regent's ceremonial Glory Day dinner in the House of Wirolla tonight. So, I understand, will the Askab Casmard and his guests. Before the evening's over, Casmard will have abdicated formally. The vacancy will be filled at the end of Glory Day."

"Casmard's an old friend of my family," Telzey said. "If you're determined to set yourselves up in Tamandun, you could make an arrangement with him. He isn't much interested in remaining Askab. I'd see to it that he didn't remember afterwards there'd been psis involved in the matter."

Sams shook his head. "I'm afraid we can't do that. It's too late for it. We're prepared to deal with Toru and the Servant of the Stone tomorrow. The manifestations we've scheduled will make it easy to do and we'll have enthusiastic public approval. But it needs exact timing. We've made Toru's plans for Casmard part of our plan. If Casmard were still alive and still Askab on Glory Day, everything would have to be revised. At best, we'd wind up with something less effective."

"Aside from not interfering ourselves," Hatzel added, "we must also, of course, make sure that no one else does—in any way! And while we know Miss Amberdon's a telepath, it hasn't yet been established what Miss Argee's special abilities are."

"I have no special psi abilities," Trigger said shortly.

"Now that," one of the other men remarked, "is an interesting lie. I've been attempting to probe that young woman's shield since she entered the room. I can vouch for the fact that it's an extraordinary psi structure—unanalyzable and of extreme resistive power."

Trigger shrugged. "Somebody else developed the shield for me. I couldn't have done it. Not that it makes any difference."

Sams smiled at her. "I agree! And I'm sure you both realize that we can't run the risk of letting you upset our plans. Once Glory Day's over, it doesn't matter what you do. We'll be glad to see you safely off Askanam then, assuming Toru's let you remain alive, which might seem rather doubtful if you won't join forces with us. Until that time, at any rate you will have to allow the group to control what you say and do. It's really the only safe way, isn't it?"

"Forget it, Sams!" Telzey said. "Our screens stay tight."

"Will they?" Sams said mildly. "I don't like to put pressure on you, but we still have too much work to get done today to waste more time over this. . . ."

The room went quiet. Then a wave of heat washed over Telzey. It ebbed, returned, and intensified. Trigger gave her a quick, startled glance. Telzey shifted her shoulders.

"So you have a pyrotic with you," she remarked.

Sams smiled. "We have several. Their range is excellent! Even if we allowed you to leave this room and building—though we won't—you couldn't get away from the effect. You don't want your blood to start boiling, do you? Or find your hair and clothes catching fire—as a start?"

Trigger, sweat beginning to run down her face, looked at Telzey. "Do you know who's doing it?"

Telzey nodded across the room.

"The tall thin man two seats left of Dovari."

Trigger's hand went to her cosmetics purse, and the gun made its abrupt appearance.

She said to the thin man, "I won't kill you if this

doesn't stop immediately. But I'll stun you so solidly you won't have begun to come awake by the end of Glory Day. And it'll be two weeks after that before your nerves stop jumping."

The heat faded away. The group sat staring at Trigger. She jerked, made a choked sound of surprise, looked down at her hand. The gun had vanished from it.

Sams and a few of the others were laughing. Sams said, "Neat enough, Hatzel! Ladies, let's stop this nonsense. Since you can't win, why not give up gracefully? Telzey, you at least are aware you can both be killed in an instant as you're sitting there."

Telzey nodded. "Oh, I do know that, Sams. But I haven't just been sitting here. I've found out Hatzel's shielded, and, of course, all you telepaths have your psi shields. But six of your most valuable people aren't shielded at all, and apparently couldn't operate if they were. Six psi minds—wide open! It would take an instant to kill us, and you can be quite sure that in that instant you'd lose those six. So I don't think you'll try it."

Sams stared at her. The others were silent a moment. Then one of the women said sharply, "Sams, she's bluffing! You said she's good, but between us all we certainly can block her as she strikes out. Then we can handle both of them as we wish."

Sams shook his head slowly. "I wouldn't care to count on it."

Dovari said in a strained voice, "Nor I! And I don't want to die while you're finding out whether you can, or can't, block her. Let them go, Sams! If they try to interfere, you can still deal with them in some other manner."

5

Trigger glanced back at the closed building door behind them. She looked both furious and relieved. "What do we do now?" she muttered.

"Keep walking," Telzey said. "Back to the Regent's palace. And we walk rather fast until we reach those trees ahead. I've still got my contacts back there. Some talk going on . . . Hatzel seems to be second in command to Sams. So he's a teleport—" She glanced at Trigger. "Too bad you lost your gun."

"That's not all I lost."

"Eh?"

"My underpants went with the gun."

"Well," Telzey said after a moment, "a minor demonstration, as Sams would say. A teleport at Hatzel's level is a very dangerous person. He didn't have to do that, of course. They were trying to make us feel helpless."

Trigger nodded. "And it worked just fine with me! I've never felt more helpless in my life." She looked over at Telzey. "Touch and go for a moment, wasn't it? I didn't think you were bluffing!"

"I wasn't. A bluff like that wouldn't have got past Sams."

"What makes them that kind of people?" Trigger said. "With everything they can do—"

"That's partly it. Most of that group are bored psis. They've used their abilities to make things too easy for themselves. It's stupid but some do it. Now they've run out of fun and are looking for something new—almost anything that seems new."

They'd reached the trees, were hurrying along a path leading through the grove. Trigger checked suddenly, glanced down at the cosmetics purse. She slapped it. The gun popped into her hand.

"Well!" she said. "I felt the weight in the purse

just now." She reached into the purse, pulled out a silky garment, shoved it into a pocket. "Briefs returned with the gun." She bit her lip. "Perhaps I should feel grateful. Somehow I don't!"

"Come on!" Telzey turned away, broke into a trot. "They did that to show you your gun doesn't impress them at all. But now you have it back, you might get a chance to express your lack of appreciation to Hatzel. We'll have to hurry!"

"What do you mean?"

"Can you set it to stun somebody for just a short time—a few minutes?"

"That's a bit tricky, but, yes, I can. Five minutes, say."

"Fine. Hatzel's been called to the palace to talk to the Regent. He'll be coming through the gardens on a scooter. If we get far enough ahead, we may be able to spot him and cut him off."

"All right. And I stun him. Then?"

"That's no telepath's shield he's using. It's a gadget. And if the gadget's the kind I think it is, I can open it and get to his mind before he comes around. Sams or somebody might realize what's happening, of course. That's a risk we'd better take. The quicker we get it over with, the less likely we are to be noticed."

They crouched presently at the edge of a terrace, winded and hot from the run, shrubbery about them. "He might still turn off on another route," Telzey remarked. "But it looks like he'll be coming by here now, doesn't it?"

Trigger nodded. "Seems to be heading this way."

"That break in the bushes is the place to take him. How far will we have to work down to it?"

"We won't. Right here is fine. He's just chugging along."

"That's a good fifty yards, Trigger," Telzey said doubtfully.

"And I'm a good fifty yards marksman. Some day I'll have to teach you how to use a gun."

"Perhaps you should. I never warmed up to guns. When I've had to use one, I just blasted away."

"What are your contacts doing?"

"Back to rehearsing their Glory Day surprises. They're not thinking about us at the moment. Sams might be, now and then. It's hard to be sure about him. But we should be able to get away with this."

Hatzel's scooter came chugging up shortly. Trigger touched the gun's firing stud, and Hatzel was sagging sideways off the scooter as the machine went out of sight behind bushes again. They worked their way hurriedly down to the path through the shrubs, found the scooter on its side, turning in slow circles. Trigger shut it off while Telzey went over to Hatzel who lay on his back a dozen yards away.

She knelt quickly beside him, lifted his head. Trigger joined her.

"Should be at the base of the skull, under a skin patch," Telzey said. "Here it is!"

She peeled off the tiny device, blinked absently at Hatzel's face. "Open psi mind—yes, I can do it." She was silent then.

Trigger glanced presently at her watch, said, "Four minutes plus gone, Telzey. He could start coming around any moment now. Shall I tap him again?"

"No, I've got him. He won't come around till I'm ready."

"I'll go plant the rock then," Trigger said.

She went a dozen yards back up the terrace where ornamental rockwork enclosed a flower bed, returned with a sizable rock which she placed on the path ten feet from where Hatzel was lying.

"I'd think it was a little peculiar I hadn't noticed that rock," she observed. "But I suppose you're taking care of that?"

"Yes. He'll wake up with a small headache from having banged his skull. He'll see the rock lying there and be irritated, but that will explain it, and he won't want to tell anyone he wasn't looking where he was going." Telzey replaced the shield which wasn't operative at the moment, smoothed in the skin patch, stood up and brushed sand from her knees. "Finished. Let's move!"

They restarted the scooter, left it lying on its side, pushing itself awkwardly about in the grass, went quickly back up to the terrace and along it through the shrubbery, until they reached a grove of trees and came to another path.

Hatzel, still unconscious, reached into a pocket and switched his mind shield back on. He awoke then, sat up with a muttered curse, felt his head, looked around, saw the rock on the path and the struggling scooter in the grass. He nodded in annoyed comprehension, and got to his feet.

He couldn't be left unshielded because one of the telepaths would have been bound to notice it. Every five minutes, however, Hatzel now would switch the shield off for a moment, unaware of what he did. If there was reason to take him under active control, Telzey would make use of such a moment. They had a glimpse of him presently on the network of paths ahead of them, nearing the Regent's palace.

"Reacting just as he's supposed to, isn't he?" Trigger said.

Telzey nodded. "Uh-huh! It was a stupid accident, and that's all. He's got more important things to think about." She added, "I'd like to give Casmard some idea of what's going on, but there's no way I can keep them from looking into his mind or Vallain's, and anything we told him they'd soon know. We'll have to work out this side of it strictly by ourselves."

6

As they were approaching the palace entrance by which they'd left, a tall, splendidly uniformed man emerged from it and came toward them.

He introduced himself as Colonel Euran, head of the Regent's Palace Guard. "It's come to my attention," he said, "that you weren't informed of a security regulation requiring guests to surrender personal weapons for the period of their visit in the palace. I thought I should correct the oversight, to save you possible embarrassment. It's merely a formality, of course—but do you happen to have weapons in your room or on your persons?"

Since they'd known their encounter with the cheola had been observed, they weren't surprised. Trigger took the cosmetics purse from her belt and handed it to him.

"There's a Denton inside," she said. "Take good care of it, Colonel. It's an old friend."

He bowed. "Indeed, I will."

Telzey said, "Could there be other regulations we don't know about?"

Colonel Euran smiled pleasantly. "It's no regulation. But the Regent Toru told me to suggest that you remain within the palace itself until he has the pleasure of meeting you again at dinner tonight. He's concerned about your safety."

"You mean the Regent's own gardens aren't safe?" Trigger asked.

"No, not always during the periods of arena games. There are subterranean levels here where beasts and criminals who've been condemned to the arena are kept. And it happens on occasion that some very dangerous creature eludes its keepers and appears unexpectedly in the palace grounds."

They thanked him for the warning, went inside. Following the directions given them by Vallain, they presently located the suite of Perial Casmard and announced themselves at the door. He opened it immediately.

"Come in! Come in!" he said, drawing them into the room and closing the door again. He looked at them, shook his head. "I'm very glad to see you," he said. "I wasn't at all sure you were still alive! Shortly after you'd left, Toru hinted in his pleasant manner that he had some particularly brutal end prepared for you. I went down to the gardens to find you, but no one could tell me where you'd gone."

They told him about the cheola. Telzey said, "We went on then and met some Federation people who've organized the Glory Day games for Toru this year. We thought we might be able to talk them into smuggling us out, but they weren't interested in getting involved in an intrigue against the Regent."

Casmard said he couldn't blame them too much. "If Toru found out about it, they might become more intimately involved in the games than any sensible man would wish to be."

"And we're confined to the palace now," Trigger said.

"That's good—since it probably means that Toru is planning no further immediate steps against you. But the situation remains extremely difficult. Have you eaten?"

"Not since breakfast," Telzey said, "and we didn't eat much then. Now that you've mentioned it, I notice I'm very hungry."

Casmard had lunch for them brought to the suite. He watched pensively while they ate, said at last, "There was an explosion a while ago on the Regent's living level. Not badly timed—he'd entered the level shortly before the device went off. However, only one of his guard dogs was killed. Toru escaped injury."

They looked at him expectantly. He shrugged. "Vallain's now confined to his quarters. Toru rarely acts hastily. He'll wait for the pre-Glory Day dinner in the House of Wirolla tonight before pursuing the matter."

When they'd finished lunch, he said, "I'm reasonably certain the Regent also will hold his hand now as far as you two are concerned. However, it would be best if you went to your room and stayed there, so as to bring yourselves as little as possible to his attention."

Telzey said, "You still don't see how we can get out of this?"

"Oh, I'm not entirely at the end of my resources," Casmard told her. "I shall meet the Regent again during the afternoon and may be able to persuade him to accept less drastic arrangements than the one he has in mind."

They left to go to their apartment. Trigger inquired reflectively, "You had the impression Casmard wanted us out of the way?"

"Yes, he does want us out of the way," Telzey said.

Trigger glanced at her. "Picked up things over lunch, huh?"

"Yes. Something about an elderly character in the palace who used to act as poisoner for Casmard's mother, and seems to have kept his hand in. Casmard's promised him a high spot in the nobility if he can get to Toru before dinner, and the old boy's game to try it."

Trigger shook her head. "Life expectancies would be awkward to calculate around here! Does Casmard think it will work?"

"Not really. He's getting desperate. If he did get rid of Toru, there'd still be a serious problem with the Servant of the Stone—Lord Ormota."

"How does he fit in?"

"After Toru, he's apparently the most powerful man in Tamandun. If Toru died, he'd have a great deal more power here in the Regent's palace than Casmard and Vallain combined could bring up. So he'd probably simply become the next Askab, with no other change in the proceedings."

"The Stone he's the Servant of is presumably the Stone of Wirolla, where they cut out people's hearts?"

"Yes."

"And the House of Wirolla, where they'll be holding the ceremonial dinner we're supposed to attend—that's where the Stone is?"

"Yes," Telzey said. "I got that from Hatzel. Big black hall. The Regent's table stands right across from the Stone."

"Should be a great dinner party for ghouls!" Trigger said after a moment.

"Well, it all seems part of their local religion or whatever you want to call it."

In a closet of their room they found games, provided for the entertainment of guests. They were unfamiliar and looked complicated enough to be interesting. They set up one designed for two players. It was cover—Telzey would be mentally active on other levels.

Hatzel's shield had been opening regularly on schedule. She'd caught the opening a few times, checked him out briefly. There was nothing of interest there at present. She'd dropped her contacts with the unprotected minds in Sams's group. They had no immediate value.

She spent a little time hunting around for traces of the navigator of Casmard's space yacht, located him finally and told Trigger, "Kewen's not in the palace any more. He's been transferred to the place they keep the criminals they'll start feeding into the arena games tomorrow. That's what's scheduled for him."

Trigger looked startled. "Does he know it?"

"He knows, but I sort of tranquilized him this morning after I picked him up. It isn't bothering him."

"It bothers me," Trigger said. "Of course, he might last longer than the rest of us, at that."

"Yes. And if we get out of it, we should be able to get him out."

A palace courier had announced himself discreetly at the door half an hour after they'd returned to their room, and handed them a formal invitation from the Regent. They would be sitting at his table during dinner in the House of Wirolla that night.

Telzey spent the remaining hours scanning the minds in the palace and its vicinity. There were many she could have entered without much trouble, but finding minds that would be useful in the present situation was more difficult. Colonel Euran of the Palace Guard had been a primary target but turned out to be as thoroughly mind-shielded as the Regent and the Servant of the Stone. Telzey wasn't too disappointed. Toru hardly would want someone in that position to be subject to hostile psychic influences.

She developed some selected contacts presently. There were others she would have preferred, but they couldn't be made available to her quickly enough.

Then it was time to prepare themselves to be taken to the House of Wirolla. It was one of the buildings on the Palace grounds, serving both as a personal palace for the Servant and as a temple for the Stone.

7

The ceremonial hall in the House of Wirolla lived up to Trigger's expectation that it might have made a good place for the festivities of ghouls. Walls, ceiling and floor were of black stone. On the lower level, the only light was provided by torches flaring sullenly from the walls and along the tables, where the top rank of Tamandun's nobility and dignitaries dined tonight. It was separated from the upper level by a flight of low stairs, running the width of the hall.

On the upper level, there was light. The curved table of the Regent stood there by itself, the Regent's honor guests seated along the outer edge of the curve. The arrangement provided them with a good view of the Stone of Wirolla on the far side of the hall. The Stone was huge and seemed almost formless, while somehow suggesting a hunkered shape which could have been human as much as Wirollan. It was gray-green, and there was an indication of scales over parts of its surface. A thick hollowed projection near the lower end might represent a pair of cupped and waiting hands. Supposedly, the Stone had been in the Hub for some centuries, having been found on the destroyed flagship of a Wirollan war fleet. But the early part of its history was uncertain.

Nowadays, at any rate, it represented a deity, or demon, who periodically indicated an appetite for human sacrifices. Traditionally, it should indicate that appetite tonight. The circumstances didn't make for light-hearted dinner conversation, but most of those who sat along the curving table, Casmard and Vallain among them, hadn't seemed much affected. Hatzel, three seats from Telzey, ate in stolid silence. From the lower level came an indistinct sound of voices. Glory Day music washed through the air, incongruously bright and brisk.

Weapons weren't allowed in the hall. But guns pointed through concealed openings in the three walls of the upper level; and the Palace Guards who held them had every section of both levels under observation in scanners.

Three of those Palace Guards and their guns were now Telzey's. The Regent's guard dog, a great arena hound standing twelve feet back of its master's chair, was nearly hers. It was, at any rate, no longer the Regent's.

It wasn't till dinner drew near its end that tensions began to be noticeable. At last, Telzey became aware of a faint tremor in the stone floor under her feet, in the chair on which she sat. It continued only a moment; but when it stopped, all talk had ended and the music had faded away.

Now the tremor returned, grew stronger, swelled into an earthquake shuddering. Again it lasted only a few seconds. By then, no one near Telzey was stirring. She found herself holding her breath, released it. A third time it came, accompanied by a distant roaring sound, suggesting a blurred giant voice. As that stopped, a low black table was rising out of the floor before the Stone of Wirolla. Two gray-clothed men, gray masks covering their faces, came out from behind the Stone on either side and stopped at the ends of the table, ropes held in their hands.

Lord Ormota, Servant of the Stone, got to his feet and strode out in front of the Regent's table. He raised his arms, and his amplified voice sounded deeply through the hall.

"The Stone of Wirolla will take two hearts tonight!"

Ormota paused, bearded face turned up in an attitude of listening. The roaring sound came again; the black hall shook, and grew still. Ormota turned toward the Regent.

"Two traitors to Tamandun sit with the Regent Toru tonight, believing themselves unknown! The Stone of Wirolla will point them out and receive their hearts."

Two traitors? Vallain, whose face had paled at last, must be one. The other? Telzey had seen in Casmard's mind that while his poisoner had found no opportunity to practice his arts on the Regent, he'd at least aroused no suspicions. But perhaps Casmard was mistaken in that. Or perhaps—

Telzey's thoughts broke off. Out of the hollowed projection on the Stone a black object like a cane or wand floated up into sight. It lifted swiftly into the air, impelled by a mechanism which Ormota presumably controlled. It hung quivering for a moment in the center of the upper level of the hall. Then, emitting a high singing note, it drifted down toward the Regent's table, swinging left and right like a compass needle. No one moved at the table; but there was an expectant stirring on the lower level, as diners shifted about to have a better view at the instant the Stone's device would indicate the night's sacrifices.

It came closer, still swinging back and forth along the curve of the table. Then, the singing note surging shrilly upward, it halted, pointed at Hatzel.

Telzey felt the shock of utter surprise in Hatzel's mind, saw for an instant a look of incredulous consternation on Ormota's face.

The wand vanished.

There was a crystal shattering against the face of the Stone. Black shards clattered down into the hollow below. The Regent Toru staggered half up out of his chair, eyes and mouth grotesquely distended, made a groaning sound and went over backward with the chair. Ormota clutched his chest, looked for a moment as if he were trying to scream, collapsed in turn.

One of the gray-clothed men uttered a high-pitched yell of horror. His shaking hand pointed at the hollowed projection of the Stone.

Two human hearts thumped and thudded bloodily about in it. A din of screaming arose in the black hall.

"Your Askab showed such extraordinary presence of mind in taking charge of the situation that I'm convinced you're controlling him," Hatzel told Telzey and Trigger in hurried undertones. "However, that was, in fact, the best immediate way of handling this unexpected turn of events. Toru obviously intended treachery against our group. I had to make him and the Servant appear to be the Stone's intended sacrifices or allow myself to be butchered."

He added, "I'll have to let Larking know about this at once—but first I want to warn you. Your lives and those of Casmard and Vallain are no longer endangered, so be satisfied with that! Don't try to make use of what's happened to interfere with our plans. They remain essentially unchanged, though details must be modified now. Sams Larking, in other words, will still be the new Askab of Tamandun at the end of Glory Day. Casmard and you two will be seen to a Federation spaceport, and if you're wise you won't lose too much time then getting off the planet!"

A bleak smile touched his face.

"This should in fact improve our future position," he remarked. "The discovery that Toru's and Ormota's bodies showed no outward sign of injury after the Stone had taken their hearts has made many new believers in the supernatural tonight." He turned away, concluding, "Remember what I've told you!" and walked off.

They looked after him. Unaware that he was doing it, Hatzel reached into a pocket and switched his mind shield back on. It would stay on now.

Trigger said thoughtfully, "No way those telepaths can find out you had him point the Stone's wand or whatever it was at himself?"

"No," Telzey said. "I released my controls on him just a moment ago. Sams is naturally suspicious, but if he looks over Hatzel's mind, it will seem everything happened exactly as Hatzel thinks it did."

8

The Glory Day games began. The Grand Arena's spectator sections were astir with rumors, curiosity, and interest. Word had spread of great and strange events in the House of Wirolla the night before—the Regent Toru and the Servant of the Stone had been revealed as traitors and slain by the Stone itself, and the long-absent Askab Perial Casmard again ruled Tamandun, supported unanimously by the nobility. The general expectation was that there would be omens and signs to make this year's Glory Day one to be long remembered.

Five sat in what previously had been the Regent's box—the Askab Casmard, Lord Vallain, Telzey, Trigger, and Hatzel, Lord of the Games. Casmard and Vallain were in an undisturbed state of mind. They were undisturbed because they knew that the occurrence in the House of Wirolla, horrifying—though very fortunate—as it had appeared at the time had been the work of a friendly psi. They knew it because the friendly psi had told each of them so mentally; and they'd compared notes. They didn't know who the psi was and had been instructed not to try to find out. They wouldn't. Casmard intended to announce his abdication in favor of Lord Vallain at the end of the day's games—

Sams Larking and his group were aware that Telzey was controlling Casmard and Vallain, but there was no reason for them to object. The two had needed support and guidance in a critical situation, and she was supporting and guiding them in a way which avoided problems for Sams. Hatzel, when he appeared in the arena box, had murmured to Telzey and Trigger, "Larking tells me you're cooperating nicely. That's fine! Let's be sure it stays that way." He'd smiled gently at them. He had no doubt it would stay that way. He'd demonstrated his potential for instant deadliness, if there'd been any question about it. And one of Sams's telepaths was remaining in good enough contact with Casmard and Vallain to catch any suspicious maneuvers Telzey might attempt through them. If she attempted any, Hatzel would be informed at once and was to take whatever steps seemed required. The group was playing for keeps and had made the fact clear.

There was another mind on which Telzey was keeping tabs—that of the yacht navigator. Kewen had been released from the arena pens to which he'd been transferred; and it occurred to Casmard then that a fine seat at the Glory Day games should compensate the poor fellow in part for his unnerving experiences. He wasn't far from the Askab's box. One of the telepaths had checked him and found Kewen had been in a state of shock and was coming gradually out of it, held under calming control by Telzey.

As far as the psi group was concerned, that took care of Telzey. She'd been neutralized. She mightn't like what they were doing, but it didn't matter. They each had their work to handle now, playing out rehearsed roles in the ascending series of thrills and marvels which would wind up with Sams Larking being roared into office as the new Askab by the people of Tamandun.

The opening events of the games were brisk and colorful enough, but still tame stuff by Tamandun's standards—mere preludes to what the day should bring. The crowds watched in tolerant appreciation for the most part, details of the action being shown in enlarging screens above each arena section.

Then what seemed to be happening in the arena was no longer what was shown to be happening in the screens. Dovari's illusions were putting in an appearance. The spectators realized it gradually, grew still, fascinated—the Stone of Wirolla was manifesting in ways it hadn't manifested before! The illusions weren't disturbing in themselves. But uncanniness was touching that area of Tamandun.

Dovari was an excellent illusionist, Telzey thought. And now it seemed to be time. She gave Trigger the signal they'd agreed on. Trigger smiled in response, slipped a knockout pill into her mouth, swallowed it.

Ten seconds later, a shock of fright jolted through Kewen's drowsy complacence. And Kewen responded. Telzey erased her shielding screens in that instant, brought all personal psi activity to an abrupt stop.

Hatzel, sitting behind Casmard, jerked violently, and disappeared. Trigger slumped limply back in her seat, eyes closed. The illusions in the arena whirled in a wild, chaotically ugly turmoil.

Shock waves of alarm could almost be sensed rising from the spectator sections. Perial Casmard calmly switched on the amplifying system before him. His calm voice spoke throughout the Grand Arena, telling his subjects that what they were witnessing wasn't merely another manifestation but one which, by its very violence, must be regarded as an augury of an approaching great period in Tamandun's history . . .

It was a rehearsed speech, but Casmard didn't know it. And it was effective. There was no general panic.

"There's one type of psi," Telzey had told Trigger some hours before, "no other psi wants to run into. They call him the howler. A howler has just one talent—he can kick up such a hurricane of psi static that the abilities of any other psis in his range fly out of control and start working every which way. That's pretty horrible for those psis, especially for the ones with plenty of equipment. The more they can do, the more's gone suddenly wrong—and the harder they try to hang on to control, the worse the matter gets!"

"You and I got hit by a howler when Casmard's

yacht was attacked. It was our navigator. Kewen didn't know he was doing it; he doesn't know he's a psi. But when he gets frightened, he howls. It's an unconscious defensive reaction with him. He was frightened then—and your shield began to batter itself with psi energy instead of repelling it. You felt as if your head were being pounded with clubs. I can't really say how I felt! I went crazy instantly in several different ways. Fortunately, it was just a few seconds before the stun beam they used knocked us and Kewen out—"

This time, Kewen was going to stay frightened for something like three minutes. That, Telzey thought, certainly should be enough. Then his fears would shut off automatically. She'd arranged for that.

Trigger would be unconscious meanwhile, oblivious to the fact that her shield was drawing torrents of hammering energy on itself. While Telzey, awake and unshielded, would have divorced herself from anything remotely resembling an ability to handle psi until the howler had gone out of action again.

9

Some four hours after the official conclusion of Glory Day in Tamandun, Telzey and Trigger were sitting in a lounge of an Orado-bound liner. Sams Larking walked in, glanced around and came over to their table.

"Why, hello, Sams!" Telzey said. "We didn't know you were aboard."

"I know you didn't," Sams said. His eyes seemed slightly glazed. He sat down, ordered a drink through the table speaker, sighed and leaned back in his chair.

"To tell you the truth, I'm not in the best of condition," he said. "But I didn't feel I needed to be hospitalized. I came on just before takeoff, rather expecting to find you around somewhere."

"How are the rest of them doing?" Telzey asked. It had taken a while to locate the members of Sams's group individually and get them under sedation; but they'd all been rounded up at last and transferred to the Federation's base hospital on Askanam.

Sams shrugged. "They're not well people, but they'll recover. They're shipping out on a hospital boat tomorrow. None of them felt like hanging around Askanam any longer than they had to." He shook his head. "So you ran in a psi howler on us!"

Telzey lifted her eyebrows. "I did?"

"Since you two are in fine shape, yes. There aren't that many howlers around. It wasn't a coincidence that brought one to the Grand Arena, and set him off just as we were going into action. How long did he go on blasting?"

"Three minutes, more or less."

"It seemed a lifetime," Sams said darkly. "A hideous, insane lifetime!" His drink came; he emptied it, reordered. "Ah, now!" he said. "That's a little better. It was rougher on the special talents, you know. Dovari was still running waking nightmares when I left—and those are pretty badly singed pyrotics!"

"Hatzel and the other teleport should have got only a touch," Telzey said.

Sams nodded. "And that's what shook them up so completely. Only a touch—and Hatzel found he'd flipped himself halfway around Askanam! The other one didn't go quite that far, of course; but neither had done that kind of thing before, and neither wants to do it again. They can't remember how they did it. And they keep thinking of the various gruesome things that can happen to a teleport at the end of a blind flip—those two are very, very scared."

His second drink came. He took a swallow, set it

down, smacked his lips. "Beginning to feel more like myself!" He gave them a brief grin.

Trigger said, "Are you going to try any more operations on Askanam?"

Sams shook his head.

"Too much bother. I'd have to build up a new gang. Besides, I decided Telzey was right—I'd get bored to death in a year playing games like that. Who's Askab in Tamandun now, by the way?"

"Vallain," Telzey said. "Casmard abdicated publicly in his favor at the end of Glory Day. A popular decision, apparently. Casmard doesn't intend to go back to Askanam again either."

"He's on board?"

"Uh-huh."

Trigger said, "He was telling us in confidence a short while ago that he and Vallain had personal proof there'd been a mysterious but well-intentioned psi involved in the downfall of Toru and Ormota and the various other strange Glory Day events. He said it was something that shouldn't be discussed, at the psi's special request."

"Well, there's been no significant breach of secrecy then," Sams said. "The Service might have got stuffy on that point." He reflected, grinned. "I was sure Toru and Ormota would be taken out one way or another after you two ambushed Hatzel in the gardens."

"You knew about that, eh?" Telzey said.

"Knowing you," said Sams, "I didn't expect you to pass up any opportunities. It wasn't a surprise."

"Why didn't you try to do something about it?"

He shrugged. "Oh, I figured I could spot you Hatzel and still win the game. And if you hadn't come up with the howler, I'd have done it."

Telzey smiled. "Perhaps you would, Sams—perhaps you would!"

CHILD OF THE GODS

1

The ivory gleam of the Jadel Tower, one of the great inner city hotels, appeared ahead and to the left beneath the flow of the traffic lanes. The urge became now to turn out of the lane and go to the Jadel Tower; and there was a momentary impression that on arriving there she would be directed to set the car down on a terrace of the tall structure. Telzey tensed slowly. If she could hold out against any one specific command, she might be able to loosen the entire set of controls. She kept the car on lane course.

The urge simply grew stronger. The psi hold on her was crude and incomplete, but whoever had obtained it knew what he was doing and had force to spare. In seconds, her muscles began to tremble, and sweat started out on her face. She gave in abruptly. The Cloudsplitter dropped out of traffic, went slanting down. She settled back in the seat, sighing. Let him get the impression she'd resigned herself to what was happening. She knew he hadn't invaded enough of her mind so far to be able to read her thoughts.

Moments later, the car moved clear of the main traffic—and now she should act at once before he realized she was about to attempt escape by a different route! She pushed the door open suddenly, tried to thrust herself out of the car.

Tried to. She felt a start of surprise on his side,

then an instant painful clenching of her muscles, which held her frozen in position on the seat. After a moment, her arm flexed slowly, drew the door shut, locked it.

A flick of sardonic approval came from him. He'd guessed what she intended, checked her just in time . . . and, for the moment, she'd run out of tricks and would have to patiently wait for a new opportunity to come along.

She let herself relax physically. Mentally, tension remained. Not only to keep the other psi from increasing the advantage he held—if he gave her any kind of opening, she might still be able to jar him enough to shake him off. So far he'd been careful. In the two hours since she first encountered him, she'd gained hardly any impression of his personality, none at all of his purpose. She'd been at ease, doing a casual telepathic scan of whatever happened to touch her attention as she rested, half napping, when she sensed an unfamiliar pattern, a light, drifting, gentle awareness. Wondering what manner of creature was producing it—something small and fluffy and friendly seemed to fit—Telzey reached out toward the gentleness. But that appeared to cause alarm; it faded to a trace, almost vanished. So it had psi sense, too! Intrigued, she approached again, gradually and reassuringly. This time, whatever it was didn't withdraw; after a moment, it seemed to be responding to her.

Then, in a flash, she knew that this was no natural impression but a trick, that while her defenses were relaxed, her attention distracted, a stealthy intrusion of her mind had begun. Instantly, she threw in every block she could to check the invader—nothing small and fluffy and friendly, but a human psi, a dangerously accomplished one. Her reaction kept him from taking complete control of her then and there, as he otherwise should have done. But she couldn't do much else, however furiously she fought to break the holds he'd secured, or to reach his mind in turn. He'd already established control enough to leave her effectively helpless; and when she realized it, she stopped struggling, though she continued to watch for any momentary weakening of the control pattern or any move on his part to extend it.

There were no indications of either. She discovered next that she couldn't get outside help. She was unable to inform anyone of her predicament; it was simply impossible. She had to act as if nothing had happened. For a while, there was no significant change in that situation. Then came an impulse to get out her car and start toward the center of Orado City, and she couldn't prevent herself from following the impulse. She knew he was making her come to him, and presently that he waited somewhere in the Jadel Tower. But after he canceled her attempt to jump out of the car and let the dropcatch system immobilize her, there was no way she could keep from going there.

Unless he slipped up at the last moment . . .

He didn't slip up. The Jadel Tower drifted closer; his controls remained locked on her mind, incomplete but adequate, and if it was causing him any stress to hold them, there was nothing to show it. She turned the Cloudsplitter toward a parking terrace at around the fiftieth level. A dozen private cars stood on it; a few people were moving about them. She set her car down in an empty slot, left the engine idling, unlocked the door on the driver's side, and shifted over to the adjoining seat.

A few seconds later, the car door opened. A man settled himself in the driver's seat and closed the door. Telzey looked over at him as the Cloudsplitter lifted back into the air.

His face was a featureless blur to her—he was covering up. Otherwise, she saw him clearly. He appeared to be fairly young, was of medium size, athletically built. And no one she knew.

The blurred face turned toward her suddenly. Telzey sensed no specific order but only the impulse to shift sideways on the car seat and put her hands behind her back. She felt him fasten her wrists together with light cuffs. Then she was free to resume her previous position and discovered that meanwhile the view outside the car also had blurred for her, as had the instrument console.

It reassured her somewhat. If he didn't want her to know what he looked like, or where she was being taken, he must expect that she'd be alive and able to talk after this business was over. She settled back in the seat and waited.

Perhaps half an hour went by. Telzey remained wary, but while the mental hold the strange psi had on her didn't relax in the least, he didn't try to develop it. At last, he set the car down, shut off the engine and opened the door on his side. Suddenly, she could see her surroundings again, though what she saw wasn't very revealing. They were in a car-port; beyond it spread a garden with trees, a small lawn, some flowering shrubbery. Patches of white-clouded sky showed above the trees; nothing else.

The man, face still a blur, walked around the car and opened the door on her side.

"Get out, please!" The voice was quiet, not at all menacing. He helped her climb out of the car, then took her by the elbow and guided her to a door in the back of the carport. He unlocked it, motioned her into a passage and locked the door behind them. "This way—"

She sensed a psi-block around them which might enclose the entire building. The appearance of the passage suggested it was a private residence. Probably the home of her kidnapper.

The blurred face said from behind her, "You did intend to jump from your car back there, didn't you?"

She nodded. "Yes."

"Aerial littering!" He sounded amused. "If you'd alerted the dropcatch system and been picked up by a sprintcar or barrier, you'd have found yourself in rather serious trouble! Rehabilitation's almost the automatic sentence for a city jumper."

Telzey said impatiently, "I could have got out of that. But I'd have been kept under investigation for three or four days, with no way to get to you, whatever I tried. I don't think you could have held on to me for three or four days."

"Not even for one!" he agreed. "It was a good move—but it didn't work."

"Am I going to be told why I'm here?"

"You'll be told very quickly," he assured her, stopping to open another door. The room beyond was sizable and windowless, gymnastic equipment set up in it. The man followed Telzey inside. "We haven't been acquainted long," he remarked, "but I've already discovered it's best not to take chances with you! Let's get you physically immobilized before we start talking."

A few minutes later, she stood between two uprights near the center of the room. There were cuffs on her wrists again, but now her arms were stretched straight out to either side, held by straps attached to the cuffs and fastened at the other end to the uprights. It was a strained position which might soon become painful.

"This is a psi-blocked house, as you probably know," his voice said from behind her. "And it's mine. We won't be disturbed here."

Telzey nodded. "All right. We won't be disturbed. So now, who are you and what do you want?"

"I haven't decided yet to tell you who I am. You see, I need the help of another psi. A telepath."

"I'm to help you with what?"

"That's something else I may tell you later. I'll have to make sure first that I can use you. Not every telepath would do, by any means."

"You think I might?" Telzey said.

"If I weren't almost sure of it, I wouldn't have hung on to you," he told her dryly. "You gave me a rather bad time, you know! If I'd realized how much trouble you were going to be, I doubt I'd have tackled you in the first place. But that's precisely why you should turn out to be the kind of dependable assistant I want. However, I can't say definitely until you let me take over all the way."

"Would you do that, in my place?" Telzey asked.

"Yes—if I were aware of the alternatives."

She kept her voice even. "What are they?"

"Why, there're several possibilities. Drugs, for example. But I suspect they'd have to depress your psi function to the point where I couldn't operate on it. So we'll pass up drugs. Then I might be able to break your remaining blocks by sheer force—after all, I did manage to clamp a solid starting hold on you. But force could do you serious mental harm, and since you'd be of no use to me then, I'd try it only as a last resort. There's a simple approach I can follow which should be effective enough. See if you can use your pain shutoffs."

Telzey said after a moment, "I . . . well, I seem to have forgotten how to do it."

"I know," his voice said. "I was able to block that from your awareness before you noticed what was happening. So you don't have that defense at present—and now I'll let you feel pain."

There was a sudden intolerable cramping sensation in her left arm. She jerked violently. The feeling faded again.

"That was a low-intensity touch," he said. "I suppose you've heard of such devices. As long as their use is confined to arms and legs, they can't kill or do significant damage, but the effect can be excruciating. I know somebody I could bring to the house in a few minutes who'd be eager to help me out in this because he likes to hurt people. If you were being jolted constantly as I jolted you just now, I doubt you could spare enough concentration to hold up your blocks against me. Because there'd be nothing to distract me, you see! I could give full attention to catching any momentary weakening of your defenses, and I'd say it would be at most an hour then before I had complete control. But meanwhile you would have had an acutely uncomfortable experience for no purpose at all. Don't you agree?"

Unfortunately, she did. She said, "Let me think about it."

"Fair enough," he told her. "I happen to be in something of a hurry, but I'd much sooner settle this without any unpleasantness."

"How long would it take to help you in whatever it is you want to do?" Telzey asked.

"Perhaps four or five days. A week at most."

"You'll let me go when it's finished?"

"Of course," he said reassuringly. "I'd have no reason to keep you under control any longer."

That might be a lie. But a good deal could happen in four or five days, and if he were to make use of her as a psi, he'd have to leave her some freedom of action. "All right," she said. "I'll give up the blocks."

"How do you feel?" his voice asked presently.

"My arms are beginning to hurt." He hadn't released her from the uprights and he was still somewhere in the room behind her where she couldn't see him.

"I didn't mean that," he told her. "You're aware of the changes in you?"

Telzey sighed. "Oh, yes. I know how I felt before you started."

"And now?"

She reflected. "Well . . . I'll do anything you tell me to do, of course, or try to. If you haven't given me specific instructions, I'll do whatever is to your advantage. That's more important now than anything else."

"More important than your life?"

"Yes," she said. "I know it's not at all sensible, but it is more important than my life."

"Not a bad start!" There was satisfaction in his voice. "You're aware of the manner in which you're controlled?"

She shook her head. "If I were, I might know how to break the controls. That wouldn't be to your advantage. So I can't be aware of it."

"How do you feel about the situation?"

Telzey considered again. "I don't seem to have much feeling about it. It's the situation, that's all."

"And that's also as it should be," his voice said. "I noticed you have connections with the Psychology Service, but if you keep your shield tight—as you will—that won't be a problem. So aside from a few additional modifications, which I'll take care of presently, we'll consider the job done. Let's get you out of those cuffs."

She was freed a moment later and turned to look at him, rubbing her, arms. He was smiling down at her, face no longer a blur. It was an intelligent and rather handsome face but not one to which she'd feel drawn under ordinary circumstances. Of course, that didn't matter now.

"I make it a rule," he remarked, "to use psi only when necessary. It lessens the chance of attracting undesirable attention. We'll observe that rule between us. For example, we don't talk on the thought level when verbal communication is possible. Understood?"

She nodded. "Yes."

"Fine. Let's have some refreshments, and I'll explain why I want your help. My name is Alicar Troneff, by the way."

"Should you be telling me your name?" Telzey asked. "That is, if it's your real one."

He smiled. "It's my real name. Why not? Federation law doesn't recognize human psi ability, so this is hardly a matter on which you could take me to court. And the Psychology Service makes it a rule to let independent psis settle their own differences. Your friends there might interfere if they knew what was happening, but they'll take no steps later on."

"I might tell them Alicar Troneff is a psi, though," Telzey remarked.

He grimaced. "Unfortunately, they already have me on record as one! It's made some of my operations more difficult, but I have ways of getting around that obstacle."

Over plates of small cakes and a light tart drink in a room overlooking the garden, Alicar came up at last with some limited information. "You know what serine crystals are?" he inquired.

Telzey nodded.

"A fossil deposit," she said. "Mined on Mannafra, I think. The cosmetic industry uses it."

"Correct on all counts! I located a serine bed last year, acquired rights to the area and brought mining equipment in to Mannafra to extract the crystals. It isn't a large mine, but it could easily produce enough to meet all my financial requirements for the next dozen years. I went back to Mannafra two days ago after an absence of several months and discovered I had a problem at the mine. I need a telepath with high probe sensitivity to investigate it further for me. You should be perfect in that role."

She looked at him. "A psi problem?"

"Psi seems to be involved. I won't tell you what I noticed, or think I noticed, because I want your unbiased opinion."

"And you think an investigation might be dangerous," Telzey added. "Or you'd do it yourself."

Alicar smiled. "That's possible. I've told you as much as you need to know at this stage. You're to think of some good reason now for being absent from Orado for about a week, and, of course, you'll avoid arousing anybody's curiosity. We'll leave in my private cruiser whenever you're ready. How long will it take you to make the arrangements?"

She shrugged. "A few hours. We can start this afternoon if you like. Anything special I should take along?"

"The kind of clothing you'd want in a desert climate with a wide range of temperature," Alicar said. "We might be going outdoors—at least, you might be. I'll take care of everything else."

He added, "One other thing before you go. While I was setting up my controls, I checked over a few of your past experiences and realized belatedly that I'd taken more of a chance in trapping you than I'd thought. It seems that if I'd made any mistake in that initial encounter, I might have been fortunate to get away with my life!"

Telzey nodded. "Perhaps. If I could have reached you, I'd have slammed you with everything I had."

"Yes." He cleared his throat. "Well, I'm going to install a prohibition against your use of psi bolts, and another one against your techniques for controlling others as I control you at present."

"But why?" she said, startled. "I might need all I know if I'm to handle a psi problem, and particularly a dangerous one, for you. I wouldn't use anything against you now. I couldn't!"

Alicar's handsome face hardened, and became thereby rather ugly.

"Probably not," he said. "But I had to leave considerable flexibility in the control patterns to let you function satisfactorily, and there might be moments

when my overall hold on you will become a little lax.
I'm making sure there'll be no disagreeable surprises
at such moments! If a situation calls for it, I can
always rearm you—but I'll be the judge of that. You'll
go blank now on what happens during the next few
minutes."

2

Alicar Troneff had approached Mannafra on the night
side and activated a psi-block in his spacecruiser's hull
while they were still high above the surface. Nine-
tenths a desert world from pole to pole, Mannafra
looked almost featureless under the starblaze. Mining complexes and an occasional government post
dotted some areas; between them, the sand dunes
rolled from horizon to horizon, broken here and there
by dark mountain ranges. Perhaps an hour after they'd
entered atmosphere, Alicar's cruiser dropped down
behind such a range, moved through winding passes,
and presently came to rest on a wide rock shelf high
above the desert floor.

"We're now about fifteen miles from the mine,"
Alicar said, shifting the engines to idling, "and that's
as close as I intend to get to it until you've done some
preliminary scouting."

"I'm to scout the mine from the car?" Telzey asked.
There was a small aircar stored in the rear of the
cruiser near the lock.

Alicar handed her a respirator.

"Fit that over your face," he said. "We may use
the car later, but at present you're simply going
outside. You wouldn't actually need a respirator, but
it'll be more comfortable, and it has a mike. Put on
a long coat. You'll find it chilly."

"You're staying in the cruiser?"

He smiled. "Definitely! Behind its psi-block. The scouting job is all yours."

She got out her warmest coat, put it on, and fastened the respirator into place. They checked the speaking attachment.

"What am I to do when I'm outside?" Telzey said.

An image appeared in her mind. "Take a look at that man," Alicar told her. "It's Hille, the mine's manager and chief engineer. I want you to identify him at the mental level. Think you can do it?"

"At fifteen miles? I might. How many other people are around?"

"Twelve in all at the mine. It's run by a Romango computer. There isn't another installation within nine hundred miles."

"That'll make it easier," Telzey acknowledged. "Anything else?"

Hille's image vanished; that of another man appeared. "Ceveldt, the geologist," said Alicar. "Try him if you can't locate Hille. If you can't find either, any of the minds down there should do for now. But I'd prefer you to contact one of those two."

She nodded. "No special difficulties? Any probe-immunes among them?"

Alicar shrugged. "Would I have a probe-immune working for me?"

"No, I guess you wouldn't," Telzey said. "All right. Is there something specific I'm to scan for?"

"No. Just see what general impressions you pick up. Above all, probe cautiously!" He cleared his throat. "It's possible that there's a telepathic mind at or near the mine. If you get any indication of that, withdraw your probe at once. We'll consider then what to do next."

She reflected a moment, not greatly surprised. "Could the telepath be expecting a probe?"

"I don't know," Alicar said. "So be careful about what you do. You'll have plenty of time. I want as much information as I can get before daybreak, but it'll be another two hours before it begins to lighten up around here."

Even in her coat, it was cold on the shelf of rock where Alicar had set down the cruiser. But the shelf extended for about fifty feet ahead of her before the mountain sloped steeply down. To right and left, it wound away into night dimness. She could move around; and that helped.

So now to find out what was going on at the serine crystal mine! The crystals were skeletal remains of a creature belonging to an early geological period when there still had been water on Mannafra. Sizable deposits had been found here and there at what presumably were former lake sites. Their commercial value was high because of a constant demand for the processed product; and no doubt there were outfits around that'd be interested in pirating a working serine mine.

Nevertheless, Telzey felt sure Alicar was holding back information. He'd said the mine wasn't a large one, and competent psis had no reason to involve themselves in criminal operations at a relatively minor level. When they had larcenous inclinations, it still simply was too easy for them to come by as much money as they wanted without breaking obvious laws. If psis were creating a problem at Alicar's mine, the cause wasn't serine crystals; and he probably knew what it was. At a guess, she thought, some enemies had trailed him to this point on Mannafra and were waiting for him to return. It wasn't at all difficult to imagine Alicar Troneff making enemies for himself among other psis.

Well, she'd see what she could do for him . . .

She opened her mental screens, sent light search

thoughts drifting through the starlit night. The desert world wasn't dead; whisperings of life began to come into her awareness. But for a while, there was nothing to indicate human life or thought, nor any guarded and waiting telepathic mind. Alicar, watching her in the cruiser's screens, remained silent.

Perhaps half an hour later, Telzey opened the respirator's mike switch, said, "Getting touches of human mind stuff now! I'll let it develop. Not a psi, whoever he is."

"Good," said Alicar's voice. "Take your time."

A few minutes passed. Then Telzey went on. "Someone called Ponogan—"

"Yes," Alicar said. "One of the mining technicians. You're there! Specific impressions?"

"Nothing useful. Imagery. He's probably asleep and dreaming. It could be a drug fantasy. Something like a big round drop of water rolling across the desert toward him . . . Traces of another mind now."

"Yes?"

"Haven't made out much about it so far. Shall I work on that, or probe directly for Hille?"

Alicar said after a moment, "Try Hille first."

She projected Hille's name and appearance lightly among the mental impressions she was touching, sensed, seconds later, a faint subconscious response. "Hille, I think," she said. And after a pause: "Yes, it is. Self-awareness. He's awake . . . Calculating something . . . Alone . . ."

"Don't try probing in depth!" Alicar said quickly. "Simply retain light contact and see what impressions you get."

She said, with a touch of irritation, "That's what I'm doing." Couldn't he trust her to handle this? Another minute or two went by. She murmured, "Picking up that other mind again. No, wait!" She shifted to Ponogan, strengthened her contact with him.

"Now here's something odd!" she said suddenly. "Both Hille and Ponogan—" She hesitated.

"Yes?" There was alert interest in Alicar's voice.

"I'm not sure what it means," Telzey said. "But each of them seems to have a kind of psi structure attached to him. Quite complicated structures! They seem almost part of their minds, but they're independent—sort of pseudominds." She hesitated again. "And I think—" She stiffened. "Djeel oil!"

"What?"

"Djeel oil! Hille's thinking about it. Alicar, they're processing djeel at your mine."

There was silence for a moment. Then Alicar's voice said: "Come back inside."

He looked around from the console as Telzey came into the cruiser's control section. But the face wasn't Alicar's, didn't resemble it in the least. She checked, startled.

The face smiled. "Life mask, of course," Alicar's voice said. "Nobody at the mine knows what I really look like. No need to explain why now, is there?"

She sat down. "You're mining and processing djeel ore here?"

"I am," Alicar said dryly.

She stared at him. "I didn't know there was any on Mannafra!"

He shrugged. "No way you could know. I'm reasonably sure I'm the only one to have come across it here, and I haven't advertised it."

Telzey shook her head. Djeel was a substance in a class by itself, located so far on only a handful of worlds. The processed ore yielded djeel oil—and djeel oil was believed to have unidentified properties which had scooped a hundred-mile semiglobular section out of a planetary surface, producing cataclysmic secondary effects. Any djeel detected since then had been confiscated by the Federation for removal and disposal

in space. She said, "Aren't you likely to work yourself into the worst kind of trouble? If you get caught
importing djeel anywhere in the Hub, they'll hang
medals on whoever shoots you!"

"I haven't imported it anywhere in the Hub," said
Alicar. "The oil processed by the mine in its first three
months of operation is at present stored away on an
asteroid chunk only I can identify. The reason I came
back three days ago was to pick up a new load. Let's
drop that subject for the moment. Just before Hille
started thinking about djeel, you seemed to have an
idea about those psi structures associated with him
and Ponogan. What was it?"

"Well, that," Telzey said. "I'd have to check a lot
more closely to be sure. But I think they're automatic
control mechanisms—something that lets the men
seem to function normally but cuts in if they're about
to think, or do, something that isn't wanted. Was that
what you noticed three days ago?"

"Yes," Alicar said. "But I didn't stay around long
enough to analyze it. Apparently everyone at the mine
has been equipped with such a mechanism—we can
check on that presently. The immediate question is
why it was done."

Telzey nodded. "Do you have any ideas?"

"Nothing definite," he said. "Look, let me give
you the background on this—I want your opinions.
I was scouting around last year, looking for good
investment possibilities. Most of Mannafra's mining
is concentrated in sections where rich strikes have
been made. This whole general area has been almost
completely neglected. But something about the for-
mations down there looked interesting to me. It was
mainly a hunch, but I came down, and inside an
hour I knew I'd found a quite respectable deposit
of serine crystals."

"If I hadn't been doing my own analysis, that's as
far as it would have gone. There were djeel traces

in the samples I'd taken." Alicar smiled. "Those, naturally, weren't the samples submitted with my application for mining rights, and I got the rights under an identity which goes with this appearance." He tapped the life mask's cheek.

"Well, now wait!" Telzey said. "Why did you want djeel oil in the first place? If they're right about what happened on Tosheer, it's horribly dangerous. And I've never heard that it was supposed to be good for anything. Though—" She paused abruptly.

"So now it's occurred to you!" Alicar nodded. "Something capable of releasing energies of that magnitude isn't going to be simply ignored. You can be sure the djeel ore the Overgovernment obligingly hauls off wherever it's found isn't being dumped into some solar furnace, though that's the story."

"You know that?"

"I know it. A good many other people suspect it." Alicar chewed his lip. "I spent a large part of the past year trying to find out just what is being done with it, but that's one of the best-guarded operations around. I couldn't even establish what government branch is involved. Incidentally after we've cleaned up the problem here, continuing that investigation may be your next assignment."

Telzey said after a moment, "I didn't think you really intended to let me go again."

He laughed. "No, not for a while! You're too useful. I have several jobs lined up for you. You can see that a supply of djeel oil would have a fabulous value if the right people can be contacted safely."

"You want to sell it?"

"I might. I'd prefer to set up a research project designed to harness djeel, but I may decide it's too risky. Because that's where djeel oil becomes dangerous—the experimental stage! It's not general knowledge, but it's been processed and stored without incident in much greater quantities than this mine, for example, would produce in years. Unfortunately, nobody seems to know what kind of experiments that industrial outfit on Tosheer was conducting with djeel when the planet's mantle erupted."

"Now to get back to the present situation. The mine went into operation roughly seven months ago. It took careful preparation, and the personnel had to be hand-picked. Of the twelve men down there, nine knew only that we'd be producing serine crystals—which, aside from serving as our cover, has turned out to be sufficiently profitable in itself. The three involved in the processing of djeel oil are Hille, Ceveldt and Gulhas, who is the Romango computer technician."

Telzey said, "You were controlling those three?"

"No. As I've told you, I use psi only when it's necessary. I did check their personalities carefully, of course, and knew they'd go along with me dependably in the matter of the djeel. During the first month, we worked only serine. Then the secret djeel operation began. As soon as it was underway, I left Mannafra."

"Why?"

"Because I intend to stay in the clear in this, Telzey! The chance of discovery seemed remote. But if it happened, all Hille and his colleagues could point government investigators to is this substitute identity of mine. It was created to give me cover in other activities which might have brought me into conflict with various authorities. I can drop it at any time."

Telzey said, "If you still are in the clear, wouldn't this be a good moment to back out of the djeel project and discard your cover identity for good? You'd be safe then."

Alicar smiled. "No doubt. But I'm not going to give up that easily!"

"We don't know at all what's happened here," she pointed out. "Supposing we go on with the investigation and I get caught."

"That would be unfortunate," Alicar told her. "I wouldn't like to lose you."

"I suppose it was a stupid question," Telzey said after a moment. "You'd simply kill me before I could give you away—"

"I'd have to, wouldn't I?" Alicar said. "But we'll take every reasonable precaution to keep you from getting caught. You know as much as I can tell you now, so let's get on with this. You say we don't know what's happened here. But we do know one thing, don't we? A psi's been operating on Hille and Ponogan, and probably on all the mine personnel. In other words, they're now controlled."

"That's what it looks like," Telzey agreed. "But so far, the picture doesn't make sense."

"Why not?" said Alicar, watching her.

"Well—somebody outside realizes djeel is being processed at the mine. If that somebody is government, they'd want to catch the absent owner—"

"Mr. Ralke," supplied Alicar. "It's the Ralke Mine."

"All right—Mr. Ralke. They can't locate him elsewhere in the Hub because he becomes nonexistent there. So, knowing he's come back once to pick up the processed djeel oil, they stake out the mine. In your other activities, have you given anyone reason to suspect Mr. Ralke might be a psi?"

He shook his head. "I doubt it very much."

"But it's possible?"

Alicar shrugged. "Let's say it's possible."

"If that were discovered," Telzey said, "it would bring in government psis—the Psychology Service. But then why control the mine people with mechanisms that would make any probing telepath suspicious? They have to assume that Mr. Ralke, psi, does probe his employees before showing himself at the mine."

Alicar scratched his chin. "It really doesn't make very much sense, does it?"

"None at all," Telzey said. "If it were the Service

and they thought Ralke might be a psi, everything at the mine would look completely normal now. In fact, it would be normal—except that there'd be a strike group sitting up here in the mountains somewhere, one of them a third-string Service telepath. And he'd be in watch-contact with someone at the mine, probably Hille, and as soon as you came back, he'd know."

Alicar pursed his mouth, frowning. "Well, let's say it's not the Service then. How does an independent psi operator like myself look to you?"

"Not much better," Telzey said. "Unless it's someone you know."

"Huh? Why that?"

"Somebody who doesn't like you," she explained. "It probably would be a hot-shot psi, because if those mechanisms are as complicated as they seemed to me, I don't think either you or I would be able to construct something like them."

The expression on Alicar's life mask indicated he didn't enjoy the suggestion. "There might be someone like that," he said slowly. "What would be his purpose?"

Telzey said, "He needn't be interested in djeel as such. But he knows you own the mine and will come back to it. So he sets up a psi phenomenon you're bound to detect and which you'll have to investigate before you risk setting foot in the mine." She grimaced briefly. "In that case, something very unpleasant—I don't know what—is supposed to happen to you while you're probing the phenomenon. What he couldn't know, of course, is that you'd do your probing by proxy."

Alicar's eyebrows had lifted. "An interesting theory!"

Telzey went on. "It isn't some psi who doesn't know you and simply wants to take over the djeel project. Because, while he might have some reason for constructing those mechanisms, he'd certainly slap shields on Hille and the others besides, so nobody else could catch them leaking thoughts about djeel."

"Yes, that omission's a curious aspect," Alicar said. He regarded her a moment. "Any more theories?"

"Only one—that's completely wild."

He smiled. "You've been doing well so far! Let's hear the wild one."

"I was wondering whether it might be the djeel that created those psi mechanisms."

"The djeel?" Alicar repeated.

"It's supposed to be a unique form of matter, isn't it?" Telzey said. "Mystery stuff?"

"Yes, it's that. But still—" Alicar shook his head. "Well, we're speculating! And we seem to have speculated sufficiently. In the light of what's actually established, what do you suggest as our next step?"

"Our next step? That's obvious. Let's get out of here!"

He laughed. "No. You might be surprised at how quickly I could get out of here if I had to. But I don't intend to do that unless we come across a very definite reason for it."

She sighed. "Then I'll have to go on probing. And if I go outside again and do it from here, there's too much chance of diffusion. A telepath might pick me up."

"I can work you in a good deal closer," Alicar said.

"How much closer? I suppose your Romango computer has defensive armament?"

"Of course. That's standard in a region like this. There's an automatic defense zone with a three-mile radius. Normal sensor range is three times that, and can be extended."

"Nine miles," said Telzey. "That's still hardly an ideal condition."

"One and a half miles," Alicar said. "We'll use the aircar and the arrangement will be the same. You'll be outside, and I'll be in the car and behind a psi-block. The car's gun, incidentally, will be pointing at you in case something goes wrong. So try to make sure nothing does."

"How are we going to get within one and a half miles of the mine?"

He grinned. "There're blind spots in the defense system because of the surrounding dunes. I checked them out when we first set up the installation. A car that's hugging the ground can avoid the sensors. I'll take you there. The rest will be up to you."

3

To Telzey's right, the section of sky beyond the gray-black mountain range where Alicar had left his spacecruiser was beginning to lighten. Morning wasn't far away. The top of the sloping hill of sand which hid the Ralke Mine from her, as it hid her from the mine computer's sensors, was thirty feet above her head. She sat, shivering, knees drawn up under her coat, arms wrapped around them, looking back down the slope at the small aircar which had brought them here. It hovered eight feet above a straggly patch of dune vegetation, shifting back and forth in occasional surges of wind. Concentrated on what she was doing, she wasn't aware of it.

Then Alicar's voice came suddenly from the speaker in her respirator. She gave a slight start.

"Anything new?" There was an edge of impatience in his voice.

She cleared her throat. "Nothing that seems important. Gulhas is in the computer control room now. He was thinking about you a minute or two ago."

"In what connection?"

"That blip the Romango picked up and identified

as an aircar before you ducked behind the dunes. Gulhas thought of it and wondered then when you'd be coming back to Mannafra. That's all. It slipped from his mind again immediately."

There was a moment of dissatisfied silence before Alicar said, "You're sure you didn't miss anything? There should have been further reflections associated with that."

"There should have been," Telzey agreed. "But there weren't. I wouldn't have missed them. You're apparently one of the subjects they don't have reflections about there now! Gulhas simply has his mind on what he's doing. Routine start-of-day checks. Nothing else."

"What about the rest?"

"No change. Ceveldt and his assistant are at their operational stations. They don't think about what's being brought up, so it's probably djeel ore. Hille's fast asleep now, and the remaining three are still sleeping. When they dream, the dreams have nothing to do with the Ralke Mine. And there's still no mind or life trace of the other five people who should be there. Unless they're behind the psi-block around your office area—"

Alicar interrupted. "I told you it's out of the question that anyone could be in there! To open the office in my absence would take something like a blast almost heavy enough to flatten the mine."

"Well, in that case," Telzey said, "those five are either dead; or they're gone. And whichever it is, nobody thinks about them either."

Alicar swore in exasperation. Telzey shrugged.

"That's the way it is," she said. "The controls have been extended since I did the first probe from the mountain. The men are more limited in their thoughts, apparently including even their dreaming thoughts. Whether that's a temporary precaution, connected with the fact that the Romango recorded a passing aircar,

I can't tell. It might be a reaction to my earlier scan-ning—say, a prearranged defense pattern against a telepathic encounter. The men think of nothing, remember nothing, that has to do either with djeel or with anything abnormal in the situation at the mine. That goes on down through the unconscious levels. The mechanisms block out the prohibited material."

"A reaction like that could be an automatic one," Alicar remarked.

"It could be. But at a guess, there's a psi around, and he's on guard."

"If there is one around, he couldn't be physically at the mine?"

"No, definitely not. With established controls, he wouldn't have to be there, of course. I should have picked up some trace of him by now if he were even within ordinary scanning range."

There was a pause until Alicar said, "Could you take one of those control mechanisms apart?"

"Taking them apart shouldn't be difficult in itself," Telzey told him. "They're only mechanisms, after all, and they don't hold much energy. But I'm rather sure we'd get a drastic reaction if I started doing it. There must be a kind of shared sentience between them to explain what's going on. So it would be noticed."

"What if you and your subject were behind a psi-block?"

"Then it wouldn't be noticed," Telzey said. "What psi-block?"

"My offices at the mine. I'm beginning to believe I can get us inside without undue risk."

"Well," Telzey said after a moment, "I suppose they might let us in. And, frankly, I wouldn't mind get-ting out of the cold. But I think you'd be stepping into a trap."

"No, it should be the other way around. When I first got the Romango, I arranged to have it accept voice override from me against any other instructions given it. Once we're there, I can take over the internal and external defense system at any time. Nobody at the mine knows about that. I'll have you work the psi controls off one or two of the men in the office area, and we should soon know exactly what the situation is and what we can do about it."

Alicar added, "You'll have to put up with the cold a little longer. I still intend to reduce the risks as much as I can, so we won't leave this place until shortly before daybreak. You're to remain alert for any changes in the situation at the mine—and in particular, of course, for any indications of activity on the part of a psi."

The starblaze was fading by the time Telzey finally climbed back into the car. She'd had nothing of significance to report in the interval; and as the door closed behind her, her residual contacts with the mentalities at the mine were shut off abruptly by the car's psi-block. She took off her coat, grateful for the warmth, sat down, pulled off the respirator and massaged her chilled face.

Neither of them spoke while Alicar maneuvered the car back along the low ground between the dunes until they were well beyond the range of the Romango computer's sensors. Then they lifted into the air and headed west, away from the mountains.

"Nothing showing in the screens," Alicar observed presently.

Telzey glanced at him. "Did you think somebody would follow us?"

"Somebody might—if they suspected I was around."

"What would you do if we did get trailed?"

"Lead them toward the Federation's Mannafra Station. If that didn't discourage them, I'd feel we were dealing with the Psychology Service, after all, and I can't afford to play around with that outfit! I'd cut back to the cruiser in that case, and get out."

"Supposing we're overtaken?"

He grunted. "This is a modified racing car. There's not likely to be anything on Mannafra that could overtake it, but for emergencies it has a very powerful little gun. Besides"—he indicated a distant brown-tinted cloudbank—"you never have to look far here to find some sizable dust storm to lose yourself in. Enough of the dust's metallic to blind sensors. Don't worry about that part of it. Now let's get that mind shield of yours open and make sure you're still the completely dependable little helper you're supposed to be . . ."

He remained silent for the next few minutes, blinking in concentration now and then. Telzey couldn't sense the scan, so that specific awareness had been sealed away, too. Presently her shield locked again.

"Well, you've done your best to carry out your assignment so far, and the opinions you've given me were honest ones," Alicar acknowledged. "I think I have you safe enough!"

There didn't seem to be much question about it. Telzey said after a while, "It wouldn't really explain anything, but those five men who've disappeared from the Ralke Mine—you said they didn't have anything to do with the djeel operation."

Alicar nodded. "They didn't. At the time I left, at any rate, it was still simply a serine crystal mine as far as they were concerned."

"Supposing," Telzey said, "they found out about the djeel and decided they didn't want to be involved in something like that? Couldn't they have gone to the authorities?"

"Meaning that's why the mine is staked out now?" Alicar shook his head. "No. Aside from the fact that it doesn't, as you say, explain the present situation, it's unlikely in itself. The system we developed was automatic and foolproof. The only way those five could have got information about the djeel would be accidentally through one of the three men in the know." He added, "And if that had happened, they wouldn't have gone bearing tales to the authorities! Hille and Gulhas control the computer, and you can be sure Hille would have rigged up some plausible mining accident. I was careful to choose the right kind of man to be manager here."

The screen scanners picked up several dozen air vehicles in the next few hours, but none were moving in the same direction, none came near them, and certainly none seemed interested in following their car. Alicar appeared to be going out of his way to advertise their presence. They flew past a number of installations, coming close enough to one to alert its defense zone and draw a standardized communicator warning from the guard computer, followed by discourtesies from the computer's operator. The car's cooling system had switched on shortly after Mannafra's yellow-white sun lifted above the horizon—the days evidently were as hot in this region of the planet as the night had been cold. Alicar said finally, "Close to noon! We've given any interested parties plenty of time to take action, and they haven't. So now we'll tackle the Ralke Mine! If there's no hitch on the approach, we'll go in, and once we're inside, we'll move fast. I'll take over the Romango at once from my offices, in case we run into difficulties."

Telzey said nothing. She felt uneasy about the prospect; but from Alicar's point of view, regaining control of the djeel oil operation was worth taking some personal risks. There was nothing she could do about it. Something less than two hours later, the car began to slant down toward the Ralke installation. The pink glow of a semiglobular force field appeared abruptly in the forward viewscreen, centered above the mine structures. The communicator went on simultaneously.

An uninflected voice said, "Warning! You are approaching the defense zone of the Ralke Mine, which is visible at present in your screens. You are required by law to provide verbal or code identification, or to change your course and bypass the zone. Failure to comply promptly will result in the destruction of your vehicle."

Alicar tapped out a signal on the communicator. The pink glow vanished, and the voice resumed. "Your identification is acknowledged. The defense zone has been neutralized. Your approach to the vehicle storage section is clear."

The communicator shut off. Alicar said in a taut voice, "That part of it is normal anyway! Let's waste no time . . ."

The car swept down, skimming the tops of surrounding dunes, toward the central building of the Ralke Mine. A circular door opened at the building's base—a door easily large enough to have let Alicar's spacecruiser pass through. He snapped over a switch, said to Telzey, "Psi-block's off! Start checking!" and she felt the block fade about her.

She'd been waiting for it; and her mind reached out instantly toward the minds she'd previously contacted here, picking them up one by one, aware that Alicar's mental screens had tightened into a dense shield. The car slid into the vehicle section. Telzey was opening the door on her side as it stopped. She slipped out, glancing around. A big loading crane stood in one corner; otherwise the section was empty. Alicar was beckoning to her from the other side of the car; she joined him and trotted along beside him as he walked rapidly toward a door in the back wall. It opened as they came up. Simultaneously, the entry door snapped shut.

They went through into a passage. A man was coming along it toward them, moving with a quick, purposeful stride. Ceveldt, Telzey told herself, the mine's geologist, one of the three involved with Alicar in the original djeel conspiracy.

"Mr. Ralke!" Ceveldt said, smiling. "We'd been wondering when you'd return." He looked questioningly at Telzey. "This young lady—"

"Nessine, my assistant." Alicar's right hand was in his pocket, and Telzey knew the hand rested on a gun. He went on. "She's part of our private operation. Everything still going smoothly there?"

Ceveldt's smile widened. "It couldn't be going better!"

Alicar nodded. "There've been some highly promising developments outside in the meantime. I want to see you and Hille in my office in about five minutes."

"I'll inform Hille," Ceveldt said.

He went toward a door leading off the passage. Alicar glanced briefly at Telzey. "Come along, Nessine!"

They didn't speak on the way to his offices. It took Alicar some seconds to open the massive door, which evidently was designed to respond to the keys he produced only after it had registered his body pattern. As it swung shut behind them, the psi-block installed about the area closed and cut off Telzey's contacts with the mine group again. They passed through an outer office into a larger inner one. There Alicar motioned to Telzey to remain silent, then spoke aloud.

"Code Alicar!" he said.

The Romango computer's voice responded promptly from a concealed speaker. "Code Alicar in effect. Verbal override acknowledged. Instructions?"

"Scan my companion for future reference," Alicar said.

"The companion has been scanned."

"Her name is Nessine. You'll recognize her?"

"I will."

"No further instructions at present," said Alicar. "I'll repeat the code before giving you new ones." He drew in a breath, looked at Telzey. "Well, that's in order!" he remarked. "I control the Romango. Now, what's happened here since this morning? Ceveldt acted as if nothing had changed after I left."

Telzey nodded. "And that's how it seems to him now! The mechanisms have modified their control patterns again. Not just for Ceveldt—as far as I could make out, the same thing seems to have happened to everyone else here. Of course, they all still have the impression that everything is normal at the Ralke Mine. But the three who should know about djeel now know about it; the others have no suspicion it's being hauled up and processed. I believe the shift was made as soon as you identified yourself from the aircar."

"To give me the initial impression that everything was normal here," Alicar said. "That much could be preplanned and automatically activated by my arrival. But, obviously, I wouldn't retain the impression very long. For one thing, I'd soon be asking what happened to the five missing members of the staff. So this setup is intended simply to gain a little time! For someone who isn't at present at the Ralke Mine."

"Enough time for the next move," Telzey said.

"A move," said Alicar, "which I should have already forestalled by shifting ultimate control of the computer to myself . . ."

A bell sounded as he spoke. He turned to a desk, switched on a small viewscreen. It showed the passage outside the offices, Ceveldt and another man standing before the door. "Ceveldt and Hille." Alicar switched off the screen. "We'll soon know now!" He pressed a button, releasing the outer door.

"Gentlemen, come in—be seated!" he said as Hille and Ceveldt appeared in the door of the inner office. "Nessine, get the files I indicated."

He hadn't indicated any, but she went back into the outer office, stood there waiting. After some seconds, Alicar called, "All right, you can come back in!"

Hille and Ceveldt were slumped in chairs when she rejoined him. Alicar had placed a facemask and a short plastic rod on the table beside him. "They both got a good whiff of the vapor and should be fairly limp for a while," he told her. "If necessary, I'll repeat the process. Now get them unhooked from those mechanisms enough so they can tell me what's been going on."

Telzey said, "I could do it easier and faster, and perhaps safer, if you'd knock a few of your controls off me! At least, until I finish with these two."

He grinned, shook his head. "Not a chance! I like you better on a short leash. You're doing fine as you are. Get to work!"

She sat down in another chair, went to work. Alicar remained standing, gaze shifting alertly between her and the men. Two or three minutes went by.

Telzey closed her eyes, carefully wiped sweat from her face.

"Getting results?" she heard Alicar inquire.

She opened her eyes, looked at him.

"Yes!" she whispered.

"Well?"

She shook her head.

"I can tell you one thing right now," she said. "We should get away from here as fast as we can!"

"I'd need to hear a very good reason for that," Alicar said.

"Ask them!" she said. "They can talk to you now. Perhaps they'll convince you."

Alicar stared at her an instant, swung to Hille. "Hille?"

Hille sighed. "Yes, Mr. Ralke?"

"What's happened here since I went away?"

Hille said, "Soad came and made us see what we'd been doing."

"Soad?" Alicar repeated.

Ceveldt nodded, smiling. "The Child of the Gods. You see, djeel oil is god matter, Mr. Ralke! It wasn't intended for men. Only the Children of the Gods may use it. Soad wants djeel oil, so we've been processing it for him. He's forgiven us for taking it for ourselves."

Alicar looked exasperated. "Telzey, get them out of this trance or whatever they're in!"

"They're in no trance," she told him. "I've neutralized the control mechanisms enough to let them say what they really think. The Child of the Gods converted them, don't you see? They believe him. The only djeel oil stored at the mine at this moment is what's been processed during the past week. He comes by regularly to collect what they have on hand for him."

"Who is that Child of the Gods?"

She giggled helplessly. "A great big drop of liquid rolling like mercury across the desert at night! Ponogan was dreaming about it when I checked the mine from the mountain. I mentioned it, remember? That's Soad. And, believe me, he is big!"

Alicar stared at her. "There's no creature like that on Mannafra!"

Ceveldt said, "Soad came from far away. He needs djeel oil to return, and it's been our privilege to provide him with what we could. But it isn't enough."

Hille added, "Mr. Ralke, he wants the djeel you took away from Mannafra. That was terribly wrong of you, but you didn't know it. Soad's forgiven you and has been waiting for you to return. He'll come tonight, and you'll understand then why you must go with one of his servants to bring back his djeel."

" 'Servant' meaning one of those control mechanisms," Telzey put in.

Alicar looked startled. "I doubt he could do that to a shielded psi mind!"

She giggled again. "Couldn't he? Remember how you stumbled across the djeel ore in the first place? You said you were flying by overhead and turned down on a hunch to take mineral samples—possibly at the one point on Mannafra where djeel can be found. On a hunch! Doesn't it look like Soad was waiting for someone to come within psi range who could dig up and process the stuff for him? He slipped up then in letting you get away with the product of the first three months of operation. He'd like it back, of course. And he put full controls on the people who remained at the mine after you'd left, to make sure nothing like that could happen again."

She added, "Whatever he is, he has a use for a ready supply of protoplasm, too! He's collected the five missing members of your mine personnel along with his djeel."

"Well," Ceveldt said mildly, "it was required. The desert offers insufficient nourishment for Soad. Naturally, we're no longer interested in mining serine crystals, and those men weren't needed in the full production of the oil. It was an honor for them to serve him in another way."

4

Alicar shook his head, drew a deep breath. "Code Alicar!" he said sharply.

The Romango computer's flat voice came into the office. "Instructions?"

"Close and seal every section of the installation to make sure the personnel stay where they are. Free passage at will is permitted only for myself and Nessine!"

"Complying," said the computer.

"Unlock the vehicle section and open its exit."

"Complying."

"Accept no further orders until I address you again."

"Understood."

"End of instructions." Alicar jerked his head at Telzey, started for the door to the outer office. "Come along!"

Hille and Ceveldt began to push themselves up from their chairs, the vapor-induced weakness still evident in clumsy motions.

"Mr. Ralke," said Hille, "you mustn't attempt to leave! That's against Soad's wishes!"

Alicar swung around to them, and now his gun was in his hand.

"Shut up!" he said savagely. "Stay in those chairs! If you try to follow, you're dead men . . . Come on, Telzey!"

They left Hille and Ceveldt staring after them, hurried through the outer office, along the passage.

"Soad's more than I counted on!" Alicar's voice was unsteady. "We're leaving, of course!"

"Hille was thinking the computer wouldn't obey you," Telzey told him.

"Well, he's wrong! He didn't know about the code override. You heard it acknowledge my instructions. The Romango's one thing their monster can't control. But hurry it up! I won't feel safe until I'm off the planet."

They ran back the way they'd come. There were blurred impressions of various minds in the surrounding structures, but Telzey tightened her shield and ignored them. For once, she agreed with Alicar— getting completely out of this area seemed the best immediate thing they could do. If possible.

They came to the passage leading to the vehicle section, to the door at its end. Alicar grasped the door handle, pulled at it, then strained, putting in all his strength. He swore furiously.

"Still locked! What—"

"Can you check with the computer?" Telzey asked.

"Not here! No voice pickup around!" Alicar chewed his lip, added, "Stand back!" and stepped away from the door, leveling his gun. Long darts of scarlet flame hissed around the lock. Metal flowed under the flame, hardened lumpily again. The air in the passage grew hot.

Alicar switched off the gun. He stepped forward, rammed the sole of his boot against the surface of the door. The door flew open.

"Come on!" he gasped. "We can open the exit manually!"

They started through into the vehicle section, came to a stop together.

The big work crane which had been standing in a corner when they arrived at the mine hadn't stayed there. It was near the center of the compartment, swinging around toward the door on its treads as they caught sight of it. Crushed parts of their aircar lay scattered about. The crane started rolling toward them then. They backed hastily out into the passage.

"Now what?" Telzey felt short of breath. "Your override system's a fake—a trick! Hille was right. Somebody spotted it while you were gone!"

Alicar stared at her, mouth twisting.

"Gulhas," he said. "The technician! Where is he?"

"In the computer room, I think. I'll check."

"Do it while we're on our way there. Get into full contact with him at once! Come on!"

"Alicar," she said, running along behind him. "You'd better let me—"

"I'll have you put Gulhas under control when we

reach the computer room. Don't bother me now. We might have other problems."

Telzey didn't reply. She caught an impression of Gulhas, lost it again. Contact wasn't easy. She had to give attention to keeping up with Alicar, and there was another distraction. Something was going on; she wasn't yet sure what. But—

"Alicar!"

"Come on!" He didn't glance back.

"Wait! Hille—"

Telzey broke off. They were passing through the mine's storage area; and now two men had appeared suddenly in the aisle ahead, stepping out from behind packing cases. Hille and Ceveldt. Guns in their hands, pointed at Alicar. And Alicar, hand hovering above the pocket that held his gun, came to an abrupt halt. She'd stopped twenty feet behind him.

"Mr. Ralke, don't move!" Hille said quietly, walking forward. He might still be unsteady on his legs, but his face was hard and determined, and the gun didn't waver. He went on. "The situation has changed! Your actions indicate to Soad that it might be too dangerous to send you back to get the djeel oil you stole. Therefore—"

The gun in his hand went off as Alicar threw himself to the floor and rolled sideways. It went off again, and so did Ceveldt's, and Telzey saw one of the scarlet darts of Alicar's gun flash into Hille's chest. Ceveldt fired again, and Alicar jerked violently around, the gun flying from his hand and skidding down the aisle toward Telzey. She scooped it up, darted behind a piece of machinery on her left, and crouched down, heart pounding.

There was stillness for a moment. She worked herself in farther between the machines and the wall. From there, she could see a section of the floor, Hille lying on his back. She tried to reach his mind, found it disintegrating in death. Alicar—no, Alicar wasn't

dying, not yet! But he was badly hurt and unconscious.

Slow, cautious footsteps. Ceveldt. She shifted contact to his mind. Ceveldt was uninjured and coming
watchfully toward the array of machines behind which
she crouched, not knowing exactly where she was. She
couldn't see him and didn't need to. She knew what
he was going to say before he spoke.

"Soad can't permit you to live either, Nessine or
whoever you are," his voice told her. "He knows what
you've done, and it seems you might cause a great
deal of trouble here before he made you understand
it was wrong. You can't get away—the doors are
locked now. So come on out!" He added, "It will be
painless and quick."

Did he know she had Alicar's gun? No, he didn't;
he'd seen it spinning away from Alicar's hand, but his
attention had been on the man, not the weapon. He'd
seen her dart out of sight behind the machines, and
he wanted to make sure of her before he went back
to finish off Alicar, if that was required.

She felt him reach a decision, and crouched lower.
Overhead and to her right, something thudded against
the wall; heat washed briefly over her, and when she
glanced up, she saw a small section of the wall glowing where the bolt had struck. She crept over to a
point directly beneath it. He was less likely to fire
at that exact spot again in trying to flush her into
sight.

There were a dozen more shots, some crashing into
metal, some against the wall. Then Ceveldt, not
knowing whether he had reached her or not, was
coming around the end of the array of machines
where he had seen her disappear.

She rested Alicar's gun on a piece of steel and held
it there unsteadily, thumb against the firing stud. She
nearly wasn't quick enough then. Most of Ceveldt's
strength had returned to him in the interval; he was

suddenly in view, standing beside the wall, seeing her. He shot. She fired into a blaze of light, felt a succession of shocks jolt through Ceveldt, felt intense heat above her and a spray of fire pain across her back. She dropped flat and rolled over to crush out the sparks on her shirt.

That took only moments. She turned again and crept forward until she was past the impact area of the last shot, then got to her feet. Ceveldt was down, and Ceveldt was dead. She stepped around him and came out from behind the machines.

Alicar's left thigh was an ugly, seared mess, and Hille's gun had punched a hole through his right shoulder. That wound was bleeding heavily. She could stop the bleeding and would—if she had time left for it. The control mechanisms attached to Hille and Ceveldt might not understand death, but she sensed them reacting to the fact that their charges weren't performing as they were supposed to perform. That reaction was being picked up by the other mechanisms here—and, no doubt, being communicated to Soad.

She started to kneel down beside Alicar, then hesitated. A sound behind her? She turned quickly, bringing the gun around. For a moment, she stood frozen.

Hille's body had turned on its side. His hand was groping with slow, fumbling awkwardness toward the gun he had dropped. He hadn't come back to life— Soad's mechanism was forcing the corpse into a semblance of action. The fingers stretched and curled, reaching. The boots scratched against the floor.

Unnerved, Telzey hurried toward the contorting thing, snatched up the gun, then ran to check on Ceveldt. And dead Ceveldt, too, was being driven to attempt to regain the weapon he'd lost.

She had both weapons now; but there was a furious

thudding on a distant door as she ran back to Alicar, and a feeling of despair came to her. Ceveldt and Hille had secured the doors to the storage area from within; and if that lock system had been under the Romango computer's control, the doors would have reopened by now. So it wasn't. But it could be only minutes before Soad's other slaves forced their way in by one means or another; they'd come armed, and that would be the end. Given more time, she might have pried them away from their psi mechanisms in turn. Given the capabilities of which Alicar had so carefully deprived her—

Realization blazed through Telzey.

She thought: "But of course!"

She stood staring down at Alicar then in such utter concentration that the racket of the assault on the door receded completely from her awareness. Seconds went racing by. Here was where he'd blocked her—and here! And here! The controls dissolved as she came to them. Abruptly, she knew she was free.

She drew a deep breath, reached confidently for one of the minds she'd touched before, restored contact. Psi flashed over the line of contact, struck with calculated violence. That mind went blank.

Barely a minute later, there was only one human mind besides her own still functioning consciously at the Ralke Mine. It was that of Gulhas, computer technician.

Gulhas was as much a convert to the Child of the Gods as Hille and Ceveldt had been, but he became Telzey's property before he knew what was happening. She detached Soad's mechanism from him, disintegrating it carefully in the process, and had him come with a float carrier and medical kit to the storeroom where he helped her do what could be done immediately for Alicar. Then they placed Alicar on the carrier and went to the Romango's control room with him.

As they arrived there, Soad found Telzey. There was a cold surging of psi, and the palms of her hands were suddenly wet. For a long moment then, Soad was looking at her as a man might look at a domestic animal which has turned unexpectedly intractable. She was prepared for an immediate attack, but none came. Gradually, the awareness of Soad withdrew, though not entirely.

Telzey let her breath out in a sigh. Her mind shield was tight; and whatever the Child of the Gods might be, it was unlikely that he could accomplish much in a direct assault on that shield. The danger should take other forms.

She said to Gulhas, "Give me verbal override on the computer," and to make sure there'd be no slips, she kept most of her attention on him as he went through the brief process, though he was no more able to go against her wishes now than she'd been able to go against those of Alicar. Some attention, however, she kept on the lingering shadowy presence of Soad, not knowing what that entity might be up to—and, particularly, not knowing where it was at the moment. It hadn't been in the vicinity of the Ralke Mine when she'd been scanning the area; she should have picked up some indication of the alien mentality otherwise. But the situation might have changed by now.

The Romango acknowledged her identity and control and asked for instructions.

"Activate the Ralke Mine's defense zone," she said.

"Activated."

She felt a little better. "You've been given the identification of a being called Soad, or the Child of the Gods?"

"I have. This is the recorded image."

A panel before Telzey became a viewscreen, and

in the screen appeared a picture much like the one she'd seen in Ponogan's mind as he dreamed: a great liquid-seeming globe rolling along the side of a desert dune under the starblaze.

She said, "Is Soad at present in your sensor range?"

"No."

Her tensions lessened again, but she remembered how far Alicar had been able to maneuver them in toward the mine. She said, "If you do sense it, inform us immediately."

"Complying."

She went on. "And if Soad appears within the defense zone, attack it with every weapon you have until it's destroyed."

There was the shortest of pauses. Then the computer said, "The instruction is not comprehensible."

Startled, Telzey glanced at Gulhas. He said, "That's correct. Soad told us to see to it that the mine's armament couldn't be turned against him, and the Romango was programmed accordingly. Your override doesn't affect that because the computer doesn't know it's been programmed. An order to attack Soad simply has no meaning for it."

"Then get it unprogrammed fast!" Telzey said. "But first have it put me in communicator contact with the Mannafra Federation Station." She hesitated, seeing the response in Gulhas's mind. "So it's been programmed against that, too!"

The Romango had, in fact, been programmed against letting a communication of any kind go out from the Ralke Mine. The Child of the Gods hadn't relied entirely on conversion and psi mechanisms to maintain its hold on the humans. Telzey asked a few more questions, saw how complete their isolation had been. Except for the automatic contacts with vehicles approaching the defense zone, the computer's external communication system was shut off. There was no other communicator at the mine, and the only air truck and two groundcars had been destroyed.

Nor would it be at all easy now to turn the Romango into a weapon against the Child of the Gods, or to restore the use of the communicator. Gulhas hadn't been involved in installing the prohibiting programs. Hille had let the machine calculate for him how it should be done, and how the programs then could be deleted from record and made inaccessible to its locators, leaving it unable to act on later instructions to erase something which for it had no existence.

Telzey then had Gulhas set the situation up as a theoretical problem. Could a method be developed to track down and eliminate such lost programs? The computer said it was possible, but warned that a number of the procedures involved might reduce it to uselessness before the task was accomplished.

Since it was effectively useless as it was, Telzey told Gulhas to go ahead. His pessimistic estimate was that if the job could be done, it should take several hours to carry it out. But that couldn't be helped.

She had time now to give attention again to other matters. Alicar was deeply sedated; unless and until they got him to a hospital, there was no more to be done for him. She'd scanned the remaining personnel occasionally, half expecting to find Soad's mechanisms attempting to make the same kind of awkward use of the unconscious bodies as they had of Ceveldt and Hille, but all was quiet in that area. It couldn't have made much difference in any case. The approaches to the computer room were sealed, and throughout the mine's structures every security lock controlled by the Romango had slammed shut. Even if the men had been awake, they wouldn't have been able to interfere with her here.

She turned to Soad's presence at the fringes of consciousness. Gradually and very cautiously—since she didn't know what he might do if he chose—she began to develop her awareness of him.

5

"Gulhas," she said presently.

The technician started, looked around at her. "Yes?"

"Will talking distract the computer?"

Gulhas shook his head glumly. "It's out of communication. There's nothing to indicate whether that's a malfunction or a necessary part of the tracing process. But it won't respond to any type of signal, and couldn't register our voices."

"It is still trying to trace out Hille's programs?"

"It's still doing something," Gulhas said. "I don't know what. Our problem set sections of it working against other sections. It may have destroyed itself in part and gone insane in its fashion. That was the risk we took."

"I know." Telzey reflected. "You can get a screen view of what it looks like outside, of the area around the mine?"

"Yes. A three hundred and sixty degree view. That screen on your left!" Gulhas pressed a button. The indicated screen lit up. He said, "You think Soad may be out there somewhere?"

"Not yet." Telzey's glance slipped over the screen, held on Mannafra's pale hot sun hanging low above the dunes. "How long before sunset?" she asked.

Gulhas looked at a console chronometer. "Perhaps half an hour."

"Does it get dark quickly after that?"

"Quite quickly in these latitudes. It will be night in approximately another half hour."

"I see." Telzey was silent a moment. Gulhas,

watching her, said abruptly, "You're a mentalist, aren't you?"

She glanced at him. "A telepath, a psi, yes."

"I thought you must be," Gulhas said. "It seemed the only explanation for what's happened." He cleared his throat. "I want to thank you. I still feel something like loyalty toward Soad, but I realize now that loyalty was forced on us. We never would have served such a creature of our own will."

"No, you hardly would," Telzey agreed.

"He seems to know what's been going on since you and Mr. Ralke arrived."

"Unfortunately, he does," she said.

"Then why hasn't he appeared?" Gulhas asked her. "You'd think he'd act immediately to restore the situation he created here."

Telzey said, "He can't move now. Sunlight would kill him. Even the starblaze produces more radiation than he likes, but he can stand that. He'll come when it's night. He's waiting."

"So we have till then!" Gulhas blinked at her. "That's why he always came at night for the oil—we thought it was simply that he was trying to reduce the chance of being seen from the air. You're certain he'll come?"

"Quite certain. He's changed his plans."

"In what way?"

Should she tell him? Telzey decided it could do no harm to weaken further his enforced subservience to Soad. She said, "He's given up on getting back the djeel oil Mr. Ralke took from the mine. He'd be safer having it, but he's been experimenting with what he's collected and thinks he already has as much as he really needs—especially if he adds to it what's been processed here during the past days. So he'll come for that."

"Then he'll leave?" Gulhas asked, staring at her.

"That's what he intends. We gave him a surprise

he didn't like today. He hadn't expected to have any trouble with humans."

"In that case, why not let him know he's welcome to the djeel oil?" Gulhas suggested. "Perhaps—"

Telzey shook her head.

"If we did, he wouldn't just pick it up and go," she said. "Everybody at the mine, dead or alive, would be going with him. He isn't leaving anybody behind to talk about the Children of the Gods—or about what they use djeel oil for either."

"No," Gulhas said after a moment. "You're right. He wouldn't want that." He reflected. "Can't you use telepathy to have someone outside send over a few aircars to pull us out of here?"

"It's not too likely," she told him. "I've been trying, but that kind of thing generally doesn't work when you most want it to."

"I see." Gulhas sighed heavily. "I'm not really myself yet," he remarked. "I know I should be horrified by this situation, but somehow I'm not extremely alarmed. It's as if someone else were sitting here . . ." He shrugged. "Well, I'll keep watching the Romango. If it gives me an opening, I'll cut in and let you know. Then we might be able to do something. But our prospects don't look good there either."

He swung about in the chair and settled himself again before the console. Telzey said nothing. There was no reason to tell Gulhas that she hadn't been letting him feel frightened. He knew enough now to make sure there'd be no lingering subjective hesitation to help her act against the Child of the Gods if the opportunity came. She'd equipped him with a provisional psi screen, which should reduce Soad's awareness of what went on in the technician's mind. But it couldn't be completely effective. The less Gulhas was told of what really counted here, the better.

She returned her attention fully to Soad. She'd found out a great deal about that entity. Soad didn't seem to have the equivalent of a human psi's shield; and apparently it was a while before he began to suspect that she might be gathering information through the contact between them. Then he'd suddenly interposed a confusion of meaningless psi impressions, which she wasn't trying to penetrate at present.

Soad was in a machine in the desert west of the Ralke Mine. Telzey wasn't sure of the distance, but it might be something like forty miles. The machine was almost completely buried in sand drifts and screened against metal-locating devices. She'd thought at first it was a spaceship; but it wasn't that, though it could serve as one. It was more like Soad's permanent home and base of operations, and in time of need apparently also his fortress—a single massive block threaded by a maze of chambers and narrow tunnels, through which his protean, semi-metallic body flowed with liquid smoothness. He'd been stranded on Mannafra with the machine for a long time.

He needed djeel oil to get away. He might have enough now, but his tests indicated it would be enough by a narrow margin at best. That made it essential to add the oil on hand at the Ralke Mine to his stores. If Telzey hadn't made an unanticipated nuisance of herself, there would have been no problem about it.

It seemed likely that his kind hadn't developed the ability to shape psi energy into killing bolts, as she and other human psis had done. Otherwise, he should have attacked as soon as he saw that she was threatening to interfere, at least temporarily, with his plans. So far, she'd made only a restrained use of the weapon herself, in knocking out the mine personnel.

Used to its full extent, she thought it might stop Soad. But that was a possibility to hold in reserve.

There was no doubt that the Children of the Gods were savagely formidable beings. They preyed on other species and warred regularly among themselves; and minds like that must be dangerously equipped, in ways still unknown to her. Any serious mistake she made about Soad now was likely to be a fatal one.

So she attempted no immediate new moves. She maintained light contact with the meaningless-seeming flow of psi impressions which veiled Soad's mentality, and probed cautiously at the mentality itself whenever she could, trying to outline further its alien strengths and weaknesses. She thought Soad might be doing much the same thing.

More distantly, Telzey probed also for the touch of any human mind she might use to inform the Federation Station of Soad's presence on Mannafra, and of the plight of the survivors at the Ralke Mine. She'd need luck there, particularly since she could afford to give only partial attention to it; and as the minutes passed, it seemed luck wasn't going to be with her. In the viewscreen, the dune shadows lengthened while the sun dropped toward the horizon. Then the sun was gone and the desert lay in shadow everywhere. Above it, the starblaze was brightening.

And, finally, there was a development.

Telzey wasn't immediately sure what it was. There was psi charge building up, and building up here, at the mine. She waited. Something took shape, was formed swiftly. And now she knew. Soad, having studied her, was constructing a slave mechanism specifically designed for her, an involved and heavily charged one. She didn't think it could affect her seriously through her shield, but she didn't care to take chances with the alien device. Her psi knives slashed through it, shredded and tore it apart, then took care of two designs she found beginning to attach themselves to Gulhas and Alicar.

Now she and Soad again had learned something about the other's capabilities; but Soad had learned more than she. That couldn't have been avoided; and since she was no longer giving anything away, she destroyed the other control mechanisms still functioning at the mine in quick sequence in the same manner. Frustrated anger washed about her as she did it—so he had intended to use those constructions in some way when he came.

Minutes later, she realized suddenly that he already was on the move.

"Gulhas," she said, "any change?"

He shook his head without looking around.

"None whatever!"

Telzey reached through the defensive screen she'd closed about his mind, and took full control of him.

She was sitting in the Romango's operator chair soon afterwards, while Gulhas lay stretched out on the floor beside Alicar's carrier. Both men were in an unconscious paralysis from which nothing, specifically new mechanisms employed by Soad, was likely to arouse them during the next few hours. So was everybody else at the mine. At least, Soad wouldn't be able to turn enslaved minds against her again in some still unpredictable way.

The Romango type of computer was unfamiliar, but that didn't make much difference now. If the machine resolved the blocks they'd set it to work against, a panel on the console before Telzey would turn green, informing her that the communication systems had been released. She'd be able to take the Romango under voice control then, assuming it was still functional. Her eyes moved between the panel and the screen which showed the surrounding desert, scanners defining every detail of the landscape as clearly as in bright daylight. Somewhere on the dunes, Soad would presently appear.

She knew the moment wasn't far away; and if the computer remained out of commission, the Ralke Mine's mechanical barriers would be no obstacle to Soad. His strange body could form its substance into heavy battering rams; he'd break through, flow inside, and when he came to her at last, she'd be destroyed. If that wasn't to happen, she must prevent it herself. Her psi weapons were ready, but she wouldn't begin to use them until she caught sight of the swiftly moving great shape in the screens. There was a personal limit to the sheer quantity of destructive energy she could channel into a single bolt, a personal limit also to the number of such bolts she could handle within a given time period. Having tested herself to the danger point, she knew rather closely what the limits were. At peak effort, she might last a little more than four minutes. If Soad could absorb such an assault and keep coming, she couldn't stop him. Nor would she know she'd failed. She'd be unconscious, probably close to death.

So she waited. Then it was Soad who struck first.

Telzey didn't realize at once that it was an attack. There'd been a gradual increase in the vividness of the random psi impressions Soad was pouring out as if he were trying to shroud himself more completely during his approach. The impressions were distracting enough; she had to give conscious effort now to maintain awareness of him. Then something like lines of fire flickered behind her eyes, blurring her physical vision, and a psi storm burst about her like shrieking sound, an impossibly swift swirling of hallucinations at every sensory level.

She knew then what was happening. Soad wasn't able to reach her mind directly through its shield. But he could let her face chaos. None of it was real, but she couldn't ignore what seemed to hammer at all her senses simultaneously. Her attention was torn this way and that.

It was sweeping to her through her psi contact with Soad. She could stop it in an instant by breaking the contact.

And that, of course, was what Soad intended. If he put her out of effective action during the critical period, the mine would have no defense against him. Telzey thought that if she waited any longer, he'd succeed. She either would lose contact with him and find herself unable to regain it in the short time left, or get bludgeoned into temporary insanity.

She lashed out with the heaviest bolt she could muster, sensed shock pass through Soad. The storm of illusion faltered. She struck again at once, and illusion was gone, replaced by reactions of agonized violence.

Soad had expected nothing like this. His kind never had encountered such a weapon. Telzey, committed now, slamming in bolt after bolt, searching for vital centers in the alien mind, felt him slow to a wavering halt, knew then that he'd already almost reached the perimeter of the mine's defense zone.

Stop him there—paralyze him . . .

His desperation and fury howled at her. Troublesome as she'd been, Soad had looked on the human psi as an essentially insignificant opponent. Belatedly now, he drove himself into the full destructive action he would have taken in an encounter with one of his own grim species. Chaos crashed at Telzey again, intensified, and her mind seemed to flow apart. She clung to shreds of awareness of Soad, of herself, slashed blindly into something horribly damaged but unyielding, was whirled through an exploding universe and knew abruptly that she was no longer reaching Soad, while the tumult still seemed to increase. Vast thunders shook her then, and blackness folded in about her.

"No, I didn't do it," Telzey said. "That Child of the Gods was simply too much for me! I was finished.

I did hurt him rather badly and slowed him down, but even so he'd come halfway through the defense zone when the computer finally got itself unblocked."

"And you ordered it to attack the creature?" asked Alicar Troneff. He was lying in a narrow hospital vat half filled with something that looked like green mud and smelled like vinegar, in the process of getting his beam-mangled left leg restructured.

Telzey shook her head.

"No. I was completely out of it by then. But I didn't have to give the order. I'd told the Romango earlier to cut loose on Soad if he showed up in the defense zone, and the instruction was recorded. So that's the first thing it did. The radiation guns finished him at once then, of course. He couldn't even stand sunlight. That was an awfully close call, Alicar!"

"Yes, it was," he agreed. He regarded her a moment. "And it seems I'm no longer in control of you—"

She smiled. "No."

"I never did trust you!" Alicar remarked dourly. "But how did it happen? You shouldn't have been able even to try to identify my controls, let alone tamper with them."

Telzey said, "If you'd left it at the specific controls, I probably wouldn't have been able to do it. At least, not in time. But you put me under a binding general injunction besides, remember? Whatever I did had to be what was best for you—in your interest. That overrode everything else. After you'd been shot, I realized it would be very much in your interests if I got back every scrap of ability I'd had, fast." She laughed. "And that broke the whole spell, Alicar! Including the injunction itself, since considering what might, or might not, be to your advantage from moment to moment in that situation certainly would have handicapped me in dealing with something like Soad."

He grunted, scratched his chin with his left hand. "Mind telling me where I am at present then?"

"Well, you're not going to like that part of it," Telzey said. "You're on a hospital ship of the Psychology Service."

He swore softly and bitterly. "I suspected something of the sort! I noticed the area is psi-blocked."

"Yes, it is," Telzey said. "But don't take it too hard. If I'd been looking out only for you, this still is exactly where you'd have wound up."

"What do you mean?"

"Soad wasn't the only problem we had there."

"Huh?"

"His supply of djeel," she said. "After we got to the mine and he decided it might be too risky to send you back for the oil you'd taken away, he began experimenting with what he'd collected to find out how close he was to the minimum he'd need. He miscalculated finally and started a reaction—the same kind of reaction that tore up Tosheer. That's why he was desperate to get what was at the mine. He needed it at once to balance out the reaction."

Alicar had paled. "And did—"

"No, it didn't," said Telzey. "But I'd picked that up from him at the end, and as far as I knew, it was going to happen. So as soon as I started thinking again, I had the Romango connect me with the Federation Station. When I mentioned psi was involved, the Service moved in, and everyone on Mannafra was evacuated in an awful hurry."

"But the djeel didn't go off then, after all?"

"Oh, it went off, all right," she said. "Four hours later. All it did though was to leave a hole in the desert about five hundred yards across where Soad's machine had been. It seems there simply hadn't been enough djeel affected by the reaction to do more than that."

❖   ❖   ❖

Alicar said after a moment, "Not that the information is likely to be of much use to me, but exactly what does djeel oil do?"

"I don't know exactly what it does," Telzey said. "And I'm not going to try to find out. In general though, processed djeel oil interacts with psi energy. The Service already knew that, though they haven't talked about it. As to what it does when it works as it's intended to, the Children of the Gods use it in connection with psi as their main form of transportation. They still have accidents with it, at least planned ones. Soad seems to have been in a fight with some of the others, and they started an uncontrolled psi reaction in the djeel of his machine that whipped him and the machine across intergalactic space—"

"Intergalactic space?" Alicar repeated.

Telzey said, "That's not really the way to put it. He was simply somewhere else, and then he was here in the Hub. But that somewhere else doesn't seem to have been even one of our neighbor galaxies! Still, he could have made it back to his starting point with a fresh supply of djeel oil. The reaction had almost exhausted what he had, and the nearest ore bed his machine could detect was on Mannafra. Soad barely made it there. But he had no way of processing the ore, so he had to wait then for something with enough intelligence to do it for him to come along. He waited a long time. Finally, you came."

Alicar nodded. "And, of course, that clears me! If I was under that monster's influence, I can't be held responsible for what's happened."

Telzey looked at him a moment.

"Well, Alicar," she said, "If you think you'll get the Service to believe that, give it a try! Since they've been checking around in your mind while you were out, I doubt you'll have much luck. And, frankly, I don't feel you should get away with it. Seven men died at your djeel mine; and the way you made use of me was cold-blooded, to say the least. Besides, I think—though that's not my business now—that I had several predecessors who didn't last very long as your controlled psi proxies. You've been letting others take chances for you for quite a while."

She added, "All things considered, I understand they're letting you off rather lightly. You were thinking of experimenting with djeel oil, and you'll get the chance, in one of the Service's high-risk space projects. You know too much about it to be turned loose anyway."

Alicar glowered at her.

"What about yourself?" he demanded. "You know at least as much as I do!"

Telzey stood up. "True," she said. "But the Service found out a while ago that I'm good at keeping secrets. I'll be starting back to Orado in a few minutes. I just stopped in to say good-bye."

He didn't reply. She went to the door, looked back at him.

"Cheer up, Alicar!" she told him. "It's still better than working for Soad until he decided to make a meal of you—which is what you would have been doing if things had turned out just a little differently!"

TI'S TOYS

1

An auburn-haired, petal-cheeked young woman who belonged in another reality came walking with feline grace along a restaurant terrace in Orado City where Telzey had stopped for lunch during a shopping excursion.

Telzey watched her approach. This, she decided, was quite strange. Going by her appearance and way of moving, the woman seemed to be someone she'd met before. But she knew they hadn't met before. She knew also, in a curiously definite manner, that the woman simply couldn't be on this terrace in Orado City. She existed in other dimensions, not here, not now.

The woman who didn't exist here glanced at Telzey in passing. There was no recognition in the look. Telzey shifted her chair slightly, watched the familiar-unfamiliar phantom take another table not far away, pick up an order disk. A very good-looking young woman with a smooth unsmiling face, fashionably and expensively dressed—and nobody else around seemed to find anything at all unreasonable in her presence.

So perhaps, Telzey reflected, it was her psi senses that found it unreasonable. She slipped out a thought probe, held it a moment. It produced no telepathic touch response, no suggestion of shielding. If the woman was psi, she was an atypical variety. She'd

265

taken a snack glass from the table dispenser by now, was sipping at it—

Comprehension came suddenly. No mystery after all, Telzey told herself, half amused, half disappointed. A year ago, she'd gone with some acquaintances to take in a Martridrama. The woman looked and walked exactly like one of the puppets they'd seen that evening, one who played a minor role but appeared enough of an individual to have left an impression in memory. No wonder it had seemed a slightly uncanny encounter—Martri puppets didn't go strolling around the city by themselves.

Another thought drifted up then, quite idly.

Or did they?

Telzey studied the pale profile again. Her skin began prickling. It was a most improper notion, but there might be a quick way of checking it. Some minds could be tapped easily, some with varying degrees of difficulty, some not at all. If this woman happened to be one of the easy ones, a few minutes of probing could establish what she was—or wasn't.

It took longer than that. Telzey had contact presently, but it remained tenuous and indistinct; she lost it repeatedly. Then, as she re-established it again, a little more definitely now, the woman finished her snack drink and stood up. Telzey slipped a pay chit for her lunch into the table's receptacle, waited till her quarry turned away, then followed her toward a terrace exit.

A Martri puppet was a biological organism superficially indistinguishable from a human being. It had a brain which could be programmed, and which responded to cues with human speech and human behavior. Whether something resembling the human mind could be associated with that kind of brain was a point Telzey hadn't found occasion to consider before. She was no Martriphile, didn't, in fact, particularly care for that form of entertainment.

There was mind here, and the blurred patterns she'd touched seemed human. But she hadn't picked up enough to say it couldn't be the mind of a Martri puppet. . . .

The woman took an airtaxi on another terrace of the shopping complex. As it rose from the platform, Telzey got into the next taxi in line and told the driver to follow the one that had just left. The driver spun his colleague's car into his screen.

"Don't know if I can," he said then. "He's heading up into heavy traffic."

Telzey smiled at him. "Double fare for trying!"

They set off promptly in pursuit. Telzey clung to her contact, began assembling additional data. Some minutes later, the driver announced, "Looks like we've lost them!"

She already knew it. Distance wasn't necessarily a factor in developing mind contact. In this case it had been a factor. The crosstown traffic stream was dense, close to the automatic reroute point. The impressions she'd been receiving, weak at best, had begun to be flooded out increasingly by intruding impressions from other minds. The car they'd been pursuing must be several miles away by now. She let contact fade, told the driver to return to the shopping complex, and settled back very thoughtfully in her seat.

Few Martriphiles saw anything objectionable in having puppets killed literally on stage when a drama called for it. It was an essential part of Martri realism. The puppets were biological machines; the emotions and reactions they displayed were programmed ones. They had no self-awareness—that was the theory.

What she'd found in the mind of the auburn-haired woman seemed less important than what she hadn't found there, though she'd been specifically searching for it.

That woman knew where she was, what she was doing. There'd been scraps of recent memory, some moment-to-moment observations, an intimation of underlying purpose. But she appeared to have no personal sense of herself. She knew she existed—an objective fact among other facts, with no more significance than the others.

In other words, she *did* seem to lack self-awareness. As far as Telzey had been able to make out, the term had no meaning for her. But the contact hadn't been solid enough or extensive enough to prove it.

On the face of it, Telzey was telling herself an hour later, the thing was preposterous. She'd had a wild notion, had tried to disprove it and failed. She'd even turned up some evidence which might seem to favor the notion. It remained wild. Why waste more time on the matter?

She bit her thumb irritably, dialed an information center for data on Martridramas and Martri puppets, went over the material when it arrived. There wasn't much there she didn't already know in a general way. A Martri stage was a programmed computer which in turn programmed the puppets, and directed them during a play under the general guidance of the dramateer. While a play was new, no two renditions of it were exactly the same. Computer and puppets retained some choice of action, directed always toward greater consistency, logic, and effect. Only when further improvement was no longer possible did a Martridrama remain frozen and glittering—a thing become perfect of its kind. It explained the continuing devotion of Martriphiles.

It didn't suggest that such a thing as a runaway puppet was a possibility.

The Martri unit which had put on the play she had seen was no longer on Orado. She could find out where it was at present, but there should be simpler ways of determining what she wanted to know immediately. A name had turned up repeatedly in her study of the Martri material . . . Wakote Ti. He was locally available. A big man. Multilevel scientist, industrial tycoon, millionaire, philanthropist, philosopher, artist, and art collector. Above all, a Martri specialist of specialists. Wakote Ti designed, grew, and merchandised the finest puppets in the Hub, built and programmed the most advanced Martri stages, had written over fifty of the most popular plays, and was a noted amateur dramateer.

A Martriphile relative of one of Telzey's friends turned out to be an admirer and business associate of Wakote Ti. He agreed to let Telzey know the next time the great man appeared at his laboratories in Draise, and to arrange for an interview with him.

"The legality of killing a puppet is regarded as unarguable," said Wakote Ti.

A college paper she'd be preparing on the legal niceties involved in the practice had been Telzey's ostensible reason for requesting the interview.

He shrugged. "But I simply couldn't bring myself to do it! They have life and a mentality, however limited and artificial they may be. Most importantly, they have personality, character. It's been programmed into them, of course, but, to my feeling, the distinction between puppets and humanity is one of degree rather than kind. They're unfinished people. They act always in accordance with their character, not necessarily in accordance with the wishes of the composer or dramateer. I've been surprised many times by the twists they've given the roles I assigned to them. Always valid ones! They can't be forced to deviate from what they are. In that respect they seem more honest than many of us."

Ti gave Telzey an engaging smile. He was a large, strongly muscled man, middle-aged, with a ruddy complexion and grizzled black hair. There was an air of controlled energy about him; and boundless energy he must have, to accomplish as much as he did. There was also an odd gentleness in gesture and voice. It was very easy to like Ti.

And he had a mind that couldn't be touched by a telepath. Telzey had known that after the first few minutes—probe-immune. Too bad! She'd sooner have drawn the information she wanted from him without giving him any inkling of what she was after.

"Do you use real people as models for them?" she asked. "I mean when they're being designed."

"Physically?"

"Yes."

Ti shook his head. "Not any one person. Many. They're ideal types."

Telzey hesitated, said, "I had an odd experience a while ago. I saw a woman who looked so exactly like a Martri puppet I'd seen in a play, I almost convinced myself it was the puppet who'd somehow walked off the stage and got lost in the world outside. I suppose that would be impossible?"

Ti laughed. "Oh, quite!"

"What makes it impossible?"

"Their limitations. A puppet can be programmed to perform satisfactorily in somewhere between twenty and thirty-five plays. One of ours, which is currently in commercial use, can handle forty-two roles of average complexity. I believe that's the record.

"At best, that's a very limited number of specific situations as compared with the endlessly shifting variety of situations in the real world. If a puppet were turned loose there, the input stream would very quickly overwhelm its response capacity, and it would simply stop operating."

"Theoretically," said Telzey, "couldn't the response capacity be pushed up to the point where a puppet could act like a person?"

"I can't say it's theoretically impossible," Ti said. "But it would require a new technology." He smiled. "And since there are quite enough real people around, there wouldn't be much point to it, would there?"

She shook her head. "Perhaps not."

"We're constantly experimenting, of course." Ti stood up. "There are a number of advanced models in various stages of development in another part of the building. They aren't usually shown to visitors, but if you'd like to see them, I'll make an exception."

"I'd very much like to!" Telzey said.

She decided she wasn't really convinced. New technologies were being developed regularly in other fields—why not in that of Martri puppetry? In any case, she might be able to settle the basic question now. She could try tapping the mind of one or the other of the advanced models he'd be showing her, and see how what she found compared with the patterns she'd traced in the mystery woman.

That plan was promptly discarded again. Ti had opened the door to a large office, and a big-boned young man sitting there at a desk looked up at her as they came in.

He was a telepath.

The chance meeting of two telepathic psis normally followed a standard etiquette. If neither was interested in developing the encounter, they gave no sign of knowing the other was a psi. If one was interested, he produced a mental identification. If the other failed to respond, the matter was dropped.

Neither Telzey nor the young man identified themselves. Ti, however, introduced them. "This is Linden, my secretary and assistant," he said; and to Linden, "This is Telzey Amberdon, who's interested in our puppets. I'm letting her see what we have in the vaults at present."

Linden, who had come to his feet, bowed and said, "You'd like me to show Miss Amberdon around?"

"No, I'll do that," said Ti. "I'm telling you so you'll know where I am."

That killed the notion of probing one of the puppets in the vaults. Now they'd met, it was too likely that Linden would become aware of any telepathic activity in the vicinity. Until she knew more, she didn't want to give any hint of her real interest in the puppets. There were other approaches she could use.

The half hour she spent in the vaults with Ti was otherwise informative. "This one," he said, "is part of an experiment designed to increase our production speed. Three weeks is still regarded as a quite respectable time in which to turn out a finished puppet. We've been able to do a good deal better than that for some while. With these models, starting from scratch and using new hypergrowth processes, we can produce a puppet programmed for fifteen plays in twenty-four hours." He beamed down at Telzey. "Of course, it's probably still faulty—it hasn't been fully tested yet. But we're on the way! Speed's sometimes important. Key puppets get damaged or destroyed, and most of some Martri unit's schedule may be held up until a replacement can be provided."

That night at her home in Orado City, Telzey had an uninvited visitor. She was half asleep when she sensed a cautious mental probe. It brought her instantly and completely awake, but she gave no immediate indication of having noticed anything. It mightn't be a deliberate intrusion.

However, it appeared then that it was quite deliberate. The other psi remained cautious. But the probing continued, a not too expert testing of the density of her screens, a search for a weakness in their patterns through which the mind behind them might be scanned or invaded.

Telzey decided presently she'd waited long enough. She loosened her screens abruptly, sent a psi bolt flashing back along the line of probe. It smacked into another screen. The probe vanished. Somebody somewhere probably had been knocked cold for an hour or so.

Izey lay awake a while, reflecting. She'd had a momentary impression of the personality of the prowler. Linden? It might have been. If so, what had he been after?

No immediate answer to that.

2

There was a permanent Martri stage in Orado City, and Telzey had intended taking in a show there next day—a Martridrama looked like the best opportunity now to get in some discreet study on puppet minds. Her experience with the psi prowler made her decide on a shift in plans. If it had been Wakote Ti's secretary who'd tried to probe her, then it could be that Ti had some reason to be interested in a telepath who was interested in Martri puppets, and her activities might be coming under observation for a while. Hence she should make anything she did in connection with the puppets as difficult to observe as she could—which included keeping away from the Orado City stage.

She made some ComWeb inquiries, arrived presently by pop transport shuttle in a town across the continent, where a Martridrama was in progress. She'd changed shuttles several times on the way. There'd been nothing to indicate she was being followed.

She bought a ticket at the stage, started up a hall toward the auditorium entry—

She was lying on her back on a couch, in a large room filled with warm sunshine. There was no one else in the room.

Shock held her immobilized for a moment.

It wasn't only that she didn't know where she was, or how she'd got there. Something about *her* seemed different, changed, profoundly wrong.

Realization came abruptly—every trace of psi sense was gone. She tried to reach out mentally into her surroundings, and it was like opening her eyes and still seeing nothing. Panic began to surge up in her then. She lay quiet, holding it off, until her breathing steadied again. Then she sat up on the couch, took inventory of what she could see here. The upper two-thirds of one side of the room was a single great window open on the world outside. Tree crowns were visible beyond it. Behind the trees, a mountain peak reached toward a blue sky. The room was simply furnished with a long table of polished dark wood, some chairs, the low couch on which she sat. The floor was carpeted. Two closed doors were in the wall across from the window.

Her clothes—white shirt, white shorts, white stockings, and moccasins—weren't the ones she'd been wearing.

None of that told her much, but meanwhile the threat of panic had withdrawn. She swung around, slid her legs over the edge of the couch. As she stood up, one of the doors opened, and Telzey watched herself walk into the room.

It jolted her again, but less severely. Take another girl of a size and bone structure close enough to her own, and a facsimile skin, eye tints, a few other touches, could produce an apparent duplicate. There'd be differences, but too minor to be noticeable. She didn't detect any immediately. The girl was dressed exactly as she was, wore her hair as she wore hers.

"Hello," Telzey said, as evenly as she could. "What's this game about?"

Her double came up, watching her soberly, stopped

a few feet away. "What's the last thing you remember before you woke up here?" she asked.

Her voice, too? Quite close to it, at any rate.

Telzey said guardedly, "Something like a flash of white light inside my head."

The girl nodded. "In Sombedaln."

"In Sombedaln. I was in a hall, going toward a door."

"You were about thirty feet from that door," said her double. "And behind it was the Martri auditorium. . . . Those are the last things I remember, too. What about psi? Has it been wiped out?"

Telzey studied her a moment. "Who are you?" she asked.

The double shrugged. "I don't know. I feel I'm Telzey Amberdon. But if I weren't, I might still feel that."

"If you're Telzey, who am I?" Telzey asked.

"Let's sit down," the double said. "I've been awake half an hour, and I've been told a few things. They hit me pretty hard. They'll probably hit you pretty hard."

They sat down on the edge of the couch. The double went on. "There's no way we could prove right now that I'm the real Telzey. But there might be a way we can prove that you are, and I'm not."

"How?"

"Psi," said the double. "Telzey used it. I can't use it now. I can't touch it. Nothing happens. If you—"

"I can't either," Telzey said.

The double drew a sighing breath.

"Then we don't know," she said. "What I've been told is that one of us is Telzey and the other is a Martri copy who thinks she's Telzey. A puppet called Gaziel. It was grown during the last two days like other puppets are grown, but it was engineered to turn into an exact duplicate of Telzey as she is now. It has her memories. It has her personality. They were programmed into it. So it feels it's Telzey."

Telzey said, after some seconds, "Ti?"

"Yes. There's probably no one else around who could have done it."

"No, I guess not. Why did he do it?"

"He said he'd tell us that at lunch. He was still talking to me when he saw in a screen that you'd come awake, and sent me down here to tell you what had happened."

"So he's been watching?" Telzey said.

The double nodded. "He wanted to observe your reactions."

"As to which of you is Telzey," said Ti, "and which is Gaziel, that's something I don't intend to let you know for a while!" He smiled engagingly across the lunch table at them. "Theoretically, of course, it would be quite possible that you're both puppets and that the original Telzey is somebody else. However, we want to have some temporary way of identifying you two as individuals."

He pulled a ring from his finger, put both hands under the table level, brought them to view again as fists. "You," he said to Telzey, "will guess which hand is holding the ring. If you guess correctly, you'll be referred to as Telzey for the time being, and you," he added to the double, "as Gaziel. Agreed?"

They nodded. "Left," Telzey said.

"Left it is!" said Ti, beaming at her, as he opened his hand and revealed the ring. He put it back on his finger, inquired of Linden, who made a fourth at the table, "Do you think she might have cheated by using psi?"

Linden glowered, said nothing. Ti laughed. "Linden isn't fond of Telzey at present," he remarked. "Did you know you knocked him out for almost two hours when he tried to investigate your mind?"

"I thought that might have happened," said Gaziel.

"He'd like to make you pay for it," said Ti. "So watch yourselves, little dears, or I may tell him to go ahead. Now as to your future—Telzey's absence hasn't been discovered yet. When it is, a well-laid trail will lead off Orado somewhere else, and it will seem she's disappeared there under circumstances suggesting she's no longer alive. I intend, you see, to keep her indefinitely."

"Why?" Telzey asked.

"She noticed something," said Ti. "It wouldn't have seemed too important if Linden hadn't found out she was a telepath."

"Then that *was* your puppet I saw?" Gaziel said. She glanced over at Telzey, added, "That one of us—Telzey—saw."

"That *we* saw," Telzey said. "That will be simplest for now."

Ti smiled. "You live up to my expectations! . . . Yes, it was my puppet. We needn't go further into that matter at present. As a telepath and with her curiosities aroused, Telzey might have become a serious problem, and I decided at once to collect her rather than follow the simpler route of having her eliminated. I had her background checked out, which confirmed the favorable opinions I'd formed during our discussion. She should make a most satisfactory subject. Within the past hour, she's revealed another very valuable quality."

"What's that?" Telzey said.

"Stability," Ti told her. "For some time, I've been interested in psis in my work, and with Linden's help I've been able to secure several of them before this." He shook his head. "They were generally poor material. Some couldn't even sustain the effect of realizing I had created an exact duplicate of them. They collapsed into uselessness. So, of course, did the duplicates. But look at you two! You adjusted immediately to the situation, have eaten with every indication of a good appetite, and are no doubt already preparing schemes to get away from old Ti."

Telzey said, "Just what is the situation? What are you planning to do with us?"

Ti smiled at her. "That will develop presently. There's no hurry about it."

"Another question," said Gaziel. "What difference does it make that Telzey's a psi when you've knocked out her psi ability?"

"Oh, that's not an irreversible condition," Ti informed her. "The ability will return. It's necessary to keep it repressed until I've learned how to harness it, so to speak."

"It will show up in the duplicate, too, not just in the original?" Gaziel asked.

Ti gave her an approving look. "Precisely one of the points I wish to establish! My puppets go out on various errands for me. Consider how valuable puppet agents with Telzey's psi talent could be—a rather formidable talent, as Linden here can attest!"

He pushed himself back from the table. "I've enjoyed your questions, but I have work to take care of now. For the moment, this must be enough. Stroll about and look over your new surroundings. You're on my private island. Two-thirds of it is an almost untouched wilderness. The remaining third is a cultivated estate, walled off from the forest beyond. You're restricted to the estate. If you tried to escape into the forest, you'd be recaptured. There are penalties for disobedience, but more importantly, the forest is the habitat of puppet extravaganzas—experimental fancies you wouldn't care to encounter! You're free to go where you like on the estate. The places I wouldn't wish you to investigate at present are outside your reach."

"They have some way of knowing which of us is which, of course," Gaziel remarked from behind

Telzey. They were threading their way through tall flowering shrubbery on the estate grounds.

"It would be a waste of time trying to find out what it is, though," Telzey said.

Gaziel agreed. The Martri duplicate might be marked in a number of ways detectable by instruments but not by human senses. "Would it disturb you very much if it turned out you weren't the original?" she said.

Telzey glanced back at her. "I'm sure it would," she said soberly. "You?"

Gaziel nodded. "I haven't thought about it too much, but it seems there's always been the feeling that I'm part of something that's been there a long, long time. It wouldn't be at all good to find out now that it was a false feeling—that I was only myself, with nothing behind me."

"And somebody who wasn't even there in any form a short while ago," Telzey added. "It couldn't help being disturbing! But that's what one of us is going to find out eventually. And, as Ti mentioned, we may both be duplicates. You know, our minds do seem to work identically—almost."

"Almost," said Gaziel. "They must have started becoming different minds as soon as we woke up. But it should be a while before the differences become too significant."

"That's something to remember," Telzey said.

They emerged from the flower thicket, saw the mountain again in the distance, looming above the trees. It rose at the far end of the island, in the forest area. The cultivated estate seemed to cover a great deal of ground. When they'd started out from a side door of the round gleaming-white building which stood approximately at its center, they couldn't see to the ends of it anywhere because groups of trees blocked the view in all directions. But they could see the mountain and had started off toward it.

If they kept on toward it, they would reach the wall which bordered the estate.

"There's one thing," Telzey said. "We can't ever be sure here whether Ti or somebody else isn't listening to what we say."

Gaziel nodded. "We'll have to take a chance on that."

"Right," Telzey said. "We wouldn't get very far if we stuck to sign language or counting on thinking the same way about everything."

They came to the estate wall ten minutes later. It was a wall designed to discourage at first glance any notions of climbing over it. Made of the same gleaming material as the central building, its smooth unbroken surface stretched up a good thirty-five feet above the ground. It curved away out of sight behind trees in either direction; but none of the trees they saw stood within a hundred feet of the wall. They turned left along it. Either there was a gate somewhere, or aircars were used to reach the forest.

They came to a gateway presently. Faint vehicle tracks in the grass led up to it from various directions. It was closed by a slab set into the wall, which appeared to be a sliding door. They could find no indication of a lock or other mechanism.

"Might be operated from the house."

It might be. In any case, the gateway seemed to be in regular use. They sat down on the grass some distance away to wait. And they'd hardly settled themselves when the doorslab drew silently back into the wall. A small enclosed ground vehicle came through; and the slab sealed the gateway again. The vehicle moved on a few yards, stopped. They hadn't been able to see who was inside, but now a small door opened near the front end. Linden stepped out and started toward them, scowling. They got warily to their feet.

"What are you doing here?" he asked as he came up.

"Looking around generally like Ti told us to," said Gaziel.

"He didn't tell you to sit here watching the gate, did he?"

"No," Telzey said. "But he didn't say not to."

"Well, I'm telling you not to," Linden said. "Move on! Don't let me find you around here again."

They moved on. When they glanced back presently, the vehicle had disappeared.

"That man really doesn't like us," Gaziel remarked thoughtfully.

"No, he doesn't," Telzey said. "Let's climb a tree and have a look at the forest."

They picked a suitable tree, went up it until they were above the level of the wall and could see beyond it. A paved road wound away from the area of the gate toward the mountain. That part of the island seemed to be almost covered with a dense stand of tropical trees; but, as on this side, no trees grew very close to the wall. They noticed no signs of animal life except for a few small fliers. Nor of what might be Ti's experimental Martri life.

Telzey said, "The gate controls are probably inside the cars they use when they go out there."

"Uh-huh—and the car Linden was in was armored." Gaziel had turned to study the surrounding stretches of the estate from their vantage point. "Look over there!" she said.

Telzey looked. "Gardening squad," she said after a moment. "Maybe we can find out something from them."

3

A flotilla of sixteen flat machines was gliding about purposefully a few inches above the lawns among the trees. An operator sat on each, manipulating controls. Two men on foot spoke now and then into communicators, evidently directing the work.

Gaziel nodded. "Watch that one!"

They'd approached with some caution, keeping behind trees for the most part, and hadn't yet been observed. But now one of the machines was coming in directly from the side toward the tree behind which they stood. The operator should be able to see them, but he was paying them no attention.

They studied him in uneasy speculation. There was nothing wrong about his motions; it was his expression. The eyes shifted around, but everything else seemed limply dead. The jaw hung half open; the lips drooped; the cheeks sagged. The machine came up almost to the tree, turned at a right angle, started off on another course.

Telzey said softly, "The other operators seem to be in about the same condition—whatever it is. But the supervisors look all right. Let's see if they'll talk."

They stepped out from behind the tree, started toward the closer of the two men on foot. He caught sight of them, whistled to draw his companion's attention.

"Well," he said, grinning amiably as they came up. "Dr. Ti's new guests, aren't you?" His gaze shifted between them. "And, uh, twin. Which is the human one?"

The other man, a big broad-shouldered fellow, joined them. Telzey shrugged. "We don't know. They wouldn't say."

The men stared. "Can't you tell?" the big one demanded.

"No," said Gaziel. "We both feel we're human." She added, "From what Dr. Ti told us, you mightn't be real people either and you wouldn't know it."

The two looked at each other and laughed.

"Not likely!" the big man said. "A wirehead doesn't have a bank account."

"You do? Outside?" Gaziel said.

"Uh-huh. A healthy one. My name's Remiol, by the way. The little runt's Eshan."

"We're Telzey and Gaziel," said Telzey. "And maybe you could make those bank accounts a lot healthier."

They looked at her, then shook their heads decidedly.

"We're not helping you get away, if that's what you mean," Remiol said. Eshan added, "There'd be no way of doing it if we wanted to. You kids just forget about that and settle down! This isn't a bad place if you keep out of trouble."

"You wouldn't have to help us get away exactly," Telzey said. "How often do you go to the mainland?"

There was a sudden momentary vagueness in their expressions which made her skin prickle.

"Well," Remiol said, frowning and speaking slowly as if he had some difficulty finding the words, "about as often as we feel like it, I'd say. I . . ." He hesitated, gave Eshan a puzzled look.

"You could take out a message," Gaziel said, watching him.

"Forget it!" said Eshan, who seemed unaware of anything unusual in Remiol's behavior. "We work for Dr. Ti. The pay's great and the life's easy. We aren't going to spoil that setup!"

"All right," Telzey said after a moment. "If you don't want to help us, maybe you won't mind telling us what the setup is."

"Wouldn't mind at all!" said Remiol, appearing to return abruptly to normal. He gave Telzey a friendly grin. "If Dr. Ti didn't want us to talk to you, we'd have been told. He's a good boss—you know where you are with him. Eshan, give the wireheads a food break and let's sit down with the girls."

They sat down in the grass together. Gaziel indicated

the machine operators with a hand motion. "You call them wireheads. They aren't humans but a sort of Martri work robot?"

"Not work robots," Remiol said. "Dr. Ti doesn't bother with those. These are regular puppets—maybe defectives, or some experiment, or just drama puppets who've played a few roles too many. When they get like this, they don't last more'n a year—then back they go to the stuff they grow them from. Meanwhile they're still plenty good for this kind of work."

"Might be a few real humans among them," Eshan said reflectively, looking over at the operators. "After a while, you don't think about it much—they're all programmed anyway."

"How do real humans get to be in that kind of shape?" Gaziel said.

The men shrugged. "Some experiment again," said Remiol. "A lot of important research going on in the big building here."

Telzey said, "How did you know one of us was a wirehead?"

"One of the lab workers told us," said Eshan. "She said Dr. Ti was mighty happy with the results. Some of his other twinning projects hadn't turned out so well."

Remiol winked at Telzey. "This one turned out perfect!"

She smiled. "You ever been on the other side of the wall?"

They had. Evidently, it was as unhealthy as Ti had indicated to go there unless one was in one of the small fleet of armored and armed vehicles designed for the purpose. The only really safe place on the forest side was a small control fort on the slope of the mountain, and that came under occasional attack. Eshan and Remiol described some of the Martri creations they'd seen.

"Why does Dr. Ti keep them around?" Gaziel asked.

"Uses them sometimes in the Martridramas he puts on here," said Remiol.

"And wait till you've seen one of those!" said Eshan. "That's real excitement! You don't see shows like that anywhere else."

"Otherwise," Remiol said, speaking of the forest puppets, "I guess it's research again. I worried at first about one of them coming over the wall. But it's never happened."

"Well, well!" said Ti. "Having a friendly gossip?"

He'd come floating out of a grove of trees on a hoverdisk and stopped a few feet away, holding the guide rail in his large hands.

"Hope you don't mind, Doctor," Remiol said. He and Eshan had got to their feet as Ti approached.

Ti smiled. "Mind? Not in the least. I'm greatly pleased that the new members of our little community have begun to make acquaintances so quickly. However, now we'll all be getting back to work, eh? Telzey and Gaziel, you can stand up here with me and we'll return to the house together."

They stepped up on the disk beside him, and it swung gently around and floated away, while the gardening machines lifted from the ground and began to reform into their interrupted work patterns.

"Fine fellows, those two!" said Ti, beaming down at Gaziel and Telzey. "They don't believe in overexerting themselves, of course. But then that isn't necessary here, and I prefer a relaxed and agreeable atmosphere around me."

Telzey said, "I understand it's sometimes rather exciting, too."

Ti chuckled. "That provides the counterpoint—the mental and emotional stimulus of the Martridrama! I need both. I'm always at my best here on the island! A room has been prepared for you two. You'll be shown there, and I'll come then shortly to introduce you to some of the most interesting sections of our establishment."

The groundcar Linden had been operating stood near the side door Telzey and Gaziel had used when they left the building. The hoverdisk went gliding past it to the door which opened as they approached, and into the building. In the hall beyond, it settled to the floor. They stepped down from it.

"Why, Challis!" said Ti heartily, gazing past Telzey. "What a pleasant surprise to see you back!"

Telzey and Gaziel looked around. A pale slender woman with light blue hair was coming across the hall toward them.

"This is my dear wife," Ti told them. He was smiling, but it seemed to Telzey that his face had lost some of its ruddy color. "She's been absent from the island for some time. I didn't know she was returning . . ." He turned to Challis as she came up. "These are two very promising recruits, Challis. You'll be interested in hearing about my plans for them."

Challis looked over at them with an expression which was neither friendly nor unfriendly. It might have been speculative. She had pale gray eyes and delicately beautiful features. She nodded slightly; and something stirred eerily in Telzey's mind.

Ti said, "I'll send someone to show you two to your room." He took Challis by the arm. "Come, my dear! I must hear what you've been doing."

He went off toward a door leading from the hall, Challis moving with supple ease beside him. As the door closed on the pair, Telzey glanced at Gaziel.

Gaziel said blandly, "You know, Ti's wife reminds me of someone. But I simply can't remember who it is."

So she's noticed it, too—the general similarity in appearance and motion between Challis and the auburn-haired puppet who'd come walking along the restaurant terrace in Orado City. . . .

A brisk elderly woman appeared a few minutes later. She led them to a sizable room two building levels above the hall, showed them what it contained, including a wardrobe filled with clothing made to their measurements, and departed after telling them to get dressed and wait here for Dr. Ti.

They selected other clothes, put them on. They were the sort of things Telzey might have bought for herself and evidently had been chosen with considerable care. They opened the door then and looked out. No one was in sight. They went quickly and quietly back downstairs to the entrance hall.

Linden's armored car still stood where they had seen it. There was no one in sight here either. They went over to the car. It took only a moment to establish that its two doors were locked, and that the locks were of the mechanical type.

They returned hurriedly to their room.

4

"Here," said Ti, "you see my current pool of human research material."

They were on an underground level of the central building, though the appearance of the area didn't suggest it. It was a large garden, enclosed by five-story building fronts. Above was a milky skylight. Approximately a hundred people were in sight in the garden and on the building galleries. Most of them were young adults. There were few children, fewer of the middle-aged, no oldsters at all. They were well-dressed, well-groomed; their faces were placid. They sat, stood, moved unhurriedly about, singly and in groups. Some talked; some were silent. The voices were low, the gestures leisurely.

"They're controlled by your Martri computer?" Telzey asked.

Ti nodded. "They've all been programmed, though to widely varying degrees. Since they're not being used at the moment, what you see is a random phase of the standard nonsleeping activity of each of them. But notice the group of five at the fountain! They've cued one another again into the identical discussion they've had possibly a thousand times before. We can vary the activity, of course, or reprogram a subject completely. I may put a few of them through their paces for you a little later."

"What's the purpose of doing this to them?" said Gaziel.

Ti said, "These are converging lines of study. On the one hand, as you're aware, I'm trying to see how close I can come to turning a Martri puppet into a fully functioning human being. On the other hand, I'm trying to complete the process of turning a human being into a Martri puppet, or into an entity that is indistinguishable from one. The same thing, of course, could be attempted at less highly evolved life levels. But using the human species is more interesting and has definite advantages—quite aside from the one that it's around in abundance, so there's no problem of picking up as much research material as I need, or the type I happen to want."

"Aren't you afraid of getting caught?" Gaziel said.

Ti smiled. "No. I'm quite careful. Every day, an amazing number of people in the Hub disappear, for many reasons. My private depredations don't affect the overall statistics."

Telzey said, "And after you've done it—after you've proved you can turn people into puppets and puppets into people—what are you going to do?"

Ti patted her shoulder. "That, my dear, needn't concern you at present. However, I do have some very interesting plans."

Gaziel looked up at him. "Is this where the one of us who's the original Telzey will go?"

"No," Ti said. "By no means. To consign her to the research pool would be inexcusably wasteful. Telzey, if matters work out satisfactorily, will become my assistant."

"In what way?"

"That woman puppet you were so curious about—you tried to investigate its mind, didn't you?"

Gaziel hesitated an instant. "Yes."

"What did you find?"

"Not too much. It got away from me too quickly. But it seemed to me that it had no sense of personal existence. It was there. But it was a nothing that did things."

"Did you learn what it was doing?"

"No."

Ti rubbed his jaw. "I'm not sure I believe that," he remarked thoughtfully. "But it makes no difference now. I have a number of such puppet agents. Obviously, a puppet which is to be employed in that manner should never be developed from one of the types that are in public dramatic use. That it happened in this case was a serious error; and the error was Linden's. I was very much annoyed with him. However, your ability to look into its mind is a demonstration of Telzey's potential value. Linden, as far as I can judge the matter, is a fairly capable telepath. But puppet minds are an almost complete blur to him, and when it comes to investigating human minds in the minute detail I would often prefer, he hasn't been too satisfactory. Aside from that, of course, he has many other time-absorbing duties.

"We already know that Telzey is a more capable telepath than Linden in at least two respects. When her psi functions have been restored, she should become extremely useful." Ti waved his hand about. "Consider these people! The degree of individual awareness they retain varies, depending on the extent and depth of the programming they've undergone. In some, it's not difficult to discern. In others, it's become almost impossible by present methods. That would be one of Telzey's tasks. She should find the work interesting enough."

"She'll be a wirehead?" Telzey said.

"Oh, yes, you'll both be programmed," Ti told her. "I could hardly count on your full collaboration otherwise, could I? But it'll be delicate work. Our previous experiments have indicated that programming psi minds presents special difficulties in any case, and I want to be quite sure that nothing goes wrong here. Your self-awareness shouldn't be affected for one thing." He smiled. "I believe I've come close to solving those problems. We'll see presently."

Telzey said, "What do you have in mind for the one who isn't Telzey?"

"Ah! Gaziel!" Ti's eyes sparkled. "I'm fascinated by the possibilities there. The question is whether our duplication processes have brought on the duplication of the original psi potential. There was no way of testing indirectly for that, but we should soon know. If they have, Gaziel will have become the first Martri psi. In any case, my dears, you can rest assured, whichever you may be, that each of you is as valued by me as the other and will be as carefully handled. I realize that you aren't reconciled to the situation, but that will come in time."

Telzey looked at him. Part lies, part truth. He'd handle them carefully, all right. Very carefully. They had value. And he'd weave, if they couldn't prevent it, a tightening net of compulsions about them they'd never escape undestroyed. What self-awareness they'd have left finally might be on the level of that of his gardening supervisors. . . .

"Eshan and Remiol are wireheads, too, aren't they?" she said.

Ti nodded. "Aside from Linden and myself and at present you two, everyone on the island is—to use that loose expression—a wirehead. I have over a hundred and fifty human employees here, and, like the two with whom you spoke, they're all loyal, contented people."

"But they don't have big bank accounts outside and aren't allowed off the island by themselves?" Telzey said.

Ti's eyebrows lifted.

"Certainly not!" he said. "Those are pleasant illusions they maintain. There are too many sharp inquiring minds out there to risk arrangements like that. Besides, while I have a great deal of money, I also have a great many uses for it. Why should I go to unnecessary expense?"

"We didn't really think you had," Gaziel said.

"And now," said Ti, stopping before a small door, "you are about to enjoy a privilege granted to none other of our employees! Behind this door is the brain and nerve center of Ti's Island—the Dramateer Room of the Martri computer." He took out two keys, held their tips to two points on the door's surface. After a moment, the keys sank slowly into the door. Ti twisted them in turn, withdrew them. The door—a thick ponderous door—swung slowly into the room beyond. Ti motioned Telzey and Gaziel inside, followed them through.

"We're now within the computer," he said, "and this room, like the entire section, is heavily shielded. Not that we expect trouble. Only Linden and I have access here. No one else even knows where the Dramateer Room is. As my assistants-to-be, however, you should be introduced to it."

The room wasn't large. It was long, narrow, low-ceilinged. At the end nearest the door was a sunken control complex with two seats. Ti tapped the wall.

"The computer extends downward for three levels from here. I don't imagine you've been behind a Martri stage before?"

They shook their heads.

"A good deal of mystery is made of it," Ti said. "But the difficulty lies in the basic programming of the computer. That takes a master! If anything at all is botched, the machine never quite recovers. Few Martri computers in existence might be said to approach perfection. This one comes perhaps closest to it, though it must operate on a much wider scale than any other built so far."

"You programmed it?" Telzey asked.

Ti looked surprised. "Of course! Who else could have been entrusted with it? It demanded the utmost of my skills and discernment. But as for the handling of the computer—the work of the dramateer—that isn't really complicated at all. Linden lacks genius but is technically almost as accomplished at it as I am. You two probably will be able to operate the computer efficiently and to direct Martridramas within a few months. After you've been here a year, I expect to find you composing your own dramas."

He stepped down into the control complex, settled into one of the seats, took a brimless cap of wire mesh from a recess and fitted it over his head. "A dramateer cap," he said. "It's not used here, but few dramas are directed from here. Our Martri Stage covers the entire island and the body of water immediately surrounding it, and usually Linden and I prefer to be members of the audience. You're aware that the computer has the capability of modifying a drama while it's being enacted. On occasion, such a modification could endanger the audience. When it happens, the caps enable us to override the computer. That's almost their only purpose."

"How does it work?" Gaziel asked.

Ti tapped the top of his head. "Through micro-contacts in my skull," he said. "The dramateer usually verbalizes my instructions, but it's not necessary. The thought, if precise enough, is sufficient. It's interesting that no one knows what makes that possible."

He indicated the wall at the far end of the room with a nod. "A check screen. I'll show you a few of the forest puppets."

His hands flicked with practiced quickness about the controls, and a view appeared in the screen—a squat low building with sloping walls, standing in a wide clearing among trees. That must be the control fort Remiol and Eshan had talked about.

The screen flickered. Telzey felt a pang in the center of her forehead. It faded, returned. She frowned. She almost never got headaches. . . .

Image in the screen—heavily built creature digging in the ground with clawed feet. Gaziel watched Ti, lips slightly parted, blue eyes intent. Ti talking: "—no precise natural counterpart but we've given it a viable metabolism and, if you will, viable instincts. It's programmed to nourish itself, and does. Weight over two tons—"

The pain—a rather mild pain—in Telzey's head shifted to her temples. It might be an indication of something other than present tensions.

An inexperienced or clumsy attempt by a telepath to probe a resistant human mind could produce reactions which in turn produced the symptom of a moderately aching head.

And Linden was a clumsy psi.

It could be the human original he was trying to probe, Telzey thought, but it could as well be the Martri copy, whose head presumably would ache identically. Linden might be playing his own game—attempting to establish secret control over Ti's new tools before he had normal psi defenses to contend with. . . . Whichever she was, that could be a mistake!

If she was resisting the attempt, then some buried psi part of her of which she hadn't been conscious was active—and was now being stimulated by use.

Let him keep on probing! It couldn't harm at all. . . .

"What do you think of that beauty?" Ti asked her with a benign smile.

A new thing in the screen. A thing that moved like a thick sheet of slowly flowing yellowish oil along the ground between the trees. Two dark eyes bulged from the forward end. Telzey cleared her throat. "Sort of repulsive," she remarked.

"Yes, and far from harmless. Hunger is programmed into it, and it's no vegetarian. If we allowed it to satisfy its urges indiscriminately, there'd be a constant need to replenish the forest fauna. I'll impel it now into an attack on the fort."

The flowing mass abruptly shifted direction and picked up speed. Ti tracked it through the forest for a minute or two, then flicked the screen back to a view of the fort. Moments later, the glider came out into the clearing, front end raised, a fanged, oddly glassy-looking mouth gaping wide at its tip. It slapped itself against the side of the fort. Gaziel said, "Could it get in?"

Ti chuckled comfortably. "Yes, indeed! It can compress itself almost to paper thinness, and if permitted, it would soon locate the gun slits and enter through one of them. But the fort's well armed. When one of our self-sustaining monsters threatens to slip from computer control, the fort is manned and the rogue is directed or lured into attacking it. The guns will destroy any of them, though it takes a good deal longer to do than if they were natural animals of comparable size." He smiled. "For them, too, I have plans, though those plans are still far from fruition."

He shut off the screen, turned down a number of switches, and got out of the control chair. "We're putting on a full Martridrama after dinner tonight, in honor of your appearance among us," he told them. "Perhaps you'd like to select one you think you'd enjoy seeing. If you'll come down here, I'll show you how to scan through samples of our repertoire."

They stepped down into the pit, took the console seats. Ti explained the controls, moved back, and stood watching their faces as they began the scan. Telzey and Gaziel kept their eyes fixed on the small screens before them, studied each drama sample produced briefly, went on to the next. Several minutes passed in silence, broken only by an intermittent muted whisper of puppet voices from the screens. Finally Ti asked blandly, "Have you found something you'd like?"

Telzey shrugged. "It all *seems* as if it might be interesting enough," she said. "But it's difficult to tell much from these samples." She glanced at Gaziel. "What do you think?"

Gaziel, smooth face expressionless, said, "Why don't you pick one out, Ti? You'd make a better selection than we could."

Ti showed even white teeth in an irritated smile. "You aren't easy to unsettle!" he said. "Very well, I'll choose one. One of my favorites to which I've added a few twists since showing it last." He looked at his watch. "You've seen enough for today. Run along and entertain yourself! Dinner will be in three hours. It will be a formal one, and we'll have company, so I want to see you come beautifully gowned and styled. Do you know your way back to your room from here?"

They said they did, followed him out of the Dramateer Room, watched as he sealed and locked the door. Then they started back to their room. As they turned into a passage on the next level up, they checked, startled.

5

The blue-haired woman Ti had called Challis stood
motionless thirty feet away, looking at them. Pale eyes,
pale face . . . the skin of Telzey's back began to crawl.
Perhaps it was only the unexpectedness of the
encounter, but she remembered how Ti had lost color
when Challis first appeared; and the thought came
that she might feel this way if she suddenly saw a
ghost and knew what it was.

Challis lifted a hand now, beckoned to them.
They started hesitantly forward. She turned aside as
they came up, went to an open door, and through
it. They glanced at each other.

"I think we'd better see what she wants," Telzey
said quietly.

Gaziel nodded, looking quite as reluctant about it
as Telzey felt. "Probably."

They went to the door. A narrow dim-lit corridor
led off it. Challis was walking up the corridor, some
distance away. They exchanged glances again.

"Let's go."

They slipped into the corridor, started after Challis.
The door closed silently behind them. They came out,
after several corridor turns, into a low wide room,
quite bare—the interior of a box. Diffused light
poured from floor, ceiling, the four walls. The sur-
faces looked like highly polished metal but cast no
reflections.

"Nothing reaches here," Challis said to them. "We
can talk." She had a low musical voice which at first
didn't seem to match her appearance, then did. "Don't
be alarmed by me. I came here only to talk to you."

They looked at her a moment. "Where did you
come from?" Gaziel asked.

"From inside."

"Inside?"

"Inside the machine. I'm usually there, or seem to be. I don't really give much attention to it. Now and then—not often, I believe—I'm told to come out."

"Who tells you to come out?" Telzey said carefully.

Challis' light-gray eyes regarded her.

"The minds," she said. "The machine thinks on many levels. Thinking forms minds. We didn't plan that. It developed. They're there; they do their work. That's the way they feel it should be. You understand?"

They nodded hesitantly.

"He knows they're there," Challis said. "He sees the indications. He can affect some of them. Many more are inaccessible to him at present, but it's been noted that he's again modified and extended the duplicative processes. He's done things that are quite new, and now he's brought in the new model who is one of you. The model's been analyzed and it was found that it incorporates a quality through which he should be able to gain access to any of the minds in the machine. That's not wanted. If the duplicate made of the model—the other of you—has the same quality, that's wanted even less. If it's been duplicated once, it can be duplicated many times. And he will duplicate it many times. It's not his way to make limited use of a successful model. He'll make duplicates enough to control every mind in the machine."

"*We* don't want that," Gaziel said.

Challis' eyes shifted to her.

"It won't happen," she said, "if he's unable to use either of you for his purpose. It's known that you have high resistive levels to programming, but it's questionable whether you can maintain those levels indefinitely. Therefore the model and its duplicate should remove themselves permanently from the area of the machine. That's the logical and most satisfactory solution."

Telzey glanced at Gaziel. "We'd very much like to do it," she said. "Can you help us get off the island?"

Challis frowned.

"I suppose there's a way to get off the island," she said slowly. "I remember other places."

"Do you remember where they keep the aircars here?" said Gaziel.

"Aircars?" Challis repeated. She looked thoughtful. "Yes, he has aircars. They're somewhere in the structure. However, if the model and the duplicate aren't able to leave the area, they should destroy themselves. The minds will provide you with opportunities for self-destruction. If you fail, direct procedures will be developed to delete you."

Telzey said after a moment, "But they won't help us get off the island?"

Challis shook her head. "The island is the Martri stage. Things come to it; things leave it. I remember other places. Therefore, there should be a way off it. The way isn't known. The minds can't help you in that."

"The aircars—"

"There are aircars somewhere in the structure. Their exact location isn't known."

Telzey said, "There's still another solution."

"What?"

"The minds could delete him instead."

"No, that's not a solution," said Challis. "He's essential in the maintenance of the universe of the machine. He can't be deleted."

"Who are you?" Gaziel asked.

Challis looked at her.

"I seem to be Challis. But when I think about it, as I'm doing at this moment, it seems it can't be. Challis knew many things I don't know. She helped him in the design of the machine. Her puppet designs were better than his own, though he's learned much more than she ever knew. And she was one of our most successful models herself.

Many puppet lines were her copies, modified in various ways."

She paused reflectively.

"Something must have happened to Challis," she told them. "She isn't there now, except as I seem to be her. I'm a pattern of some of her copies in the machine, and no longer accessible to him. He's tried to delete me, but minds always deflect the deletion instructions while indicating they've been carried out. Now and then, as happened here, they make another copy of her in the vats, and I'm programmed to it and told what to do. That's disturbing to him."

Challis was silent for a moment again. Then she added, "It appears I've given you the message. Go back the way you came. Avoid doing what he intends you to do. If you can deactivate the override system, do it. When you have the opportunity, leave the area or destroy yourselves. Either solution will be satisfactory."

She turned away and started off across the glowing floor.

"Challis," said Gaziel.

Challis looked back.

"Do the minds know which of us two is the model?" Gaziel asked.

"That's of no concern to them now," said Challis.

She went on. They looked after her, at each other, turned back toward the corridor. Telzey's head still ached mildly. It continued to ache off and on for another hour. Then that stopped. She didn't mention it to Gaziel.

There were thirty-six people at dinner, most of them island employees. Telzey and Gaziel were introduced. No mention was made of a puppet double, and no one commented on their identical appearance, though there might have been a good deal of silent speculation. Telzey gathered from her table companions that they regarded themselves as highly privileged to be

here and to be working for Dr. Ti. They were ardent
Martriphiles and spoke of Ti's genius in reverent terms.
Once she noticed Linden watching her from the other
end of the table. She gave him a pleasant smile, and
he looked away, expression unchanged.

Shortly after dinner, the group left the building by
the main entrance. Something waited for them outside—a shell-like device, a miniature auditorium with
curved rows of comfortable chairs. They found their
places, Telzey sitting beside Gaziel, and the shell lifted
into the air and went floating away across the estate.
Night had come by then. The familiar magic of the
starblaze hung above the island. White globe lights
shone here and there among the trees. The shell
drifted down presently to a point where the estate
touched a narrow bay of the sea, and became sta-
tionary twenty feet above the ground. Ti and Linden,
seated at opposite ends of the shell, took out override caps and fitted the woven mesh over their heads.

There was a single deep bell note. The anticipatory
murmur talk ended abruptly. The starblaze dimmed
out, and stillness closed about them. All light faded.

Then—a curtain shifting again—they looked out at
the shore of a tossing sea, a great sun lifting above
the horizon, and the white sails of a tall ship sweeping
in toward them out of history. There was a sound in
the air that was roar of sea and wail of wind and
splendid music.

Ti's Martridrama had begun.

"I liked the first act," Telzey said judiciously.

"But the rest I'd sooner not have seen," said Gaziel.

Ti looked at them. The others of his emotionally
depleted audience had gone off to wherever their
quarters in the complex were. "Well, it takes time to
develop a Martriphile," he observed mildly.

They nodded.

"I guess that's it," Telzey said.

They went to their room, got into their beds. Telzey lay awake a while, looking out through the big open window at tree branches stirring under the starblaze. There was a clean salt sea smell and night coolness on the breeze. She heard dim sounds in the distance. She shivered for a moment under the covers.

The Martridrama had been horrible. Ti played horrible games.

A throbbing set in at her temples. Linden was working late. This time, it lasted only about twenty minutes.

She slept.

She came awake again. Gaziel was sitting up in bed on the other side of the room. They looked at each other silently and without moving in the shadowed dimness.

A faint music had begun somewhere. It might be coming out of the walls of the room, or from beyond the window. They couldn't tell. But it was music they'd heard earlier that night, in the final part of the Martridrama. It swelled gradually, and the view outside the window began to blur, dimmed out by slow pulsing waves of cold drama light which spilled into the room and washed over the floor. A cluster of vague images flickered over the walls, then another.

They edged out of bed, met in the center of the room. For an instant, the floor trembled beneath them.

Telzey whispered unsteadily, "I guess Ti's putting us on stage!"

Gaziel gave her a look which said, *We'll hope it's just Ti!* "Let's see if we can get out of this."

They backed off toward the door. Telzey caught the knob, twisted, tugged. The knob seemed suddenly to melt in her hand, was gone.

"Over there!" Gaziel whispered.

There was blackness beyond the window now. A blackness which shifted and stirred. The outlines of the room were moving, began to flow giddily about them. Then it was no longer the room.

They stood on the path of a twisting ravine, lit fitfully by reddish flames lifting out of the rocks here and there, leaping over the ground and vanishing again. The upper part of the ravine was lost in shadows which seemed to press down closely on it. On either side of the path, drawn back from it only a little, was unquiet motion, a suggestion of shapes, outlines, which appeared to be never quite the same or in the same place from moment to moment.

They looked back. Something squat and black was walking up the path toward them, its outlines wavering here and there as if it were composed of dense smoke. They turned away from it, started along the path. It was wide enough to let them walk side by side, but not much wider.

Gaziel breathed, "I wish Ti hadn't picked this one!"

Telzey was wishing it, too. Perhaps they were in no real danger. Ti certainly shouldn't be willing to waste them if they made a mistake. But they'd seen Martridrama puppets die puppet deaths in this ravine tonight; and if the minds of which Challis had spoken existed and were watching, and if Ti was *not* watching closely enough, opportunities for their destruction could be provided too readily here.

"We'd better act exactly as if it's real!" Telzey murmured.

"I know."

To get safely out of the ravine, it was required to keep walking and not leave the path. The black death which followed wouldn't overtake them unless they stopped. Whatever moved along the sides of the ravine couldn't reach them on the path. There were sounds and near-sounds about them, whispers and a hungry whining, wisps of not quite audible laughter, and once a sharp snarl that seemed inches from

Telzey's ear. They kept their eyes on the path, which mightn't be too stable, ignoring what could be noticed along the periphery of their vision.

It shouldn't go on much longer, Telzey told herself presently—and then a cowled faceless figure, the shape of a man but twice the height of a man, rose out of the path ahead and blocked their way.

They came to a startled stop. That figure hadn't appeared in the ravine scene they'd watched. They glanced back. The smoky black thing was less than twenty feet away, striding steadily closer. On either side, there was an abrupt eager clustering of flickering images. The cowled figure remained motionless. They went on toward it. As they seemed about to touch it, it vanished. But the other shapes continued to seethe about now in a growing fury of activity.

The ravine vanished.

They halted again—in a quiet, dim-lit passage, a familiar one. There was an open door twelve feet away. They went through it, drew it shut, were back in the room assigned to them. It looked ordinary enough. Outside the window, tree branches rustled in a sea wind under the starblaze. There were no unusual sounds in the air.

Telzey drew a long breath, murmured, "Looks like the show is over!"

Gaziel nodded. "Ti must have used his override to cut it short."

Their eyes met uneasily for a moment. There wasn't much question that somebody hadn't intended to let them get out of that scene alive! It hadn't been Ti; and it didn't seem very likely that it could have been Linden. . . .

Telzey sighed. "Well," she said, "everyone's probably had enough entertainment for tonight! We'd better get some sleep while we can."

6

Ti had a brooding look about him at the breakfast table. He studied their faces for some moments after they sat down, then inquired how they felt.

"Fine," said Telzey. She smiled at him. "Are just the three of us having breakfast here this morning?"

"Linden's at work," said Ti.

"We thought your wife might be eating with us," Gaziel told him.

Ti made a sound between a grunt and a laugh.

"She died during the night," he said. "I expected it. She never lasts long."

"Eh?" said Telzey.

"She was a defective puppet," Ti explained. "An early model, made in the image of my wife Challis, who suffered a fatal accident some years ago. A computer error which I've been unable to eradicate causes a copy of the puppet to be produced in the growth vats from time to time. It regards itself as Challis, and because of its physical similarity to her, I don't like to disillusion it or dispose of it." He shrugged. "I have a profound aversion to the thing, but its defects always destroy it again within a limited number of hours."

He gnawed his lip, observed dourly, "Your appetites seem undiminished! You slept well?"

They nodded. "Except for the Martri stuff, of course," said Gaziel.

"What was the purpose of that?" Telzey asked.

"A reaction test," said Ti. "It didn't disturb you?"

"It was scary enough," Telzey said. "We knew *you* didn't intend to kill us, but at the end it looked like the computer might be getting carried away. Did you have to override it?"

Ti nodded. "Twice, as a matter of fact! It's quite

puzzling! That's a well-established sequence—it's been a long time since the computer or a puppet attempted a logic modification."

"Perhaps it was because we weren't programmed puppets," Gaziel suggested. "Or because one of us wasn't a puppet at all."

Ti shook his head. "Under the circumstances, that should make no difference." His gaze shifted from one to the other. For an instant, something unpleasant flickered in his eyes. "You may be almost too stable!" he remarked. "Well, we shall see—"

"What will we be doing today?" Telzey asked.

"I'm not certain," Ti said. "There may be various developments. You'll be on your own part of the time, at any rate, but don't go roaming around the estate. Stay in the building area where I can have you paged if I want you."

They nodded. Gaziel said, "There must be plenty of interesting things to see in the complex. We'll look around."

They had some quite definite plans for looking around. The longer Ti stayed busy with other matters during the following hours, the better . . .

It didn't work out exactly as they'd hoped then. They'd finished breakfast and excused themselves. Gaziel had got out of her chair; Telzey was beginning to get out of hers.

There was something like a dazzling white flash inside her head.

And she was in darkness. Reclining in some kind of very comfortable chair—comfortable except for the fact that she was securely fastened to it. Cool stillness about her. Then a voice.

It wasn't mind-talk, and it wasn't sound picked up by her ears. Some stimulation was being applied to audio centers of her brain.

"You must relax and not resist," she heard. "You've

been brought awake because you must try consciously not to resist."

Cold fear welled through her. Ti had showed them the programming annex of the Martri computer yesterday. She was there now—they were trying to program her! Something was fastened about her skull. Feelings like worm-crawlings stirred in her head.

She tried to push the feelings away. They stopped.

"You must relax," said the voice in her audio centers. "You must not resist. Think of relaxing and of not resisting."

The worm-crawlings began again. She pushed at them.

"You are not thinking of relaxing and not resisting," said the voice. "Try to think of that."

So the programming annex knew what she was and was not thinking. She was linked into the computer. Ti had said that if a thought was specific enough—

"We've been trying for almost two hours to get you programmed," Ti said. "What was your experience?"

"Well, I couldn't have been awake for more than the last ten minutes," Telzey said, her expression sullen. "I don't know what happened the rest of the time."

Linden said from a console across the room, "We want to know what happened while you were awake."

"It felt like something was pushing around inside my head," Telzey said.

"Nothing else?" said Ti.

"Oh, there was a kind of noise now and then."

"Only a noise? Can you describe it?"

She shrugged. "I don't know how to describe it. It was just a noise. That was inside my head, too." She shivered. "I didn't like any of it! I don't want to be programmed, Ti!"

"Oh, you'll have to be programmed," Ti said

reasonably. "Let's be sensible about this. Were you trying to resist the process?"

"I didn't know how to resist it," Telzey said. "But I certainly didn't want it to happen!"

Ti rubbed his chin, looking at her, asked Linden, "How does the annex respond now?"

"Perfectly," Linden said.

"We'll see how the other subject reacts. Telzey, you wait outside—that door over there. Linden will conduct you out of the annex in a few minutes."

Telzey found Gaziel standing in the adjoining room. Their eyes met. "Did you get programmed?" Gaziel asked.

Telzey shook her head.

"No. Some difficulty with the annex—almost like it didn't want me to be programmed."

Gaziel's eyelids flickered; she nodded quickly, came over, watching the door, slipped something into Telzey's dress pocket, stepped back. "I suppose it's my turn now," she said.

"Yes," Telzey said. "They were talking about it. It's like little worms pushing around inside your head, and there's a noise. Not too bad really, but you won't like it. You'll wish there were a way you could override it."

Gaziel nodded again.

"I hope it won't take with me either," she said. "The idea of walking around programmed is something I can't stand!"

"If it doesn't work on you, maybe Ti will give up," Telzey said.

The door opened and Linden came out. He looked at Gaziel, jerked his thumb at the doorway. "Dr. Ti wants to see you now," he told her.

"Good luck!" Telzey said to Gaziel. Gaziel nodded, walked into the other room. Linden closed the door on her.

"Come along," he said to Telzey. "Dr. Ti's letting

you have the run of the building, but he doesn't want
you in the programming annex while he's working on
the other one."

They started from the room. Telzey said,
"Linden—"

"Dr. Linden," Linden said coldly.

Telzey nodded. "Dr. Linden. I know you don't like
me—"

"Quite right," Linden said. "I don't like you. You've
brought me nothing but trouble with Dr. Ti since you
first showed up in Draise! In particular, I didn't
appreciate that psi trick you pulled on me."

"Well, that was self-defense," Telzey said reasonably. "What would you do if you found someone trying
to pry around in your mind? That is, if you could do
what I did. . . ." She looked reflective. "I don't suppose you can, though."

Linden gave her an angry look.

"But even if you don't like me, or us," Telzey went
on, "you really should prefer it if Ti can't get us
programmed. You're important to him because you're
the only telepath he has. But if it turns out we're both
psis, or even only the original one, and he can control us, you won't be nearly so important anymore."

Linden's expression was watchful now. "You're
suggesting that I interfere with the process?" he said
sardonically.

Telzey shrugged. "Well, whatever you think you can
do."

Linden made a snorting sound.

"I'll inform Dr. Ti of this conversation," he told
her. He opened another door. "Now get out of my
sight!"

She got. Linden had been pushed as far as seemed
judicious at present.

She took the first elevator she saw to the third floor
above ground level, went quickly to their room. The
item Gaziel had placed in her pocket was a plastic

package the size of her thumb. She unsealed it, unfolded the piece of paper inside, which was covered with her private shorthand. She read:

Comm office on level seven, sect. eighteen. It's there. Usable? Janitor-guard, Togelt, buttered up, won't bother you. Comm man, Rodeen, blurs up like Remiol on stim. Can be hypnoed straight then! No one else around. Got paged before finished. Carry on. Luck.

Me.

Telzey pulled open the wardrobe, got out a blouse and skirt combination close enough to what Gaziel had been wearing to pass inspection by Togelt and Rodeen, went to a mirror and began arranging her hair to match that of her double. Gaziel had made good use of the morning! Locating a communicator with which they might be able to get out a message had been high on their immediate priority list, second only to discovering where the island's air vehicles were kept.

Telzey went still suddenly, eyes meeting those of her mirror image. Then she nodded gently to herself. The prod she'd given Linden had produced quick results! He was worried about the possibility that Ti might acquire one or two controlled psis who could outmatch him unless he established his own controls first.

Her head was aching again.

Preparations completed; she got out a small map of the central complex she'd picked up in an office while Ti was conducting them around the day before. It was informative quite as much in what it didn't show as in what it did. Sizable sections of the upper levels obviously weren't being shown. Neither was most of the area occupied by the Martri computer, including the Dramateer Room. Presumably these were all places barred to Ti's general personnel. That narrowed down the search for aircars considerably.

They should be in one of the nonindicated places
which was also near the outer wall of the complex.

Rodeen was thin, sandy-haired, in his early twen-
ties. He smiled happily at sight of Telzey. His was a
lonely job; and Gaziel had left him with the impression that he'd been explaining the island's communication system to her when Ti had her paged. Telzey
let him retain the impression. A few minutes later,
she inquired when he'd last been off Ti's island.
Rodeen's eyes glazed over. He was already well under
the influence.

She hadn't worked much with ordinary hypnosis
because there'd been no reason for it. Psi, when it
could be used, was more effective, more dependable.
But in her general study of the mind, she'd learned
a good deal about the subject. Rodeen, of course, was
programmed against thinking about the communicator
which would reach other points on Orado; it took
about twenty minutes to work through that. By then,
he was no longer in the least aware of where he was
or what he was doing. He opened a safe, brought out
the communicator, set it on a table.

Telzey looked it over, asked Rodeen a few questions. Paused then. Quick footsteps came along the
passage outside the office. She went to the door.

"What did Togelt think when he saw you?" she
asked.

"That I was your twin, of course," Gaziel said.
"Amazing similarity!"

"Ti sure gave up on you fast!"

Gaziel smiled briefly. "You sure got that programming annex paralyzed! Nothing would happen at all—
that's why he gave up. How did you override it?"

"It knew what I was thinking. So I thought the
situation was an override emergency which should be
referred to the computer director," Telzey said. "There
was a kind of whistling in my head then, which
probably was the director. I referred to the message

we got from Challis and indicated that letting us be
programmed by Ti couldn't be to the advantage of
the Martri minds. Apparently, they saw it. The annex
went out of business almost at once. Did Ti call for
Linden again?" Her headache had stopped some five
minutes ago.

Gaziel nodded. "We'll have some time to ourselves
again—Ti'll page us when he wants us."

She'd come in through the door. Her gaze went
to the table, and she glanced quickly at Telzey's face.
"So you found it. We can't use it?"

"Not until we get the key that turns it on," Telzey
said, "and probably only Ti knows where it is. Nobody
else ever uses the gadget, not even Linden."

"No good to us at the moment then." Gaziel looked
at Rodeen, who was smiling thoughtfully at nothing.
"In case we get hold of the key," she said, "let's put
in a little posthypnotic work on him so we can just
snap him back into the trance another time. . . ."

They left the office shortly, having restored Rodeen
to a normal condition, with memories now only of
a brief but enjoyable conversation he'd had with the
twins.

Telzey glanced at her watch. "Past lunch time," she
remarked. "But Ti may stay busy a while today. Let's
line up the best spots to look for aircars."

The complex map was consulted. They set off for
another upper-level section.

"That blur-and-hypnotize them approach," said
Gaziel, "might be a way to get ourselves a gun—if
they had armed guards standing around."

Telzey glanced at her. So far, they'd seen no armed
guards in the complex. With Ti's employees as solidly programmed as they were, he didn't have much
need even for locked doors. "The troops he keeps to
hunt down rambunctious forest things have guns, of
course," she said. "But they're pretty heavy caliber."

Gaziel nodded. "I was thinking of something more inconspicuous—something we could shove under Ti's or Linden's nose if it got to be that kind of situation."

"We'll keep our eyes open," Telzey said. "But we should be able to work out a better way than that."

"Several, I think," said Gaziel. She checked suddenly. "Speaking of keeping our eyes open—"

"Yes?"

"That's an elevator door over there, isn't it?"

"That's what their elevator doors look like," Telzey agreed. She paused. "You think that one doesn't show on the map?"

"Not as I remember it," Gaziel said. "Let's check—section three seventeen dash three."

They spread the map out on the floor, knelt beside it. Telzey shifted the scale enlargement indicator to the section number. The map surface went blank; then a map of the section appeared. "We're—here!" said Gaziel, finger tapping the map. "And, right, that elevator doesn't show—doesn't exist for programmed personnel. Let's see where it goes!"

They opened the door, looked inside. There was an on-off switch, nothing to indicate where the elevator would take them. "Might step out into Ti's office," Telzey said.

Gaziel shrugged. "He knows we're exploring around."

"Yes. But he could be in a pretty sour mood right now." Telzey shrugged in turn. "Well, come on!"

They stepped into the elevator. The door closed, and Telzey turned the switch. Some seconds passed. The door opened again.

They stood motionless, looking out and around. Gaziel glanced over at Telzey, shook her head briefly.

"It can't be as easy as *that*!" she murmured.

Telzey bit her lip. "Unless it's locked . . . or unless there's a barrier field that won't pass it. . . ."

The door had opened at the back of a large sun-filled porch garden. Seemingly, at least, the porch was open to the cloudless sky beyond. There were rock arrangements, small trees, flower beds stirring in a warm breeze. Near the far end was a graveled open area—and a small aircar was parked on it. No one was in sight.

No, Telzey thought, escape from Ti's island couldn't be so simple a matter! There must be some reason why they couldn't use the aircar. But they had to find out what the reason was. . . .

They moved forward warily together, a few steps, emerged from the elevator, looked around, listening, tensed. Gaziel started forward again. Telzey suddenly caught her arm, hauled hard. Back they went stumbling into the elevator.

"What's the matter?" Gaziel whispered.

Telzey passed her hand over her mouth, shook her head. "Close!" she muttered. "The sun—"

Gaziel looked. Her eyes widened in comprehension. "Should be overhead, this time of day!"

"Yes, it should . . ." It wasn't. Its position indicated it might be midmorning or midafternoon on the garden porch.

The garden porch—a Martri stage.

"They set it up for us!" Gaziel murmured. "We asked Challis where we could find aircars."

Telzey nodded. "So they spotted us coming and spun in a scene from some drama—to get us out there, on stage!"

"They almost did. . . . Look at it now!" Gaziel said softly. "Nothing's moving."

The garden porch had gone still, dead still. No eddy of air disturbed the flower beds; no leaf lifted. There was total silence about them.

"They've stopped the scene," Telzey whispered. "Waiting to see if we won't still try to reach the car."

"And find out we've become part of the action! Wonder what— It's moving again!"

The garden growth stirred lazily, as before. A breeze touched their faces. Some seconds passed. Then they heard a hoarse shout, a high cry of fear, and, moments later, running steps. A young man and a young woman burst into view from behind a cluster of shrubs, darted toward the aircar.

The Martri scene began to fade. Off to the left, another man was rising out of concealment, holding a gun in both hands. He took unhurried aim at the pair as they pulled open the door of the car. Then flame tore through the two bodies, continued to slash into them as they dropped writhing to the ground, dimming out swiftly now with everything about them.

Telzey turned the elevator switch. The door slid shut. They looked at each other.

"If you hadn't noticed the sun!" Gaziel said. She drew in a long breath. "If we'd— The computer would hardly have had to modify that scene at all to get us deleted!"

"Wish those minds weren't in quite such a hurry about that," Telzey said.

The elevator door opened. They stepped out into the hall from which they'd entered it.

7

"Oh, certainly we have permanent Martri stages here in the complex," Ti said at lunch. "They're generally off limits to personnel, but you two are quite free to prowl about there if you like. The equipment's foolproof. Remind me to give you a chart tomorrow to help you locate some of them."

He appeared affable, though bemused. Now and

then he regarded them speculatively. He'd spent all
morning, he told them, trying to track down the
problem in the programming annex. The annex, a
relatively simple piece of Martri equipment, was
Linden's responsibility; but Linden was limited.

Ti shrugged.

"I'll work it out," he said. "It's possible I'll have
to modify the overall programming approach used on
you. Meanwhile—well, Linden has business offices on
the level above your room. I'd like you to go there
after you finish. He's to carry your general indoctrination a step further this afternoon. Go up the stairs
nearest your room and turn left. You won't have any
trouble finding him."

They didn't. They came to a main office first, which
was a sizable one where half a dozen chatty and
cheerful-looking young women were at work. One of
them stood up and came over.

"Dr. Linden?" she said. "Oh, yes. He's expecting
you."

They followed her through another room to Linden's
private office. He arose behind his desk as they came
in.

"Dr. Ti informed me you were on your way here,"
he said. He looked at the young woman. "I'll be out
of the office a while. Take care of things."

"How long do you expect to be gone, sir?" she
asked.

"Between one and two hours." Linden gave Telzey
and Gaziel a twisted smile. "Let's go!"

He led them up a narrow passage to an alcove
where sunlight flooded in through colored windows.
Here was a door. Linden unlocked it but didn't open
it immediately.

"I'll explain the situation," he said, turning back
to them. "I told Dr. Ti in Draise that Telzey might
become dangerous, and advised him to have her
destroyed. But he was intrigued by the possibilities

he felt he saw in her, and in creating puppet doubles of her." Linden shrugged. "Well, that's his affair. He's been attempting to shake you up psychologically— Martri programming takes hold best on minds that have been reduced to a state of general uncertainty. However, his methods haven't worked very well. And he now suspects you may have deliberately caused the malfunction of the programming annex this morning. So he's decided to try a different approach— and for once in this matter, I find myself in complete accord with him!"

"What's the new approach?" Telzey asked guardedly.

Linden smiled.

"We have devices in the room behind that door," he said, "which were designed to put difficult subjects into a docile and compliant frame of mind. I'm happy to say that various phases of the process are accompanied by intense physical pain—and believe me, you're getting the full treatment!"

Telzey said, "One of us is Gaziel. She hasn't done anything to you. Why do you want to give her the full treatment?"

Linden shrugged. "Why not? Subjectively you're both Telzey, and as far as I'm concerned, you're equally insufferable. You'll find out which of you is Telzey in fact when you're supposed to. I'll make no distinctions now. When I feel you've been sufficiently conditioned, I'll put you through the psi depressant procedure again to make sure no problems begin to develop in that area. Then I'll report to Dr. Ti that his subjects are ready for further programming sessions."

He smiled at Telzey.

"You," he said, "had the effrontery to suggest that it would be to my advantage if Dr. Ti gave up his plan to program the two of you. I don't agree. He feels now that the experiment probably will fail as such, but will produce valuable new information. So he'll continue with it until neither of you has enough mind left to be worth further study. I see nothing undesirable in that prospect!"

He opened the door he'd unlocked, glanced back down the passage in the direction of the offices.

"This kind of thing could disturb the illusions of the work staff," he remarked. "Subjects experiencing the docility treatment make a remarkable amount of noise. But the place is thoroughly soundproofed, so that's no problem. You're at liberty to yowl your heads off in there. I'll enjoy listening to it. In you go!"

He took each of them by an arm and shoved them through the door into the room beyond. He followed, drawing the door shut behind him, and locked it from inside. As he started to turn back toward them, Telzey dropped forward and wrapped herself around his ankles. Linden staggered off balance and came down, half on top of her. Gaziel came down on top of him.

It was a brisk scramble. Linden was somewhat awkward but big enough and strong enough to have handled either of them readily. Together, hissing, clawing for his eyes, clinging to his arms, kicking at his legs, they weren't being at all readily handled. They rolled across the room in a close-locked, rapidly shifting tangle, Linden trying to work an arm free and making inarticulate sounds of surprised fury. A table tipped over; a variety of instruments which had been standing on it crashed to the floor. Telzey saw one of them within reach, let go of Linden, snatched it up—mainly plastic but heavy—slammed it down on Linden's skull. He yelled. She swung down again with both hands, as hard as she could. The gadget broke, and Linden lay still.

"His keys—" she gasped.

"Got them!" Gaziel held up a flat purse.

They went quickly through Linden's pockets, found nothing else they could use. He was breathing noisily but hadn't moved again. "We'll just leave him locked in here," Telzey said as they scrambled to their feet. "That's a solid door—and he said the place was sound-proof. . . ."

They unlocked the door, drew it cautiously open. Everything was quiet. They slipped out, locked the door, started down the passage. Somewhere another door opened; they heard feminine voices, turned back and ducked into the alcove across from the door.

"Once we're past the office area, we should be able to make it downstairs all right," Telzey said softly.

Gaziel studied her a moment, lips pursed. "Now we start them thinking we're hiding out in the forest, eh?"

"Yes. Looks like the best move, doesn't it?"

Gaziel nodded. "Wish we'd had a few more hours to prepare for it, though. Getting to the aircars is likely to be a problem."

"I know. It can't be helped."

"No," Gaziel agreed. "Between Linden and Ti planning to mess up our minds and the Martri computer waiting around to introduce some fancy deletion procedure, we'd better try to clear out of here the first chance we get! And this is it."

The side door to Linden's armored car opened to the third key Telzey tried. They slipped inside, drew the door shut.

Telzey settled into the driver's seat. "I'll get it started. Look around and see what he has here."

"Handguns he has here," Gaziel announced a moment later.

"A kind we can use?"

"Well, they're heavy things. I'll find out how they work." There were clicking noises as she checked one of the guns. The car engine came to life. Telzey eased the vehicle back from the wall of the building, turned it around. It went off quickly across the lawn toward the nearest stand of garden trees. Gaziel looked over at her. "It handles all right?"

"It handles fine! Beautiful car. I'll come up on the taloaks from the other side."

"We can use the guns," Gaziel said. "I'll tie two of them to my belt for now. Nothing much else."

Taloaks made great climbing trees, and a sizable grove of them stretched to within a hundred yards of the residential area of the main building complex. Linden's car slipped up on the trees from the forest side of the estate, edged in among thickets of ornamental ground cover, stopped in the center of one of the densest clusters of growth. Its side door opened. Telzey climbed from the driver's seat to the top of the door, then onto the top of the car, followed by Gaziel. Each of them now had one of the big handguns Gaziel had discovered fastened to her dress belt. A thick taloak branch hung low over the car. They scrambled up to it, moved on.

Some five minutes later, they sat high in a tree near the edge of the grove, straddling branches six feet apart. They could watch much of the ground in front of the building through the leaves, were safely out of sight themselves. So far, there'd been no indication of activity in the area.

"It might be a while before they start looking for Linden," Gaziel said presently.

"Unless Ti checks in to see how our indoctrination is coming along," Telzey said.

"Yes, he's likely—"

Gaziel's voice broke off. Telzey looked over at her. She sat still, frozen, staring down at Linden's gun which she was holding in both hands.

"I'm sorry," Telzey said after a moment. "I wasn't really sure myself until just now."

Gaziel slowly refastened the gun to her belt, lifted her head.

"I'm nothing," she said, gray-faced. "A copy! A wirehead."

"You're me," Telzey said, watching her.

Gaziel shook her head. "I'm not you. You felt me get that order?"

Telzey nodded. "Ti's working through the computer. You were to take control of me—use the gun if you had to—then get me and Linden's car back to the main entrance."

"And I'd have done it!" Gaziel said. "I was about to point the gun at you. You canceled the order—"

"Yes. I blanked out the computer contact."

Gaziel drew a ragged breath. "So you're back to being a psi," she said. "How did that happen?"

"Linden's been trying to probe me. Off and on since yesterday. He pushed open a few channels finally. I finished doing the rest of it about an hour ago."

Gaziel nodded. "And you took him over after you knocked him out. What's the real situation now?"

Telzey said, "Ti did check. He had his own key to the treatment rooms. I woke Linden up and had him tell Ti a story that got things boiling. What it amounts to is that we put guns on Linden and got his personal standard communicator from him before we knocked him out. We plan to find a spot in the forest where we can hole up in his car and call for help. So they're coming after us with their other armored cars—eleven of them—in case the order Ti just gave you doesn't bring us back."

Gaziel stared at her a moment, face still ashen. "Ti's going with them?"

"Yes. And he's taking Linden along. They're about to start. I'm still in contact with Linden, of course, and I know how to get to the aircars. But they've stationed some guards at key points in the complex. It will take us some time to maneuver around those, and if we're seen, Ti could come back with his patrols to stop us. So we have to make sure they can't get back." She added, "There they are now!"

A groundcar swept around the curve of the building complex. Others followed at fifty-yard intervals. They arrowed across the lawns in the direction of the forest wall, vanished behind trees. Telzey said, "Ti and Linden are in five and six. We can start down." She looked at Gaziel. "You are coming with me, aren't you?"

"Oh, I'm coming with you!" Gaziel said. "I'll help any way I can. I simply want all this to stop!"

8

Telzey locked the last control into position, pushed her hair back out of her face, looked over at Gaziel watching her from the edge of the console pit. A low heavy humming filled the Dramateer Room. "We're set," she said.

"Any detectable reaction from the minds yet?" asked Gaziel.

Telzey bit her lip reflectively. "Well, they're here, all right!" she said. "Around us. I can feel them. Like a whole army. Spooky! But they're just watching, I think. They haven't tried to interfere, so it doesn't seem they're going to be a problem. After all, we are getting out. It's what they wanted, and they seem to understand that we're doing it." She added, "Not that I'd like to tempt them by walking across one of their stages! But we won't have to do that."

"Just what have you been doing?" Gaziel said. "I couldn't begin to follow it."

"I couldn't either," Telzey said. "Linden did it. I sort of watched myself go through the motions." She flexed her fingers, looked at them. "Ti's forest things have cut the groundcars off from the gate and are chasing them up to the fort. One of the cars—well, they caught it. Ti and Linden already are in the fort. Ti's tried to contact the main complex, but the comm line leads through the computer and it's been cut off there. He knows the computer must be doing it, of course, and he's tried to override."

"The override system's deactivated?"

"That's the *first* thing we did," Telzey said. "They'll need a calculated minimum of thirty-two minutes to wipe out the forest puppets from the fort."

"That will get us to the aircars?"

"It should, easily. But we'll have a good deal more time. The first groundcar that comes back through the gate into the estate will start up a section of a Ti Martridrama—the third act of *Armageddon Five*. That's about what it sounds like, and its stage is the whole estate except for the central building complex. Ti won't be able to get here until Act Three's played out—and it takes over an hour. We want to keep him bottled up as long as possible, of course—"

She jerked suddenly, went still for a moment, shook her head.

"Linden just died!" she said then. "Ti shot him. He must have realized finally I had Linden under control. Well, it shouldn't change matters much now."

She got out of the console chair. "Come on! Mainly we'll have to be a little careful. I know where the guards are, but it'll be better if we don't run into anybody else either."

It took them eighteen minutes to work their way unseen through the building, and get into the aircar depot. A line of supply trucks stood there, and four smaller aircars. They got into one of the cars. The roof of the depot opened as Telzey lifted the car toward it. The car halted at that point.

From a car window, they aimed Linden's guns at the power section of the nearest truck. After some seconds, it exploded, and the trucks next to it were instantly engulfed in flames. A chain reaction raced along the line of vehicles. They closed the window, went on up. Nobody was going to follow them from Ti's island. The energy field overhead dissolved at their approach, closed again below them. The car went racing off across the sunlit sea toward the Southern Mainland.

Gaziel sighed beside Telzey, laid the gun she'd been using down on the seat.

"I did have the thought," she said, "that if I shot you now and pushed you out, I could be Telzey Amberdon."

Telzey nodded.

"I knew you'd be having the thought," she said, "because I would have had it. And I knew you wouldn't do it then. Because I wouldn't do it."

"No," Gaziel said. "Only one of us can be the original. That's not your fault." She smiled, lazily, for the first time in an hour. "Am I dying, Telzey?"

"No," Telzey said. "You're going to sleep, other me. Don't fight it."

Some six weeks later, Telzey sat at a small table in a lounge of the Orado City Space Terminal, musing on information she'd received a few hours before.

It happened now and then that some prominent citizen of the Federation didn't so much disappear as find himself becoming gradually erased. It might be reported for a while that he was traveling, had been seen in one place or another, and eventually then that he'd settled down in quiet retirement, nobody seemed to know quite where. Meanwhile his enterprises were drifting into other hands, his properties dissolved, his name was mentioned with decreasing frequency. In the end, even former personal acquaintances seemed almost to forget he'd existed.

Thus it would be with Wakote Ti. He'd demanded a public trial. With his marvelous toys taken from him and an end made to the delights of unrestricted experimentation, he'd felt strongly that at least the world must be made aware of the full extent of his genius. The Federation's Psychology Service, which sometimes seemed the final arbiter on what was good for the Federation and sometimes not, decreed otherwise. The world would be told nothing, and Ti would be erased. He'd remain active, however; the Service always found a use for genius of any kind.

"What about all the new principles he discovered?" Telzey had asked Klayung, her Service acquaintance. "He must have been way ahead of anyone else there."

"To the best of our knowledge," said Klayung, "he was very far ahead of anyone else."

"Will that be suppressed now?"

"Not indefinitely. His theories and procedures are being carefully recorded. But they won't be brought into use for a while. Some toys seem best reserved for wiser children than we have around generally at present."

It was on record that Ti had deeded a private island to the planetary government, which would turn it into the site of a university. The illusory bank accounts of his innocent employees had acquired sudden reality. The less innocent employees were in Rehabilitation. His puppets and Martri equipment had disappeared.

And Gaziel—

Telzey watched a girl in a gray business suit come into the lounge, sent out a light thought to her.

"Over here!"

Acknowledgment returned as lightly. The girl came up to the table, sat down across from Telzey.

"You're taller than I am now, aren't you?" Telzey said.

Gaziel smiled. "By about half an inch."

Taller, more slender. The hollows under the cheek-
bones were more pronounced. There'd been a shift
in the voice tones.

"They tell me I'll go on changing for about a year
before I'm the way I want to be," Gaziel said.
"There'll still be a good deal of similarity between
us then, but no one would think I'm your twin." She
regarded Telzey soberly. "I thought I didn't really want
to see you again before I left. Now I'm glad I asked
you to meet me here."

"So am I," Telzey said.

"I've become the sort of psi you are," said Gaziel.
"Ti guessed right about that." She smiled briefly.
"Some of it's surprised the Service a little."

"I knew it before we left the island," Telzey said.
"You had everything I had. It just hadn't come awake."

"Why didn't you tell me?"

"I didn't dare do anything about you myself. I just
got you to the Service as quickly as I could."

Gaziel nodded slowly. "I was on the edge then,
wasn't I? I remember it. Have they told you how I've
been doing?"

"No. They wouldn't. They said that if you wanted
me to know, you'd tell me."

"I see." Gaziel was silent a moment. "Well, I want
you to know. I hated you for a while. It wasn't reasonable, but I felt you were really the horrid change-
ling who'd pushed me out of *my* life, away from *my*
family and friends. That was even after they'd taken
the puppet contacts out of my head. I could think
of explanations why Ti had planted them there, in the
real Telzey." She smiled. "We're quite ingenious, aren't
we?"

"Yes, we are," Telzey said.

"I got past that finally. I knew I wasn't Telzey and
never had been. I was Gaziel, product of Wakote Ti's
last and most advanced experiment. Then, for a while
again, I was tempted. By that offer. I could become

Gaziel Amberdon, Telzey's identical twin, newly arrived on Orado—step into a ready-made family, a ready-made life, a ready-made lie. Everything really could be quite simple for me. That was a cruel offer you made me, Telzey."

"Yes, it was cruel," Telzey said. "You had to have a chance to see if it was what you wanted."

"You knew I wouldn't want it?"

"I knew, all right. You'd have stayed a copy then, even if no one else guessed it."

Gaziel nodded. "I'm thanking you for the offer now. It did help me decide to become Gaziel who'll be herself and nobody's copy."

"I'd like to think," Telzey told her, "that this isn't the last time we'll be meeting."

"When I'm free of the Telzey pattern and have my own pattern all the way, I'll want to meet you again," Gaziel said. "I'll look you up." She regarded Telzey a moment, smiled. "In three or four years, I think."

"What will you be doing?"

"I'll work for the Service a while. Not indefinitely. After that, I'll see. Did you know I was one of Ti's heirs?"

"One of his heirs?"

"He isn't dead, of course. I drew my inheritance in advance. I used your legal schooling and found I could make out a rather strong case for paternal responsibility on Ti's part toward me. It was quite a lot of money, but he didn't argue much about it. I think I frighten him now. He's in a nervous condition anyway."

"What about?" Telzey said.

"Well, that Martri computer he had installed on the island is supposedly deactivated. The Service feels it's a bit too advanced for any general use at present. But Ti complains that Challis still comes around now and then. I wouldn't know—nobody else has run into her so far. It seems he arranged for the fatal accident the original Challis had. . . ." Gaziel glanced at her watch, stood up. "Time to go aboard. Good-bye, Telzey!"

"Good-bye," Telzey said. She looked after Gaziel as she turned away. Klayung, who wouldn't discuss Gaziel otherwise, had said thoughtfully, "By the time she's through with herself, she'll be a remarkably formidable human being—"

Gaziel checked suddenly, looked back. "Poor old Ti!" she said, laughing. "He didn't really have much of a chance, did he?"

"Not against the two of us," Telzey said. "Whatever he tried, we'd have got him one way or another."

THE SYMBIOTES

1

Trigger had been shopping at Wehall's that morning, winding up with lunch on one of the store's terrace restaurants. She had finished, and was leaning back in her chair contemplatively when a tiny agitated-sounding voice spoke to her.

"Good lady," it said, "you have a kind face! I'm a helpless fugitive and an enemy is looking for me. Would you let me hide in your handbag until he goes away?"

The words seemed to have come from the surface of the table. Someone's idea of a joke . . . Trigger looked casually around, expecting to discover an acquaintance. People sat at tables here and there about the terrace, but no one was at all near her. And she saw no one she knew.

"Good lady, please! There isn't much time!"

She shrugged. Why not go along with the humorist?

"Where are you?" she asked, in a conspiratorially low tone. "I don't see you."

"Between the large blue utensil and the smaller white one. I don't dare show myself. The abominable Blethro wasn't far behind me!"

Trigger glanced at the blue pitcher on the table, moved it a few inches back from a square white sandwich warmer. Her eyes widened briefly. Then she laughed.

One of Wehall's advertising stunts! A manikin, a miniature male figure, crouched beside the pitcher. Straightened up, it might have reached a height of eight inches. The features were exquisitely mobile and lifelike. Blue eyes looked imploringly at her. It wore a velvety purple costume—the finery of an earlier century.

"You really are cute, little man!" she told it. "A work of art. And just what kind of work of art are you, eh? Protohom? Robot? Telecontrolled? Do you know?"

The doll was shaking its head violently. "No, no!" it said. "Please! I'm as human as you are. Help me hide before Blethro finds me, and I'll explain everything."

Her reactions were being recorded, of course. Well, she wouldn't mind playing their game for a minute or two.

"A joke's a joke, midget," she remarked, drawing up her eyebrows. "But slipping you into my bag just might be construed as shoplifting. Do you realize you probably cost a good deal more than I make in a year?"

"They said no one would believe me," the doll told her. Tears in the tiny eyes? She felt startled. "I'm from a world you've never heard about. Our size was reduced genetically. Blethro had three of us in a box in his aircar. We agreed to attempt to escape the next time he opened the car door . . ."

Trigger glanced about. Halfway across the terrace, a man stood staring in her direction. She shifted the blue pitcher slightly to give the doll better cover. "Where are the other two?" she asked.

"Blethro seized them before they could get out of the car. If I'm to find help for them, I must get away first. But you believe I'm a toy! So I—"

And now the man was coming purposefully along the aisles toward Trigger's table. She cupped a light hand over the doll as it began to straighten up. "Wait a moment," she muttered. "Does your abominable Blethro sport a great yellow moustache?"

"Yes! Is—"

Trigger swung her handbag around behind the pitcher, snapped it open, blocking the man's line of view. "Blethro seems to have spotted you," she whispered. "Keep down and pop inside the bag. We're leaving."

Bag slung from her shoulder, she set off quickly toward the nearest door leading from the terrace. Glancing back, she saw the man with the jutting yellow moustache lengthen his stride. But he checked at the table where she'd been sitting, hastily moved a few articles about and lifted the top off the sandwich warmer. Trigger hurried on, not quite running now.

A small sign on the door read Wehall Employees Only. She looked back. Blethro was hurrying, too, not far behind her. She pushed through the door, sprinted along the empty white hallway beyond it. After some seconds, she heard a yell and his footsteps pounding in hot pursuit.

The hall ended where another one crossed it. Blank walls, and nobody in sight. Left or right? Trigger ran up the branch on the right, turned another corner—there at last was a door!

A locked door, she discovered instants later. Blind alley! Blethro came rushing around the corner, slowed as he saw her. He smiled then, walked unhurriedly toward her.

"End of the line, eh?" he said, breathing heavily. "Now let's see what you have in that bag."

"Why?" Trigger asked, slipping the bag from her shoulder.

Blethro grinned. "Why? Why were you running?"

"That's my business," Trigger told him. "Perhaps I felt I needed the exercise. Unless you're something

like a police officer—and can prove it—you'd be well
advised to leave me alone! I can make very serious
trouble for you."

The threat didn't seem to alarm Blethro, who was
large and muscular. He continued to grin through his
moustache as he came up. "Well, perhaps I'm a
Wehall detective."

"Prove that."

"I don't think I'll bother." He held his hand out,
the grin fading. "The bag! Fast!"

Trigger swung away from him. He made a quick
grab for her. She let the bag slide to the floor, caught
the grabbing arm with both hands, moving solidly
back into Blethro, bent and hauled forward. He flew
over her head, smacked against the locked door with
satisfying force, landed on the floor more or less on
his shoulders, made an unpleasant comment and
rolled back up on his feet, face very red and angry.

Then he saw the handbag standing open on the
floor beside Trigger and a gun pointed at him. It
wasn't a large gun, but its appearance was sleek and
deadly; and it was held by a very steady hand.

Blethro scowled uncertainly. "Here—wait a minute!"

"I hate arguments," Trigger told him. "And I did
warn you. So just go to sleep like a good boy now."

She fired and Blethro slumped to the floor. Trigger glanced down. The doll figure was clinging to the
rim of the handbag, peering at her with wide eyes.
"Did Blethro have friends with him?" she asked.

"No. He came alone in the car. But he'd indicated
he was to meet someone here."

Trigger considered, nodded. "We'll put this away
again." She slipped the gun into a cosmetics purse
she'd been holding in her left hand, closed the purse
and placed it in the bag. Then she knelt beside
Blethro, began going quickly through his pockets.

"Is he dead?" the small voice inquired from behind
her.

"Not dead, midget. Nor injured. But it'll be an hour or two before he wakes up. Good thing I nailed him first—he carries a gun. What's your name, by the way? Mine's Trigger."

"My name's Salgol. What are you doing?"

"Something slightly illegal, I'm afraid. Borrowing Blethro's car keys—and here they are!" Trigger straightened up. "Now let's arrange this a little differently." She picked up Salgol, eased him into her blazer pocket. "You stay down in there when there's anyone around. Blethro left his car and the box with your friends in it on a lot next to the restaurant terrace?"

"Yes."

"Fine," Trigger said. "You point the car out to me when we get there. Then we'll all go somewhere safe, and you'll tell me what this is about so we can figure out what to do."

"Thank you, Trigger!" Salgol piped from her pocket. "I did well to trust you. I didn't have much hope for Smee and Runderin, or even for myself."

"Well, we may not be out of trouble yet. We'll see." Trigger snapped the bag shut, slung it from her shoulder. "Let's go before someone happens by here. Ready?"

"Ready." Salgol dipped down out of sight.

A few people glanced curiously at Trigger as she came back out on the restaurant terrace. Apparently they'd realized something was going on between her and Blethro, and were wondering what it had been about. She thought it shouldn't matter. Everyone having lunch here would have finished and left before Blethro regained his senses. She sauntered across the terrace, went along a passage to the parking lot, stopped at the entrance. There was no attendant in sight at the moment. She waited until a couple who'd just got out of their car went past her. All clear now . . .

"Salgol?"

She could barely hear his muffled reply from the pocket.

"Take a look around," she told him quietly. "We're there."

Salgol stuck his head out and identified Blethro's aircar as one of those standing against the parapet on the street side of the parking lot—the seventh from the left. Then he disappeared again until Trigger had unlocked the car door, stepped inside and locked the door behind her.

The car was of a fixed-canopy, one-way-view type. Trigger didn't take off immediately. The box in which Salgol's companions were confined stood on a back seat, and she wanted to make sure they were in there. She worked the latches off it and opened the top.

They were there—two tiny, charming females in costume dresses which matched Salgol's outfit. They stared apprehensively up at her. She lifted Salgol into the box and he spoke a few unintelligible lilting sentences to them. Then they were beaming at Trigger, though they said nothing. Apparently they didn't know Translingue. She smiled back, left the box open, sat down at the controls and took the car up into the air.

2

The hotel room ComWeb chimed, and Trigger switched it on. Telzey's image appeared on the screen.

"I came home just now and got your message," Telzey said. "I'm sorry there was a delay." Her gaze shifted around the room. "Where are you?"

"Hotel room."

"Why?"

"Seems better to keep away from the apartment just now."

Telzey's eyebrows lifted. "Trouble?"

"Not yet. But there's more than likely to be. I ran into something unusual, and it's a ticklish matter. Can you come over?"

"As soon as you tell me where you are."

Trigger told her, and Telzey switched off, saying she was on her way.

There was a world called Marell . . .

Trigger said, "The Old Territory people who set up the genetic miniaturization project did it because they thought it had been proved there'd be a permanent shortage of habitable planets around. So that sets it back about eleven hundred years, when they'd begun to get range but didn't yet know where and how to look."

They'd discovered Marell, which seemed eminently habitable, and decided to populate it with a human strain reduced in size to the point where a vast number could be supported by the planet without crowding it. A staff of scientists and technicians of normal size accompanied the miniature colony to see it safely through any early problems.

On Marell, a plague put an abrupt end to the project before it could get under way. It wiped out the supervisory staff and more than half of the small people; and no Old Territory ship touched on the planet again. The survivors were left to their own resources, which were slender enough. They came close to extermination but recovered, began to develop a technology, and in the course of the following centuries spread out until they'd made a sizable part of Marell their own.

"Steam and electricity," said Trigger. "They'd got up to that, but not beyond it. One group knew what actually had happened on Marell, but they kept their records a secret. Some others had legends that they were descendants of Giants who flew through space and that kind of thing. Not many believed the legends. Then the Hub ship came."

It had been a surveyor ship. It moved about in Marell's skies for weeks before coming down to take samples of the surface. It also took a section of a Marell town on board, along with about a hundred of its inhabitants. Then it left.

"When was that?" Telzey asked.

"Salgol was one of the first group they picked up, and he was the equivalent of eleven standard years old at the time," said Trigger. "That makes it fifteen standard years ago."

"Most of the people they took with them then died," Salgol told Telzey. "They didn't treat us badly but they gave us bad diseases. They found out what to do about the diseases, and taught Translingue to those of us who were left, and some of the Giants learned one of our main languages."

Telzey nodded. "And then?"

"We went back to Marell. They knew we had an electrical communication system. They used it."

The Hub ship issued orders. Geologically, Marell was a rich world, and the Hub men wanted the choicest of its treasures. They were taking what was immediately on hand, and thereafter the Marells would work to provide them with more. Quotas were set. The ship would return each year to gather up what had been collected.

"How many Marells were there now?" Telzey asked.

Salgol shook his head. "That isn't definitely known. But when I was there last, I was told there might be sixty million of the people."

"So, even with limited equipment, it adds up to a very large annual haul of precious stones and metals."

"Yes, lady, it has," said Salgol.

"And you don't have weapons against space armor."

"No. The people do have weapons, of course, and good ones. There are huge animals there—huge as we see them—and some are still very dangerous. And the nations have fought among themselves, though not since the ship came. But they aren't like your weapons. One town turned its cannon on the Giants when they came to collect. The Giants weren't hurt, but they burned the town with everyone in it."

Trigger said, "Besides, there were threats. The Marells were told they'd better be thankful for the current arrangement and do what they could to keep it going. If the Hub government ever learned about them, the whole planet would be occupied, and any surviving Marells would be slaves forever."

"Did you believe that?" Telzey asked Salgol.

"I wasn't sure, lady. The Hub people I've met before today might do it, if they saw enough advantage in it. Perhaps you had a very bad government."

"Then why did you run away from Blethro? Wasn't that endangering your world, as far as you knew?"

Salgol glanced at his companions. "There's a worse thing beginning now," he said. "Those they took away before were to become interpreters like myself, or to provide some special information. But now they plan to collect the most physically perfect among our young people and sell them in the Hub like animal pets. I felt I had to take the chance to find out whether there weren't some of you who would try to prevent it. I thought there must be, since you don't seem really different from us except for your size."

Telzey said after a moment, "They'd risk spoiling the present setup with something like that?"

"It wouldn't spoil it, Telzey," Trigger said. "Blethro was acting as middleman. He was to make a contact today to sell the idea, with Runderin and Smee as samples and Salgol filling in as their male counterpart.

If the deal went over, the merchandise would get amnesia treatment and be taught Translingue before delivery to the distributor. They'd be sold undercover as a protohom android speciality. They'd think it's what they were, and I doubt it would be possible to disprove it biologically. They'd be dead in ten years, before they could begin to show significant signs of aging. They were to be treated for that, too."

Telzey remarked, "Developing self-aware intelligence in protohom products is illegal, of course."

"Of course. But if the results could be made to look like those two, somebody would find it profitable."

Telzey regarded the tiny ladies with their beautiful faces, elaborate coiffures and costumes. They gave her anxious smiles. Replaceable erotic toys. Yes, the exploiters of Marell might have hit on a quite profitable sideline.

She said to Salgol, "Could you tell someone how to get to Marell?"

He shook his head. "Lady, no. I've tried to find out. But the Hub men were careful not to let me have such information, and the people's astronomy isn't advanced enough to establish a galactic reference. All I can say is that it took the ships on which I've been three months to make the trip in either direction."

Trigger closed the door to the suite's bedroom, where the Marells had returned to their box. "Well?" she said. "How does it check out telepathically?"

"They are human," Telzey said. "Allowing for their backgrounds, they can't be distinguished mentally from Hub humans. Salgol's near genius grade. It's a ticklish situation, all right. How long's it been since Blethro might have come awake?"

"Not much more than an hour."

"How well are you covered?"

Trigger shrugged. "Blethro can give them my

description, of course. I dumped his car, taxied back to where I'd left mine, left that in a garage, and taxied here. I really didn't leave much of a trail."

"No. But we'll assume Blethro contacted his principals at once. That's obviously a big outfit with plenty of money. And the matter's important to them. You could upset their entire Marell operation and land them in serious trouble. They're probably looking hard for you."

Trigger nodded. "They'd try for a quick pick-up first. I figured our best chance to get a line on them would be while they're still looking for me. In fact, it might be the only real chance for a century to find out where Marell is. If they can't locate me and those three, they could dissolve the project and wipe out the evidence, and they probably will."

"Where do you want to take this?" Telzey said.

"Psychology Service, top level."

"That seems the best move. Why didn't you go directly to their city center?"

"Because I didn't want to have it fumbled by some underling," Trigger said. "I don't know the local Service group. You do."

"All right." Telzey looked at the room ComWeb. "Better not use that. I'll call the center from a public booth. They should have an escort here for you and the Marells in minutes."

She left. Trigger returned to the bedroom, told Salgol what they intended. He was explaining the situation to the other two while she closed and latched the box. She put on her blazer, glanced at her watch, sat down to wait.

Some three minutes later, she heard the faintest of clicks. It might have come from the other room. Trigger picked up the gun she'd left lying on the table beside her, stood up quietly, and listened. There were no further sounds. She started moving cautiously toward the door.

The air about her seemed to sway up and down, like great silent waves lifting and falling. Trigger stumbled forward into the waves, felt herself sink far down in them and drown.

3

"How do you feel?" a voice was saying; and Trigger realized her eyes were open. She looked at the speaker, and glanced around.

She was sitting in a cushiony deep chair; there was a belt around her waist, and her hands were fastened to the belt on either side. There was a tick in her right eyelid. Other nerves jerked noticeably here and there. The man who'd addressed her stood a few feet away. Another man, who wore a gold-trimmed blue uniform, sat at an instrument console farther up in the compartment. He'd swung around in his chair to look at her. This was a spaceyacht; and that splendid globe of magenta fire in the screen might be a sun she'd seen before.

"Nerves jumping," she said in reply to the question. She ran the tip of her tongue over her lips. "And thirsty. This is the Rasolmen System?"

The uniformed man laughed and turned back to the console. The other one smiled. "Good guess, Miss Argee! You're obviously awake at last. You had me worried for a while."

"I did?" Trigger said. He'd shoved back the flap of his jacket as he spoke, and she had a glimpse of a gun fastened to his belt.

"It was that knockout method we used on you," he explained. "it's one of the safest known, but in about one out of every three hundred cases, you can run into side effects. You happen to be that kind of case. Frankly, there were a couple of times I wasn't too sure you mightn't be going into fatal convulsions. But you should be all right now." He added, "My name is Wrann. Detective by profession. I'm the man responsible for picking you up—also for delivering you in good condition to my employer. You'll understand my concern."

"Yes, I do," Trigger said. "How did you find me so quickly?"

He smiled. "Good organization—and exceptionally good luck! We had your description; and you'd been lunching at Wehall's. There was a chance you were among the store's listed customers. We ran your description against the list in the Wehall computer and had a definite identification in no time at all."

"I thought that list was highly confidential," said Trigger.

Wrann looked somewhat smug. "Few things remain confidential when you come up with enough money. You were expensive, but I'd been told to find you and a certain box, and find both fast, and ignore the cost. We'd thrown in a small army of professionals; but, as it turned out, you'd selected one of the first hotels we hit with your pictures and name. The name was no help. The pictures were. That identification came high, and the suite keys higher, but we got both. We were taking you out of there minutes later."

"What was hotel security doing all that time?"

Wrann grinned. "Looking the other way. Amazing, isn't it, in a fine establishment like that? Enough money usually does it. You were very expensive, Miss Argee. But my employer hasn't complained. And now we've almost reached our destination. Feel able to walk?"

Trigger moved her elbows. "If you'll take this thing off me."

"In a moment." The detective helped her stand up, nodded at a passage behind them. "We had a comfortable little cell ready for you, but I was keeping you up front as long as you were in trouble and conceivably could need emergency treatment to pull you through. You'll find drinking water in the cell. If you'll do me the favor, you might straighten yourself out a bit then, before I hand you over at the satellite. You look rather rumpled."

She nodded. "All right. Did you bring along my makeup kit?"

"I brought along whatever you had at the hotel," Wrann said. "But I was told to keep your property together. You'll find a kit in the cell."

There were two barred cells then, facing each other at the end of the passage. Trigger stopped short when she saw who was in one of them. Wrann chuckled.

"Surprise, eh?" he said. "My employer also wants to see Mr. Blethro. Mr. Blethro was reluctant to make the trip. But here he is."

He unlocked the door to the other cell and slid it back, while Blethro stared coldly at Trigger. Wrann motioned her in, shut the door and locked it. "Now, if you'll back up to the bars—"

Trigger moved up to the door, and Wrann reached through the bars, unfastened the belt from around her waist and freed her wrists. "If you need anything, call out," he said. "Otherwise I'll be back after we've docked." He went off down the passage to the front of the yacht.

Trigger drank a cup of water thoughtfully, returned to the cell door. Blethro sat on a chair, moody regard fixed on the floor. The yellow moustache drooped. She heard Wrann say something to the pilot in the forward compartment. The pilot laughed.

"Blethro!" Trigger said softly.

Blethro gave her a brief, unpleasant glance, resumed his study of the floor.

Trigger said, "Are you in trouble with whoever it is we're being taken to see?"

Blethro growled something impolite.

"It is my business," Trigger said. "I know how we can get out of this. Both of us."

He lifted his head, moustache twitching with sudden interest. "How?"

"You heard what Wrann said about that knockout stuff they used on me?"

"Some of it," Blethro acknowledged. "I heard you earlier."

"Oh? What were the sound effects?"

Blethro considered, watching her. "Someone choking to death. Gasps—hoarse! Groaning, too."

"Fine!" said Trigger. "And I'll now have some dandy convulsions right here in this cell. As soon as I start, yell for Wrann. If I can get his gun and keys, we'll go after the pilot next."

Blethro stared at her a moment longer, grinned abruptly.

"Why not?" he said. "I've become inconvenient to them—I've got nothing to lose." He stood up, came over to the bars of his cell. "You might even do it! But you'd better be quick. Wrann's a tough boy—tougher than he looks."

Trigger raked fingernails down the side of her face and dropped to the floor. Blethro bellowed, "Wrann! Better have a look at that girl! She's throwing a fit or something!"

Footsteps pounded along the passage before he finished. Trigger, contorting, eyes drawn wide, clutching her throat, breath rasping, heard Wrann's shocked curse. Then the bars rattled as the cell door slid open. Wrann came down on his knees beside her, reaching for an inner coat pocket.

Trigger's right hand speared stiffly into his throat. Wrann's head jerked back. She turned up on her left elbow, slashed her hand edge across the bridge of his nose, saw his eyes glaze, gripped his head in both hands, hauled him down across her and rammed his skull against the floor. Wrann made a gurgling sound.

Stunned but not out. His gun first—and she had it, hearing the pilot call, "Need some help back there, Wrann?" and Blethro's, "No—he's handling her all right!" as she squirmed out from under Wrann's weight and got to her knees. Wrann clamped a hand around her ankle then, pushing himself up from the floor; and she twisted around and laid the gun barrel along the side of his head. That was enough for Wrann. He dropped back, face down; and Trigger came to her feet.

She went quickly over to the cell door, Blethro watching in silence. Wrann's key was in the lock. Trigger took it out, glanced along the passage. She couldn't see the pilot from the door; but he could see the passage and anyone in it if he was at the console and happened to look around. She whispered, "Catch!" and Blethro nodded quickly and comprehendingly and put a big cupped hand out between the bars. She tossed the key over to him. He caught it. A moment later, he had his cell door unlocked and drew it cautiously open far enough to let him through.

They slipped out into the passage together. The pilot sat at his console, back turned toward them. Blethro muttered, "Better let me take the gun!"

"I can handle it." Trigger eased off the gun's safety, indicated Wrann. "Lock him in if you can do it quietly. But wait till I'm in the control section."

She started off down the passage without waiting for his reply. She wasn't exactly trusting Blethro. Her own gun would have been preferable, but if her luck held, shooting wouldn't be necessary anyway. The magenta sun was sliding upward out of the yacht's screen; the pilot was using his instruments. She came up steadily behind him.

He reached out, pulled over a lever, then leaned back in his chair and stretched. "Wrann?" he called lazily. He turned, beginning to get out of the chair, saw Trigger ten feet away, gun pointed. He stared.

"Get up slowly," she told him. "That's right. Now keep your hands up and go over to the wall."

She knew Blethro had entered the compartment; now he came into view on her right. He grinned. "I'll check him."

The pilot shook his head, began to laugh. "Damndest thing I've seen in a while! Awake five minutes, and you almost had the ship!"

"Almost?" said Trigger.

"Look at the screen."

She looked. The screen was blank. "Ship power went off just now," the pilot explained. "We're riding a beam."

Trigger said, "Check him out, Blethro. " Then, some moments later: "Where's your gun? You're bound to have one."

The pilot shrugged. "You're welcome to it! That drawer over there."

Blethro jerked open the drawer, took out the gun. "Now," Trigger said, "we have two guns on you, and we're in a bad jam. Don't be foolish. Sit down at the console, switch ship power back on and break us out of that beam. And don't tell me you can't do it!"

"I am telling you that." The pilot settled himself in the control chair.

"I'll go through any motions you like. Nothing will happen. You can check for yourself. The people here don't want anyone barging in on them under power, so the satellite's overriding my console now, and we'll stay on their beam till it docks us. Sorry, but this simply hasn't done you any good."

After a minute or two, it became evident that he'd told the truth. Blethro had begun to sweat. Trigger said, "How long before we dock?"

The pilot looked at a chronometer. "Should be another six minutes."

"Wrann brought a handbag of mine on board along with a box. Where did he put the bag?"

"There's a bulkhead cabinet beside the passage entry," the pilot told her. "It's not locked. The bag's in there."

"All right," Trigger said. "Get out of the chair. Blethro, put on his uniform. Hurry! If he's got a cap, put that on, too. I'll get my gun."

The pilot climbed out of the chair. Blethro frowned. "What'll that do for us?"

"We dock," Trigger said. "We come out. For a moment anyway, they may think you're the pilot. I'm a prisoner. We'll have three guns. We may be able to knock out the override controls and take off again."

The pilot shook his head. "That won't do you any good either."

Blethro grimaced, baring his teeth. "It can't hurt. They're dumping me, friend." He jerked his gun. "The uniform off! Fast!"

There was a faint hissing sound. Startled, Trigger looked around. Sudden scent of not-quite-perfume—

Oh, no! Not again!

The pilot spread his hands, almost apologetically. "They don't take chances! We might as well sit down."

He did. Blethro was staggering backwards; the gun fell from his hand. Trigger stood braced for an instant against the armrest of the control chair, felt herself slide down beside it, while the pilot's voice seemed to go on, drawing slowly off into distance: " . . . told you . . . it . . . would . . . do . . . no . . ."

4

Again she came awake.

This was a gradual process at first: the expanding

half-awareness of awakening—a well-rested, comfortable feeling. But then came sudden knowledge of being in a dangerous situation. There was a shield which guarded her mind, and that now had drawn tight as if it sensed something it didn't like. Full recollection returned as she opened her eyes.

She was in a day-bright room of medium size with colored crystal walls, unfurnished except for a carpet and the couch on which she lay. The day-brightness wasn't the natural kind; the room had no windows or view screens. There was one rather small square scarlet door which was closed. The room was silent aside from the minor sounds made by her own motions and breathing. She wasn't wearing the clothes she'd had on but a short-sleeved sweater of soft gray material, and slacks of the same material which ended in comfortably fitting boots.

Probably, though not necessarily, she was on the solar satellite which had hauled in the unpowered yacht with its unconscious pilot and passengers. Rasolmen was an open system. It had no planets and very little space debris. It did have, however, a sizable human population whose satellites circled the magnificent sun along their charted courses, as occasional retreats or permanent residences of people who liked and could afford that style of living. Large yachts sometimes joined them for a few weeks or a year. There was almost no commercial shipping in the system beyond that which tended to the requirements of the satellite dwellers.

If the purpose had been only to silence her, it would have been simpler to kill her than to bring her here. So they must want to find out how much she'd learned about their operation, and whether she'd talked to others before she was caught.

It seemed a decidedly sticky situation, but she wasn't improving it by lying where she was until someone came to get her. Trigger got off the couch and went over to the scarlet door. There was a handle. She turned it, and the door swung open into a dark corridor with walls and floor of polished gray mineral in which there were flickering glitters. She moved out into the corridor.

Not many yards away, the corridor opened on a room which seemed to be of considerable size. Through the room poured a river of soundless fires, cascading down through the air, vanishing into the carpeting.

Trigger stood watching the phenomenon. Its colors changed, sometimes gradually, sometimes in quick ripples and swirls, shifting from yellow through pink and green to sapphire blue or the rich magenta blaze of the Rasolmen sun. No suggestion of heat or cold came from the room, no crackle of energy. It seemed simply a visual display.

She started cautiously toward the room. There was no other way to go; the corridor ended beside the door through which she'd come. Immediately, the flow shifted direction, surged toward her and became a fiery wall, barring her from the room.

Less sure now that it was only a display, Trigger waited, ready to retreat through the door. But when nothing more happened, she moved forward again. Again the phenomenon responded. It blurred, reformed as a vortex, lines of dazzling color spiraling swiftly inward to a central point which seemed to recede farther from her with every step she took. Trigger shook her head irritably. There was a strong hypnotic effect to that whirling mass of light. For a moment, she'd come to a stop, staring into it, her purpose beginning to fade from her mind. But warned now, she went on.

And the vortex in turn drew back, away from her, freeing the entry to the room. Once more it changed, became the descending river of fire it had first appeared to be. Faces and shapes came sweeping down with the flow, sometimes seen distinctly, sometimes only as dim outlines within it. They whipped past, now beautiful, now horrible, growing more menacing as Trigger came closer. Then another abrupt blurring; and what took form was a squat anthropoid demon, mottled and hairless, with narrow pointed ears, standing in the room. He wasn't as tall as Trigger, but he seemed almost as broad as he was tall; and his slanted cat eyes were fixed avidly on her. The image was realistic enough to give her a start of fright and revulsion. Then, as she reached the room, it simply vanished. There was a musical giggle on her right.

"You're hard to scare, Trigger!"

"Why were you trying to scare me?" Trigger asked.

"Oh, just for fun!"

She might be twelve or thirteen years old. A slender, beautiful child with long blond hair and laughing blue eyes. She closed the instrument she'd been operating, an instrument about which Trigger hadn't been able to make out much except that it seemed to have multiple keyboards.

"I'm Perr Hasta," she announced. "They told me to watch you until you woke up, and I've been watching almost an hour and you were still just lying there, and it was sort of boring. So I started playing with my image-maker, and then you did wake up, and I wanted to see if I could scare you. Did I?"

"For a moment at the end," Trigger admitted. "You have quite an imagination!"

Perr Hasta seemed to find that amusing. She chuckled.

"By the way," Trigger went on, "who are 'they'?"

"They're Torai and Attuk," said Perr Hasta. "And don't ask me next who Torai and Attuk are because I told them when you woke up, and I'm to take you to see them now. They can tell you."

"Do you live here on the satellite?" Trigger asked as they started toward a doorway.

"How do you know you're on the satellite?" Perr said. "That was hours ago they brought you there. They could have taken you somewhere else afterwards."

"Yes, I suppose so."

Perr smiled. "Well, you are still on the satellite. But don't think you can make me take you to a boat lock. Torai is watching you now, and we'd just run into force screens somewhere. She's anxious to talk to you."

"I wouldn't want to disappoint her," Trigger said.

Attuk was a rather large, healthy-looking man with squared features and a quite bald head, who dressed with casual elegance and gave the impression of enjoying life thoroughly. Torai appeared past middle age—a brown-skinned woman with a handsome face and fine dark eyes. Her clothes and hair style were severe, but her long fingers glittered with numerous rings. Something ornate, which might have been a musical instrument in the general class of a flute, or perhaps a functional computer control rod, hung by a satin strap from her belt. Trigger decided it was a computer control rod.

A place had been set for Trigger at a small table near the center of the room, and refreshments put out—fruit, a chilled soup, a variety of breads, two loaves of meat. The utensils included a sizable carving knife.

The others weren't eating. They sat in chairs around the wide green and gold room, which had a number of doors and passages leading from it. Torai was closest to Trigger, some fifteen feet away and a little to Trigger's left. Perr Hasta, beyond Torai, had tilted her chair back against the wall, feet supported by one of the rungs. Attuk was farthest, on Trigger's right, beside a picture window with an animated seascape at which he gazed when he wasn't watching Trigger.

"I had the impression," Torai remarked, "that you recognized me as soon as you saw me."

Trigger nodded. "Torai Sebaloun. I've seen pictures of you. I've heard you're one of the wealthiest women on Orado."

"No doubt I am," Torai said. "And Attuk and Perr Hasta are my associates in the Sebaloun enterprises, though the fact isn't generally known."

"I see." Trigger sliced a sliver of meat from one of the loaves and nibbled at it.

"You created something of a problem for us, you know," Torai went on. "In fact, it seemed at first that it might turn into a decidedly serious problem. But we moved in time, and had some good fortune in those critical first few hours besides. You've talked freely meanwhile and told us what we needed to know. You don't remember that, of course, because at the time you weren't aware of doing it. At any rate, there's nothing to point to us now—not even for the Psychology Service's investigators."

Trigger said, "I've seen something of the Service's methods of investigation. Perhaps you shouldn't feel too sure of yourself."

Attuk grunted. "I must agree with our guest on that point!"

"No," Torai said. "We're really quite safe." She smiled at Trigger. "Attuk favors having Telzey Amberdon picked up, to find out what she can tell us about the Service's search for you. But we aren't going to try it."

"It would be a sensible precaution," Attuk observed, looking out at the restlessly stirring seascape. "We could have a new mercenary group hired, with the usual safeguards, to do the job. If anything went wrong, we still wouldn't be involved."

Torai said dryly, "I'd be more concerned if nothing went wrong and she were delivered safely to our private place!" She looked at Trigger. "We obtained a dossier on Amberdon, as we previously had on you. What we found in it hardly seemed disturbing. But what you've told us about her is a different matter. It appears it would be a serious mistake to try to maintain control over a person of that kind."

Attuk made a disparaging gesture. "A mind reader, a psi. They can be handled. I've done it before."

"Well, you are not having that particular mind reader brought to the satellite for handling!" Torai told him. "The information we might get from her isn't worth the risk. She can't harm us as long as we keep well away from her. My decision on that is final. To get back to you, Trigger. Your interference made it necessary to terminate the very lucrative Marell operation at once. Now that it's known such a world exists, we can't afford to retain any connections with it."

Trigger said evenly, "I'm glad about that part, at least. You three have all the money you can use. You had no possible excuse for exploiting the Marells. They're as human as you are."

They stared at her a moment. Then Attuk grinned and Perr Hasta chortled gleefully.

"That's where you're mistaken," said Torai Sebaloun.

Trigger shook her head. "I don't think so."

"Oh, but truly you are! The Marells may be human enough. We aren't."

The statement was made so casually that for a moment it seemed to have almost no meaning. Then there was a crawling between Trigger's shoulder blades. She looked at the smiling faces in turn. "Then what are you?" she asked.

Torai said, "It may sound strange, but I don't know what I am. My memory never goes back more than fifty or sixty years. The past fades out behind me. I keep permanent records to inform me of past things I should know about but have forgotten. And even the earliest of those records show that I didn't know then what I was. I may have forgotten that very long ago." She looked over at Attuk. "Attuk isn't what I am, and neither is Perr Hasta. And neither of them is what the other is. But certainly none of us is human."

She paused, perhaps expectantly. But then, when Trigger remained silent, she went on. "It shouldn't be surprising, really. A vast culture like this one touches thousands of other worlds, often without discovering much about them. And it alerts and attracts other beings who can live comfortably on its riches without revealing themselves. An obvious form of concealment, of course, is to adopt or imitate the human form. With intelligence and experience and sufficiently long lives, such intruders can learn in time to make more effective use of the human culture than most humans ever do."

Trigger cleared her throat, then: "There's something about this," she remarked, "that doesn't fit what you're telling me."

"Oh?" Torai said. "What is it?"

"Torai Sebaloun herself. The Sebaloun family goes back for generations. It was a great financial house when the War Centuries ended. It's less prominent now, of course, but Torai must have been born normally. Her identification patterns must be on record. She must have grown up normally. Where a member of the Sebaloun family was involved, nothing else could possibly have escaped attention. So how could she be at the same time a long-lived alien who doesn't remember what it really is?"

Torai said, "You're right in assuming that Torai Sebaloun was born and matured normally. I sought her out when she was eighteen years old. I'd been watching her for some time. She was a beautiful woman, in perfect health, intelligent as were almost all members of the Sebaloun line, and wealthy in her own right, not to mention her family's great wealth. So I became Torai Sebaloun."

"How?"

"I transferred my personality to her. The body I'd been using previously died. I forced out Torai's personality. I acquired her body, her brain and nervous system, with its established habit patterns and memories. I was Torai Sebaloun then, and I let the world grow gradually accustomed to the various modifications I wanted to make in its image of her. There were no problems. There never are.

"That's how I exist. I'm a personality. I take bodies and use them for a while. Before I discovered human beings, I was using other bodies. I know that much. And when my host body no longer seems satisfactory, I start looking around for a new one. I'm very selective about that nowadays, as I can afford to be! I want only the best."

She smiled at Trigger. "Of late, I've been looking again. I was on Orado when you took my property from Blethro. Since he's shown himself to be a most capable individual, I was interested in the fact that you'd been able to do it. As soon as we had your name, I was supplied with a dossier on you. I found that even more interesting, though it left a number of questions unanswered. So I had you brought to our satellite to make sure of what I'd come across. You've had a medical examination during the past hours, which confirms that you're in superior physical condition. Our interrogation revealed other excellencies. In short, I find no disqualifying flaw in you."

Trigger glanced at the other two. They had the expressions of detachedly interested listeners.

She told Torai carefully, "Perhaps you'd better go on looking. There are obvious reasons why it wouldn't be advisable for you to try to take over my identity."

"No, I couldn't do that," Torai agreed. "So this time we'll create a new one. Your appearance will be surgically altered. So will your identification patterns. And, of course, I don't intend to give up the Sebaloun empire. All the necessary arrangements were made some while ago. Torai is the last of her family, and her sole heiress is a young protégée to whom the world will be gradually introduced after Torai's death. All that remained then was to find the protégée. And now—"

Torai broke off.

Barely fifteen feet between them, Trigger had been thinking. She could be out of her chair and across that distance in an instant. Attuk sat a good eight yards away. Perr Hasta, relaxed, chair tilted back against the wall, could do nothing to interfere.

Then, with the carving knife held against the brown neck of Torai Sebaloun, and Torai herself held clamped back against Trigger, they could bargain. Torai was in charge here; and whether it was insanity that had been speaking or an entity which, in fact, could make another's body its own, Torai obviously placed a high value on her life. She could keep it, on Trigger's conditions.

So, as Torai seemed about to conclude the outline of her plans for Trigger, Trigger came out of the chair.

She'd almost reached Torai when something stopped her. It was neither solid barrier nor energy screen; there was no jolt, no impact—all she felt was its effect. She could come no closer to Torai, whose face showed startled consternation and who'd raised her hands defensively. Instead, she was being forced steadily away. Then she was lifted into the air, held suspended several feet above the carpet, and something pulled at her right arm, drawing it straight out to the side. She realized the pull was on the blade of the knife she still held; and she let go of it, which was preferable to getting her fingers broken or having her arm hauled out of its socket by what she knew now must be an interacting set of tractor beams. The knife was flicked away and dropped lightly to the surface of the little lunch table.

Torai Sebaloun was smiling again. Her hands remained slightly raised, fingers curled, knuckles turned forward, toward Trigger; and all those glittering rings on her fingers clearly had a solid functional purpose.

"Quick! Oh, she was quick!" Perr Hasta was saying delightedly. "You were right about her, Torai!"

"Yes, I was right." Torai didn't turn her eyes away from Trigger. "And still she was almost able to take me by surprise! Trigger, it was obvious from what we'd learned about you that at some early moment you'd try to make me your hostage. Well, you've tried!"

Her fingers shifted. Trigger was carried back across the room, still held clear of the carpet, lowered and set on the edge of a couch against the far wall. The intangible beam complex released her suddenly; and Torai dropped her hands and stood up.

"The transfer is made easier by suitable preparations," she said, "and they've now begun. It's why I told you what I did. A personality that knows what is happening is more readily expelled than one which has remained unaware and unsuspecting until the last moment. You may not yet believe it's going to happen, but you won't be able to avoid thinking about it; and that's enough to provide a satisfactory level of uncertainty. Meanwhile, be at liberty to discover how helpless you are here, in fact, in every way. I'll be engaged in sensitizing myself to the personal articles I had brought to the satellite with you."

Perr Hasta also had come to her feet. "Then I can go to Blethro now?"

Torai shrugged. "Why not?"

She turned toward a door. Perr Hasta darted across

the room to another door, pulled it open and was gone through it. Attuk got out of his chair, glanced at Trigger and smiled lazily as he started toward a hallway.

Somewhat incredulously, Trigger realized that they were leaving her here by herself. She watched Torai open the door, got a brief glimpse of the room beyond it before Torai shut it again. Attuk had gone off down the hall.

She looked around. The lunch table was sinking through the richly patterned carpet, accompanied by the chair she'd used. Both were gone before she could make a move to recover the knife. The seascape Attuk had studied shut itself off. The chair on which Torai had been sitting followed the example of the lunch table. The one used by Perr Hasta moved ten feet out from the wall, did a sharp quarter turn to the left and remained where it was. The green and gold room was rearranging itself, now that three of its four occupants had left.

Possibly she didn't rate as an occupant of sufficient significance to be considered. Trigger got up from the couch and started toward the door left open by Perr Hasta. She glanced around as she got there. The couch had flattened down and was withdrawing into the wall.

From the doorway, she looked out at a vast sweep of wilderness—a plain dotted with sparse growth, lifting gradually to a distant mountain range. Somewhat more than a hundred yards away, Perr Hasta was running lightly toward a great sloping boulder. A dark rectangle at the base of the boulder suggested a recessed entrance.

Blethro was there? What was this place?

Perr Hasta could answer that. Trigger set off in pursuit.

She checked almost at once. For an instant, as she came through the door, she'd had the impression of the curving walls of a large metallic domed structure, in which the door was set, on either side of her. Then the impression vanished; and, looking back in momentary bewilderment, she saw neither structure nor door, but only the continuation of the great plain on which she stood.

No time to ponder it. Perr Hasta already was halfway to the boulder. Trigger started out again—and, within a hundred steps, she again slowed to a stop, rather abruptly. What halted her this time was the sudden appearance of a sheet of soft, rosy light in the air directly ahead. She'd come up to a force screen. And the whole view beyond the screen had blurred out.

5

When she passed through the door leading from the green and gold room, she'd entered a maze, a series of stage settings blending a little of what was real with much more that was projected illusion. To the eye, the blending was undetectable, and other senses were played upon as skillfully. Force screens formed the dividing walls of the maze, unnoticed until one reached them, responding then with a soft glow which extended a few feet to right and left. Trigger would turn sideways to such a screen, feeling its slick coolness under her fingertips, and move on along it, accompanied by the glow. Perhaps within a dozen yards, the screen would be gone, and she'd find herself in another part of the maze with a different set of illusions about her—and, presently, other force screens to turn her in new directions.

She'd simply kept moving at first, trying to walk her way out, while she watched for anything that might be an indication to the pattern of the maze.

One point became apparent immediately. She couldn't go back the way she had come; the maze's transfer mechanisms operated only in one direction. She passed through a forest glade where a light rain dewed her hair and sweater, and a minute later, was walking along the crest of a barren hill at night, seeing what might be city lights in the distance, while thunder growled overhead. Then a swamp steamed on either side and sent fog drifting across her path. Sounds accompanied her—animal voices, an ominous rustling in a thicket, sudden loud splashes. Something else soon became established: nothing had been left lying carelessly around here that might be considered a weapon. Trigger saw stones of handy size and broken branches, but they were illusion. Vegetation that wasn't illusion was artificial stuff which bent but wouldn't break. She hadn't been able to pull off even a leaf or pry loose a tuft of springy moss.

The settings presently took on an increasingly bizarre aspect. A grotesquely costumed bloated corpse swung by its neck from a tree branch, turning slowly as Trigger went by below. Immediately afterwards, she was in a place where she saw multiple replicas of herself all about, placed in other scenes. In one, she swayed in death beside the bloated horror, suspended from the same branch. In another, she strode across a desert, unaware of a gaunt gray shape moving behind her. An on-the-spot computer composition, initiated by her appearance in this part of the maze—

A few minutes later, she sat down on a simulated beach. There was nothing bizarre here. The white sand was real, and water appeared to sweep lazily up it not many yards away. Sea smells were in the windy air; and there were faint sounds which seemed to come from flying creatures circling far out above the water.

The maze section she'd just emerged from was one she'd passed through before. The illusion view had been new, but she'd recognized the formation of the ground. And when she'd gone through it before, she hadn't come out on the beach.

So the maze wasn't a static construction. The illusion views could be varied and exchanged, and there might be easily thousands of such views available. The positions of force screens and transfer points could be shifted, and had begun to be shifted. The actual area of the maze might be quite limited; and still she could be kept moving around in it indefinitely. If she came near an exit point, she could be deflected past it back into the maze. In fact, nobody needed to be watching to take care of that. The controlling computer would maneuver her about readily enough if that was intended.

Whatever purpose such an arrangement served the satellite's owners, it was no friendly one. The multiple-image area showed malice; a number of displays were meant to shock and frighten. Others must have walked in the maze before this, bewildered and mystified, while their reactions were observed. She'd been tricked into entering it as she attempted to follow Perr Hasta, perhaps to reduce her resistance and make her more easy to handle.

At any rate, she had to get out. The satellite was a complex machine; the machine had controls. The smaller the staff employed by Torai Sebaloun—and there'd been no indications of any staff so far—the more intricate the controls must be. Somewhere such a system was vulnerable. But she had no more chance here to discover its vulnerabilities and try to change the situation in her favor than she would have had behind locked doors.

Therefore, do nothing. Stay here, appear reasonably relaxed. If somebody was studying her reactions as seemed likely, that couldn't be too satisfactory; and if they wanted to prod further reactions out of her, they'd have to make some new move. Possibly one she could turn to her advantage.

✧   ✧   ✧

"Hello, Trigger!" said Perr Hasta.

Trigger looked around. The blond child figure stood a dozen feet away.

"Where did you come from?" Trigger asked.

Perr nodded at a stand of bushes uphill, which Trigger had reason to consider part of the beach scene's illusion setup. "I saw you from there and thought I'd come find out what you were doing," Perr said.

"A short while ago," Trigger remarked, "there was a force screen between that place and this."

Perr smiled. "There still is! But there's a way around the screen if you know just where to turn—which isn't where you'd think you should turn."

She sat down in the sand, companionably close to Trigger. "I've been thinking about you," she said. "There's an odd thing you have that didn't want you to be hypnotized."

Which seemed to be a reference to the Old Galactic mind shield. Trigger didn't intend to discuss that, though she might already have told them about it. "I've never been easy to hypnotize," she said.

"Hm-m-m," said Perr. "Well, we'll see what happens. You're certainly unusual!" She smiled. "I was hoping Torai would let Attuk bring your psi friend here. It should have been an interesting situation."

"No doubt."

"Of course, Attuk doesn't really care what Telzey knows," Perr went on. "Her dossier shows what she looks like, and Attuk forms these sudden attachments. He can be quite irresponsible then. He formed a strong attachment to you, too—but you're Torai's! So Attuk's been sulking." She chuckled.

Trigger looked at her. The three of them might be deranged. "What kind of being is he?" she asked, as casually as she could.

"Attuk?" Perr shrugged. "Well, he is what he is. I don't know what it's called. A crude creature, at any rate, with crude tastes. He even likes to eat human flesh. Isn't that disgusting?"

"Yes, I'd call it disgusting," Trigger said after a moment.

"He says there was a time when he had human worshipers who brought him human sacrifices," Perr said. "Perhaps that's when he developed his tastes. I'm sure he'd like it to be that way again, but it's not so easy to arrange now. So he makes himself useful to Torai and she keeps him around."

"How is he useful to her?" Trigger asked.

"This way and that," said Perr.

"What are you, Perr?"

Perr smiled, shook her head. "I never tell anyone. But I'll show you what I do, if you like. Would you? We'd have to leave the playground."

"This is the playground?" Trigger said.

"That's what we call it."

"Where would we go?"

"To the residence."

"Where I was before?"

"Yes."

Trigger stood up. "Lead the way!"

Getting out of the maze without running into force screens was, as Perr Hasta had indicated, apparently a matter of knowing where to turn. The turning points weren't detectably marked and there seemed to be no pattern to the route, but in less than two minutes they'd reached an open doorway with a room beyond. They went through and closed the door. There was nothing illusory about the room. They were back in the residence.

"Torai controls the satellite from the residence?" Trigger asked.

Perr gave her a glance. "Well, usually that's where she is. But she could control it from almost anywhere on it."

"Ordinarily that's done from a computer room."

"We go through here, Trigger. No, hardly anyone goes to the computer room. Only when something needs adjusting or repairs. Then Torai has someone brought out to do it."

"You mean you don't have a computer technician on hand?" Trigger said. "What would happen to the satellite if your main computer broke down?"

"Goodness. There're three main computers. Any one of them could keep the satellite going perfectly by itself—and they're hardly likely to break down all together, are they? Here we are!" Perr stopped at a passage door and slid back a panel covering a transparent section in the upper part. "There! That's what I do, Trigger."

The room was small and bare. Blethro sat on a bench with his back against the wall, facing the door. His hands were loosely folded in his lap. His head lolled to the side, and a thread of spittle hung from a corner of his mouth. His eyes were fixed on the door, but he gave no sign of being aware of visitors.

"What have you done to him?" Trigger said after a moment.

Perr winked at her.

"I drank what Torai would call his personality," she said. "Oh, not all of it, or he'd be dead. I left him a little. He can sit there like that or stand, or even walk if he's told to. But I took most."

Drugs could account for Blethro's condition, but Trigger felt a shiver of eeriness.

"Why did you do it?" she asked.

"Why not? It was a kindness really. They weren't going to let Blethro live. He's Attuk's meat. But that won't bother him now." Perr Hasta slid the window shut. "Besides, that's what I do: absorb personalities or whatever it is that's there and different in everybody. Some seem barely worthwhile, of course, but I may take them while I'm waiting for a prime one to come along. Or I'll sip a bit here and there. That's barely noticeable. I'm not greedy, and when I find something that should be a really unusual treat, I can be oh-so-patient until the time comes for it. But then I have a real feast!" She smiled. "Would you like me to show you where the computer room is?"

Trigger cleared her throat. "Why do you want to show me that?"

"Because I think you want to know. Not that it's likely to do you much good. But we'll see. It's this way, Trigger."

They went along the passage. Perr glanced sideways up at Trigger. "Blethro wasn't much," she remarked. "But you have a personality I think I'd remember for a long, long time."

"Well, keep away from it," Trigger said.

"That odd mind thing of yours couldn't stop me," Perr told her.

"Perhaps not. There might be other ways to stop you."

Perr laughed delightedly. "We'll see how everything goes! We turn here now. And that's the passage that leads to the computer room. The room's probably locked though—"

She took a step to the side as she spoke, and a door that hadn't been noticeable in the wall was suddenly open, and Perr Hasta was going through it. Trigger reached for her an instant too late. She had a glimpse of the smiling child face turned back to her as the door closed soundlessly. And even before she touched it, Trigger felt quite sure there'd be no way in which she could reopen that door. Its outline had disappeared again, and there was nothing to distinguish it from the rest of the passage wall.

6

There was another door at the end of the passage Perr Hasta had said led to the computer room. The computer room might very well lie behind it. It was a massive-looking door; and while there were no visible indications of locks, it couldn't be budged.

Its location, at any rate, was something to keep in mind. And now, before she ran into interference, she'd better go through as much of the residence area as possible to see what useful articles or information it might provide.

The search soon became frustrating. The place seemed to be laid out like a large house with wings, extending through a number of satellite levels. Some of the doors she came to along the passages and halls wouldn't open. Others did. The rooms they disclosed were of such widely varying styles that this might have been almost a museum, rather than a living place furnished to someone's individual preferences. As a rule, very little of the furnishing would be in sight when Trigger first came into a room; but it began to emerge from walls and flooring then, presenting itself for use. The computers were aware of her whereabouts.

Unfortunately, they weren't concerned with her needs of the moment. Nothing they offered was going to be of any help on the Sebaloun satellite. There must be some way of controlling the processes, but she didn't know what it was. Verbal instructions produced no effect.

She came back presently to the green and gold room to which she'd been conducted when she came awake. The door through which Torai had gone was closed. Trigger glanced at it, went to the passage along which Attuk had disappeared. The first door she opened there showed a fully furnished room. Something like an ornate bird cage with a polished black nesting box inside was fastened to one wall about five feet above the floor; and standing in the cage, grasping a bar in either hand, and gazing wide-eyed at Trigger as she peered around the door, was Salgol.

She came quickly inside, drew the door shut and went to the cage. "Where are Smee and Runderin?"

Salgol nodded at the box. "In there. They're afraid of these people!"

"I don't blame them." Trigger gave him a low-voiced condensed account of her experiences. Runderin and Smee came out of the box while she was talking, and Salgol passed the information on in the Marell language. "Do you think they really aren't human?" he asked.

"I don't know what to think," Trigger admitted. "So far I've seen no evidence for it. But at any rate, it's a bad situation because they control the satellite. They may not intend to harm you three physically."

"We'd still be prisoners, and that's bad enough," Salgol said. "Isn't there something we can do to help?"

"There might be. Let's see if I can open the cage lock."

The lock wouldn't open, but Trigger found she could bend the bars with her hands. She pried two of them far enough apart to let Salgol squeeze through. "Now," she said, "I know where Torai probably is keeping my gun. If you found it, do you think you could move it?"

"Perhaps not by myself. But two of us could." Salgol spoke to his companions. They replied quickly in voices like miniature flutes. "They both want to help," he told Trigger.

"Good. But if two of you can handle the gun, one of them will help best by staying in the cage."

"Why that?"

"To make it seem you're all still there, in case someone comes into the room."

Salgol spoke to his companions again, reported, "Runderin will come. She's the stronger. Smee will stay."

Runderin peeled out of her colorful but cumbersome outer clothes, and Salgol took off his purple coat. They arranged the clothing in the sleep box so it could be seen indistinctly by someone looking into the cage. Then the two squirmed out between the bent bars, and Trigger set them on the floor. She squeezed the bars back into place, gave Smee, who was now sitting on display in front of the box and looking rather forlorn, a reassuring smile, and left the room with two Marells tucked under her sweater.

The reduced furnishings in the green and gold room would have given her no place to hide; but Salgol and Runderin were quickly concealed behind chair cushions near the door Torai had used. From what Torai had said, Trigger's personal belongings should be in the room beyond the door. If she came out and left the door open, the two would try to get the gun as soon as she was out of sight. If they found it, they'd hide it and wait for an opportunity to let Trigger know where it was.

With the gun, she might start to even up the odds around here rather quickly.

Trigger resumed her wary prowling. The Sebaloun residence remained silent. In empty-seeming rooms, the satellite's mechanisms responded to her presence and produced the room equipment for inspection. She inspected, went on.

Then a door let her into a wide low hall. Not far ahead, the hall turned to the right; and on the far side of the turn was another door. Trigger stood listening a moment before she went down the hall, leaving the door open behind her. Thirty feet beyond the turn, the hall was open on a garden. She glanced over at it, went to the door in the far wall, and found it locked.

She'd had no intention of checking the garden, nor did she go into the branch of the hall that led to it.

It seemed too likely it would prove to be another trick entry point to their playground maze. But as she came back to the door by which she'd entered the hall, she found it blocked by a force screen's glow.

It sent a jolt of consternation through her, though it had been obvious that the satellite's masters would act sooner or later to limit her freedom of motion. But if the only exit from the hall was now the garden, and if the garden was in fact part of the maze, she'd been driven back to her starting point. Venturing a second time into those shifting computer-controlled complexities would be like stepping deliberately into quicksand.

She went part way down the branch of the hall and looked out at the garden from there. It was of moderate size, balanced and beautiful, laid out in formal lines. A high semicircular wall enclosed it; and above the wall was the milky glow of a light dome. There was no suggestion of illusory distances.

It might be part of the residence, and not a trap. But Trigger decided she wouldn't take a chance on it while she had a choice. If she stayed where she was, something or other must happen presently.

And then something did happen.

Abruptly, the figure of a man appeared on one of the garden paths, facing away from Trigger. He glanced quickly about, turned and took a few steps along the path before he caught sight of her.

It was Wrann, the Sebaloun detective who'd engineered her kidnapping in the Orado City hotel.

7

Trigger watched him approach. He showed marks of their encounter on the yacht—bruises around the eyes and a plastic bandage strip along the side of his head where she'd laid him out with the barrel of his gun. Wrann's feelings toward her shouldn't be the friendliest, but he was twisting his mouth into an approximation of a disarming grin as he came quickly through the garden toward her. He stepped up into the hall, stopping some twelve feet away. She relaxed slightly.

"I'll be as brief about this as I can," he said. "My employers haven't forgiven me for nearly letting you and Blethro get away. I'm in as bad a position as you two now! I suggest we consider ourselves allies."

"Somebody may be listening," Trigger said.

"Not here," Wrann told her. "I know the place. But they may find out at any time that I'm no longer locked up and block our chance of escape. Minutes could make the difference!"

"We have a chance of escape?"

"At the moment," he said impatiently. "The delivery yacht we arrived in has left. It never stays long. But there's a separate spacelock where Sebaloun keeps her private cruiser. Unfortunately, I found an armed guard there. I didn't expect it because they rarely allow personnel on the satellite when they're here themselves. Sebaloun may have considered the circumstances unusual enough to have made an exception. At any rate, the man is there. I didn't let him see me. He knows me and isn't likely to know I'm no longer Sebaloun's trusted employee. But he'd check with her before letting me into the lock. So I came back to get a weapon."

"You know where to find a weapon?"

"I know where Attuk keeps his guns. It seemed worth the risk of being seen."

"It probably would be," Trigger agreed. "But unless you can unlock that door over there, we can't get into the residence from this hall. The other door's sealed with a force screen. Or was, a few minutes ago, after I came out here."

Wrann looked startled. "Let's check on that!"

The force screen was still present; and Wrann said he didn't have the equipment to unlock the other door. "I'm afraid we'll have to forget about Attuk's guns."

"Why?" said Trigger. "You know your way around here. Can't we go to another entry to the residence?"

Wrann shook his head. "I wouldn't want to try it. The garden's part of a mechanism they call their playground—"

"I've been there," Trigger said. "A maze effect."

"Yes, a maze effect. When somebody's let into the maze unaccompanied by one of the residents, the controlling apparatus develops an awareness of the fact and begins to mislead and confuse the visitor."

"How did you get through it just now?"

Wrann said, "I've been shown the way. I've had occasion to use it. And I didn't stay in the playground long enough to activate the mechanisms significantly. Working around to another residence entry would be another matter!" He shook his head again. "We'd never make it."

Trigger said, "We do have to go through the playground to get to the lock?"

"It's the only way that isn't blocked for us." Wrann looked at her. "I can get us there. Between us, we shouldn't need a weapon to take the guard."

"You're Torai's detective; I'm the prisoner, eh?"

"Right. I'm to put you on the Sebaloun cruiser. You have your hands on your head. When we get to the guard, you create a diversion." Wrann grinned sourly. "You'll think of something! I jump the guard. We can be off the satellite two minutes later."

Leaving the Marells behind. Trigger said, "And then?"

"We get in touch with the authorities immediately. I don't want to give Sebaloun a chance to get off the satellite. With luck, we'll be back with the law before she even knows we're gone."

Trigger said, "Don't you have a few things to hide yourself, Wrann?"

"Normally I'd have enough to hide," he agreed. "I understand your suspicions. But I have no choice. We're dealing with very dangerous people, Miss Argee! How long do you think I'd live—or you, for that matter—if those three stay at large, and the Sebaloun money is looking for us? As of now, I'll be glad to settle for Rehabilitation!"

Trigger nodded. "All right. Let's go! It could be a trap, of course."

Wrann looked startled. "What do you mean?"

"That door mightn't have been sealed because I was in the hall but because someone knew you were on your way back to the residence."

"I see. We'll have to risk that." As they started down into the garden, Wrann added, "Stay close behind me. I'll hurry as much as I can, but we must be careful. Setting off even one force screen would alert the playground—and then we'll have had it!"

Wrann moved quickly, if cautiously, sometimes half running, rarely hesitating for more than a moment. Trigger concentrated on following in his steps. The maze remained silent and unresponsive as half a dozen illusion scenes slipped past. A stretch of flowering meadow was briefly there, and twice patches of mossy turf where Wrann's greater weight made him sink in almost ankle deep at every step, though Trigger didn't have much difficulty.

Then he vanished ahead of her again. She slowed, carefully took the same stride she'd watched him take—and went stumbling through pitch-blackness. She caught her balance, stood still, feeling sand under the soles of her boots.

"Wrann?" she said quietly.

There was no reply. Her heart began to race. Dry, musty odors, warm stirring of air . . . She listened, lips

parted, barely breathing, and heard sounds then, soft
ones, as if someone moved cautiously over the sand.
The sounds didn't seem close to her.

After a moment, they stopped, and Trigger realized the darkness was lifting. A dim, sourceless glow
had come into the air. It strengthened slowly into a
sullen light; she began to make out something of her
surroundings. It looked like a stretch of steep-walled
gully filled with sand, a dry watercourse. No way to
tell yet what part was real, what part was illusion.

Then she saw something else. A shape stood on
the other side of the gully, farther along it, back
against the overhanging rock wall.

It didn't move. Neither did Trigger, watching it,
between moments of scanning the sand about her. A
simulated dry watercourse might have contained some
real rocks, and she would have felt better with a rock
in either hand at the moment. She saw nothing but
sand.

She didn't think that shape was Wrann.

The glow strengthened again. The shape remained
motionless and indistinct; but an abrupt jolt of fright
had gone through her, for now she recognized the
squat demon figure Perr Hasta's image maker had
showed her after she came awake. The thought that
Perr was at play again flicked up, but she discarded
it at once. The image maker had been used to introduce her to the satellite. It wouldn't be involved here.

With that, she saw the anthropoid creature move
away from the gully wall, start slowly toward her. There
was a point some twenty feet to her left where the rock
bank wasn't too steep. She should be able to scramble
up there, but she didn't want to try it yet. She didn't
know what was above; a blur of light shrouded the
upper levels of the gully. She looked back. The watercourse seemed to twist out of sight beyond its bank
fifty feet away. She thought she was likely to meet a
force field before she got nearly that far.

She could see the approaching anthropoid more clearly now than she liked. The dwarfishly broad body looked tremendously strong. He made crooning sounds which at moments seemed almost to become slurred words. The yellow eyes stared. Trigger felt a surge of revulsion, began to back away. He continued his unhurried advance as if he knew she wasn't retreating far—and once those great hands closed on her, all her skills weren't likely to be of much further use . . .

There was the glow of a force field behind her. Trigger edged toward the left along the glow. The stalking creature angled in slowly to corner her between screen and bank. She shifted to the right and, as he swerved, back to the left. He came at her suddenly then, thick arms reaching, and she ducked, scooping up two handfuls of sand, slashed sand full into the yellow eyes, and was past him.

She heard snarling as she made a dash for that not-quite-vertical section of the gully's bank, scrambled a dozen feet up it, and stopped. A screen had acquired glowing visibility overhead. She looked back. The anthropoid had followed, digging at his face with his hands. She dropped down, slipped under his swift lunge. Fingers clawed along her back and almost ripped the sweater from her, but then she was away and coming up with her hands full of sand again. As he swung around after her, she let him have the second dose. He uttered a gurgling howl.

Full daylight flooded the gully. Torai Sebaloun's amplified voice announced from above, "I am seriously annoyed with you, Attuk!"

Trigger, moving back, glanced up. The haze effect was gone. A view-screen had taken its place; and the enlarged faces of Torai and Perr Hasta were looking down through it.

Torai appeared very angry, while Perr obviously was

enjoying herself. The anthropoid peered up at them, blinking painfully, before he turned and lumbered away. Abruptly, his shape blurred, seemed about to flow apart, then reassembled itself. What it reassembled into was the quite human appearance of Attuk, elegantly clothed. He stalked over to the wall of the gully, vanished into it. The screen had gone blank.

Trigger pulled down her sweater, brushed sand from her palms and turned as Torai and Perr Hasta came walking up the gully behind her.

"So now you know Attuk's a shape-changer!" Perr said smilingly to her. "What you saw here is what we think is his own shape. It's the one he almost always uses when he gets someone into his place in the playground. A crude creature, isn't he? He would have been rather careful with you, of course."

"Careful or not," said Torai, "if he'd damaged the body in the least, I should have killed him! As it is, I'll have to think up a suitable punishment for Attuk. But that can wait." She added curtly to Trigger, "I'm ready to transfer. You'll come along now."

Trigger went along, having no choice in the matter. Torai's ring beams held her hemmed in as she walked ahead of the two, and the beams controlled the pace at which she could and must walk. Once she tried to slow her steps, and they simply lifted her and carried her on a few yards before she was set down to start walking again.

"Attuk did Wrann very well," Perr Hasta was saying chattily from a little behind her. "The voice and manner of speaking, too! Of course, Attuk always is very good with voices."

Torai said, "I'm also somewhat annoyed with you, Perr! You shouldn't have let it go that far. Their bodies can die of fright, as you know. What good would this one have been to me then?"

"Oh, I called you in time!" said Perr. "Trigger's charts show she isn't the kind to die of fright." She laughed. "Wasn't it beautiful, the way she sanded up his eyes?"

The insane conversation went on until they were back in the residence. There Torai's beams steered Trigger into a narrow room and to an armchair set up at its far end, turned her around and placed her in the chair. Torai took the computer control rod hanging from her belt in one hand and brought her thumbnail down on a point near its lower end. The beam effect released Trigger.

"Stretch your hand out toward me," Torai said.

Trigger hesitated, reached out, saw a screen glow appear in the air a few feet ahead of her. She drew back her hand. The glow vanished.

"You're sealed into that end of the room," Torai told her. "So you might as well relax." She turned her rings toward another armchair in the room, and the beams drew the chair over to a point opposite Trigger, about twelve feet from her. Torai settled herself in the chair, and Perr Hasta came up and stood beside her, smiling at Trigger.

Torai studied Trigger a moment then, with an expression that seemed both hungry and contented. She nodded slowly.

"Yes, a good selection!" she remarked. "I should be well satisfied with that one. And I see no reason for further delay." She leaned back and closed her eyes.

Trigger waited. Presently, something began to happen; and she also shut her eyes to center her attention on it. A sense of eager greed and momentary scraps and bursts of what might be somebody's thinking were pushing into her awareness. She studied them a moment, then started blanking out those impressions with clear strong thoughts of her own which had nothing to do with Torai Sebaloun or the Rasolmen satellite, but with people and events and things far away, back in time. It went on a while. Her defense appeared rather effective, though new Torai thoughts kept thrusting up, quivering with impatience and anger now, until Trigger blanked them away again. The Old Galactic shield remained tight, and it might be Torai hadn't counted on that. Frustration grew in the thoughts still welling into Triggers awareness; then, abruptly, anxiety and acute alarm.

"Perr—you're not helping! Perr! Perr Hasta!"

No reply from Perr. A sudden soft thumping noise, and Torai screamed once; and Trigger's eyes flew open.

Torai had fallen out of the chair and lay shaking on the carpet; and Perr Hasta was on her knees beside her, peering down into her distorted face with much the same avidity Trigger had seen in Torai's own expression and in the yellow eyes of anthropoid Attuk. Perr looked up at Trigger then, and laughed.

"I knew it!" she said. "She got stuck in that mind thing of yours, Trigger! If she had any difficulty, I was to start absorbing your personality to make it easier for her, but I didn't. She can't get through, and she can't get back."

Perr looked down at Torai again. "And—now, now, now! I've waited a long time for the personality of the Torai thing, and now I'll take it all, and there's nothing it can do about it."

The child face went blank, though a smile still curved its lips; and Perr's body began weaving gently back and forth above Torai.

Trigger got quietly out of her chair.

8

If Torai Sebaloun had succeeded in implanting her personality in Trigger's body, she would have found herself behind the force screen which now held Trigger imprisoned at this end of the room, with the computer control rod which had switched on the screen fastened by its satin strap to the belt on the dead Torai body on the far side of the screen.

Hence, since Torai must regard Attuk and Perr Hasta as somewhat uncertain allies, there should be a device to release the screen on this side. Trigger had been waiting for an opportunity to start looking for that device; and now, with Torai helpless and Perr Hasta preoccupied, the opportunity was there.

Unfortunately, the switch, button, or whatever mechanism it was, seemed well hidden. Trigger went quickly over the smooth walls, glancing now and then at the two outside. Something that might be Torai's thoughts still flickered occasionally through her mind, but they were barely perceptible, and she no longer bothered to blank them out. Perr Hasta, completely absorbed, showed no interest in what was happening on this side of the screen.

When the walls provided no clue, Trigger began searching the armchair. Engaged with that, she discovered suddenly that Perr was back on her feet and watching her. At the same time, she realized she could sense no more Torai thought impressions, and that Torai, who'd been stirring feebly when she looked last, was now quite motionless. Perr Hasta gave her a slow, dreamy smile.

"Torai was very good," she said. "Every bit as good as I'd expected! So you'd like to get out?"

"Yes," Trigger acknowledged. "Do you know what I have to do in here to turn off the screen?"

"No."

Trigger bit her lip. "Look," she said. "If you'll take that control rod on Torai's belt—"

"Goodness," said Perr, turning away. "I wouldn't know how to use the thing. Besides, why should I let you out? I must go find Attuk."

She sauntered out of the room, humming. Trigger gritted her teeth and resumed her search. One night-mare was down; but two were still up and around. She had to get out, fast!

A tiny voice cried, "Trigger!"

She jerked about. Salgol and Runderin were danc-ing up and down on the other side of the glowing screen.

"We found your gun!" Salgol piped. "Is she dead? What is this thing between us?"

Trigger let out a breath of partial relief. "You have my gun? Good! Yes, she's dead, but the other two might show up any time. That's a force screen between us. Now, look—"

She explained rapidly about the computer control rod. She'd been watching Torai and was able to describe exactly where Torai had pressed on the rod to turn on the screen. There must be some kind of switch there.

The Marells confirmed there was a button there. In fact, the rod was covered with grouped rows of tiny buttons. The trouble was that depressing the button in question proved to be beyond their com-bined strength. Trigger, watching their struggles, exclaimed suddenly, "Stuff in my handbag!" They looked at her, breathing hard. "Keys!" she went on. "Something Salgol can slam down on the button—"

They'd turned and darted halfway out of the room while she was still speaking. Trigger resumed her investigation of the armchair. It seemed to her she'd already looked everywhere. In frustration, she banged her fist down on the chair's padded backrest. There was a sharp click.

She stood frozen for an instant, swung back toward the screen, reaching out to it.

No glow . . .

No screen!

She stepped through the space where it had

blocked her and unfastened the control rod from
Torai's belt with shaking fingers. Manipulating the ring
beam mechanisms probably would take plenty of
practice—no time to bother with that now! She ran
out of the room after the Marells.

The playground maze was still trying to be a problem; but the computer rod made the problem rather
easy to handle. The force screen controls seemed to
be grouped together at one end. When they encountered a screen now, Trigger hit the studs there in
quick succession until she came to the one that
switched off the screen; and they'd hurry on until
checked again. Salgol, Runderin and Smee had no
trouble keeping up with her. Her interference with
the screens might be confusing the overall maze
mechanism. Sound effects soon died away, and the
scenery took on a static appearance. At this rate, it
shouldn't be long before they'd passed through the
playground area.

Force screens, however, might not be the only
difficulty. If Attuk was aware Torai's transfer attempt
had failed and that Trigger was again free, he could
be waiting to intercept her with a gun near the
periphery of the playground. He'd said an armed
guard had been stationed at the spacelock; and if that
was true, she might, in fact, have two guns to deal
with before she got off the satellite. When the surrounding scenes began to look unfamiliar, she moved
with growing caution.

One more screen went off. Trigger started forward
over springy moss, along the side of a simulated weath-
ered stone wall, watching the top of the wall and the
area ahead. The Marells followed close on her heels.
Some thirty feet on, the wall turned to the right. She
checked at the corner. The wall disappeared in dense
artificial vegetation not far away. More of the stuff on
the left. A path led between the two thickets.

Had a shadow shifted position in the shrubbery at the moment she appeared? Yes. She could make out something there now. It seemed to be a rather small dark shape.

She glanced down at Salgol who was peering up at her. She whispered, "Be careful, you three!" and started slowly toward the thicket. She stopped again. The shrubbery stirred—the half-glimpsed shape was moving. Something familiar about it?

A hand parted branches; a quite familiar face looked out warily. Telzey's blue eyes went wide.

"Trigger! You're here! "

"I didn't know you were here, Telzey."

"I woke up just a few minutes ago." Telzey shook her head. "Last thing I—"

Trigger said hastily, "Better wait with that! We're on a private satellite, Rasolmen System. Somebody had unpleasant plans for both of us, but I'm on my way to a spacelock now. With luck, if we move fast enough, we can make it." She turned to the left. "Come on!"

Telzey stepped out from the thicket. Trigger's right hand went under her sweater front, came out with the gun. She shot Telzey through the head, jumped back as she staggered, stitched a line of fire down the front of her body as it fell and began to blur; then stood there, gun held ready, watching it change into something much larger.

Anthropoid Attuk wasn't dead, somewhat to her surprise. But then it was a life form she didn't know much about. It was down, at any rate, making watery sounds as it tried to lever itself up on its thick arms. She leveled the gun at the staring yellow eyes.

"No! Wait!" Perr Hasta, slipping out from the thicket, dropped to her knees beside Attuk. "Attuk, too! Oh, Trigger, I'm grateful! I wanted him almost even more than Torai. Now—"

Her face smoothed into its empty feeding look.

There was a tug at Trigger's slacks. She glanced down. The Marells were looking at her, white-faced. "What are those two doing?" Salgol's small voice asked nervously.

Trigger cleared her throat.

"The big one's dying," she said. "The other one's helping it die. It's all right—it may have saved us some trouble."

"How did you know the big one wasn't Telzey?" Salgol asked. "We thought you'd killed her!"

Well, Trigger thought, for one thing Telzey would have discovered I was around moments after she woke up. Unless something had been done to her mind after Attuk had her brought to the satellite. There'd been that doubt . . .

Trigger said, "I was almost sure as soon as I saw her. But, of course, I had to be quite sure. Did you notice how deeply she sank into the moss? She would have had to weigh almost three times as much as I do." She shrugged. "So now we'll let Perr Hasta have her treat!"

Attuk had collapsed meanwhile, and Perr Hasta was bent above him, her long silky hair almost concealing his head. Trigger added, "It won't take long. Then I'll talk to her."

Perr Hasta said drowsily, "That should last me quite a time! Why, yes, you're right, Trigger. Your gun would kill me as quickly as it did Attuk. Much more quickly, in fact. My physical structure is delicate and could be easily disrupted. You'd like me to show you to the spacelock? That will be simple. You're already past the screen barriers."

Trigger said, "There's a guard at the lock?"

"No guard," said Perr. She yawned. "Torai had the satellite planned so no humans would be needed on it, except the ones who come to deliver this and that, or to fix something. And, of course, our visitors. My!

What a visitor you turned out to be, Trigger! This has been a most interesting experience."

"All right," Trigger said. "No guard. If you're lying, you're likely to go before he does. Blethro first, then. I'm not leaving anything human here. Where is he?"

"Blethro's dead," Perr said. "Attuk's been feeding. I'll take you to what's left if you want, but you won't like what you see."

"Let's go there anyway," Trigger said.

She didn't like what Perr Hasta presently showed her, but there was no question that it had been Blethro.

"Now we'll go to the spacelock," she said.

They went there. There was no guard. One vessel was docked in the inner lock area, the Sebaloun cruiser, a luxury boat. Trigger motioned Perr Hasta into it ahead of her with the gun, the Marells following. She checked out the cruiser's controls, with Perr standing beside her, decided she understood them well enough. "Back outside, Perr!" she said.

She followed Perr Hasta outside. Lock controls next; and they were simplicity itself, computer directed, the satellite computers responding to the cruiser's signals. No operator required. "Perr—" she began.

Perr wasn't there.

Trigger looked quickly around, skin prickling. She hadn't seen Perr disappear, hadn't been aware of her disappearance. Perr had been there, standing next to her, a bare instant ago. Now Perr was nowhere in sight.

A faint giggle behind her. Trigger turned, gun pointed. Nothing. But then the giggle again. She fired. Pause, and there was giggling overhead, in the dull gleam of the inner lock. Her gun point searched for it. The giggling shifted. This way, that—

A whisper then. "I'd drink your personality now, Trigger! I was saving it up. But I can't. I'm too full. Perhaps the next time."

Trigger backed to the cruiser's entry lock, gun covering the area behind her, slipped in and dove into the pilot seat. The entry lock slammed shut. Engines already on . . . purr of power. She threw in the satellite's lock switches. The cruiser moved forward into the outer lock. Inner lock slid shut. Outer lock opened. She cut in full drive. In the same instant, it seemed, the satellite shrank into invisibility behind them, and she hit the subspace switch.

Some minutes later, Salgol addressed her tentatively from the seat beside her. "Would it distract you if I spoke to you now?"

"Huh?" Trigger looked around, saw the three of them gathered there, watching her solemnly. "No, it's all right to talk," she said. "We'll be running on automatics for a while."

Salgol hesitated. "Well, I—we noticed your face is quite pale."

"I suppose it might be." Trigger sighed. "There's some reason for it, Salgol."

"There is? We aren't safe?"

"Oh, we should be physically safe enough at the moment." Trigger shook her head. "But we may find we still have very big problems."

9

"How much did the Service tell you after I got back?" Trigger asked.

"Not much at all," Telzey said. "Just that you were safe and sound but currently incommunicado. And that your little people were all right, too." They'd been having dinner together while Trigger related her experiences on the Sebaloun satellite.

"Of course, I had my own lines out," Telzey went

on, "so I did pick up a few things. There's a flock of diplomats preparing for a trip to Marell to make official contact with its civilization, so somebody got to the group which was exploiting the Marells in time. Then I tapped a man who knew that group had a connection to the Sebaloun enterprises. When it was reported that Torai Sebaloun and two close associates had disappeared in space on her private cruiser and were presumed dead, I figured you could have had something to do with it.

"And, by the way, there were a couple of matters we were able to clean up at this end meanwhile. Some detective friends tracked down the outfit Wrann had hired to hunt for you. They were working without a license and had broken a number of unwritten rules on the job, and the big private agencies feel that sort of thing reflects on everyone. Once we'd identified them, all that was necessary was to pass the word along here and there."

"I hope they weren't treated too roughly," Trigger said.

Telzey shrugged. "I didn't ask. But I understand someone was extremely rough on the hotel security people who fingered you for Wrann and helped smuggle you out. I suppose that was regarded as the nth degree in unprofessional conduct. At any rate, you won't have problems in that area. No one seems much interested in Blethro's disappearance. He had a long, very bad record—it was almost bound to catch up with him eventually. But that still leaves a number of people who might connect you to the Sebaloun satellite and Torai Sebaloun."

Trigger said, "It turned out to be only Wrann and the yacht pilot and some of Wrann's underlings. They've had a case of group amnesia. Anyway, they're mostly in Rehabilitation."

Telzey settled back. "So, what were they keeping you incommunicado about?"

"Symbiote Control."

"Never heard of it."

"It's a special Service group," Trigger said. "Top-secret. They figured I might as well tell you since you'd be finding out anyway."

"I'd be trying to," Telzey admitted.

"Uh-huh. It seems there's a variety of immigrant creatures that keep out of sight in one way and another. They like the advantages of life in the Hub. Some pretend to be human. Mostly they're harmless, and some are considered useful. The Service likes to keep an eye on them, but sees no special reason to bother them otherwise."

"But then there are the ones that aren't harmless. Symbiote Control pumped me about everything that happened on the satellite. They already knew about the Torai type of entity and the Attuk type. The Perr Hasta type was completely new; but what I could tell them about it seemed to explain some rather mysterious occurrences they have on record."

"They knew about the first two?" Telzey said.

"Yes. They're taking care of that quietly, partly because there aren't enough of either around to be worth setting off a public panic. Attuk was a Gelver. It's their name for themselves. Gelvers get checked out individually. Most of them have sense enough not to use their shape-changing in ways they shouldn't, and they help locate others who might be doing it. They have an understanding with the Service. They can stay as long as they make no trouble."

"Where do they come from?"

"They don't know," said Trigger. "A Gelver ship got wrecked on a Hub world before humans ever reached this galactic area. The ones here now are remote descendants of the crew. They have no record of their home world and, of course, it could be almost anywhere. It's different with the Torai type of entity. They do know where that one came from and how it got here, and some other things about it. It's in the exploration records . . ."

Most of the surface of the entity's planet of origin, Trigger explained, was a watery swamp where no intelligent life had evolved. The host bodies available to it there had primitive nervous systems, and it was incapable of developing awareness which extended beyond that of its host. But a Hub expedition had spent some time on the planet and left it with numerous living specimens. The entities in the specimens began to transfer to human bodies. It was an instinctive process at that point; but with human brains, they acquired a human intelligence potential. They made use of it. Their existence wasn't suspected until decades later.

"What's been done about their world?" Telzey asked.

"It's posted. Satellite warnings in Translingue and a dozen other major Galactic languages, explicit about the danger of psychic invasion. Fortunately, the entity can't reproduce when it adopts a host outside its native ecology. There's no way to establish exactly how many were set at large in the Hub by that one expedition, but almost all of them seem to have been located by now."

"What do they do with them when they're located?"

"Not much one can do with them really, is there?" Trigger said. "They don't harm the host body. It lives and procreates and doesn't mutate out of the species. It uses its brain and may be performing a valuable function in society. To the sentient individual, of course, they're a destructive parasite. But that's how they've evolved. They get a choice between dying when the body they've currently occupied dies or going back to their world and its water creatures. I understand most of them decide to go back."

"So those three entities found one another," Telzey

said, "and formed an evil little coven, grouped about the Torai Sebaloun figure."

"For their mutual benefit," said Trigger. "You can see how Attuk and Perr could be useful to Torai. The Sebaloun family members who might have competed for control with her all seem to have died at convenient moments."

Telzey said after a pause, "There's still nothing to show what happened to Perr Hasta?"

"Nothing whatever. It was hardly three hours before I was back at the satellite in a Service ship with psi operators on board. But it was airless by then—open to space—the computer system off. And Perr was gone. It's a little odd, because the delivery lock was sealed, and there are no other facilities for a second spacecraft on the satellite. But perhaps she wouldn't need a spacecraft. After all, we don't know what she's really like. At any rate, I'm reasonably certain Perr Hasta is still around."

"And being around, she could look you up," Telzey said.

"Yes," said Trigger. "That's what makes it awkward for me. Of course, she's a capricious sort. She may have dropped the idea of absorbing my personality by now."

Telzey shook her head. "She doesn't seem to have been capricious about waiting for her chance to get at Torai and Attuk!"

"I know," Trigger said moodily. "I can't count on her forgetting about me—and that doesn't leave me much choice. I'm not going into hiding because of Perr, and I wouldn't want to have a Service operator keep me under indefinite mind-watch, even if they were willing to do it. Or even you. So I'll accept the Service offer to get those latent abilities of mine organized enough to turn me into some sort of functioning psi." She looked at Telzey. "They don't expect me to reach your level, but they think I should become easily good enough to handle Perr if she shows up. She didn't try to tackle Torai or Attuk until she had them at a disadvantage, so she must have limitations."

"They'll probably have you that far along in no time," Telzey said.

"Yes, I suppose so . . ."

Telzey smiled. "Cheer up, Trigger! It really isn't all that bad, being a functioning psi."

"Oh, I know." Trigger returned the smile briefly. "I imagine it will be fun, in a way. And it certainly has its advantages. It's just that I never planned to be one. And now that I'm about to get started—well, it still seems rather strange to me. Shall we go?"

"Might as well." They gathered their purses and rose from the table. Telzey remarked, "You won't find it any stranger than a number of things you've already done."

"No?" said Trigger doubtfully.

"Definitely not. Take tangling with three inhuman monsters on a Rasolmen satellite, for example—"

Afterword
by Eric Flint

And here we leave Telzey Amberdon, making a quip to Trigger Argee. Schmitz wrote no more Telzey stories, so we can only speculate what further adventures she might have undergone. We can only wonder, for instance, what he might have done with her new "twin," Gaziel. Of one thing, however, we can be quite certain—Trigger Argee would have figured in many of those adventures.

So let me talk about Trigger, for a moment. For she, of all the characters who appear in Schmitz's Hub universe, is my personal favorite.

Trigger, who is introduced in this second volume of James H. Schmitz's *Federation of the Hub* series, and will be central to the next volume, is less familiar to most readers than Telzey Amberdon. Yet, in the final analysis, it is around Trigger—and not Telzey—that Schmitz's Hub universe truly revolves.

Telzey, by virtue of her psi powers if nothing else, is basically a loner. When Telzey does have assistance—except for Trigger—her helpers are very

much in the nature of sidekicks, not equals. Throughout the course of Telzey's many adventures, which
comprise a much larger percentage of Schmitz's work
than Trigger's, she encounters few of the major characters who inhabit the rest of the Hub tales. And
those encounters which do occur (again, with the
notable exception of Trigger Argee), are of a relatively
brief and glancing nature. Heslet Quillan, Holati Tate
and Prof. Mantelish never appear at all, and Pilch
only once. Of the most important of Schmitz's Hub
personalities, beyond Trigger, only the Kyth detectives and Keth Deboll figure prominently in the
Telzey saga.

Trigger interacts with all of them, except the
detectives. And the interactions are neither brief nor
unimportant. Holati Tate and Pilch—even, to a
degree, Professor Mantelish—are her mentors and
teachers. Heslet Quillan is her co-adventurer and
eventual romantic interest. And Telzey, when Trigger finally encounters her, becomes both a friend and
a companion.

Trigger Argee is, without a doubt, the most well-
rounded character that James H. Schmitz ever produced. Unlike Telzey, she does *not* possess
extraordinary psi powers. True, after she encounters
Telzey, Trigger begins to realize that she does
apparently possess a considerable latent psi capability.
But that ability figures little in her exploits. For the
most part, Trigger makes her way by virtue of those
basic human characteristics of intelligence, courage,
tenacity, and a fierce sense of principle. (It doesn't
hurt, of course, that she's a crack shot with her
beloved Denton.)

There is none of the solitary splendor about Trigger
that there is about Telzey. She is sometimes hot-
tempered, frequently sarcastic and witty, always stub-
born—and occasionally childish. Where Telzey is aloof
toward romantically inclined males, Trigger's attitude

is far more complex. She is generally self-confident, true. But at other times she is hesitant, or flirtatious, or even downright prudish. And she is, in a way that it is impossible to imagine Telzey doing, quite capable of falling in love with the wrong man before she finds the right one.

None of Schmitz's characters in any of his other Hub stories are as warmly portrayed as Trigger. None are, in the end, so richly human.

In this volume, the reader was introduced to Trigger after she met Telzey. Volume 3 will go back and trace the route by which Trigger got there. Trigger—and all the people who helped to shape her into the formidable figure that she becomes. First and foremost among them being Heslet Quillan, the roguish intelligence officer who finally meets his own match in Trigger herself and becomes the "on-and-off husband" that Telzey reads about.

So. We'll be off to the Hub once again in the next volume. Telzey fans are urged to come along for the ride. Telzey will not figure in that volume, but you will find her own stories all the richer for having made the journey.

Telzey, after all, is not the only luminous star in this wonderful universe James H. Schmitz created. There is also the woman who became her closest friend and companion. Telzey had her due in Volumes 1 and 2. Volume 3 is Trigger Argee's great day in the sun.

Putting together a multi-volume, multi-story series like this one involves the work of a lot of people. I'd like to take the time here to thank the staff at Baen Books, in general, and Nancy C. Hanger in particular. Nancy is Baen's production manager, and she is the one who gets to scramble to make my last-minute changes and corrections workable. Not only does she get it done, she even manages not to curse me in the process. (As far as I know, anyway. But I'm not asking, no sirree.)

Thanks much, Nancy.

That Certain Something
by Guy Gordon

What is it that makes a Schmitz story so special? What makes them so fun so read? I don't claim to have the definitive answer, but here are some of the things people love about Schmitz:

The Twist

Number one has got to be "the twist." In all the best Schmitz stories there is that one extra plot twist at the end, that you weren't expecting.

After spending the entire story worrying about the murderous Hlat, Quillan finds out that it has actually been . . . (no, I won't tell you. Read "Lion Loose" in Volume 3). In "Balanced Ecology" (Volume 4) it isn't until the last paragraph you find out the real hero of the story. In "The Demon Breed" (Volume 4), Nile is terrorized by the Parahuans; or is it the other way around?

Schmitz sucks you into the story with action so fast,

you almost never see the twist coming. But he doesn't lie to you. The twist at the end doesn't invalidate what you thought was happening in the story. Instead, it *adds* to the story; sometimes in wondrous ways. "The Demon Breed" is the perfect example of this.

Inverted Clichés

A related Schmitz technique is the "inverted cliché." If you run across a cliché in a Schmitz story, you can be sure the author is having fun at the expense of your expectations.

Schmitz's monsters are good examples of this. In "The Winds of Time" (Volume 4), we find that a spaceship passenger has a dangerous "pet" aboard. It turns out there may be some confusion as to who is the passenger, and who is the pet.

Schmitz characters often use stereotypes as camouflage. In "The Searcher" (Volume 4), Danestar Gems conceals snooping equipment in her wigs, and conceals her wigs by the "Purloined Letter" method (i.e., in plain view, but completely unnoticed because they are so obvious). And if you chase Trigger Argee into an empty corridor, and think you have *her* cornered, think again.

James H. Schmitz wrote Space Opera. But in an area filled with clichés, he always finds a way to surprise and entertain you. A perfect example of this is "The Star Hyacinths," where he lifts a Pirate Treasure story and drops it, whole, onto a distant planet. Every cliché is there; the shipwreck, the stranded pirate, the treasure (with a curse on it, no less!). In this story, instead of turning the clichés upside down, he pokes fun at them. Blackbeard the Pirate becomes Greylock, and even keeps the parrot on his shoulder!

A "Lived-in" Future

In the Hub stories Schmitz draws a future that looks and feels like a *Jetsons* cartoon. When Holati Tate gets in his "car," he doesn't drive away; he flies away. Telzey steps through a "portal," and is instantly on the other side of the planet. Quillan puts on a spacesuit, turns up the antigravity control, and flies towards the ship.

Unlike bad SF, none of this is explained to you by the characters. Characters never stop in the middle of the story and explain to one another how the FTL drive works, or discuss portal technology. The future is assumed. These characters live in it. It's not new to them, so they don't notice it. We readers do, and we're fascinated by it. But it's all secondary to the plot and the action.

For example, take this (condensed) passage from "Compulsion" (Volume 2):

> "Very well. I can get you a report on the Siren trees."
>
> "How soon?"
>
> "It will be in your ComWeb by the time you reach your room. And I'll have a scan extract made of Miss Argee's file. You'll receive it in a few minutes."
>
> The blue reception button on the ComWeb was glowing when Telzey came into her room. She closed the door, sat down, and pulled up the report on the Sirens. The report began flowing up over the reading screen at her normal scanning rate.

Here is Schmitz, in 1970, describing business being done on "Internet time." And his "ComWeb" may be the best presagement of the Internet in all of science fiction.

Exotic Locations

James Schmitz is the *best* travel agent. "The Demon Breed" takes place on the water world of Nandy Cline, where giant floatwood forests travel around the globe on ocean currents, and are filled with strange plants and animals. These each have a part in the story and are not there just for decoration.

Schmitz transports you to Nandy Cline. He imparts the feel of the storm coming: the smell of the moist air, the agitation of the animals, the gusts of the wind. After reading "The Demon Breed" you can easily identify a dozen species that inhabit the floatwood forests, which are useful, and which to avoid.

In the opening of "Balanced Ecology," we unobtrusively learn about the plants and animals of the Diamondwood forests from the play of two children. In "Glory Day" (Volume 2), Telzey and Trigger visit a world that maintains a medieval culture, for a hidden purpose. No reader will forget the decaying portal circuit of "Lion Game" (Volume 1), or mistake it for Melna park on Orado; even if, in both cases, you are being chased by something big and scary.

Craftsmanship

The pieces of a Schmitz story fit together like a well-integrated machine. There are no superfluous scenes, no unnecessary characters, no extra verbiage. The plots are tight, with possible objections answered before they come up. There is a careful balance among description, action, and dialog.

In this respect Schmitz is like Heinlein: he is an excellent storyteller. His writing does not call attention to itself. He uses the standard props of science fiction: spaceships, FTL travel, ESP (psi), strange worlds, and aliens. But these props are used as shortcuts to get on with the story. They are *not* what the story is about. Furthermore, no "sci-fi" ideas are thrown in because they sound cool, or just because they appeared in *Scientific American* last month.

Characters

Another example of Schmitz's craftsmanship are his characters. Schmitz is known for his strong, believable female characters—which can be extremely difficult to write into an action story. Schmitz makes great effort to avoid or counter the cultural bias of his audience.

For example, his characters' names are deliberately gender neutral (Nile, Ticos, Trigger, Telzey, Gefty, Danestar). Equality of women in the Schmitz future is not an issue. It is simply a feature taken for granted, just like the spaceships.

Characters of both genders are introduced to the reader *doing* something, and doing it well. Nile is piloting her craft around a typhoon. Trigger is taking out her frustration by killing targets at a practice range. Ticos is lying his head off to his interrogators—and getting away with it. The reader is immediately encouraged to identify with the proper character.

In general, when you meet a Schmitz hero, he (or, just as likely, she) is going about his own business. He is not out looking to save the universe. She's taking a break from college. He's captaining his ship (but happens to have a strange cargo), or he might be a research scientist whose work requires isolation in the floatwood islands, or she might be having lunch at a deluxe shopping mall when something strange turns up.

The one thing they all have in common is that when trouble starts, they don't scream for help, they don't call for the police, they *deal* with it. Again, like Heinlein, Schmitz draws strong, competent characters.

Monsters

More than any science fiction writer I can think of, Schmitz loved to put a touch of horror into his stories—usually by including a monster. Schmitz's monsters are some of the most inventive in SF. Their best feature is that they retain the ability to *scare* you. I don't know about you, but if *I* ran into a tarm prowling a floatwood forest, I'd be scared to death. And I *know* I couldn't outsmart the Goblin in Menlo Park. But Schmitz's monsters aren't just big, dangerous, and stupid. If you're going up against a janandra, you'd better realize that it's actually more intelligent than *you* are.

Besides monsters, Schmitz has also created fascinating plants and animals. One example is the Tumbleweeds in "Balanced Ecology." These are seemingly part plant, part animal.

Ilf had noticed a small one rolling straight towards a waiting slurp and stopped for a moment to watch the slurp catch it. The slurp was of average size, which gave it a tongue-reach of between twelve and fourteen feet, and the tumbleweed was already within range.

The tongue shot out suddenly, a thin, yellow flash. Its tip flicked twice around the tumbleweed, jerked it off the ground and back to the feed opening in the imitation tree stump within which the rest of the slurp was concealed. The tumbleweed said "Oof!" in the surprised way they always did when something caught them, and went in through the opening. After a moment, the slurp's tongue tip appeared in the opening again and waved gently around, ready for somebody else of the right size to come within reach.

Ilf, just turned eleven and rather small for his

age, was the right size for this slurp, though barely. But, being a human boy, he was in no danger. The slurps of the diamondwood farms on Wrake didn't attack humans. For a moment, he was tempted to tease the creature into a brief fencing match. If he picked up a stick and banged on the stump with it a few times, the slurp would become annoyed and dart its tongue out and try to knock the stick from his hand.

Notice how skillfully Schmitz has introduced you to two members of the Diamondwood ecology Already you know the tumbleweeds are harmless and dumb. And if you think about it, the slurps must be rather intelligent to understand the concept of "play." Why *don't* the slurps of Wrake attack humans?

Themes

While Schmitz wrote many stories just for entertainment value, there are three themes that reappear throughout his work: psi, ethics, and ecology.

Obviously, the Telzey stories are where Schmitz wrote out most of his ideas about psi. Sometimes he just plays with fun ideas, like how to trick a teleporting animal ("Sleep No More," Volume 1), or how to rescue someone trapped under sea ("Company Witch", Volume 2). But he also makes a serious effort to answer such questions as how society will cope with psis. His answer is his most enigmatic creation: the Psychology Service.

Schmitz stories almost always bring up a point of ethics. It is not Schmitz's style to pose ethical dilemmas for his characters. Generally, *they* know what to do. Rather, he raises those questions in *your* mind. How *should* the human race interact with other intelligent species? What if they're implacably hostile towards us?

In "The Winds of Time," when Gefty realizes the janandra is intelligent, he must shift tactics. Killing it would now be murder. What should the Hub's response be to the invasion of Nandy Cline in "The Demon Breed," or the killing of the Malatlo in "Attitudes" (Volume 4)? What if the other species won't *talk* to us, and we're not even sure if it's intelligent ("Compulsion")?

His concern with ecology shows up best in "The Demon Breed." By dropping Nile into the floatwood forest with nothing but a handgun and a tame otter, Schmitz forces her to use the forest resources to accomplish her goals. Nile could blast her way into an Incubator, but that would be wasteful. Much better to gain entry by imitating its natural symbiote. The forest provides everything from Ticos Cay's research material to a way to defeat a giant tarm.

In "Balanced Ecology," the problem is not so much how *we* should deal with aliens, but how the aliens should deal with *us*. Not only does Schmitz have immense fun creating fantastic plants and animals, but he reaches a solution consistent with the way they live together.

"Grandpa" (Volume 4) is another good example of ecology as a theme. Fifteen-year-old Cord knows in his bones how the ecology of Sutang works. When Grandpa, a large floating plant used for transportation, exhibits new behavior, Cord knows a basic rule that some of his elders ignore: If you don't understand it, it can kill you. When the trouble hits, Cord uses his knowledge of the local ecology to figure out a solution.

Like any good mystery writer, Schmitz has given us all the information we need to see the solution. If Schmitz were a bad writer, those clues would be obvious. Near the beginning of the story, someone would casually explain the importance of symbiotic pairs to another character. But Schmitz gives you the pleasure of discovering the solution along with Cord.

Conclusion

For all my efforts to analyze Schmitz's style, I can't claim to have discovered his secret. I seriously doubt you could write a "Schmitz story" by applying the above observations as a formula. Mostly, Schmitz stories are just *fun to read*.

When it comes to the best
in science fiction and fantasy,
Baen Books has something for *everyone!*

IF YOU LIKE ...
YOU SHOULD ALSO TRY...

Marion Zimmer Bradley . . . . Mercedes Lackey,
Holly Lisle

Anne McCaffrey . . . . Elizabeth Moon,
Mercedes Lackey

Mercedes Lackey . . . . . Holly Lisle, Josepha Sherman,
Ellen Guon, Mark Shepherd

Andre Norton . . . . Mary Brown,
James H. Schmitz

David Drake . . . . David Weber, John Ringo,
Eric Flint

Larry Niven . . . . James P. Hogan,
Charles Sheffield

Robert A. Heinlein . . . . Jerry Pournelle,
Lois McMaster Bujold

Heinlein's "Juveniles" . . . . Larry Segriff,
William R. Forstchen

Horatio Hornblower . . . . David Weber's
"Honor Harrington" series,
David Drake, *With the Lightnings*
and *Lt. Leary, Commanding*

The Lord of the Rings . . . . Elizabeth Moon,
The Deed of Paksenarrion

IF YOU LIKE ...
YOU SHOULD ALSO TRY...

Lackey's "SERRAted Edge" series . . . . . . Rick Cook,
Mall Purchase Night

Dungeons & Dragons™ . . . . . . "Bard's Tale"™ Novels

Star Trek . . . . James Doohan & S.M. Stirling,
The Rising and *The Privateer*

Star Wars . . . . Larry Niven, David Weber
The "Wing Commander"™ series

Jurassic Park . . . . Brett Davis, *Bone Wars*
and *Two Tiny Claws*

Casablanca . . . . Larry Niven, *Man-Kzin Wars II*

Elves . . . . Ball, Lackey, Sherman,
Moon, Cook, Guon

Puns . . . . Rick Cook, Spider Robinson
Harry Turtledove, *The Case of the Toxic Spell Dump*

Alternate History . . . . Gingrich and Forstchen, *1945*
James P. Hogan, *The Proteus Operation*
Harry Turtledove (ed.), *Alternate Generals*
S.M. Stirling, "Draka" series
Eric Flint & David Drake, "Belisarius" series
Eric Flint, *1632*

SF Conventions . . . . Niven, Pournelle & Flynn,
Fallen Angels
Margaret Ball, *Mathemagics*
Jerry & Sharon Ahern, *The Golden Shield of IBF*

Quests . . . . Mary Brown, Elizabeth Moon,
Piers Anthony

Greek Mythology . . . . Roberta Gellis, *Bull God*

IF YOU LIKE . . .
YOU SHOULD ALSO TRY . . .

Norse Mythology. . . . David Drake, *Northworld Trilogy*
Lars Walker, *The Year of the Warrior*
Lars Walker, *Wolf Time*

Arthurian Legend . . . Steve White's "Legacy" series
David Drake, *The Dragon Lord*

Computers . . . . Rick Cook's "Wiz" series
Spider Robinson, *User Friendly*
Tom Cool, *Infectress*
Chris Atack, *Project Maldon*

Science Fact . . . . Robert L. Forward,
Indistinguishable From Magic
James P. Hogan, *Rockets, Redheads, and Revolution*
James P. Hogan, *Minds, Machines, and Evolution*
Charles Sheffield, *Borderlands of Science*

Cats . . . . Larry Niven's "Man-Kzin Wars" series
Esther Friesner, *Wishing Season*

Horses . . . . . Elizabeth Moon's "Heris Serrano" series
Doranna Durgin

Vampires . . . Cox & Weisskopf (eds.), *Tomorrow Sucks*
Wm. Mark Simmons, *One Foot in the Grave*
Nigel Bennett & P.N. Elrod, *Keeper of the King*

Werewolves . . . Cox & Weisskopf (eds.), *Tomorrow Bites*
Wm. Mark Simmons, *One Foot in the Grave*
Brett Davis, *Hair of the Dog*